# kells

Cover image: *Portrait of an Augustinian Monk, identified as Fra Mariano da Genezzano* by anonymous, c. 1480. Cover and book design by Alex Dimeff.

The section-marking Chi Rho illustrations were adapted from artwork in the actual Book of Kells, accessible via the Digital Collections of the Library of Trinity College Dublin.

The poems "Adiutor laborantium," by an unknown author, and "Cantemus in omni die," by Cú Chuimne, are from *Iona: The Earliest Poetry of a Celtic Monastery*, by Thomas Owen Clancy and Gilbert Márkus, originally copyright 1995. Reproduced with permission of Edinburgh University Press Limited through PLSclear.

This is a work of fiction. Names, characters, places, and incidents are the product of the author's imagination or are used fictitiously.

Library of Congress Cataloging-in-Publication Data

Names: Crider, Amy, author.
Title: Kells : a novel of the Eighth Century / Amy Crider.
Description: First edition. | New Orleans, Louisiana : University of New
  Orleans Press, [2023]
Identifiers: LCCN 2023012253 (print) | LCCN 2023012254 (ebook) | ISBN
  9781608012503 (paperback ; acid-free paper) | ISBN 9781608012572 (ebook)

Subjects: BISAC: FICTION / Historical / Medieval | LCGFT: Novels.
Classification: LCC PS3603.R525 K45 2023 (print) | LCC PS3603.R525
  (ebook) | DDC 813/.6--dc23/eng/20230316
LC record available at https://lccn.loc.gov/2023012253
LC ebook record available at https://lccn.loc.gov/2023012254

First edition.
Printed in the United States of America on acid-free paper.

**UNIVERSITY OF NEW ORLEANS PRESS**
2000 Lakeshore Drive
New Orleans, Louisiana 70148
unopress.org

# KELLS

a novel of the eighth century

AMY CRIDER

# PART ONE

## CONNACHTACH'S CONFESSION

# CHAPTER ONE: THE CATTLE

I wasn't sentimental about the animals. As a child, my sister Oona tried to make them all pets, our cows, sheep, and pigs. She named each one, and before they were slaughtered, she prayed for their souls. One day our father inquired about her prayers and she told him, "So our pigs tomorrow will alight to heaven," and he slapped her there, under the cross. I think of this every Martinmas. It seems right that I begin to tell you my story with the slaughter. I haven't forgotten what our friend Cellach said about the hides and the pen of God written on their skin.

The last time I slaughtered for Martinmas at home, Oona and my niece Deirdre were with the children under the cross on the hill, singing a song about the approach of winter. Dermott led the last calf into the pen. From above us, the children sang:

Winter, winter coming nigh.
Hear the corncrake's lonely cry,
Winging onward to the sky.
Don't go, daylight,
Don't come, dark night.
Winter, winter fires burning,
Winter, winter seasons turning.
Hear the wind blow round and round,
Autumn cries a lonely sound.

We made sure it was calm first; you know fear gives it the taste of game. Dermott the priest swung the mallet down between the ears, and the calf, the one Oona named White Star for the white patch on its forehead, fell as if struck by lightning. We hoisted it up on the hooks and I made the lengthwise slits in its neck. The calf was unconscious while its heart beat out its blood into the cauldron below.

The boys Kevin and Enan, Dermott's twin nephews, jostled closer to watch. It was their time to learn how to do it. I cut the belly with that long, knowing knife, careful not to pierce the bladder or intestine, and tied those off before pulling them out. Then I began to work on the skin with the smaller knife. It was slow, patient work to take the hide off in one piece, with the knife dulled for this work. Nearby, half a dozen men stood watching on the other side of the willow fence. Old Fiachrach judged the scene with his high-pitched, grating voice, looking for mistakes.

"Any time now," Fiachrach said. "Is the knife too sharp?"

The knife slipped through the warm blood, curving around the ribs, then found the precious sinew at the spine. My knife was like a pen drawing the calf's shape, or a sculptor's tool smoothing flesh rather than stone.

"Connachtach is so slow."

My knife slipped, slitting the skin.

"Now you've done a careless thing," the old man said.

I stopped and took a deep breath. I looked at Fiachrach, and it must have been a dangerous look, because the old man shrunk away behind his son. Dermott spat on the ground as a retort.

I remember the day had grown warm. There had already been a frost, but now the unseasonable warmth made a Martinmas-summer day. I sweated, but it was the general noise that caused my sweat. Twenty-four lived on the strong-farm, one of the larger in Connacht. We were ten men, seven women, five children, and two elderly. Their number pressed in on me.

You know I was from Connacht, hence my name "man of Connacht." My mother had lost three sons before me and decided on something plain and simple.

We didn't slaughter more calves because Dermott was granting some to new clients. Now that I was leaving, the strong-farm was Dermott's, and he was no longer a boaire, an average-farmer, but a mruighfher, a strong-farmer, and he had the potential to raise his honor price and be a lord-of-superior-testimony.

"I need the last hide not to go in the tanning pit," I said.

Dermott nodded, stretching his big, black-haired arms. He was always the more powerful one. The nephews wheeled the cart of hides down to the stream. Quiet descended, with occasional sounds flaring up and disappearing: a voice raised in question, a laugh, the bark of a dog, a chattering squirrel, someone running. Every sound was clear and distinct, sudden and just as suddenly stopped. Nearby was a stone vat of urine, and flies hovered over it, their buzzing, too, not continuous, but rising and falling. The sounds seemed to echo, and then were swallowed by the pensive air.

I told Dermott I was going to the stream to wash and he nodded. I didn't need to ask about who would do what about rending the fat, boiling the hooves for glue, cleaning the guts. Everyone knew what to do.

The wide stream bubbled with activity. Oona, having come down from the hill to do her part, knelt on the rocky bank and scraped a hide with a smooth stone sharpened on one edge. Kevin and Enan were in the water dunking the hides alternately with Oona's scrubbing. I stripped to my linen braes, stepped into the cool water up to the thighs and rinsed my bloody hands. The nephews laughed as they played with the hides, but a deep silence beat in the air between each sound. This silence was what I looked for, strained my ears for, and it seemed it was a path of silence already being laid before me between the farm and the monastery. I was stepping into the silence, every moment drawing me closer to that destination, the monastery where silence is a vow.

Oona started singing softly to herself. She scrubbed rhythmically and her head bobbed, the black hair shaking and loosening from its hood. Her song was lilting, a song of parting and sorrow.

O if my love
Were like the swallow

That flies, up in the sky—
Then with my love
I would now follow,
And kiss my love, or I will die…

Her voice rose little by little. This sound disturbed my quiet now, and reached into me. The song brought me back to all I was leaving, all I was separating from. It was a stolen feeling, the beauty and sadness of the song no longer belonged to me, and I no longer had the right to be moved. But my throat tightened, my breath shook a little.

The boys stopped playing and dragged the hides out of the water. Oona sat back on her heels, tilted her head back, and sang the last verse with her eyes closed. When she opened her eyes, she looked straight at me and smiled because I was staring at her; she was not aware of the touching emotion of her song. I doused my face with water and came up to her on the rocks.

"Your mangy hair will be shorn and not look like a bird's nest anymore," Oona said, pushing my wet yellow hair back behind my ears.

"Only a woman would look on the vow as a change of hairstyle."

She laughed, her crinkled eyes glinting black in the low sun. "I don't think that. You'll be at peace now, I think."

"So you think? Was I not at peace?"

"No, never." Oona tucked up her own stray locks and smoothed her hands over her apron. "It's a terrible thing, though you bore it well. I don't mean to say you complained. You never did. To wait…" She sighed and put her hand over her mouth.

She meant it was a terrible thing to wait for someone to die, I knew. Our father was dead several months now, and with his death went my obligation to stay on the farm. I took her hands, wanting to contradict her, but I couldn't.

She met my gaze with a steady, confident look. "You will be happy now."

"One doesn't seek to be happy."

"You know what I mean."

"All right."

We walked up the slope from the stream with the boys, who pulled the cart to the urine vat. They spread out the hides and pushed them down into the vat with a long stick. "One of these hides is not for tanning," I said.

After the hides soaked in the urine for three days, we pulled them out and lay them one at a time over a beam that I sat behind, the beam between my knees. I scraped off the hair and fat with the curved, two-handled luna; the hair fell in a wet mass at my feet. We hauled buckets of water to fill the tub next to the barn and put in the hides to soak again.

After two days of soaking in water, the hides were ready for the pit of tanning liquor. We folded them and lay them in the pit, except for one. I picked the finest, palest skin. Oona and I stretched it over a frame and fastened it by pushing small, smooth pebbles around its edge and tying a cord around the bulge to the edge of the frame. I picked up my lunellum, a finer knife than the luna, the wide blade for scraping off the last of the flesh.

A shadow blocked the light of the doorway. "What's this you're up to?" Lemar asked. He took jaunty steps toward us and nodded to the tanning pit. "That's good. We need leather. What's that?"

"Vellum," I said. I glanced at Oona because she made a little sound from her throat. She put her hand on the frame and grasped the edge.

"We don't need any vellum," said Lemar.

"I wish to show the abbot I can still scribe. I want to bring a document with me. It's my skin."

"It's not your skin. Put it in the tanning pit."

"It was my calf when I slaughtered it. I don't remember you stringing up any calves."

"You are a monk now. You own nothing. Nothing belongs to you now. Move aside." Lemar was old Fiachrach's big adolescent son. He had made a claim on the cattle, which I'll tell you of presently.

Oona turned red and didn't move. Lemar grabbed the frame, threw the hide into the pit, and pushed it down with a stick, ruining it for writing.

"If you had asked me respectfully, I would have let you have it," he said. He leaned back, his face fat and satisfied, holding the stick out from his waist, daring me to fight him, the tanning pit between us.

I am a slight man but I had almost a decade on him. I seized the end of the stick and pulled sharply, using his weight against him. He stumbled, perched on the edge of the pit. He grabbed Oona, and Oona instinctively pulled him back. His foot dunked in the tanning liquor, but he righted himself with a gasp.

We stood each holding the ends of the stick. Then he let go and flung it at me.

"You are a better Christian than your monk brother," he said to Oona and stalked out.

Oona picked up the frame. "He owes you a face-cleansing. I wouldn't have helped him, but it was too quick for my thought."

"I've asked for a life of hardship. So it begins."

"Why does he think he has the right?"

I put my arm around her. "He sees me as having come down in the world, and he sees the world as a boat where if I am come down, but at the other end is raised up."

Oona told me later what she did as I stayed in the shed to sharpen tools: she went into the empty house. I can imagine she paused and listened. She knew what she was there for, but she glanced around as if looking for something, as if she were being watched. The chest was under a bench along the wall, almost invisible in the shadow. Its bronze clasp gleamed like the eye of a cat in the dark. She strode up to it with purpose, as if she had a legitimate need for something other than her goal; after all, it was as much her chest as Dermott's. She touched the clasp. It was as smooth as the skin of a fresh apple. When she opened the lid, a scent arose of old linen and leather.

Feeling for the book in the dark, she grasped its small square leather cover and slid the volume under her apron against her chest. Hastily, she put everything back as it was and hurried outside. She walked up the hill beyond the stream where the tall, carved wooden cross marked the place of our masses, took out Dermott's Psalter, and opened it. The question was what page to cut out, so that she could scrape the ink off and I could use it. Somewhere a psalm would be unfinished. Someday Dermott would notice. My voice in her head whispered, *You should have asked him.* She felt herself blush, and she lowered the book from her eyes.

From the top of the rise she had a view of the houses, the wall around them, the stream and shed, and the grain cribs. On the hill on the other side, figures moved rapidly among white dotted sheep and orange cattle. She looked the opposite way at the long, low valley and stream. She thought of distant places she had heard of, like Frisia, where there were markets one could pay silver coins and buy things. Lords and abbots bought parchment, skeins of wool, jars of wine, silk, all kinds of things. There was a world where not everything one could possibly have was the work of one's own hands.

Someone shouted her name, and she turned back toward the farm again. Holding the book to her chest, she waved and walked down, and up the opposite hill.

Kevin was waving. An animal lay at his feet. "Blackie's dead."

She knelt down to the big old black-faced sheep. "Not long?"

"Nay, I think not."

She stroked the sheep's long black nose. A drop of blood glistened in its nostril. "Then flay him. We need a skin for Connachtach."

## CHAPTER TWO: THE FEAST

In the morning there was a frost, casting my mind back to the last frost of spring. We had marched with torches to Rag Cruachan, fulfillment of my father's last demand to be buried among the ancestors of Connacht. At the huge mound of earth over ancient bones, we interred the old man. Nearby was the king's ritual seat of power, a rocky platform where long ago every year he married the earth. Gone with the pagan kings was the power of Connacht. Tara and its leaders blessed by Saint Patrick had displaced them.

A light frost brittled the grass over the plain on our way. On our return it warmed, and a light rain fell. With each step back without my father, my spirit rose into the damp sky. Our train was an arrow pointing away, away from my father's bones, away from the cruel words and fists. I was free.

The morning after the slaughter, I stepped outside of my hut, one of the four huts of the unmarried men beyond the low stone wall of the farm. I outstretched my arms and whispered a prayer I'd remembered for a decade:

"Adiutor laborantium,
Bonorum rector omnium,
Custos ad propugnacium,
Defensorque credentium,
Exaltor humilium,
Fractor superbentium…"

"O helper of workers,
Ruler of the good,
Guard of the ramparts

And defender of the faithful,
Who lift up the lowly,
And crush the proud..."

... From the far woods a lone wolf's howl rose through the fog, chilling my neck, and I continued:

"Ruler of the faithful,
Enemy of the impenitent,
Judge of all judges,
Who punish those who err,
Pure life of the living,
Light and Father of lights,
Shining with great light,
Denying to none of the hopeful,
Your strength and help,
I beg that me, a little man
Trembling and most wretched,
Rowing through the infinite storm
Of this age,
Christ may draw after him to the lofty
Most beautiful haven of life
An unending
Holy hymn forever.
From the envy of enemies you lead me
Into the joy of paradise.
Through you, Jesus Christ,
Who live and reign."

I brought my cupped hands together and closed my eyes, listening to the low pulse of a few autumn birds. It was as if I'd spent the last decade in a fast dance or dizzying game, and now all was quiet. I opened my eyes, turning around. The gray and brown trees and stones, the yellow stubble of the rigs moving with crows, the same as it had always been, now glowed dully in the gloom, lighted by the silence of the dawn. I tried to fix this pause in my memory, crossed myself, mouthing the name of Saint Columba, author of my prayer. The early morning had warmed enough already to melt the frost, and we were in for another Martinmas-summer day.

The house of Oona and Dermott huddled within the wall by the stream, directly under the high wooden cross that stood at the top of the hill. My eyes adjusted quickly to the darkness when I entered. The slender, pale-faced orchid near the door was Deidre asleep on her cot. She murmured my name.

"I'm here." I stoked the fire, laying on some peat.

Behind the curtain Oona and Dermott were waking, muffled voices, a few words scattered in the dark hush of the morning. The sweet, pungent smoke rose, and Deirdre stretched and came over.

She felt for my shoulders from behind, for she was nearly blind. "There's nothing like the sweet smell of a good fire to wake to." She pressed her cheek against mine. Her long red hair fell over my neck.

I gently pushed her away. "You're too old to embrace me so."

She sat on the floor beside me. "You embrace mother and she is old."

"She is my sister."

"And I am your niece."

"And for that you must mind me."

She drew her knees up to her chin. "You're leaving soon, then?"

I poked the fire. "I have one thing to do. But soon."

"Will you pick a foster-son before you go?"

"Your grandfather had ten years to pick one. Now it's up to Dermott."

"This is your home."

I didn't get angry, knowing she only wanted for me not to leave, for things to stay as they had been.

"You might not feel the same as you did," she continued. "Were you very young?"

"I was fourteen when my father demanded I leave the monastery to come back to the farm. I have waited ten years."

Deirdre drew her legs up and rested her chin on her knees like a child, though she was perhaps thirteen and as tall as Oona now. She gazed into the fire. The flame reflected in her milky eyes that glowed like opals.

"I had a bad dream just now. I dreamt I heard you reading from the Bible. You were on a stony outcropping, holding aloft the Gospel, like Saint Boniface, while a pagan raised his sword. You leapt out of the way and fell down the cliff. I awoke before you hit the ground." She stretched toward me. "I'm afraid for you."

"It was only a dream." I reached out and held her hand, which was cool and moist.

"Is there danger leaving here?"

"It meant nothing. You are afraid for me to leave, so you dreamt it."

"Dreams are not true?"

"No."

"Some of the Bible stories sound like dreams to me, when you recite them. Are the stories of the Bible true?" she asked.

"What do you mean by true?"

"You know, that they really happened?"

"In this world? Is this world the true one?"

She exhaled in a laughing sigh, delighted in my familiar riddling ways. "What do you mean?"

"The stories of the Bible are true. But it's not necessarily that they are worldly, of this world. They're truer than that. It's this world that isn't true."

"Do you mean it's like a dream, the world?"

"Something like that. A veil. The world wraps around us like a shroud, a knotted shroud of many layers, and we struggle to push it away, to see through it, to fight our way out of the darkness. What's true is beyond that darkness. For this world is death, and what's real is everlasting."

"That frightens me."

I bent and put my arms around her.

"And you, at the monastery, all the day will contemplate this mystery?" she asked in my ear.

"Every moment struggling against the veil."

"What guides you in the darkness?"

"The love of God."

I felt her body suddenly relax. She held me loosely around the waist with her head buried on my shoulder. Across from us the fire cast our single shadow on the wall.

"It isn't easy," I said after a pause, "to make this sacrifice."

Her soft, hesitant voice asked, "And it will be worth it, to make this sacrifice?"

I hugged her tightly for a moment and then pulled away, turned, and laid another turf on the fire.

If I said that I had sacrificed ten years to live at home on the farm, it would seem I didn't care for them. I cared, enough to stay and protect them from our father past the time when I was old enough to leave. Our father never weakened, he lived on, as hard as an ox bone to the end. For a moment when he breathed his last, the only illness of his life, I felt joy, as if floating like a leaf on the wind. Shame pulled my soul back down to earth as Oona prayed aloud for him.

I was free. Surely now. Dermott would have the cattle, and somehow all would be well for the family. It had to be. I couldn't keep on with life on the strong-farm, caring only for increasing the cattle, being a slave to cattle. That was life of a lord, it was slavery to animals, rivalry, and vanity. I felt as if I saw the world in a dark brass mirror, a different place than others saw. Where they saw gold I saw iron. They dreamt of kingdoms where I saw mud and waste.

Mortality breathed down my neck. Each year passed with a finger pointing, a voice that said, *You will die, and heaven will be too late to do your work.*

The work was it. The work of my dreams, which waited for me like a warm hearth after a long and storm-wracked journey. The work that was a promise, a promise that I either made or had been made to me, a promise I nourished when our father broke the dawn with spitting shouts, a promise I kept with every prayer during my few hours alone on this crowded farm.

In the chest under the table was Dermott's Psalter, to me glowing in the dark of the box. I knelt and opened the chest.

"What are you getting?" Deirdre asked.

"I just wanted to look at it. The Book."

"Will you read to me?"

I stroked the red leather cover and took it out.

"You won't be able to read to me when you're gone," she said.

"Dermott can read."

"Only a few psalms, the ones he's memorized."

I brought the book to the fire. The letters trembled in the flickering light. "Can you see the letters at all?" I asked.

I held the book up to her. She pushed back her red hair. "Like the branches of trees in the forest, all tangled. But I understand what it does. It is like magic, isn't it?"

I traced the tiny lettering on the smooth vellum page. "Not magic. It is a miracle."

Normally, the king would settle affairs of business in winter after Shrovetide, but I planned to leave soon, so with the fresh kill we held a feast. The strong-farm supported thirty-five head of cattle. My ten cattle and the calves we kept would be added to Dermott's ten. He was having a bad year. His sheep were dying, and his cows had borne no calves as if bewitched. He was counting on my ten cattle and the calves. The local king Domnais of the mac Gabrain, with his thegns, came to approve of my plans.

The king of Connacht had red hair and a closely-trimmed red beard speckled with gray. He was short and brawny; his large freckled hand patted the hilt of a short sword in his belt. He brought his poet Teague to the feast. As we ate veal and drained the keg of beer, Teague recited the story of the king's ancestors. It was not a long story, as his family had newly risen to power in the province.

When Teague had told of the end of the last wars, Kevin raised his cup toward the poet and said, "If you please, let us hear of Niall of the Nine Hostages, founder of our land."

Enan kicked Kevin's ankle, and Kevin spilled his beer with a little shout.

Everyone looked at the king, who raised his cup, too. "Of course, let us hear of Niall. We respect the Ui Neill."

Niall Noigiallach was founder of the Ui Neill line, the oldest family in Connacht, kin of all who hosted the feast. The Ui Neill were rivals of the mac Gabrain, the king's family, but no longer held the grip of power. There was still prestige in the name, but we were laid low. Teague, standing tall before us, his large face looming in the semi-dark of twilight, raised his hands and spoke with a rolling voice.

"Niall of the Nine Hostages was the fifth son, the son of Eochaid's second wife, but his first wife, Mongfind, was a jealous woman who tried to interfere from the beginning. She sent Niall's mother to labor in the field when she was heavy with child, and, afraid for him when he was born, healthy and sound, his mother gave him to the poet Torna to raise as his foster-son..."

We kin of the Ui Neill knew the stories well, but we sat still and listened with enchantment at the rolling words. The poet got to the part of Niall's test, when the druid Sithchenn determined which son would succeed his father. The sons were put into a house set afire and commanded to bring out the most important thing.

The poet turned to the children. "And what would you bring forth to save?"

A little girl said, "My spoon."

A boy said, "My knife."

Kevin raised his cup. "The beer! Save the beer!"

The crowd laughed.

Teague continued, "And so one son did save the beer. And another the hammer. And another the weapons. And another the bellows. But Niall brought forth the anvil, and the old druid said, 'Here is the one who will succeed you.'"

I said in Oona's ear, "I would save pen and ink."

When Teague was finished, Dermott raised his cup. "To Saint Columba of the Ui Neill."

The king said, "To blessed Saint Columba, and blessed Saint Patrick," for Saint Patrick was patron of the mac Gabrain. We all drank.

I felt Lemar's glance from where he sat across and a little down from me. He sat next to his father, Fiachrach. Lemar's Adam's apple bulged like a sharp stone, and he had a strong grip on his knife, which he waved in the air between stabs at his meat. A fine sweat glowed on old Fiachrach's forehead as father and son spoke to each other and the king who sat across from them.

Our trenchers were empty save for split bones, the marrow consumed. Enan held his beer to the dog's mouth. The children lay on the ground, falling asleep. The king's thegns lit torches. It was time to discuss our business.

"So, it is the white martyrdom for you," Domnais said.

"I stuck to my initial vow as best I could here," I replied. "I never took a wife."

"His father hoped he would take my daughter, Maeve," said old Fiachrach.

I didn't answer.

"There is a rival claim to your cattle," said the king.

I looked hard at Lemar, who looked away at his father. "He should speak," I said.

"I have a claim," Lemar said sullenly. "My father was foster-brother of Connachtach's father, and my older brother was his foster-son. When my brother died, Connachtach came home, but it was supposed to go to my brother, and now it should go to me." Lemar lightly sawed his knife against the edge of the table.

Old Fiachrach continued his son's line of reasoning. "Connachtach has no sons or brothers. His sister has no sons but only a blind daughter whom no one would want. Who would it go to when they are gone? It might as well be settled to us now."

The king turned to me. "And why do you want to give it over to Oona? They make sense."

"How can he even be the one to decide, withdrawing from the world as he is?" Lemar asked. "It's no decision of his."

"Let him speak," Dermott said.

I said, "As a youth Lemar went on summer raids, wildly sowing devastation. He won't take care or protect the cattle."

Some of the retainers laughed, because they had been on those raids with Lemar.

"I went mad when my brother died. I'm older now," Lemar said. "You still can't show how you would pass on the cattle."

"My two nephews, Kevin and Enan," said Dermott.

Lemar said. "Your claim is no stronger than mine. Less so."

The king drummed his fingers, calculating. "It seems to me Lemar has the stronger claim."

"There's also the plough half owned by Connachtach," Lemar said.

Dermott spoke. "The cattle are of the Ui Neill and should stay in our family."

The king waved his hand, smiling generously. "Let's not be divided. We all only want what is fair. Connachtach is determined to give up his claim."

"Let me have a word with my brother-in-law. Please." Dermott gestured to me, and I rose to go with him.

We walked up the hill to the cross. The sun purpled the western hills, and the feast was a dusky shadow from which voices and laughter dimly rose. I turned my back on the revelry, looking north, the direction I would go, where the silver stream shining in its wind crossed a broad stretch of moorland. A dark wood loomed at the moor far away.

Dermott's face was in shadow, the setting sun outlining his head in gold. "You should not go."

I kept my eyes on the stream. "It's not a choice."

"Of course it is."

"God has called me."

Dermott put his hand on my shoulder. "I know the call of God, but there are many ways to serve. I became a priest; I tend to the souls of the family here. Perhaps that is not as great a thing as you seek. But you could marry Maeve and become a deacon. We could do God's work together. There are ways you can serve."

Dermott's hand, meant to be a gentle gesture, felt heavy on my shoulder. "I must do it. It has been my goal since the beginning. I must follow my path."

The hand pressed firmer. "Perhaps you feel you are too good to work the farm? Is it pride that leads you to leave?"

"It is abject humility I follow in this way."

"And you must humble us all in the process?"

"I'm sorry. I can try to convince King Domnais. Lemar is not fit for the cattle."

"It's a lost cause. Think of Oona. Can you leave her? Think of Deirdre. Think of never knowing what becomes of them."

"I do think of it."

"But it is easy to know what will become of us. No one will marry a blind woman. Deirdre will grow old without a husband or children to care for her, dependent on cousins, on distant relations, their wives resentful of the burden. Oona will grow old knowing this, and her hope and happiness will dwindle. You could marry, have children, and keep Deirdre safe. It is not your own life you sacrifice." His voice grew hard. It was a rebuke rather than a plea.

"I don't know what is in the future or what God has planned."

"I never knew you to be so uncaring."

"I care. Your words weigh heavy on my soul. But if I stayed, if I stayed… my life would be an empty shadow. I can't describe it. Perhaps you and I together can still convince the king."

"It was God's will that you were called back here. Your father understood that without you, your family loses the cattle."

I shook off his hand. "You always defended my father, who was a cruel man who abused my mother and sister with harsh ways. I don't know why you were so blind to it."

"He was a steward to the Ui Neill and increased our cattle."

"I don't want to hear about my father."

"Perhaps in the monastery you will learn to love, for you love none of us," Dermott said, his voice breaking on the last word.

Anger caught in my throat. It was all because of the cattle, and the power, rivalry, and conflicts that cattle produced. "Don't abuse me for the sake of a few animals. Don't make yourself a stranger to me, don't end it this way."

"If I oppose Lemar, I have to go on living here and live with the consequences. It would be better for me not to make an enemy of him." He shook his head. "The king's decision is fair. It's your decision that is not."

Dermott turned and strode down the hill. I watched his shadow disappear. A lovely voice rose in the air. Oona was singing. My face was hot with shame.

I went back down and stood next to one of the glowing torches. The children had fallen asleep in various positions. The men were rapt at Oona's song, the king himself wiping away a tear. Dermott sat staring into his cup. I looked about for Deirdre, who was curled on the ground, a sleeping child in her arms.

When Oona finished her song, the king raised his cup. "You are an angel, to be sure."

Oona smiled. She came and put her arms around me, before sitting next to Dermott. He raised his head and stared hard at me.

The king sighed. "Well, is our business settled then? You are decided and set on this goal?"

My mouth was dry. "I must go. But I cannot leave as it is. Dermott does the most work of anyone here. As priest he tends to our souls, bringing blessings on us all. It is true I am giving up all power in this world. I will have only the power of prayer, a few prayers in here, and I will pray for you all. But on my last act as scion of the Ui Neill, I must ask that you not deny my sister the cattle. My family must be taken care of, no less because of their lack of heirs, but perhaps all the more so." There was a pause as the king scratched his head and nodded. "Dermott has ploughed while others played, and he has sown while others sowed mischief."

Lemar's knife flashed in the dark, pointed at me silently, a mocking smile on his face. His father rapped the table once with his fist.

"And if I deny Dermott the cattle, will you stay, keep the cattle, and take your place here as a lord of superior testimony?"

I had a sudden understanding. If I stayed, I would be the king's rival. The king was pleased for me to go, and he would made the decision that would make it easier for me to leave. "Yes," I lied, taking a chance. I was bluffing, and it pained me to see Oona's face beam at me with the hope that I might stay.

Lemar looked confused, as Fiachrach coughed and spat. The king rubbed his gray-speckled beard and quaffed his ale. He smiled, looking self-satisfied at the magnanimity of his decision.

"Then let it be divided. Half the cattle to Lemar and half to Dermott. That is the fairest decision I can make. Are we settled?"

I looked at Dermott, whose face was still hard and unsmiling in the torch light. I wished this to be enough, but I know now my wish was only that I should not feel guilty. I thought then, surely it had to be enough. Surely Dermott had no cause to resent me.

"I am satisfied," Dermott said quietly. Oona kissed his cheek.

"Then I am satisfied," I said.

Lemar drove the point of his knife into the table. "I will abide by this also, though unkind words have been spoken."

Domnais raised his cup and they all drank to his decision. "How soon do you leave?" he asked me.

"A week from today. I have one thing to do first."

Oona rushed over, putting her arms around me. "So soon? Already?"

Dermott said, "And why not sooner?"

## CHAPTER THREE: THE LEECH

There are no snakes on the island of Hibernia. Saint Patrick drove them away. The same was true of my destination, Iona; in that case Saint Columba had purged them. But I had read of serpents in the Bible and elsewhere, and dreamt of them sometimes. I dreamt that as the ink flowed out of my pen, it turned into a long writhing black snake on the page, and it slithered off the vellum, slid off the table and out through a hole in the wall, taking all the letters with it.

Waking with a start, my heart beat fast. *And it will be worth it, this sacrifice?* Deirdre had asked. The question echoed in the bare hut, which seemed especially small.

I took some deep breaths, lying still, damp with sweat. I'd been feverish in the night. I put my hand under my arm to feel the lump again. The same sort of lump that Oona told me our mother complained of the year before dying. It was the same, smooth, and the size of a pebble. I rose and checked the small leather bag that hung on the peg to see that it still held my precious objects, as if the dream had taken them away. The parchment would be ready. I hurried out.

Next to the house, Deirdre was fulling cloths of wool, stepping on the woven lengths, barefoot in the vat of cloudy urine. She was already accustomed to the smell and sang a little chant to herself.

"Good morning. Have I been long dreaming?" I asked, looking at the sky. The sun was still low over the hill. The cross on the hill was black before the sunrise.

"Not so long. Father rose early, so I joined him. I prefer to full the wool early before the sun bakes the pee, doesn't smell quite as bad."

"Good idea. Where is he now?"

"He went to drive some calves to Lemar's new base-client with Kevin."

"That's a boy's job."

"I think he wanted to be off for a little while. I'm done, will you help me out?" I lifted her out of the vat. "Shall we hang it up?"

"In a moment. I just need to fetch a little water." I picked up a small pail nearby and went to the stream.

Lemar's younger sister Maeve approached as I dipped the water. "So you leave soon?" she asked.

"Aye."

She nodded, the brisk nod natural to her bony jaw and sharp chin. She had a quickness, like a ferret. "It isn't exactly the distance I think of. It's hard to say."

I looked in her face. Her jaw and chin were strong, but her round blue eyes were deep and emotional, tinged with fear, perhaps from growing up with Lemar as a brother.

She continued. "You'll walk a long way, but it's not the distance." She sighed and rubbed her face, then put her hands on her hips and spoke with difficulty. "This is the present here. And you'll go off into the future, and we will be the *past* to you. We will still be here. I will yet exist. But I and we will be the past, and when you wake in the monastery, we will be a dream you woke from. We will just be a dream, and you will wake, and be broken from the past, like a dam in the river." She lowered her head and looked at me searchingly with her keen eyes.

This was a little different from what I was expecting, and I blinked, regarding her, thinking about this Time, like a glistening river winding through the landscape, which emptied into the ocean that was eternity.

"We all end up in the same place," I said.

"I should have expected that."

"What do you want me to say? I'll remember you, all of you, of course."

"I don't ask to be remembered. The dead are for remembering." She clenched her fists. In the distance came Lemar's voice, shouting at his father. "If you married me, that would have solved your problems," she said, meaning the cattle. Her jaw tensed at the sound of her brother's voice.

I looked into her eyes and saw the fear. I could have taken her away from Lemar, and I would have been a kind husband. Who knew what man Lemar would make her marry?

"I'm sorry," I said.

She raised her jutting chin, resolved. "You will remember ghosts, a shadow. But I will go on. I will yet exist." She turned and walked away.

I remained standing there, watching her straight back, her straight neck. It would have been interesting to marry her.

Deirdre skipped down the hill. "Mother says to come and eat." But she settled on a rock and flung her arms out, leaning back on her hands. "Was that Maeve? I thought I heard her voice."

"Yes."

"Now she'll have the cattle and the status, without marrying you." Deirdre spoke lightly and tilted her head toward the warming sun. "She'll be a fine high-born wife to someone now."

"It's not *that* many cattle."

"It's enough. It's a good start. Lemar was proud enough before—now he'll be insufferable. He'll send away to Gaul for a glass window, like an abbot. Are there glass windows where you're going?" We had no glass windows on the farm.

"Aye, there are a few in the church."

"What is the church like?"

"It has a stone foundation and painted walls. In the day it's very cool inside, like a refreshing drink for your soul, with its windows of sea-green glass. At night there are candles that shimmer like a pond in moonlight, and the light shimmers with the vibration of a hundred men chanting. The sound swells in waves rising and falling, and it lifts your soul."

"After all these years you remember the chanting?"

"All the time."

"What else is it like there?"

I sat beside her. "There are mountain ash trees with their orange berries. As Isidore says, ash trees grow in harsh places."

"You quote Isidore as if he were an old friend."

"The author of a book is like a friend."

She cocked her head and spoke out of the side of her mouth.
"Moses wrote the Old Testament, but I have a hard time imagin-
ing him as a friend. More wine, Moses? Fancy a game of knuck-
le-bones, Moses?"

"You are wicked," I said, bursting into laughter.

She laughed. "Do monks laugh?"

"Of course we laugh. Anyone who looks forward to heaven
can laugh at the queerness of the world."

Her laughter ended in a sigh. "I find it so hard to believe you'll
be really happy."

I paused, and spoke hesitantly. "Happiness isn't the goal."

"I don't know if I believe you. A kind of happiness."

I was struck with how much older she had lately become, her
long limbs outstretched on the rock. "You contradict me."

"I only seek to know why, but I want to believe you. There is
something you seek. I don't want you to leave feeling badly. I want
to know and believe it will be worth it. I want to have faith it will
be. For your sake and for ours. For mine. For my heart's peace."

The rock, stained red with blood from the hides, was cold and
hard under me, and the chill rose up my back. "I have spoiled
you, allowing you to question me."

She leaned forward and grasped my foot. I put my hand over
hers.

"I only want to know you will be happy. What if you are mistaken? You have one chance. You will take your vow and you
cannot return. How are you sure?"

I stroked her freckled hand. *Is it worth this sacrifice?* "If I arrive
and it seems that I was wrong, then I was not the man I thought
I was, and I will have to become that man."

I recalled Dermott's words: *Perhaps in the monastery you will learn
to love, for you love none of us.* The rising sun caught my eyes and
blinded me for a moment. Oona called from the house.

I said, "You wanted to know what happiness is to me. Tonight I will share with you something of this happiness. My happiest memory and what I look forward to." I took Deirdre's hand and pulled her up.

At the house, Oona said, "Deirdre, go in and pour the mash while we hang the wool."

Oona and I pulled the wool out of the vat, holding it up to drip off. Oona's muscles rippled under her sleeves. We draped the wool over the branches of a low tree, and she started to sing.

"Please don't. It makes my heart sore," I said. "You sound like our mother."

Oona looked at me, startled. "You so rarely mention her. Sometimes I think you have forgotten."

"I remember, her singing most of all. Her gentle spirit."

"She thought fine things were meant for you. Because your spirit was gentle. Too gentle," Oona said.

I took her hand, her fingers strong in my grasp. "You look like her, with your black hair and eyes. I do remember." I looked into her face. The lines around her eyes told of a life of care and hard work, early mornings stoking the fire, afternoons squinting at needle work.

"When she died, your name was on her lips. She thought you safe in the monastery, away from all his cruelty. When he sent for you to come back, I was so glad to see you again, but afraid the monks had had no nothing. Now I don't know what to think."

"Think I am finishing the journey I started."

"But do you feel anything?"

"Of course."

"You have tried not to. All these years, knowing you would leave, you have tried to forget us even as we stood before you."

I stared at her. I couldn't speak for a few moments. "You will never be dead to me. Not ever."

"I'm not sure what it's for, going now—now that he can't touch you. I know you feel you must. But I'm not sure why, why it is so certain you must go."

"Only that I must."

"What do you need that we can't provide?"

"That is the essence of it. That what I need, this life can't give to me."

She leaned into me and suddenly spoke in a fast whisper, as if needing to get the words out before she changed her mind. "I have a confession to make. When you left as a boy, I made a charm, of a bit of an old belt of yours and a feather you once cherished, bound with my spit and some mud, and I buried it under the threshold, and I made an incantation for you to someday return. When you did, I was frightened. I didn't know if I had made things happen and, if so, if I had made a mistake. And I vowed to be a mother to you and protect you, though by then you were nearly grown, and I think we took turns protecting each other."

I held her, my eyes veiled by her black hair. "There are more important things in the world to wish for than for me to be here."

She softly butted her head against my shoulder. "It is because you think that, that I know I have lost you." She pulled the bronze ring off her finger. "Will you take this?" It was an old ring that had found its way into the family from Rome long ago, incised with a cross.

I held it in my hand, remembering it on my mother's finger. "No, I prefer to take no remembrance. If I live in your heart, and you in mine, no distance between us will matter." I slid it back onto her finger, her hand strong like our mother's hand.

"Should I have never willed you back?"

"It was no magic, only the will of God. I have no regret. I'm glad that I knew you for these years. But conjure no more. I am not coming back."

As Oona pulled herself from my arms, wiping tears on the back of her hand, something moved in the distance that startled me. At the top of the hill, a strange man had stopped under the cross. The man had appeared suddenly from nowhere, a tall man dressed in rough clothes, his face shaded by his hood. As his arms were outstretched in the gesture of prayer, I didn't call out to him.

Oona saw me stare and turned to look. She fell back against me. "This man is no good," she whispered.

"Why do you say that?"

"I don't know." She put her hand to her mouth.

The man brought his hands together and caught sight of us. He came down to the gate of the wall.

"Good morrow," the man said. Now one could see he was old, with a neatly trimmed gray beard and long gray hair. He had small black eyes above a large, hooked nose, like a bird of prey. When he spoke, his voice had a surprising low softness, a coo.

"My name is Ultan, and I travel as a leech, and an interpreter of dreams. I've no land left, so I make my way as best I can."

Oona was pale, anxiously holding my hand. Her own was cold.

"Welcome Ultan. I'm Connachtach, and this is my elder sister Oona."

Ultan stood before the gate and gestured to Oona, waiting for her invitation. He seemed to sense her disapproval. Oona put her hand on the latch and paused. The question of whether she would admit him hung in the air while she took some deep breaths, staring up at the cross above them. Though I felt no harm in welcoming the stranger, I felt the weight of her concern and didn't rush her.

A red squirrel, Deirdre's pet she named Augustine, skittered along the wall toward us. Ultan held out his hand, and Augustine sniffed it eagerly. The squirrel put his paw into Ultan's hand as if to shake it, and the stranger laughed a deep, echoing laugh. Augustine chattered in response.

Oona scooped up the squirrel in her arms. "I think there is little work for a doctor here," Oona said. "But you are welcome to a meal. We must be kind to strangers." She opened the latch, setting Augustine on the wall.

Ultan's smile was bright. "You are kind."

Inside, Deirdre had spooned the mash into three wooden bowls. "We have a guest," Oona said. "Please bring another bowl. Deirdre, this is Ultan. Deirdre is my daughter."

"Good day to you," Deirdre said.

"You are without sight?" he asked.

"Almost."

"Let me see. Could we have a candle?"

I lit a candle from the fire and brought it close. Ultan put his hands around Deirdre's face and tilted her head back.

"Roll your eyes up and down for me," he said in a soft voice. He examined her. "It is strange. You have cataracts, at such a young age."

"Is there hope for her?" I asked.

Ultan let her go. "There is no cure. But I can suggest that you keep your eyes shaded from the sun as much as possible. Wear your hood out of doors."

"Thank you," Deirdre said. "Have you travelled long?"

"Not as long as I will. I have been on the roads these six months. I hope to go to Spain to see the relics of Saint James. I am much in need of divine favor. My land was stolen from me because I have no sons."

"It's bad luck," Oona said drily. She didn't speak again as we ate.

I put my hand on Ultan's shoulder when we finished. "I would speak with you further, if you will."

"Of course. I thank you for the delicious food."

"You're welcome," Deirdre said when Oona didn't reply.

I led Ultan back to my hut, leaving the door open to admit the light. We sat on the edge of my cot.

"I fear I am also in need of divine favor," I said. I pulled off my tunic and raised my arm to reveal the lump.

Ultan felt it carefully, taking the measure of it with his fingers. "How long ago did you notice it?"

"Two months, I think."

"It's the only one?"

"Yes."

Ultan gave it a gentle press, then indicated I could lower my arms.

"There's no cure, is there? My mother had it."

"How old was she when she passed?"

"About thirty. I'm twenty-four."

Ultan nodded, considering. "It's hard to say. The end could be soon, I'm afraid. But it might be longer. You'll know when more lumps appear, perhaps in the groin. Sometimes the disease does pause in its course. I can tell I can be frank with you. It will end your life. God keep you."

"I had already decided I wanted to return to the monastery where I lived for a time as a boy."

"I would recommend, if you have such a desire, not to put it off."

We stood up and recited the Lord's Prayer. I took him by the arm. "Thank you. You're welcome to stay as long as you need to."

Ultan smiled, his black eyes glinting like coals. "I fear your sister would prefer that I not."

"She's only upset because I'm leaving. She's not herself."

Ultan shrugged. "Still, you have given me a meal, and I think that's all I should ask. But I would like to return. I'm concerned about her daughter."

"Won't you stay? Would you like to see our Psalter?"

"A book! I have never seen one except once in a church at Tara."

I put my tunic back on, looking forward to showing him the book. A shadow came through the open doorway. Oona had come with a parcel wrapped in linen.

"I've wrapped some bread for you to take, and the linen will serve as a scarf for you," she said.

I was embarrassed. The seemingly kind gesture was also a request that he leave.

I took one and took the parcel. "I thank you, Oona. You are very kind."

We stood awkwardly. Ultan picked up his walking stick and we went outside together. He kissed us both on the cheek and slowly walked back up the hill, past the cross.

I took Oona by the elbow. "Why did you dismiss him like that? There are others here who might have been in need of doctoring from a leech."

Oona's eyes were wide and fearful. "I don't know. I just feel it. I hope you'll forgive me."

She sank into my arms and we stood together, while in the distance we heard the man whistling as he walked away.

## CHAPTER FOUR: THE INK

Earlier in the spring, when our father took to his bed, I walked to the monastery of Armagh with a bundle of fine wool. I entered the guest house and noticed the soft bed and abundance of costly beeswax candles. I asked to see the secnap, who came to the guest house.

He was a compact, efficient man fitted to his role of administrator, carrying a small ledger. He looked at me with darting eyes and spoke briskly. When I offered the wool to trade, he started to touch the bundle, then jerked his hand back as if it burned when I told him what I wanted.

"Gum Arabic and copperas are costly and precious," he said.

"It's fine wool. I seek to return to Iona where I spent my childhood, and I'd like to prepare a document to present to the abbot."

He smoothed his hand over his tonsured scalp. "Iona. Saint Columba's fine old place. But I'm surprised you don't seek to come here. Iona is perhaps past its prime."

"Though Patrick's star rises, Columba's is not eclipsed. I have come far. Will you trade? I only need a small bit of gum and copperas."

He unrolled the wool on the bed. It was dyed pale blue, the color of purity, from Oona's hand. "Our sheep are the finest in Connacht. Feel how soft." *Like your monastery*, I thought, noting again the feather pillows on the bed.

He stroked it and nodded. "It is still only wool for copperas. You've nothing else? No silver at all?"

"I am on a holy mission." I tried not to let my impatience cut into my voice. "I seek to be a scribe, to devote myself to a holy cause. Surely you would not discourage me or stand in my way for a few coins."

He cleared his throat and frowned into his ledger. "You only need but a little? You are perhaps preparing only a single page?"

"Yes, that is all. One page should be enough. I don't have much time to tarry. My father is dying."

He blushed. And I blush now at my rudeness.

I rolled the smooth orange rocks of gum in my hand, watching as they reflected the light, before melting them by the fire. I uncorked the glass vial of copperas and sniffed the iron smell of the pale green salt. The dozen oak galls soaked in a basin of water. The liquid was brown and slightly foamy, the color of beef broth, and I strained it through the cheesecloth several times. When it was pure, I dropped in the grains of copperas. The moment they hit the water, spots of black blossomed and spread, in another moment the ink was thoroughly black as I poured in a few drops of the melted gum.

I put a clay jar at the top of the parchment to keep it from curling, dipped the cut quill in the ink, drew a short stack of three lines, then measured that width with a pair of dividers. With that set, I walked the dividers down the page and pricked holes at each line, then ruled it with a small piece of lead and a straight edge.

Deirdre spun wool thread where she sat on her cot, the wool winding down from her drop spindle. "What's that scratching sound?"

"I'm making lines on the page. Come here." She set down her work. "This is what I wanted to show you. Here's the ink." I took her finger and lightly dipped it in the jar.

She rubbed her thumb to her forefinger. "It feels a little like blood." She sniffed. "It smells like the earth when the rain hits it on a particularly hot day."

"I'm writing Deus. That starts with D, like your name. Here, feel it." I took her hand and put it over mine and wrote. "You pull the pen down toward you, pulling the letter out of the pen. And the ink glides on the page, smooth and shiny, the black, black ink on the page white as snow. It's called ink because in Latin it means to burn. It burns into the page, and it's there forever. It turns brown after enough time, but it's there forever. Do you feel the perfection of it? It goes out into the world. The word of God will never be forgotten or changed, the book holds it inside, in this ink."

Her hand was light on my wrist, not trying to guide me, as I copied the Psalm.

"The word of God… Isn't there a line in the Book about 'in the beginning was the Word'?"

"Yes. In the beginning was the Word, and the Word was with God. It's like saying, 'First, God had a thought.' Everything begins with a thought. And writing these words, we can make our invisible thoughts, make them visible to share them, and to fix them forever. Can you imagine having a thought and then being able to write it down? Never to forget it? Never to lose it?"

She raised her hand to her mouth in wonder. "That seems fantastic when you put it that way. Men write their thoughts? They don't only copy the Psalms and the Gospels? Of course, you said something about Isidore earlier."

"There are many books. Our library was vast, with dozens of them. Excuse me, I can't talk and write at the same time." There was a pause as I filled out the page:

Lord, hear my prayer—let my cry come to you—Do not hide your face from me now that I am in distress. Turn your ear to me—when I call, answer me quickly. For my days vanish like smoke—my bones burn away as in a furnace. My days are like a lengthening shadow—I wither like the grass.

Deirdre went back to her drop spindle, winding up the length of thread. She said a prayer to Saint Brigid and put the wool in its basket. "And you want to scribe these books? What power it seems."

"I am only an instrument. When I was a boy, my teacher Brother Luke said I had the potential to be a master scribe. He said I was nimble."

"Who else was there?"

"Old Brother Nithard would smile on my work. The Abbot Bresal nodded to me when we passed outside. He knew of me. I learned very quickly. The writing would be enough, but it can be even more splendid. Sometimes, for a special occasion, the monks create a wondrous thing. When I was young I saw it, a book from the monastery of Lindisfarne, with a red leather cover bound over with silver and jewels. Inside there were pages with such intense colored inks they're called 'illuminations,' as if light were shining through them like a colored glass window."

She looked at me as if she could see me while I spoke, her face bright in the light of the dying embers. "I long to see it. Tell me more, make me see it."

"The designs were finely wrought, intricate, like an embroidered cloth, woven, braided, spiraling patterns, so that you could lose yourself in a trance. It is something that shines in my memory. It was beyond any druid's magic to create, it was the power of God's word made visible. I long to create such a book. That is what I have been waiting for these ten years. What I must do before I die."

"But you are not so old."

I hesitated. "Still, life is short."

"You must use your talent then."

"I kept my wax tablet and have practiced, the letters at least, the art unlined."

"Can I hold the parchment?" I handed the rolled up parchment to her and she held it carefully, tenderly. "It is so light. To hold such power. It is like a small bird. What if a bird could write its song?" She burst into a laugh. "It's madness, isn't it? But a miracle. There is something of madness in miracles." She held out her arm, balancing the scroll on her outstretched palm. "Here."

I took it back.

She continued, "I feel God's presence when I think of all that is beautiful for no reason. I barely see flowers now, but I often remember them and think they didn't have to be beautiful. The green hills and the sound of the wind didn't have to be, but God made them so, just to please Himself. You have this book and this work you do is beautiful, just to please God. What could be lovelier? To spend your day in a beautiful chant and twisting ink into incredible fancies, to give God pleasure. I'm glad. God gives so much, and for us all you will give something great in return."

"It is not a fanciful life. Bending over the page for hours is hard labor. When I am laboring for God, it's as if my sins are cast aside for a while, and I forget myself. We commit a hundred failures a day, but for a few perfect hours all that is forgotten, and I am not myself, weak and ashamed, but an instrument of something greater, and I touch the passion of the saints."

"So in laboring for your creation, it is what becomes of you that is the real offering."

At the time I took little notice of that remark, but it came back to me long after. For a while I forgot it, because just then Dermott entered, and a weight fell heavy on my shoulders.

"Good evening, Connachtach." He sat and turned away from me.

"Blessings. You made good time."

"They've improved the road through the waste. So you have your parchment."

"Yes." I slid the parchment into my bag, my hands clammy with sweat.

"Uncle Tach has been making a fine page of scribing," Deirdre said.

Dermott looked grim. "Where is Oona?"

"Making a pair of shoes with Maeve," Deirdre answered.

"Go to her."

I wouldn't forget Deirdre's face, cowed and surprised at his coldness. She hesitated as she stood, reaching toward me. I touched her hand, but just barely. We didn't embrace. We didn't say goodbye. She left.

Dermott cut a piece of horseradish from the table and chewed it. "Oona always finds a way to believe that everything is right and as it should be. After a while, that is wearying. Sometimes things are not right and not as they should be. She says every-thing happens for a reason. Yes, and sometimes a bad reason."

"If you're angry with me, repudiate me to my face."

Dermott looked at me with a disdain that cut me to my core. "You must do what you must do," was all he said.

"Is our friendship over now?"

"It makes no difference. You have left us never to return. If I were not a priest, I would curse your journey. But I will ask God to pardon my ill will. I think your journey is cursed in any event. As you have cursed us with your desire. For I think it is not a holy cause you seek, but you are proud."

I picked up the leather bag, slid my scribing tools into it and took some cheese and a loaf of bread. "I am gone. Tell Oona and Deirdre I love them."

"If you wish."

I waited a moment, for some last word of goodbye, but he sat back in his chair, chewing on the horseradish, and then turned to bank the fire.

I went outside and headed up the path across the footbridge to the top of the hill, stood under the cross, and looked back. In the twilight the houses were swallowed in shadow. Smoke hovered over the thatched roofs, ghost-like and dreamy, smoke and shad-ow. The sun set behind the hill opposite, and as it sank the farm melted into the dark. There was a pause of absolute darkness, and I could go nowhere. I stood still, waiting, while the stars in heaven pulled my gaze upward, away from the farm that was no longer mine. The sky behind me lightened, and I turned toward the full rising moon. Now I could see. I walked toward the moon.

## CHAPTER FIVE: THE WILD BOY

When I reached the edge of the woods, I lay down to spend the night. At sunrise, I thought about going back, saying goodbye to Oona and Deirdre, and making some peace with Dermott. But what words could there be? If it was ended, it was ended. I was entering the vow of the monastery, and my family was cut off. I would be a good monk and pray for my family. There was no way to mend things with Dermott. Going back might only bring a repetition of the previous night, more bitterness, and tears. That thought brought me to my feet, walking into the woods. But as I went, I felt the weight of knowing it was wrong to leave this way, wrong not to hold Oona and Deirdre one last time, and the uneven path, riddled with roots and strewn with acorns, hindered my feet.

As I walked into the woods, I recalled Maeve's speech about breaking with the past. I was returning to the place of my early youth. Returning, I had the dual sensation that I was walking both back into my past and ahead into the future, and I started to feel disoriented. My legs felt uncertain, as if trying to step upward but the path went down, and trying to step downward but the path went up. I stopped, my breathing labored as if I'd been running. Walking had been noisy and now that I had stopped all was silent. "Watch over me," I whispered.

I set off again more quickly and ceased thinking about the past and future. The thick leaves underfoot obscured the narrow way, and I went forward with difficulty. I had a sensation of being followed, and I stopped several times. The rustle of the leaves seemed to stop one step after mine.

A fog rose. The trees wavered in the mist. Suddenly, I thought I glimpsed someone moving ahead. "Hello," I called, hurrying.

Someone small darted between the trees and disappeared again.

I came upon a cave below a rocky outcropping, with an old foundation of a ruin within it. There were charred twigs in a fire pit and some bones but no other indication of human habitation. I set off, at first sure of the path, but the mist rose again. Again I heard the rustle of steps and saw movement. "Hello, can you help me?" I called. After a while I stopped and my heart skipped a beat as the cave entrance yawned before me. I had walked in a circle.

The boy I was following came out from the cave and looked straight at me. He wore skins and furs, and his hair was long and wild. One blue eye and one brown eye looked fearfully, and he held onto the shaft of the knife sheathed in his belt.

"Who are you?" I asked.

"Boy." His mouth was twisted.

"Do you have a name?"

He backed away.

"Don't be afraid. I've lost my way in the fog. Can you show me the way?"

The boy began to bark, and howl, and wave the knife.

I knelt to the boy's level. He picked up a stone and threw it at me, hitting my shoulder. I took out a loaf of bread and held it toward him. The boy sniffed. He inched forward, his knife raised.

"Peace to you, Boy."

In one motion the boy set the loaf between his teeth, slashed me across the back of the hand, swept up the bag, and ran.

I stumbled to my feet and ran after him. "That's mine! Stop!" I ran hard, blood spattering from my hand, until I slipped on the leaves and fell. The wood was silent. The boy was gone with my precious parchment of writing.

Now I was off the path. I headed where I thought the boy had gone. I peered at the ground, trying to tell where the leaves were disturbed. On the ground lay the white, slender quill pen. Crystals of gum Arabic were scattered on the leaves. "Please, just the parchment, God," I whispered. My heart leapt as I found the leather bag, but the bag was empty. I crushed the bag in my fist with a cry.

The wood slid down the bank of a stream where I knelt and drank water from my cupped hand. The cut stung. It was growing dark. I listened for some sound of the boy, but there was only an eerie birdsong, like a low human whistle, that repeated twice and stopped. Perhaps the boy belonged to some nearby farm. I decided to walk up the stream to try to find his family.

I rose, stiff and sore, and started to walk up the stream. After an hour I came to a stone wall and a bright, open field, purple and gold in the late sun, the sky above indigo, and in the distance were some small white houses and a barn. I headed for the first little house.

A young woman of about sixteen with red hair opened the door when I knocked. She held a baby in her arms. "I'm a traveler, a monk on my way to Iona," I told her. "Can I sleep in your barn?"

She closed the door, and I heard women's voices beyond it. Then the door opened again and she let me in. An old woman stirred a pot on the fire that smelled wonderful. The young woman laid the baby in its crib and it kicked its legs, laughing.

"So you are a monk?" the old woman asked as she ladled out a bowl of stew.

"Thank you. This is very fine." I ate hungrily. "Yes, I am going to complete a vow I made as a child. It was my desire to scribe a great Gospel, a beautiful book."

"You're brave to travel alone, and so late in the year," the girl said.

"I met someone braver. A boy living alone in the woods, fending for himself."

The girl gasped and the woman put her hand on her daughter's shoulder. "You saw him?"

"Yes. It seems very sad for such a young boy to live as a hermit."

"That was no boy," the woman said. "That was the changeling. He appears in the fog, and he steals here and there. Sometimes he's a fox, sometimes he's a crow."

"I think he was just a poor lost boy. But he took something of mine."

The woman shook her head. "It was a lost soul. For sure, he is the changeling of the wood."

"I was hoping to find him again and get back what he took."

The woman's eyes widened, and she waved her spoon. "I would never venture more than a few yards into that wood, and the saints protect me from ever seeing that lost soul."

The bread turned dry in my mouth. There would be no help to find my parchment. "There is no chance of finding him?" My voice sounded distant in my ears.

The room was darkening in the setting sun. "Surely not now, with night coming on." She strained a cup of ale for me. "But truly you should not go even in the daylight. I'm sorry if he took something valuable. He is a cursed boy, and I would not seek him. Is it something we could help you replace?"

I shook my head. "Thank you, no. It was too valuable."

"We'll pray this is not some bad omen," the old woman said.

I slept on the floor that night. In the darkness I heard a light rain falling outside. I lay awake a long time. The next morning, they fed me porridge and gave me some loaves to take. They walked me across the field. I looked back at the houses and the wood beyond it. I wanted to go back into the wood, thinking I could find the cave again, and maybe the parchment would be there. My hosts prayed for my journey. It would look foolish to go back in the opposite direction. There was no chance of finding the parchment.

## CHAPTER SIX: OVER THE SEA

I walked across broad fields and over peat bogs, on wicker tracks. Rocky hills rose along the west, and the rising path took me up to broad views under a clear sky. I stopped two more nights at kindly cottages, blessing and gaining blessings from those who would take grace from a penitent monk.

At last the hills descended to the first object of my journey. Stone walls criss-crossed the fields, dividing cattle and sheep, and among the houses was a church with a high cross. Flowing away beyond was the great river. Here there were enough strong-farms to host a cattle market every year, and every other year or so a ship came to expand the market's wares to include quern stones, wine, furs, iron, copper, tin, and bronze. The market, opening with a great dance and ending with horse races, was the highlight of one's life. I had arrived in Derry, and the river would take me to the sea, if sailors were willing to take me.

The sounds of the community, over fifty people, echoed among large houses with more than one room, built of wood and stone. Children and dogs ran up to me as I made my way, herding me, asking my name, the dogs running back and forth, the children tugging. Men pushed their way through the children to take my hand while the women tried in vain to pull the children back. We headed for the church, and the priest was quickly brought.

Father Wyn was a small, pot-bellied man with a short blond beard who looked like a gnome from pagan days. He slapped me on the back and shook my hand vigorously. "Welcome to Derry, friend. Who might you be and what brings you this way?"

"I am Connachtach mac Neill of Connacht. I'm on my way to take the vow of white martyrdom at Iona. If God would grant it, I ask for a boat to take me to the monastery."

There was a murmur. The priest said, "It is late in the year to take to the sea. We must talk to the king. He's riding now but will return by nightfall. Let us have a prayer."

After the prayer, they went out and set up tables and benches so that all could feast on pork, apples, bread, and peas. A chill wind blew in from the sea, refreshing our senses dulled by ale and food. There were many voices and the trill of birds, and I felt a little dizzy with the commotion and my tiredness. When the king and his thegns rode in on their fine black horses against the red sky of the setting sun, torches were lit.

King Donall was thick, tall, an oak tree of a man, with a broken nose and big beefy hands that clasped mine in a firm grasp.

"Welcome, Brother Connachtach. Let's eat and drink and save business for the daylight."

The king sat beside me, his six children gathering around, and he brushed them off like persistent flies. But they wanted a story and would not be denied. He quaffed his ale and raised his hand, big enough to be easily seen in the twilight, and the crowd fell quiet, anticipating a tale to take them into the night.

"Hagen the fisherman was out to sea and too far out from shore he was. A mist came over, a gray heavy mist, and he heard the voice of a woman. A beautiful voice and it spoke and called his name. 'Hagen, Hagen the fisherman. Come to me, Hagen.' And he looked, and a little away from him the mist parted, and he saw beneath the water a beautiful woman, with black eyes and long black hair floating around her face. She looked at him from below the waves and she spoke, saying, 'Follow me.' So he rowed far, far out to sea, and the sea rocked, it grew heavy and sprayed all about him. But he ignored the heavy sea and followed the voice that was luring him on. Meanwhile his companions saw him disappear into the mist, and they sought to follow and stop him, but a great pod of seals surrounded the boats so that they couldn't move, and they could not send their shafts into any of the selkies, so quick they were, swimming in circles all around them. Hagen followed the woman, and she called to him to join her in the kingdom below the waves. So he leapt over the side of the boat and drowned in the heavy sea. The mist lifted, and his boat drifted back to his companions empty, and the seals departed.

"But the most terrible is when the selkie, so large and sleek, sits on the rocks and lures a child to it, by enchantment. And the child runs as if to play with the changeling seal, and just as the child reaches it, off the seal leaps, with a swipe of its tail, and the child tumbles into the water after."

"What about Hagen?" a small girl asked.

"Well, and so a good and brave friend of Hagen the fisherman went out on the rocks and called forth the selkie, and demanded to know how his friend could be returned. And the seal woman's head rose up above the water and she spoke, saying, 'Weave a net with no linen or hemp, catch a fish with no hook or spear, touch the moon as it shines in its fullness.' And she departed. So he thought. After he thought a while, he pulled all the seaweed off the rocks and off the beach, and wove his net from the seaweed. He went out in the deep night with his seaweed net and caught fish with no hook or spear. And in the night the shining moon reflected on the water, and he touched it. Just as he touched the shining reflection of the moon, his friend Hagen burst up through the waves, retching, and nearly drowned. His friend threw the net around him and pulled him into the boat. And that was the only time ever a man returned from the changeling seal's watery doom."

That night I dreamt Oona and I were children, riding in a small boat. A storm rose, blackening the water, and the boat rocked in the fierce waves. Suddenly Oona stood up, pointing. The boat pitched and she was hurled overboard. I scrambled to the side, shouting her name as the water swirled and rain lashed my face. Then I heard the sound of a distant bell. A huge yellow moon rose through the waves. The moon in the water turned into Oona's face. I reached, and clasped her hand, pulling her up from the depths. When she burst through the surface, I awoke.

I had slept in the priest's house, where a silver cross hung over the table, gleaming in the firelight. It was the first thing I saw when I opened my eyes. It flashed as Father Wyn stoked the fire and stirred a pot of mash, his smile gentle and glowing. I thought I would like to tell him about the dream, about home and the people I left behind, but as I was deciding, there was a knock on the door. The priest let in the king.

"So it's to Iona you need to go?" he asked, sitting on a bench. "And why so far? There are monasteries here."

"I was there before, as a boy, but my father required me to return. My father has passed on. I have always planned to go to Iona and finish my life there."

"What does Iona have for you?"

I wished I still had the scribing to show him. "They have a large library and a scriptorium. I am a scribe. Though it has been many years, I still remember. My Latin is still good. I seek to offer my labor in this to God. It is truly a holy mission."

"It is late to travel over the sea."

My words rushed out in nervous excitement. "This is a blessed cause. I plan to scribe a great new Gospel. A holy book. Something that will live forever. God has called me to fulfill this destiny. Your men will be most blessed if they help me. Truly they could not do anything more deserving of grace."

The king ate his bowl of mash quietly. With a nod he said, "Let me inquire. He soon took me. I wondered if he would let me speak to the men. It is strange to me now, I never expected no for an answer. I never thought there would be any difficulty, though I was asking to travel a long way at sea in winter. I thought God would still the waves for me.

The king returned. "I have seven men here, seven brothers who sail together in the big currach. They say they are willing, as it will be a blessed mission. They will need help across the sea, and will find more sailors in Port Bhaile an Trá. They know the way, all the way to Iona. It is a hard voyage. We hope it will secure a great blessing to take you to your calling. You will pray for us at the monastery?"

"Yes, certainly."

He brought his hands together. "That's it, then. They will be ready to leave tomorrow."

We ate some more mash while Father Wyn read from the Bible, making numerous mistakes. I spent much of the day inside the church, and the brothers came to meet me. They were seven strong men in their teens and twenties, taciturn and stoic. The oldest served as their captain. They asked to pray together with Father Wyn.

The next morning, everyone gathered on the riverbank to see us off. The river would take us to Lough Foyle, a huge loch with a narrow channel that led out to the coast and sea. We would camp for the night at the estuary and then travel along the coast to Port Bhaile an Trá before heading north on the open sea.

There were prayers but it was a high song of the sea that echoed from the shore and carried us off. Six men rowed, sitting behind each other, oars on alternate sides, and the captain steered in the stern. We sat tightly together; I was sideways between two stretchers. The calm river slid under the skin of the boat.

The men rowed the long, slender oars in quiet, practiced unison. The green land stretched beyond the banks toward distant hills, the leafless autumn trees casting long shadows.

John, the captain, turned his head between beats of the oar and asked, "What is your home like?"

I stared at the dotted sheep and cattle on shore. Now it would be stopped in my memory, my sister's hair would never gray, all would be as it was, I was on the river that time emptied into, and this ocean separated me utterly from my home and the years I'd lived there. "They have a strong-farm, five head I left to Lemar, added to his, and five to my sister. They have nine houses. It's on a stream, with a cross, no church. They have a priest, he was my brother-in-law. It's a fine place they have."

"And Iona, have you been there?"

"Aye. We have a great house where all the monks sleep, it holds a hundred of us. We have a library and a scriptorium in the house, and barns, and more cattle than any strong-farm. We have a small lake at the southern end of the island, and a well by the monastery. We have an abbot, if he's the same, Abbot Bresal. His hair was white, and he accepted all the privileges of age, but his wiry arms could swing the slaughterer's mallet or fell a tree with the strength of any young man. We have boys at school, and some laborers whose wives live on the Island of Women across the sound, between Iona and the island of Mull."

The beat of the oars continued until the river emptied into the vast loch, and they hoisted the sail. Now the boat flew. The sail with its brown cross bulged overhead, and the sound of it was like a rush of wings, like an echoing drum. The straining ropes made a high-pitched keen as the spray hit our faces. The breeze was strong, and we rose and fell over the waves, each drop bouncing us in our seats, not hard, but enough to remind one to respect the power of the water and wind. Yet I felt confident in the skill of our captain and these men, and the gusts of wind slapping my face made me feel happy and alive.

At the end of the day we arrived at the Bunafebhall, the narrow mouth of Lough Feabhall, and a small beach gave us shelter in a cove. The men pulled the boat ashore and flipped it upside-down, balanced on the stretchers and oars, to sleep under.

They built a fire and cooked a pot of dried fish, pouring milk into it from a skin. The bread was still soft enough to eat; later on in the journey the dry hard bread would join the fish and milk in the pot. I gave a blessing over the food. The brothers talked quietly among themselves, but I stayed apart.

It was an early morning for the next part of their journey. As the men prepared the boat, John the captain walked a little way down the beach and stared at the sea. I sensed he wanted a word.

"We'll pick up two more at Port Bhaile an Trá, to share in the rowing. It will be nine hours from there to Islay, where we'll spend the night. That will be almost half-way. I wonder, Brother Connachtach, if you would like to share in the rowing for this bit, so that here and there one of our brothers will have a little rest?"

The sun was a bright haze behind the clouds, low and diffuse, but feverishly warm. The fire was in us, in our glowing, perspiring faces, our sweaty chests, in our rocking beat climbing the waves. The fire was in my burning shoulders and back, in my palms worn against the wood.

My arms circled up and down, in the circle of the ocean, the rhythm was a circle and time was four circling beats, under circling gannets, under the circling sun.

Sitting backward, I could not see the destination, only the past shrinking away as the rust-colored cliffs rolled by. But after two hours, the beat that had driven us changed. The captain steered for land and ordered down the sail. I turned my head to see. A crescent harbor curved into a long point, Port Bhaile an Trá. It was midday, and the low green fields and stone houses glistened, a welcome sight after the harsh cliffs. Along one side of the harbor was a stone quay with wooden posts, where a small crowd had gathered, having seen the boat coming.

When the boat was tied to the quay, I stepped out in turn, swaying unevenly. Aid put his arm around me to steady me.

A man in the front of the crowd shook hands with the captain. "John, I didn't expect you with winter so close on," he said.

John put his hand on my shoulder. "This is Connachtach, on his way to take the vow at Iona. Connachtach, meet Oswy."

All eyes were on me, and I tried to stand up straight. I felt I would vomit and locked my eyes on the horizon trying to still the swell in me.

Oswy said, "You're lucky for now, it's unusually calm and mild, but the sea could betray you at any time."

"We're bound to try," the captain said. "And we're looking for two more men to alternate the work with. The first leg to Islay is a long, hard row."

"Come, eat, and rest, and we'll see about it."

We moved up the shore. Various currachs and coracles were upturned around the houses. They brought out benches and a pottage of dried fish, the smell strong in the air.

I sat between John and Oswy. The glowing faces of the taciturn sailors reminded me of the faces of the monks in my youth, of men who didn't speak much, but felt deeply. As the ale flowed and the women laughed, they repeated the tale of the selkies, and tales of Fergus, who built the Giant's Causeway from Hibernia to nearby Staffa.

After the feast, John and Oswy talked quietly together, apart from the rest. Oswy called over two boys on the cusp of manhood. Some of the crowd watched and grew quieter. The women ceased laughing.

Oswy turned to the group and said, "Arcil and Aaron will go." He indicated the two boys. "Come, let's not be so grave. We'll have a song." A young man put a pipe to his lips and played a fast jig, and the children danced.

A woman approached me. "You must go? Wouldn't you like to wait until summer?" Her large gray eyes softly loomed at me.

"I cannot wait."

The woman turned and gazed at one of the boys. He was dancing, his brown curls bouncing with each step. She turned her gaze back to me, her face uncertain, her eyes frightened. "The seas are heavy this time of year."

"I have no fear. We are blessed on this mission." I write these words now with shame. At the time I only folded my arms and nodded with a face blank and ignorant.

She looked at me in surprise. I sensed she didn't share my confidence. She seemed to want to say more, not knowing what to say. "There are no monasteries where you are from?"

I smiled in a knowing, fatuous way. "Not like Iona. There is no other. I will scribe." I said this as if it answered everything.

Her face was puzzled and somehow pitying. Now I started to feel uncertain. She crossed herself and walked away toward the dancing children.

I sought out the captain, who was admiring a new coracle nearby.

"Will it be a very rough crossing?"

The captain tilted his head. "Yes. You may be sick."

"I didn't mean that. I meant…" I hesitated to finish.

The captain looked up calmly. "It could be rough. And if we are lost, it is a large portion of Derry men we take, and the two boys. But that is always the risk. We have a mission to honor, and we will."

I looked away at the dancing children. The woman who had spoken to me stood with her arms outstretched towards her child, who spun and danced. I held out my hand to John. "I'm very grateful to you, to all of you. But we will not be lost. God will watch over you."

He took my hand. "The risk is yours, too. But you will pray, and we will pray, and we will all be brothers together now, brothers of the sea."

The next morning, they asked me for a prayer to bless the voyage and keep the wind steady. Everyone stood together on the beach in silence as I spread my arms in prayer.

"Dear Lord, and dearest Saint Columba, we ask you to be with us on this journey that we undertake in your name. As you control the wind and move over the sea, we will know your divine presence. We seek only to do your will with all our strength and courage, knowing it is You who provide them to us. In Jesus' name, Amen."

We pushed off and raised the sail. The sun was bright over the tarnished bronze sea. Gulls followed us like persistent beggars until an eagle, silent and gliding, swept the scattering gulls away. The eagle circled over the boat, I felt, like a protective spirit, for a long while. I always saw the signs in my favor.

Saint Columba had chosen Iona because when he landed there, he could no longer see Hibernia. I wanted to know the moment that Hibernia was no longer visible. And *back*, I was going back to a place that was only a dream all these years, on the other side of this sea, the sea so wide no voice could carry across it. No voice calling from one side would reach the other; any sound would be swallowed by the vast empty space. The island slipped farther away, the little white houses growing smaller on shore.

The sound of the sail died away as the wind slackened. I turned to look ahead, but the way forward was suddenly dense with fog.

The captain said, "Shall we have another prayer?"

I glanced at their faces and uttered the same prayer I had spoken when we left. Nothing happened. The fog came closer and enveloped us. The sea began to chop, and we bounced hard in the little boat.

The wind sprang alive again, and the boat heaved as the sail filled, but it was a twisting wind and the boat spun. Quickly they worked to lower the sail. Bouncing, spinning, we rowed to counter the waves and wind. The fog lifted to reveal a school of basking sharks churning the water, their round, stretched open mouths the size of a man's head, lined with concentric teeth.

One swam under the boat, its fin scraping the thin hide of the bottom. It came up and turned to eye us.

"So proud of your teeth, are you?" the captain shouted.

The wind blew harder and the waves rose in steep hills. As we came down from a heavy chop with a hard thud, the young boy Aaron suddenly pivoted over his oar and flew out of the boat.

I grabbed the oar before it slid away. "Aaron! Grab the oar. Here it is! Grab it!"

We couldn't see him in the gray waves and mist. The captain struck his bell to give the boy a clue where the boat was.

I pulled the oar through the water. "Grab hold!" Then I prayed with words that sprang without thought, my voice hoarse and choked, "Oh God, have mercy. We are nothing but dust, sinners, and as men the weakest of all creatures. Oh God, have mercy, have mercy, because we are all guilty, and our boat is so small. Our boat is so small."

We were like a reed in the surging current. The bell echoed loudly in my brain, the sound that had to tell Aaron where to swim. The circling sharks churned the water. All was chaos. We were all wet with the fog and spray. The looming, frightened eyes of Aaron's mother filled my mind. I had promised her God's blessing. This was my promise. I couldn't pass it off to God. It was up to me, as God's instrument. As the one who promised.

We rowed against the chop to keep the boat in place. There was a shadow in the waves. Not knowing if it was man or beast, I aimed the oar towards it. Something weighed down the end. I pulled. It seemed a long while that the six foot oar came into the boat, inch by inch. It grew heavier in my hands. There were arms and legs, hands and a face. I pulled the boy in, the boat tipping close to capsizing, but the others steadied it with all their skill. The end of the oar was bitten off.

The boy fell into the boat face down, blood pouring from his foot. I slapped his back until he coughed and retched, groaning above the sound of the waves. We turned him over and tore strips from our tunics to bind his bleeding foot. The foot wasn't entirely gone. He'd lost his little toe.

"Am I alive?" he said between gasps.

I pulled him into my arms and hugged him to warm his body. I felt sick and dazed, and I ached all over as we bumped up and down. "You're alive, thanks to Connachtach," John said. This only filled me with shame.

The fog began to turn into droplets of a light rain as it lifted, and more of the great sea extended around us. The fog became lighter and more transparent until it trickled away, and some blue appeared in the sky. I didn't know which way was which in the vast gray sea. The heaving waves died down, and my stomach began to settle where it belonged. Tall brown islands of rock rose in the distance, and the captain steered with a confident face. Aaron lay down as best he could in the crowded boat. The sailors resumed their chant.

Now it was only effort, our effort alone in the sea. It was still hours of rowing, even when we could raise the sail again. We took turns, changing twice an hour, at any time two men resting. It was colder now, but it was heavy work and I sweated.

When I was too exhausted to think about how far it was or where I was going, the captain said, "The tide won't let us go to the lee side of the island. It's the ocean side for us."

I looked up. There was a green island at last. We had reached Islay, but there was still some way to go as we headed with the tide around to the western half. I wondered where we could find port among the straight brown cliffs.

But the captain knew and steered us toward a tiny beach. On the ocean side of the island, the chop was heavy, and we fought to head to the sandy stretch. Then we hit the racing tide and were almost thrown onto the beach. We pulled the boat ashore and all knelt in a silent, spontaneous prayer of thanks. I carried Aaron up the beach to a grassy spot.

A light appeared above us in the dusk. Two monks came down the hill onto the beach, one carrying a torch. The monks were freshly shaven and tonsured, their faces smooth as shells, shiny in the twilight.

"Peace to you, brothers. I am Brother Soen and this is Brother James. We saw you on the water. Will you come to the monastery and be fed? Our guest house is small, but we have a pot on the fire."

Captain John answered, "We have a wounded boy, if you could dress his wound properly we'd be grateful. We'll be grateful for a meal, and, if you have one to spare, an oar, as we lost one to a shark. Our brother here, Connachtach, is seeking to become a monk."

"You seek to join us here?"

Still breathing heavily, I put my hand over my heart. "No, Brother Soen. I am on my way to Iona. But I would like to stay for a day, if my brothers here would give me the time. I have a favor to ask of you. An offering I seek to make."

Brother James said, "Do you know of the happenings at Iona?"

"No."

"They no longer have a master scribe."

I remembered my old teacher. "Has Luke passed on?"

"No, but he has suffered a stroke. He's blind."

"He taught me. He taught me not just the skill, but the joy." I blinked back tears, trembling, overwhelmed by everything.

"Let us pray," Brother Soen said. He led us in prayer while I felt dizzy from hunger and the hard hours that had passed. Then the monks led us up the hill and across the island to their house. Brother James carried Aaron into their infirmary. A pot hung over the fire in their stone hall, and the smell of stewed pork filled the air when we joined the twenty monks of the small monastery. We ate in silence except for the echoing words of Brother Soen, who read from the Gospel.

We huddled together in the tiny guest house. It was a cold night, and I clung to the thin blanket, wrapping it around myself. The next morning Brother Soen came to me.

I knelt before him. "I have a great favor to ask."

The brother motioned for me to speak.

"I intended to bring a parchment of my scribing to show the abbot at Iona, to prove myself. I had one but lost it on this journey. May I spend the day here and have the use of your scriptorium to write a new one?"

The brother beamed at me. I felt my heart lighten.

But Soen replied, "It is up to the abbot. I will bring you to him."

A sharp wind blew outside. We took a small path between the church and the vallum to a small stone house. The tunnel-like path seemed to focus the wind into us, and the crashing sea nearby was loud as Soen knocked on the abbot's door. A voice said something inaudible over the wind and sea, and we entered.

The house was one large room. A low fire glowed in the hearth, immediately attracting my attention because I was so cold. The abbot, a middle-aged man, frail and desiccated-looking, stood at his desk. The next thing I noticed was the stack of vellum on the desk. I knelt and the abbot blessed me. Soen explained my journey. .

"How may we assist you?" the abbot asked. He had gray watery eyes. For a moment he looked like something that had been left on the beach by the sea, something worn away, salt-dried, wet at the edges. The last remains of something that, now in its final state, would never change.

I swallowed. "If I may scribe a page in your scriptorium, Father, to present to the abbot at Iona, I would be so grateful."

The abbot coughed. "Vellum is precious. Perhaps if you would work in return for it."

"Yes, of course, Father." My knees hurt on the cold stone floor.

"And you may confess to Brother Soen. He will find you something to do. Very well."

I kissed his dry, bony hand, and we went out. I hoped Soen would assign me to work with the cellarer in the kitchen where it would be warm, but Soen sent me to cut peat with James.

We worked in silence in the raw wind, with the crack of the shovels and the sucking sound of the wet peat as it pulled away from the ground. We worked until it was time to eat. Joined by the sailors, we ate a cold meal of bread and cheese. The abbot read to us from the Gospel in a hoarse, wind-stolen voice.

That night in the guest house, I could not get warm and lay awake shivering. The next morning Soen brought me to the scriptorium. It was a stone-built room with narrow glass windows. There were three quills, a horn of ink, and one page of vellum waiting for me on the slant-topped desk. Respecting the silence, I nodded my thanks to Soen and went to work.

Two other scribes were there, and the abbot entered. He read out Psalms in slow, measured tones, and we copied from his dictation. In the black ink, I saw the black sea, the rolling waves, the flying skuas, the pitch of the sea, and the long trial of this journey. I had to keep my hands from shaking.

That night, Soen asked to hear my confession as an anmchara, a brother of the heart. We went outside. It was dark on the hilltop, with only a sliver of the moon.

"I need to confess, but I am unsure whether the sin was mine." I explained about leaving my family behind, parting in bad feelings, and the injury to Aaron. I didn't mention his mother's eyes.

Brother Soen listened, looking away with a distracted air. When I finished, the brother's face grew stern. "What do you seek?"

"I seek absolution, I suppose. But I don't know that it was really my sin."

"You suppose? Do you think you are somehow free of sin?" The brother's eyes narrowed under a furrowed brow. "And what of the murder in your heart? The little everyday murders of the flawed soul? We are born in sin. You seek pardon by asking me to help you escape your responsibility."

"If God was working through me, if I was only fulfilling His plan—"

"Then you deny free will entirely?"

"No, I... I don't know. Of course I believe we have will. We choose whether to sin or not."

"Is there pride in your heart? Do you hate? Do you lust? Do you grasp? Sin lives inside you and eats like a worm in the gut. I cannot answer your question. You ask the wrong question. I do think you proud. None of us is above sin. I can hear your confession if you take responsibility. But if you do not, then I cannot help you. Confession is not contingent, it does not say, 'Absolve me *just in case* I am guilty.' Nor can one confess as a formality and expect absolution. Confession springs from remorse that burns in you, an inferno of remorse seeking the cool water of grace. I say this not as one above sin, but as one who drowns in tears of remorse. For we are all guilty, my brother, you as well as I."

"I do feel remorse. I didn't mean to deny it."

"How do you feel about Dermott now? About Lemar? "

"I don't know."

In the dark Soen's face wavered, ghost-like. "We are commanded to love. Now I think you hate them. We hate those who teach us lessons. Are you afraid?"

Fear tightened my throat. "I don't know."

"Afraid of punishment?"

"Perhaps." My heart pounded in fear.

Soen touched my arm. "I ask you one more question. What if there were no punishment? What if I could promise you that you would never be punished for what happened? I'd like to leave you with that thought a while."

I remained alone outside in the dark. The wind tore at my thin woolen clothes, stinging the swollen cut on my hand. What if there were no punishment? I imagined such a world. A world where there was no justice, random and chaotic. Anything could happen. Anything. I shook with cold and fear. The world could not be like that.

Soen returned, holding something. We did not need to speak. I leaned forward, and Soen lashed me with a bundle of long pliable twigs that snapped pain across my back. He gave me twelve lashes. The last two bled.

That night the whipping burned into my skin as I lay in bed. The heat spread from my back. I felt warm at last. I feel asleep bathed in the hot pain.

The next morning, Soen walked me to the beach where the sailors waited to go on to Nave Island. Aaron was there with fresh bandages on his foot.

"Shouldn't Aaron be sent home?" I whispered to John.

"He won't hear of it. He wants to be blessed."

Something clenched in my chest as I looked over at the boy, whose face was resolute, eager. But if he was that desirous to carry out God's will, I thought, should I stop him? I shrugged off my doubts, sinner that I was.

Soen and I embraced. He asked, "Tell me, what is the one and only thing God requires of us?"

A dozen answers flooded my mind. Fear, obedience, faith, forgiveness. But I felt none of these were what Brother Soen was looking for. I was silent.

"When you know the answer, only then will you be ready to be a monk, and scribe. Your work will be a true offering to God then."

I gave him the kiss of peace, and we pushed off. The water was calm, and the wave crests rippled like writing on the sea. The sun was bright but cold, and the spray fresh on my face.

It was a four-hour row to Nave Island, where we stopped to rest. The beach had sheltering, overhanging rock. We lit a small fire and ate bread the monastery had given us and drank milk from a skin bag. I leaned against a seaweed-covered rock and unrolled the page of scribing. The captain sat next to me and looked over my shoulder.

"Such knowledge," he said.

I held the scroll up before us, then rolled it again. "Your knowledge is more impressive. We would never survive this journey without it."

The captain gazed at the sea and said, "Sometimes you can know a great deal and still be lost. You *will* be lost, in the end. Knowing isn't protection when the gale is high. A doctor can die of the disease he knows and cannot cure, a farmer who knows the land and the rising of every moon may lose it all in a drought or sudden frost. The sailor knows every cliff and rock of the shore, the names of every wind and the rhythm of the swells, but when the gale is high, he may still be lost. Knowledge is a fine thing, but nature scorns all knowledge in the end and says, I will take you now as it pleases me, knowing or unknowing."

I followed his gaze to the ocean, dark, impenetrable. I had come so far but it was still a mystery as deep as the mystery of God, of death, of the mystery of my own heart. God knew all but provided man only with endless mysteries. In death knowledge would come, or be unnecessary. But of all the unknown, only one question, Soen's question, needed to be answered. What does God want of me?

We entered the sea again, the familiar rocking. The wind picked up, and we rode up and down over the swells, the water drumming under the skin of the boat. This time the tide was with us and it was a few hours to Colonsay where we would pass the night before the last leg of the journey.

Rust-colored cattle dotted the green slopes. The little bay was surrounded by long protruding fingers of rock. As we hauled in, children ran to the beach followed behind by their folk. The sailors scooped children into their arms, and the children cried, "Stories! Tell us!"

At the head of the parents, the king arrived, trotting on short, stubby legs, his head and face framed in blond curls and beard. He extended his hand, introducing himself as Congall. John knew him already.

"This is Connachtach, a penitent on his way to Iona."

The king tossed his head and considered, then beamed. "It might do. Come in, let's eat and we'll tell our tales. I have two creatures I might send with you."

We walked up the slope, past the cattle, to a farm of ten wattle and daub houses, their foundations green with spongy moss. The sweet smell of peat fires hung in the air. They noticed Aaron's limp immediately, his bandage soaked with blood, and some women insisted on tending to his wound. At first he resisted, but a comely girl with a wreath of flowers on her head took the lead, and he followed her, insisting he was in no pain, though his clenched jaw told otherwise.

Inside the king's house, our host sat me down on the one cushioned chair. "For he is a wise and learned man, taking the white martyrdom."

A child asked, "What is the white martyrdom?"

Congall said, "A pure life, my little rascal."

I replied, "The green martyrdom is the martyrdom of penance. The white martyrdom is exile in the monastery, giving up everything you have, including your kith and kin. And there is the red martyrdom. That is blood sacrifice."

"As many saints have given," Congall said. "And any monk is ready for."

The children looked in wonder.

"I'll show you my scribing." I got up and spread the parchment out on the table.

"Is this the Word of God?" our host asked in awe. Everyone crowded around the table to see.

"It's a psalm. In Latin it reads: 'Sacrifice and offering you do not want, but ears open to obedience you gave me. Holocausts and sin offerings you do not require; so I said, Here I am; your commands for me are written in the scroll. To do your will is my delight; my God, your law is in my heart.'"

They all listened in a hush. A sigh arose when I was finished.

"Does the Bible contain every word? If there was a word not in the Bible, can it still be written?" asked a little girl.

"I don't know if the Bible contains every word. That's a good question. I don't think that it does. But every word can be written, any word you can think of. People have written many things: histories, saint's lives, philosophy. Even in the Good Book there is a saying, 'Of the writing of books there is no end.'"

"But once you write it down, it becomes the Word of God?"

I considered. The girl's mother spoke. "Of course. Anything written is holier than sounds that fade in the wind."

I smiled. "A doctor of the church could not have answered better." And I absorbed their admiring looks, even absorbed the mother's wisdom, as if I had answered so wisely myself.

That night, to pay for my supper, I was bidden to tell a story. I told of saints. There was Molua, who as a child accidentally turned blackberry juice into wine so that he and his friends got drunk. There was Mochta, who lit a fire wizards couldn't quench, and Mullin, who rescued a wren from a cat and a fly from a wren.

I slept soundly on the floor of the king's house. The next morning when I awoke, someone was scrubbing my feet. A boy washed my feet with a soft rag.

"Who are you?"

"I am Cellach. I am a masterless slave. With your permission I'd like to join you and sell myself to the monastery."

The boy before me was slight but might have been older than he appeared. Something about the strength of his arms and the size of his hands suggested manhood, though his face was young, with no downy hair yet. Faun-like ears poked through blond curls.

I couldn't have predicted all that would pass between this boy and me, the horrible disaster to come, and the great question he brought to me. That was far in the future, beyond predicting. And yet even then when we met, there was some spark in his eyes, and I felt something, as if we had things to teach each other.

"Who was your master?" I asked.

Cellach dried my feet. "My mother was slave to this house, and I was kept. I did all I could to make myself useful, but she died and I have no place. To be honest," his voice dropped quietly, "I don't think they understand how much I do here. They will miss me, but they say they don't need me. I wished to sell myself to a lord for my keeping, but have found none who needs me."

If I said yes I would have to take responsibility for the boy, but it did not seem such a burden. "Every man needs a lord," I said.

Cellach nodded and looked at me with bright eyes. I felt there was something familiar about him but didn't know why. "Who was your father?"

"I never knew him. My mother was a widow when she had me. We aren't from here. She was widowed and came here from Nave seeking a place, and was a slave to this house. She didn't know she was with child until she arrived here." Cellach sat with his knees drawn up, and his mien was simple and modest. "They've been good to me, but I am becoming a landless man, and there's no place for me here."

"You're welcome to come with me, but of course I can give you no guarantee there will be a place for you at Iona."

Cellach gave a reserved smile. "Thank you. I have strength and skills. I only hope to prove myself."

I smiled back. "I suppose I'm in the same boat."

While we were talking, the king's family was rising, and Congall briskly ordered them to tasks. His wife, Judith, slowly combed her daughter's hair in the corner, a contrast to the bustle of activity, and I suddenly felt her eyes on me. I was going to speak to her when Congall abruptly slapped me on the back.

"So the boy Cellach will go with you, is it? It would be a great favor to us. We're sending a calf to Iona, to the monastery, and he will tend it on the journey, and tend to your needs. It's in my head that Iona is the place for him and he will serve well there. You will watch him. I see you're already attached to him. We must go and load the calf onto the boat. Come, Cellach."

Congall put his hand on Cellach's shoulder, and they went outside.

"Is Cellach going?" asked the girl whose hair Judith was combing. She was the girl who had asked me about the written word the previous night.

"Yes, he's coming with me," I said.

"I don't want him to go."

"Shush," Judith said.

The girl scrambled away from the comb. "It's not true we don't need him."

"I said enough. Go out to the coop and gather eggs, then let the chickens into the field to feed on the grubs."

"Cellach always helped me."

"Don't be selfish. You're big enough to do for yourself. Later I'll let you comb my hair."

"I won't ever comb your hair if you send him away."

Judith swatted the girl's backside. She let out a shriek. As she ran by me she said, "I hate you." I wasn't sure if she meant her mother or me.

I waited in front of Judith, sensing she was going to say something. She put the comb into a leather-covered box. Everything about her manner as she began to gather her sewing things was slow and deliberate. She picked up a blue tunic and settled it into her lap with the needle and thread. All this while, she wasn't looking at me. Now she stared down at her mending.

"You will find the boy useful," she said.

"Why don't you?"

She sewed tiny stitches in yellow thread along the hem of the garment. "His mother had the gift of second sight. She knew her place, of course, but she saw him destined for something grand. Perhaps she had her head in the clouds. I think she might have given him ideas, though. And if he has such a destiny, it's not to be here. We have a king, my husband, and he has four sons. There's no place for ambition here, if ambition he has. I think his mother had ambitions, God rest her soul." She paused in her sewing and gave me a steady look. "I don't say the boy ever acted proud or even that he believed her prophecy. But I think perhaps he does have a destiny, and here is not the place for it. Not among my sons."

I bowed my head. "I understand."

"You will find him useful, I know. Don't let me keep you."

I bowed again and went outside. On the beach the king supervised as Cellach and Congall's sons hobbled the calf and rolled her into the boat. It lowed with a piteous groan. Cellach put his arms around the calf and whispered in its ear, calming her as he stroked her head.

Aaron's foot was cleanly bandaged, and the moss they had wrapped it in had reduced the swelling. The girls fussed over him in saying goodbye, stroking his brown curls as he blushed.

The blond girl and Judith followed with a basket of food. The girl threw her arms around Cellach, and I trembled to watch, but I told myself we were blessed. Congall came up and thrust out his hand, and when I took it, he grabbed me around the neck with the other hand and embraced me.

"It's a fine holy thing, this journey. Thank you." He nodded toward the boat and Cellach.

"It was a pleasure to be here. Thank you for your hospitality."

Cellach gently pushed the little girl away, and she clung to her mother. My heart ached. I could not ignore it. Her face accused me, saying this was not merely a holy mission, but one that called for sacrifice. I told myself Cellach would have left in any event. It was not I taking him away. I repeated that to myself, but it didn't relieve the weight on my shoulders.

We pushed the boat with the lowing calf into the water and jumped in. I sat down across from Cellach, who drummed his fingers on the calf.

"And I will row?" he asked the captain.

"Yes, in your turn."

"I like to keep busy." He stroked the calf. "So you make the parchment from the calfskin, eh?"

"Parchment is from sheepskin. From a cow it's called vellum."

Cellach stroked the calf's neck and said to it, in a tender voice, "Has the pen of God already written the Gospel on your skin?" For a long while these words have stayed with me. After a pause, he asked, "Did God put everything here on earth for our use?"

"We are stewards of the earth. It's a responsibility, not a gift."

Cellach nodded. "It's a hard life is our fate. It's true, I know Jesus said, consider the lilies. Fish are plentiful in the sea, and the sun and rain grow us oats and barley. But it's a hard life no doubt.

The king has many cares. Just tell me what to do and keep me busy, and I'll sleep well."

The boy's inquisitiveness intrigued me. He seemed restless and ready to act, and his active mind did not seem like one to be content caring for animals and hoeing fields. I took the parchment from my bag and unrolled it before Cellach. "What does this look like to one who can't read the words? I'm just wondering."

The boy traced the letters with his finger. "Fish hooks, shears, pruning hooks, an ear, a snake, a cow horn, a pair of breasts, a cross."

"Have you ever seen a snake?"

"No, but I sometimes dream of them. I know they glide like a rope on the ground, with a little forked tongue that lashes the air. He spoke to Eve and his tongue touched her ear."

I smiled. "Just so. They bite with fangs like a cat."

"Really?"

"And they live long by shedding their skin when it's tight."

"Are there other creatures in the world, strange creatures we've never seen?"

"If you read the book by Isidore, he tells of all manner of strange beasts."

Cellach looked at the sea. He spoke in a quiet, distant voice, touched by wonder. "There are creatures we don't raise or feed or hunt or milk. Creatures not under our hand." There was a long pause while he thought. "Are they dangerous to man, then?"

"Isidore says dragons in the East fight with elephants, and when they shed blood, they make the red earth we use for our red ink."

Cellach looked up with bright eyes. "I like hearing new things. Tell me about this book."

I told him all I could remember of Isidore's Etymologies, until it was our turn to row. Gulls and gannets kited amid the rocky cliffs of Colonsay as we sailed around it, before we veered away north and west. We were on the open sea again, and the chop of the waves was higher. I lurched forward and back from the waist at each roll up and down, my eyes on the horizon to keep from getting sick. A thin line glowed between the low clouds and the sea. The clouds darkened and a light rain fell. I licked my chapped lips.

Young Cellach proved himself well at the oar. His slight body was one taut muscle, stronger than one would guess. I wondered if the monastery would take him or if he would have to find his way back, after all. He was taking a chance. I thought about suggesting that rather than become a slave, Cellach ask to become a monk, but perhaps he didn't have the calling.

A gannet floated overhead, so gleaming white, another small creature that was strong as any man, to hold itself aloft in the wind with taut sinew and hollow bone. It descended and skimmed over the water, showing us the way.

A dark land appeared from the clouds, behind the tall Torrance Rocks. But the tide worked against us. We rowed hard. The chop had died down, but the smooth water belied the heavy current that pulled us back. The captain struck the bell in time to keep us at the pace.

Suddenly the wind rose, a twist of the wind that caught the sail and pulled the boat with a fierce blow toward the high, jutting rocks offshore. Weather-sharpened crags loomed in the twilight, the sun glinting on their bestial orange and black stripes. We lurched toward the immovable boulders, which were ready to grind the boat into splinters.

John took the steering oar with both hands and ordered the sail down. Cellach turned to me, his face white and tense. We veered closer, the waves pounding loud against the rocks. The spray mingled with the drops of sweat flying off the sailors' heads, and we dragged the oars through the sea, the boat zig-zagging in the confusion of the tide running counter to the wind-blown chop of the waves.

For a while our rowing did nothing but keep us in place. We could make no progress. The shore was so tantalizingly close. But the wind increased, the waves rose higher, and we took on water. When we did move, we edged ever closer to the stacks of rock.

The boat rocked, and the calf bleated loudly. My breath was sucked out of my chest by the commotion. We were in danger of being swamped. We all rowed in unison now, driving the slender oars into the waves. My arms ached with trying to hold onto it in the force of the water.

The tide surged, and the captain pushed the steering oar back as we lurched only feet from being dashed on the rocks. The boat shot to the side and flew out of danger on the crest of a wave. The beach was open before us, but we still struggled with the tide, and it was a hard row to move against the current. If we could get a little closer, we could jump out and drag the boat to shore.

"Pull, only a little farther, pull," he encouraged us. We began a loud chant, bellowing over the sound of the wind and the bleating calf.

At last the men jumped into the shallows with a coordinated grace and ran the boat up onto the beach, carrying it up the shore before sinking to their knees in exhaustion and a prayer of thanks. We were on Mull.

"Iona tomorrow," the captain said to me. "A short distance now."

I put my trembling hand on the captain's shoulder. "Tomorrow."

"I think I aged a few years on that one," Cellach said with a rueful, relieved smile.

I smiled back. "I feel like I've been on this boat for years, since I was a boy."

## CHAPTER SEVEN: ARRIVAL

It had been such an arduous test to arrive that my goal was almost forgotten. Oona once told me that in the effort of giving birth, she scarcely remembered there would be a baby in the end. That was how I felt. Though Iona is only a short row from the large island of Mull, it wasn't possible to see Iona from where we had landed. Its presence so nearby was ghostly. I thought I could hear the bell struck for the evening chant, and I trembled.

To spend ten years waiting for this new life… I can't explain it. That I lived, that no illness or accident or ocean terrors prevented me. It was a miracle. Our friend Cellach and I laughed with the sailors that night, as they told stories on each other, joyous men together.

My ankles shook as we pushed off that morning. I couldn't stop shaking. We rounded the point, and Iona lay there in the sea, the long thin island surrounded by a halo of silver sea, its central rocky spine sharply rising over the monastery. It was only a half-hour row then, and the miracle was before me. I recalled Deirdre saying something about the madness of miracles. Here was the small beach—called the Bay of the Dead because here kings of Scotia were brought for burial in the holy cemetery. And there were the monks on shore, who would one day be my true brothers.

We beached the curragh. I realized the monks were Brother Reuben and Brother Marcus, and I was still shaking, surprised that I recognized them after so long. Reuben had hardly changed, a little fatter in his round face, but I knew that ironic smile. And Marcus, my school fellow, tall and grown now, but

I knew his piercing dark eyes that always seemed to look right through me.

John introduced himself to them as the boys unloaded the excited calf. "Good day, God bless you brothers. I bring a penitent who knows this place."

I put my hand on Reuben's shoulder. "Do you know me, Brother? I have changed much, though you have hardly at all. It has been ten years."

Reuben tilted his head and regarded me. I knew I looked a hideous sight, my hair and beard long and matted, my clothes damp with sea and sweat.

Marcus suddenly threw his arms around me. "Connachtach!" We hugged as tears came to my eyes.

"I have returned."

"Like a wild man!"

I laughed through my tears. Reuben put an arm around me. "Welcome, Brother, my old student. I remember."

Finally, I pulled back. "This is Cellach. He'd like to sell himself to the monastery. He brings the calf with him."

They greeted him, and the sailors too, and we walked up the Road of the Dead, and all was strange and familiar. The stone pillars by the road incised with crosses, the cross-road where Marcus and Cellach turned to lead the calf to the west side. The rest of us continued up to the guest house, just past the cemetery of the kings and saints.

To the left was the guest house nestled at the foot of the rocky outcropping; to the right on the little plain between that spine and the sea was the round wooden House—the monastery—within a low embankment—the vallum—with the little stream, and church, and abbot's house. The sweet smell of peat hung in the air. The sun was a gold star in the cold, clear sky. I stood and stared at this little world that was my home now. I was home. The bell was struck. Suddenly a hundred monks appeared like a flock of doves and descended toward the church in a whirl of white robes.

Reuben ushered us into the guest house. "It's time for Tierce. Will you wait?"

"Of course."

The sailors and I huddled by the fire. Reuben must have acted quickly because the bell was barely finished when a boy came with bread and whey.

I could scarcely eat around the lump in my throat, because the chant rose from the church, booming through the air, filling the dark room with the passion of a hundred holy men. As it rose, I remembered.

"Cantemus in omni die
  concinentes varie
  conclamantes deo dignum
  hymnum sanctae Mariam..."

"Let us sing every day,
  Harmonizing in turns,
  Together proclaiming God
  A hymn worthy of holy Mary.

In two-fold chorus, from side to side,
  Let us praise Mary,
  So that the voice strikes every ear
  With alternating praise.

Mary of the Tribe of Judah,
  Mother of the Most High Lord,
  Gave fitting care
  To languishing mankind.

Gabriel first brought the Word
  From the Father's bosom
  Which was conceived and received
  In the Mother's womb.

She is the most high, she the holy
  Venerable Virgin

Who by faith did not draw back,
But stood forth firmly.

None has been found, before or since,
Like this mother—
Not out of all the descendants
Of the human race.

By a woman and a tree
The world first perished;
By the power of a woman
It has returned to salvation.

Mary, amazing mother,
Gave birth to her Father,
Through whom the whole wide world
Washed by water, has believed.

She conceived the pearl
—They are not empty dreams—
For which all sensible Christians
Have sold all they have.

The mother of Christ had made
A mouth of a mouth is no one
Christ's death accomplished,
It remained this by casting of lots.

Let us put on the armor of light,
The breastplate and helmet,
That we might be perfected by God,
Taken up by Mary.

Truly, truly, we implore,
By the merits of the Child-bearer,

That the flame of the dread fire
Be not able to ensnare us.

Let us call on the name of Christ,
Below the angel witness,
That we may delight and be inscribed
In letters in the heavens."


"*Truly, truly, we implore…*" I repeated. I put my hands over my wet face. I thought of all I had known, the voices I would never hear again. These now would be the voices of my family. The sailors were listening too, respectfully silent. I stood and grasped each of their hands in turn and went out the door.

Beyond the earthen vallum, the wildflowers were brown and gone to seed. The odd song of a corncrake croaked from the meadow, a sound like wood rubbing against wood. Though the buildings were close to the low drop-off of the shore, the gentle surf here made no sound. The church was before me, and the round house where the monks lived to the right of it. It was all smaller than I remembered, except for the four giant stone crosses before the church. When I'd left ten years earlier, there were only two crosses, Saint Oran's cross and Saint Matthew's.

Most of the crosses on the island, those that line the Road of the Dead, are simple pillars incised with crosses. These four had arms and were elaborately carved. The crosses seemed to speak. Surely Saint Oran had something to say. The legend was that when Saint Columba and his disciples arrived, the ground had to be consecrated by burying one of their company. Columba's Uncle Oran volunteered and was duly buried in the cemetery now named for him. After three days Columba ordered him dug up. He was still alive, in a way, and started to speak of heaven, saying, "It is not what you think at all." Columba ordered his mouth to be filled with dirt and to rebury him. It was the oldest of the crosses, a pale sandy color and not quite as tall, the carved design a jumble of images. On the arms giant serpents threatened a human head, the soul crying for help.

I looked more closely at one of the new crosses. It was covered
with snakes twisting like vines, the symbol of rebirth, and bosses
like roses. The other new cross was covered with stories. In the
center was carved a portrait of Mary and the infant Jesus. Below
that was Daniel in the lion's den, two standing lions on each side
of him. Below David was Abraham with his raised sword, holding Isaac by the hair. Then there was David playing the harp
and David slaying Goliath with a catapult. It was an ambitious
undertaking, this cross. It had the voice of authority. Unlike the
other crosses, it had long arms, with a circular support.

Deirdre had thought that here, I would find answers. But this
was a place of seeking. The answer comes with death. And what
was the question? I thought of the question the monk on Islay
had left me with: *What does God ask of me?* Of all the many questions in the wide world, that was the only question.

A breeze bearing the chill of Advent rustled the grass. I turned
toward the house. The ground floor contained the refectory, the
school, and the scriptorium. The monks slept on the upper floor,
entered from stairs wrapping around the exterior of the building.
I wondered if I could go in. Surely it would be no affront, just to
step in and look. I didn't feel the ground underfoot as I walked
with quickening pace. The door swung easily inward. It seemed
too easy to enter. I felt I should have suffered more for this arrival.

It was dark with smoky shadows. It came back to me and connected to my memory, making my attention alive to the vivid reality of the place. Yes, it was like this, yes, the green glass windows,
the tables, the bookcases, yes, it was like this.

Twelve tables filled the space on the side toward the door, in
more than half of the round, sixty foot room. This had been my
school. This was where I scratched Latin words onto my orange
wax tablet and was praised for it. Luke and Reuben had taught
me then, Luke a vigorous teacher, and Reuben, with his subtle,
biting wit. This was where I learned about books.

Four cupboards, with prominent locks, divided the space between the refectory and school and the smaller writing area, the
scriptorium. Centered between the book cupboards was a desk

with large ledgers to keep track of their lending. I could glimpse the slanted writing desks on the other side of the cupboards, on the far side of the room. There were more windows on that side, the greater light beyond.

With slow, deliberate steps, feeling as if I were floating down a stream, I passed by the tables and cupboards and entered the writing area. My sense of the space was distorted, jumbled with childhood memory; it was smaller than I remembered, the desks close together, the floor criss-crossed with shadows. Across the slanted desks hung straps weighted at each end, swaying slightly, that held down the curling vellum. There were four desks and stools. Each desk had a slot for the ink horn and a foot rest. A small table along the side held straight edges, chalk, quills stripped of their barbs, dividers, and a jar of ink. The desks faced a lectern for the times when the scribes copied books read aloud to them.

This was the heart of the place. This was where my life had worth. I examined an unfinished page on one of the desks. The letters were too long, too slanted, looking like the tendrils of a vine instead of the good, solid square script I composed. *I write as least as well as that*, I thought. I wondered who wrote it. Who would be so florid, perhaps holding back wild emotion? Could this be Marcus? I went on to another desk with another unfinished page. Here the letters were too short and wide. Here was someone constrained, who held the pen tight and too upright from the page, and cut the quill narrow. I picked up the pair of dividers perched on the desk and measured the line spacing, which I knew were off. I held the dividers in my right hand and felt the sharp points of it with my left thumb and forefinger. Slowly I pushed the point into my thumb until a drop of blood squeezed out. I set the dividers down again and put my thumb between my lips.

On another desk, the writing was round, the letters rocked a bit in a loosely-held grip. This was jovial Reuben.

I went to the lectern and picked up the volume Reuben had been copying from. Here was something interesting. I felt the crest of the rhythm. It was careful, written slowly, square, very studied, as if copied from a master, but without roundness or spontaneity.

There were no mistakes, but the scribe was trying too hard, trying to be perfect but in a way that lacked grace or confidence, and somehow the scribe was hiding, hiding in this careful perfection, hiding himself in conformity. This was a scribe who longed for genius and missed the mark.

I read the words. It was a hymnal, and the hymn was Chu Chuimne's, the very one they were chanting now. I turned the page. At the end of the hymn was a small letter "c" in red. I stared and drew in my breath; my face turned hot. This was the manuscript I had copied myself ten years ago.

I sat down with it and turned back to the beginning. *I only wanted to be perfect. I've nothing to be ashamed of.* Absorbed in my reading, the sound of many tramping feet startled me. I'd forgotten to listen for the chant to end. I bolted up, but there was no way to run out without running right past everyone in the refectory. I stood frozen, my heart pounding.

Monks entered the house, then two men entered the scriptorium and stopped, staring at me in surprise. I knew them later as Jeremiah and old Gormgal, the master of the library. Jeremiah looked down his hawkish nose at me, his light blue eyes quizzical and cold.

"Who are you?" he asked, startled enough to speak, against the vow. This attracted everyone's attention in the silent house, and they crowded in to see. I faced a sea of monks staring at me, and I felt stupid.

"I am Connachtach, a penitent seeking my place, with a longing to scribe a great new Gospel. I meant no affront."

Gormgal's thin, wrinkled face relaxed into a smile. Jeremiah crooked his finger at me, and we went outside, squeezing past the wondering monks.

Jeremiah looked at me sternly. "Untonsured and unsworn, you don't belong inside yet. I am Brother Jeremiah, the abbot's assistant."

"I've been sworn these ten years. I was here as a boy. My name is Connachtach."

"You were an oblate, and now you still await the ceremony."

"It is a matter of an hour." I felt inexplicable anger. There was something about this man I didn't like.

"Yes, it is a matter of an hour. That is all the more reason for patience."

I swallowed around a lump in my throat. "I only longed to see again what my heart has desired all these years."

"Your feelings are not important. These feelings are what you leave behind. If you follow every little emotion you experience, you will not last here."

After all I had been through, I wanted to hit him. I breathed deeply and tried to quell this rotten feeling.

"I have been scribing still, practicing when I could. I've brought a parchment to show the abbot. And I have heard of my dear Luke's blindness. I've come to scribe. You will have a use for me."

Jeremiah raised an eyebrow with a slight shrug of his shoulder. "I don't know that we have the need or the resources for a great new Gospel. The hides from the slaughter are in the tanning pit. We need shoes."

# CHAPTER EIGHT: THE RULE

Jeremiah invited the sailors and me to pray in the church for thanksgiving for our successful voyage. The church, too, was smaller than I remembered, but the paintings on the walls of Saint Columba, doves of peace, lambs, and worshiping monks glowed against the whitewash. I stood shoulder to shoulder with the sailors, my brothers who brought me to my new brothers.

We ate a good meal in the guest house, and I said goodbye. They would wait for the tide, then go back to Mull to spend the night before their perilous voyage home. Did I pray for their safe return? Did I think of the danger I had put them through? I was only thinking of what I wanted, impatient to start.

Jeremiah brought me to the abbot's house. I had thought Bresal was old when I knew him before, but he was probably not so very old then. He was shorter than I remembered and had grown thin and wiry with age. His hair around the tonsure was speckled white and gray.

Jeremiah spoke first. "This is Connachtach, who was here as a boy, seeking to return to his vow."

I knelt before the abbot and kissed his hand.

"Connachtach, let me remember." He closed his eyes. I felt he couldn't remember me. He thought a few moments. "You learned with Brother Marcus?"

"Yes! I've brought a parchment to show you." I handed it to him.

"Ah, this is fine. Very nice. I recall you did do some scribing. It's coming back to me."

"Thank you, dear Father. I would like to scribe again and create a beautiful Gospel, like the one from Lindisfarne that I once saw here."

The abbot rolled the parchment back up. "We'll see. I'm afraid that's beyond our needs for the moment. You must go back to the beginning, I think. You will spend a penitential year. First things first."

"Yes, Father, but I have heard that Luke was struck blind. I will be useful to you."

From behind me, Jeremiah cleared his throat.

"There are many ways to be useful," Bresal said. "Don't fear. There is always work."

"I feel I have a gift to share with you. I've left my family behind. There has been much sacrifice."

"Of course." Bresal held the scrolled parchment, tapping it absently.

I felt he had hardly seen how fine it was. "If you would examine it closely," I said. My knees ached on the stone floor.

"You've only just arrived. We don't know you. A year of penitence will show us what you're made of," Jeremiah said. "You must have patience. Don't let pride lead you."

I clenched my fists. "It is not pride. It is not pride at all. It is a gift from God."

Bresal put two fingers on my shoulder. "It is not proper to argue. Calm yourself."

I seethed, to be told to calm myself. My body was rigid as I knelt on the hard stone floor. His fingers pressed into me.

"Breathe slowly and pray deeply," he said.

I closed my eyes. I tried to do as he said, taking a deep breath. If only I could be alone with him, without Jeremiah thwarting me.

"Let us have the ceremony, seeing as how eager you are," Bresal said. "Pray, and God will examine you. You have much to learn." I looked up at him and I don't know what expression I had, but he said, "You have nothing to fear." Did I look afraid?

"You will need an amchara," said Jeremiah. "I think Brother Luke would have much to teach you. As you know, he was a great scribe and it has now been taken from him."

"Yes," said Bresal. "Brother Luke will guide you well. Unburden yourself to him. Confession will clean your soul."

I swallowed and muttered, "Yes, thank you Father."

"The problem with humility," Bresal said, "is that it is the most painful of lessons to learn."

I looked up at him, aching all over. His face was smiling, but it was a stern smile. I couldn't speak.

There was a public ceremony outdoors as Reuben shaved me, cut my hair, and shaved my tonsure. I swore to oppose the devil. I was given a clean white robe.

We were one hundred and twenty men on the island, and men only. The great house was where the ninety-five monks slept. The rest were laymen, mostly housed between the monastery and the Bay of the Dead along the east coast where the land was fairly flat, in a dozen small houses between rigs of wheat and rye, vegetables, herbs and meadow, and a few outbuildings.

Bresal, Gormgal, Nithard, and Luke were the ancient old men, fifty years old or more. Reuben and a small handful of others were in their middle age, the rest ranging from their teens, and a few young oblates at school. We were thin with self-denial, strong with sinew and muscle, mostly bearded, brown-haired, brown-eyed, some tall. At a glance, we were similar, a family of Christian brothers, but with familiarity we took on our unique characteristics: above the bearded chin one had a bent nose, another pockmarked, another freckled and pale, Rueben with his round, fleshy face often smiling ironically, Marcus with his frank, darkly penetrating eyes.

Ninety-five young, strong men, in an ordinary life would rule strong-farms, take wives, concubines, command children, increase their cattle, take base-clients, fight in battles or protect their land against a king's wanton raids. But these men did not choose that life. They lived among other men and gave up autonomy to a life that was regulated every day, not just by season and climate, but regulated by the hour. They lived to pray. They prayed together and alone, prayers that were the same on rotation week to week, and prayers that varied in subtle ways, their private prayers different from unison chant, the chants different when it was hot or humid or cold and dry, the timber of their voices softly changing, echoing the pattern of the year. They prayed through hunger. They prayed in the joy of sacrifice, the freedom of sacrifice.

These were men who lived together and were silent, except for the three hours between Tierce and Nones, when they heard instruction or confessed. These were men who felt the weight of their sins and offered each other forgiveness, warmth, wordless understanding, because all were the same. In the tiny, packed church our sweat warmed the air.

There were offices of chanting approximately every three hours, from Prime at dawn to Compline just before bed in the evening, with the deep of night interrupted for Matins. Between Prime and Compline were Tierce, Sext, Nones, and Vespers. There was a meal in the morning after Tierce and another after Nones, except for the fast days of Wednesday and Friday when there was only the one morning meal. During times of hard work, we might have some cheese and milk before Compline.

This was the Rule. The Rule was not to talk in the House and as little as possible within the monastic enclosure. The Rule was the rejection of idleness, the spurning of vanity, and devotion to God. The Rule was hunger. The Rule was love for one's brothers, obedience to the abbot, pity for all sinners, and mercy to all who repented. One prayed for guidance from the saints—from Saint Columba and from a hundred others. One sought to be perfect and know, with deep remorse, one's failings. One sought peace above all, the peace of Columba, the peace of Christ, peace between men, peace within one's soul.

In our vow of silence, hand signals and facial expressions were the only communication. Marcus sneezed and I made the sign of the cross: *bless you*. Gormgal made a slight tugging motion as if milking a cow: *pass the milk*. I passed the jug of milk and noticed that Gormgal was eating like a penitent, only milk and bread. Gormgal touched his gray bristled chin: *thank you*. I stroked my cheek: *you're welcome*. Gormgal caught my eye and crooked his finger, then dipped it, meaning, *Follow me, afterward*.

There were a half a dozen boys, younger oblates, who cleared the tables. I followed Gormgal outside, into Columba's crypt. I ducked in the low-ceilinged room and knelt before the stone sarcophagus that held the saint's bones. Gormgal took down a small silver reliquary. He placed it before me.

Inside was a pair of dividers, a straight edge, and a quill. Gormgal gestured to it. I picked up the quill. The tip was stained with brown ink. I stroked it. It was hardened, smooth, and dry. I had never touched Columba's relics before. I felt very blessed, and smiled at Gormgal.

It had been made clear to me that the abbot saw no need to scribe a new Gospel, and in general there was no need for much scribing at the moment in any event. Days passed and the effort to quell my disappointment, and to keep it from becoming bitterness, made me sweat on the cold winter days.

In the crypt, Gormgal whispered, and I don't know how he knew of my longing, "I think of a new Gospel also. Armagh is rising up, raising up the legends of Patrick. They are raising him up, up above Columba! They are puffed up with pride, and they act as if Patrick were the mightiest, the patron saint of all Ireland. It is galling beyond endurance!" He turned red. "I fast against them. I eat but once, every day. I fast against them in the name of Jesus Christ. They will come down! Columba must be remembered!"

He put a trembling hand on my shoulder and caught his breath. I put my hand around his. We sat still for a while, Gormgal's raspy breath echoing in the tomb.

I couldn't help smiling, bowing my head to hide it. We prayed more before we left. Outside, Gormgal leaned against me, weak with hunger. He was light as a bird, just air and bone. I held the old man, who swayed like a thin willow branch, for a minute or two.

"Perhaps you should eat," I whispered.

As if to prove wrong such an offensive idea, Gormgal immediately straightened himself, planting his feet. He clasped his hands and raised them, shaking them to the moon.

There was still some time left before Compline. I went to Luke's private cell to make my daily confession. Abbot Bresal had chosen him to be my amchara, my brother of the heart. I knocked on the door.

"Come in, Brother."

A white cat darted in between my feet. "Here's Pangur Bán," said Luke when the cat leapt into his lap. Luke sat up in his cot. His blind sunken eyes were shaped like two tiny fish. The old scribe spent his days privately praying in a little cell near the crypt. "Do you have a wax tablet, Connachtach? There should be one here. I've composed a little poem I'd like you to scribe for me. I'd like to send it to my dear old confessor at Lindisfarne when next we send monks there."

I settled myself at the desk and Luke recited:

I and Pangur Bán, my cat
'Tis a like task we are at;
Hunting mice is his delight
Hunting words I sit all night.

Better far than praise of men
'Tis to sit with book and pen;
Pangur bears me no ill will,
He too plies his simple skill.

'Tis a merry thing to see
At our tasks how glad are we,
When at home we sit and find
Entertainment to our mind.

Oftentimes a mouse will stray
In the hero Pangur's way:

Oftentimes my keen thought set
Takes a meaning in its net.

'Gainst the wall he sets his eye
Full and fierce and sharp and sly;
'Gainst the wall of knowledge I
All my little wisdom try.

When a mouse darts from its den,
O how glad is Pangur then!
O what gladness do I prove
When I solve the doubts I love!

So in peace our tasks we ply,
Pangur Bán, my cat, and I;
In our arts we find our bliss,
I have mine and he has his.

Practice every day has made
Pangur perfect in his trade;
I get wisdom day and night
Turning darkness into light.

Luke asked, "What do you think?"

As he couldn't see my smile, I took Luke's hand and pressed it to my lips and cheeks. "It's very endearing."

Luke stroked the cat and purring filled the dark room. "How are you getting on? Can you take instruction?"

"Of course."

"Can you? I remember instruction rankled you."

"Did it? But I'm not a boy now."

"But I think you feel you are finished, you are arrived, that you have entered your vocation and you have nothing more to learn. But this is only the beginning. You are stripped of all, and emptied, and must be made new. Your soul is like iron, to be smelted in the holocaust and beaten hard and steady. Do you feel your soul like iron?"

I shuddered. "Yes."

"So it is. Fired and beaten it must be, until it softly glows. Do you see the faces of the other monks, how they glow?"

"Some."

Luke put his fingertips to his forehead. "That is the worst part about my blindness. Not seeing the faces, and having to speak to communicate. In the silent world inside, much is communicated through expression. You must be aware of that."

I considered this. There was Gormgal, red-faced and emotional, and Reuben had a sideways glance and a wry, ironic smile. Many of the monks did have a glow. I wondered what my face revealed. I felt I had things I wanted to keep secret.

"I wish you could see me," I said. I took his hands and put them on my face.

"You are tense," he said.

I kept his cool hands on my cheeks. "I came with a purpose and it is thwarted. I've left my family, left them in want, and the mission that I felt blessed my journey is for naught."

"So is mine," he said quietly. "Let us help you."

I didn't want to speak. I had said more than I wanted to.

He said, "It is desire for things that causes pain. You must let God in. How little you mention God."

"It is not a desire for a thing. It is a mission from God that I came on. My work is my prayer. I am being denied God," I said, with uncontrolled anger in my voice.

He was silent for a long pause as my words hung in the air. "If you could only hear yourself. If you could only know yourself. Do you want help?"

"Of course."

"I am giving you the best help I can. You don't want it."

I rose. "I will leave, and perhaps next time you will have something else to say."

"I wish you would allow me into your heart."

"I have bared my soul."

"Your heart is hard. You must soften your heart. Connachtach."

I left.

After Compline we all marched up the stairs of the house to our cots. There were some coughs, a sneeze that echoed. I lay awake under the thin woolen blanket, still dressed as we all were. In a few hours we would get up again for Matins, halfway between night and dawn. I felt the presence of almost a hundred breathing men. What I tried to think was that we were all the same, all monks devoted to the chant and loving God. At home, my former home, I had been different because I had stuck to my vow. Now that I was here, where I belonged, I still felt different. I thought of my soul like iron, and dreamt of the anvil pounding my hard heart until it was soft as a ripe peach.

In the second sleep, from Matins to Prime, I dreamt I was deep under the dark sea, breathing like a fish. I was a salmon, searching for my schoolmates, struggling to return. I dreamt someone was standing in the water, and I, Connachtach the salmon, was swimming around the man's legs, and I thought of the salmon that the otter brought to Saint Kevin, and wondering if I were that salmon, sacrificed to feed a saint, *and is that all? Is that all there is?*

## CHAPTER NINE: AEDITH

There were places I could be alone. Behind the monastery was the steep hill, called Dun I, up which I would often hike. Near the top was a little hollow from which the monastery could not be seen. I would sit in it facing the western sea where the ocean rolled on to the end of the world. Only the legendary lands of Saint Brendan's voyage were beyond that horizon.

Oona had loved the story of Saint Brendan, and listened to it with pleasure every time I told it. To the north were tinier hermitages, Tiree and Coll, islands remote and barren but for the clash of thousands of birds. I wondered if I should retire there and get farther away from faces, from eyes glowing under brows furrowed from exhaustion and smiles beatific and certain. Perhaps go to a solitary island completely alone, living on crabs and snared gannets.

Then I walked back down, with my hands clasped before my chest, through the early morning mist before Prime, the weak winter sun barely risen over the isle of Mull across the sound. I took the road from the cemetery down to the Bay of the Dead, past the many crosses and the few small buildings, the field of winter wheat, and meadows of drying brown-headed flowers.

The beach was faintly red in the sunrise, the gentle tide a quiet hush. The silence was broken by the piercing song of a redshank wading nearby, and I turned my head toward the bird hopping on its thin orange legs. It raised its long curved beak and cried again. I lifted my gaze. Something dark was out in the waves, rolling with the tide. A seal, I thought. It bobbed and tumbled, inching closer toward the rocks. It did not seem to be swimming, but floating and rolling in the water. I wondered if the seal were

dead. A larger wave turned it over. A flash of pale skin. An arm,
a bare foot.

I ran to the brown boulders that made a natural jetty and
climbed over the rocks, not thinking. Time seemed to slow down.
I could see every crevice to avoid, every tangle of seaweed as I
raced, not feeling the speed. A white face loomed below. I waded
in among the uneven rocks, and a heavy wave pulled the body
back as I reached for her hand. She was tangled in seaweed. I
grasped the seaweed and pulled. The heavy weight of the creature surprised me and I slipped, falling backward, in the frigid
water. I struggled in my soaked woolen robes, blinded by the
wave, losing sight of her. I pushed through the water to the mass
of seaweed rolling out of my reach. Stumbling over the rocks I
grabbed the slimy seaweed, pulling and pulling through the white
foam as salt spray splashed into my panting mouth. I lifted her up
and carried her to the beach to lay her down. Something swung
from her wet clothes.

She was a girl of about Deirdre's age, her long red hair tangled in a mass around her head, her cheek bruised from the rocks,
her lips gray. I pulled the seaweed from around her and put my
head on her chest. There was a rasp; she was alive.

I tried to lift her to turn her over. Again there was a weight
that surprised me now that she was no longer bound in the seaweed. I lay her back down and felt her waist. Her linen apron was
knotted with rocks, the swollen knots too hard to untie. I yanked
the apron off over her head.

Turning her over in a crouch, I pushed my fists against her
stomach in three quick, hard thrusts. She coughed and retched,
her little body shaking. I turned her over again and rubbed her
hands and legs vigorously, but she remained still, and I picked
her up and carried her to the guest house, meeting Cellach on
the way.

"Fetch the doctor."

Cellach didn't ask questions and went quickly. In the guest
house, I laid the girl on the mattress and stoked the fire high, slid
a pillow under her head, and laid a blanket over her. The doctor,

Brother Kay, came in with strong smelling herbs. He waved them under her nose, and she began to cough violently. When she tried to sit up, the doctor held her and gently eased her back. Her thin face was ashen.

Brother Kay threw some herbs on the fire, and their scent filled the air. The girl coughed for a while then finally stopped, and the doctor brought her a cup of water.

"What happened, Aedith?" he asked her.

She sipped the water, staring at the fire, her blue eyes reflecting the sparks. She didn't answer.

"You fell in?" the doctor continued.

She slowly nodded. "I must have. I don't remember."

I wondered when and if I should say something about the stones in her apron, but I felt now was not the time. "You're from the island of women?" I asked.

She nodded.

The doctor said, "She's Brother Jeremiah's niece."

She looked up at us with worried eyes. "What will you say?"

The doctor stroked her hand. "What is there to tell? You fell into the tide. We'll take you back to the island as soon as you're well. Gwyn must be worried sick for you."

Aedith started crying. "I didn't think," she said between heavy breaths.

"Quiet now," the doctor said. "You'll be fine. We must go and tell the abbot, and get you some hot milk. You'll be home to your mother in no time."

Cellach was waiting outside as I left Aedith with the doctor, and I told him to fetch hot milk. I went to the abbot's house and knocked. Jeremiah came out.

"A girl from the other island washed ashore, nearly drowned. Aedith, your niece."

Jeremiah cocked his head in bafflement. "I've never heard of such a thing. Is the doctor tending to her? Is she all right?"

"Yes. I'd like to go along when they take her back to her home."

"I'll tell the abbot. I'm sure that will do. Father Bresal's niece Morgan is in charge there."

I returned to the guest house, meeting Cellach with the jug of milk outside.

"What happened?" Cellach asked.

I said, "Something strange. A mystery."

"Was the devil involved in this?"

"I think perhaps he was."

"I will pray for her."

"So will I."

I took the jug and went in. The doctor was stoking the fire as Aedith lay still, her eyes open. I brought her the milk and she sat up.

"I'm going to fetch some more herbs to throw on the fire. They will clear her lungs," the doctor said. "Rest, my dear."

He left, and I sat beside Aedith while she sipped the warm milk. She looked at me awkwardly.

"Did you speak with my uncle?"

"Yes."

"What did you tell him?"

I folded my arms and leaned toward her. "What should I tell him?"

Tears slipped from her eyes. "What did you say?"

"That you fell in the tide. But for your soul—"

She put her hands over her face, trembling. "Please don't tell him. His way to heal my sin will be to punish me. And for my mother—I couldn't bear anyone to know. Forgive me. Forgive me." She cried into her hands.

I sat on the edge of the bed and put my hands on her shoulders. "I don't know what is best. There was a time when I thought I always knew what was right. Now I don't. So I won't tell for now. Calm yourself, be easy."

She grabbed my hands and pressed them against her cheeks. "Thank you. Thank you. What is your name?"

"Brother Connachtach."

"Thank you, dear Brother Tach."

The bell was struck for Prime, and I smoothed her cheeks, wiping her tears on my sleeve. "Rest. Will you be ready to return this afternoon?"

"Yes, I think so. I had better prepare myself." She sat up and rubbed her head.

"Yes, prepare yourself and be strong."

"Thank you."

I got up and went to the church for Prime. As I chanted, it was hard to think about the words. The mystery of the girl felt like a haze around me, and when I thought about her, Deirdre's face also came to my mind.

When I returned to the guest house, Aedith was sitting up with Marcus, who was amusing her with shadow figures on the wall. The doctor came in after me.

"How are you breathing?" he asked her. He put the herbs on the fire, the air redolent with sage. He checked her pulse. "Healthy as a horse," he said, patting her head. "Ready to see your mother?"

Her smile faded. She looked around the room. "I suppose."

"She's most likely very worried," the doctor said.

"Yes, I must go to her. I didn't think. I didn't think."

Marcus put his arm around her. "Hush, there now, there's no blame. We must go. You're dry now. We'll float you across the water, nice and easy." He helped her up from the mattress, and she took his hand.

We went down to the shore where the coracles were beached. It was a short row to the other island, the island to which Saint Columba had banished women, a few yards off the shore of Mull. A silver light on the water surrounded it as the mist rose, and it lay silhouetted like a seal on the water. The island was even smaller than Iona, with a rocky coast. Where the rocks were even with the water we scrambled over the slippery stones to shore. The island was ringed with rocky outcroppings, dipping into a center of green meadow. Marcus went there from time to time on Fridays to help the women, but I had never been there, though I had seen it well enough from the top of Dun I.

There was a cry. A tall woman stood on the peak, careering down to us with her arms outstretched. Aedith stumbled up the narrow path into her arms.

"Where have you been, child?" she asked between laughter and sobs.

"I don't know. I must have fallen."

I assumed the woman was Aedith's mother, but Aedith said, "Morgan, forgive me. Where is my mother?"

Morgan held her tightly in her muscular arms. "She is inside, as always."

We climbed up and over the boulders, down into the green hollow dotted with cows where five houses were nestled. In the center were gathered a dozen women and an equal number of children, praying in a circle, who shouted when they spotted Aedith coming down. The noisy group clamored around them, all trying to hold Aedith at once.

Morgan pulled Aedith away. "Be still! She must rest."

The women shushed the children. The group spread apart and Morgan, her arm around Aedith's waist, walked her into the small round house. I followed them in.

The house was dark. A low fire burned in the center, the smoke dully rising. The darkness resolved into beds, a bench, stools, pots, and blankets. Morgan let go of Aedith, who stepped into a muttering shadow on the other side of the fire. On the bed was a red blanket with a fold in it. The fold was a blade-thin woman, whispering, her bony bare arms clasped in front of her chest, her eyes closed.

"Mama," Aedith said in a timid voice.

The muttering grew slightly louder, a prayer, a mixture of the Latin Our Father and Scots calling for saints Brigid and Kevin.

"Mama, I'm here."

Her mother opened her eyes, large and gleaming with visions of another world. "The angels brought you," she whispered. She held out her arms, and Aedith slid into the bed with her.

"I'm here, Mama. I fell in the water."

Her mother hushed her, stroking her hair. "I won't let the sea take you. The angels brought you back, just as I prayed. God would not refuse me, not this time." Her bright eyes danced with tears. "My treasure, my only treasure." She closed her eyes and hugged Aedith tightly.

Morgan turned and gestured for me to follow. Outside she said, "Gwyn doesn't always notice that someone is there. You are a new monk?" Her gaze was frank and her manner brisk.

"Yes, I'm Connachtach. I was the one who found her on the beach across the way."

Morgan held out her hand. "Thank you."

I took her hand, and she squeezed mine in a strong grip. "Tell me about her," I asked.

"She has a large imagination."

"It's a small island," I said

Morgan gave me a rueful smile, and I smiled back shyly. Her eyes were a bold lapis blue, and there was a wine stain on her temple, as if God had put his thumbprint on her. I tore my eyes from her gaze.

"We'll let the children play until dinner," she said. "I thought Fiona would help, but the flighty woman is off somewhere, of course. Excuse me." She left me.

I didn't know where Marcus had gone to. The bell for Tierce was struck on Iona, echoing over the water. One boy was playing with a collection of shells. I went and knelt beside him.

The boy turned to me with bright eyes and picked up the shells one by one. "This is a periwinkle. This kind, the pretty ones, lives on the wrack, the seaweed with the big leaves. You turn the leaf over and there they are. But this kind, the rough kind, lives on the rocks. This is a dog whelk. Do you see the hole in this mussel shell? The dog whelk drills a hole into the shell and eats the little soft creature. But you must see this. Do you see anything unusual about this?" He handed me a spiral univalve shell with a glossy pink mouth.

"No, what is it?"

The boy clutched the shell and gestured as if to a classroom. "Usually the opening is to the right. But this one is very rare. It opens to the left. This might be the only one you ever see. Behold it." He put it into my hand, and I examined it.

"You know a great deal."

"Yes. I know all about shells. If anyone has a shell question, they know to come to me."

A small girl came running up to us. "Here, Brion," she said with a shy smile. She presented him with a brown and white striped shell.

"That's fine, Emer," he said, tracing the whorls with his finger. "That's a topshell. Thank you." He thanked her with a modest, adult air that was gentle and formal. The girl held her hands behind her back and swayed back and forth, watching him fondly. He nodded to her, and she smiled broadly and ran off. I had a premonition of the boy growing to manhood, undisturbed by female affection, not cold but diffident, respectful and unrequiting. Brion seemed accustomed to this girl's attentions, and he was friendly but not familiar.

"Will you be coming to the monastery to take instruction?" I asked him.

Brion looked puzzled. "Why?"

"Because you have aptitude. Watch." I picked up the shells and made a B with them. "That's the first letter of your name."

Brion shrugged. "That is not the order they go in." He took the B apart and rearranged them. "I think you don't know about shells," he said.

The other children ran up to us. Emer, the littlest girl, said, "Tell us about the winds."

I sat on the ground with them. "King Setna dreamt his wife Eithne swallowed a star, and nine months later, Saint Maedoc was born."

Emer lay on her back and opened her mouth.

Another child said, "You'll more likely swallow a bug."

She closed her mouth and pulled her knees under her chin.

I continued, "Saint Mochuda imprisoned a demon in a standing stone, and used the monolith as a boundary for his monastery. And you know how we pray, with arms outstretched. Saint Kevin stood in the forest praying for so long that a small brown bird made a nest in his hand. He stayed there until the chicks were fledged." I told them these stories until a light rain began to fall, and Morgan came outside to call us in to eat.

The house was smoky from the humid air. Aedith helped Morgan dish out the stewed meat. It seemed that the normal routine was restored, but the children begged Aedith to tell what happened despite the women telling them to be quiet.

Aedith's eyes met mine. She flushed and gave an embarrassed smile at the group's attention, and said, "The seal was as big as a big man, and so black and shining. Its eyes glowed like coals, and it stared into mine so that I was enchanted. It seemed I could hear music, a pipe playing. It seemed to nod and turn its head, and I followed. I was pulled into the water, and I couldn't feel the wet, cold waves, or the rain as it fell like a curtain. The water parted before me, and I entered it, like entering a house, the house of the changeling seal. It was before me, swimming on, and I swam on, and then the waves started to turn, to spin around, so that down I was pulled toward my watery doom." She stopped and glanced again at me, but I betrayed nothing. "But then I heard cries, human cries, of rescue. I heard my mother's voice in prayer, calling me back. Someone was carrying me, this dear monk. And I lived to tell you the whole story."

As Aedith told her story, Gwyn lay on the bed, propped on her elbow, her face lighted by the fire. I could see the resemblance to her brother Jeremiah in her beaky nose, gaunt cheeks, and sallow skin. Her eyes glowed with a weird light. She looked as if she had not been outdoors in a long time. Her light brown hair was well combed, perhaps by Aedith, and its thick luster contrasted her hollow, aging face. Now, as she listened to her daughter's animated speech, she beamed, her thin mouth smiling at the fantastic tale. Unlike the children, she wasn't frightened; unlike Morgan, she didn't frown disapprovingly. She either was happy her daughter had escaped, or enjoyed the entertaining fiction. It was all the same to her.

Emer handed Aedith a doll. "Eithne is afraid. You have to tell her it's all right."

Aedith took the doll and addressed it tenderly and with confidence. "Of course it's all right. The spell is broken now. It lost its chance, and now it will be gone forevermore."

Morgan looked up. "And it's best to speak of it no more." Her voice was sharp.

Aedith blushed and then gave the doll a kiss, and then kissed Emer, who threw her arms around her.

"Me, too," Gwyn said. Emer brought the doll over for her kiss. Gwyn scooped the little girl into her arms and fell back on the bed.

Aedith added a turf to the fire, and the sparks danced. When she looked up, our eyes met. The challenge on her face melted into a deep sadness before she turned back to stir the pot.

"We should go before the tide turns back," I said.

"You've had enough to eat?" Morgan asked.

"Yes, I've broken my penance."

Marcus came inside just then. Aedith handed him a bowl of bread and meat.

"We were about to leave," I said.

"Of course, just a bite or two," Marcus said. He began to wolf down the food.

Another woman entered from outside. She was a plump woman, her blond hair falling from her hood. "You ate early, I was going to help," she said.

"Fiona, I think your second name is 'I was going to help.'" Morgan said.

Fiona laughed, not offended. She helped herself to a bowl of food. "All is well?"

Emer said, "You missed the story."

"And it won't be repeated," said Morgan.

Fiona sat next to Emer and stroked her hair. "Did you help Brion find shells?" she asked.

"Yes, I found a good one."

"Perhaps Aedith brought shells with her from the sea."

The room fell silent and uncomfortable. Fiona burst into a laugh. "All is well, children, all is well. I'm sorry, Aedith. But all is well. I am just so relieved, I can only be merry."

Aedith went and hugged her. "Darling Fiona, what would we do without you?" Fiona kissed her forehead.

Marcus finished eating and set the bowl on the table. "It's never dull here." He popped a last piece of bread in his mouth, smiling on Aedith and Fiona.

"I'll walk you back to the boat," Morgan said.

"And I," said Aedith.

The children all started to shout that they would go, too.

Morgan shushed them. "No, you must stay and not be darting about everywhere. It's like herding cats with you."

We walked across the green, up and over the hill to the rocky shore where we had beached the boat. Aedith stood close to me. I suddenly grabbed Aedith's hand. I drew the letters of her name on her palm, spelling it aloud.

"This is your name, Aedith."

Her eyes started and she gaped. "It is?"

"I am a scribe at the monastery."

"Will you teach me?" Her face was open and expectant. She would not be denied.

"I don't know. You can't come to Iona. I doubt I'll be coming here."

"You can come with Marcus. He has business here helping Morgan and Fiona. He comes here most Fridays."

I looked at her urgent face. Her eyes were wide and direct in mine, ready to convince me.

"I don't know. We'll see."

"I'll pray for it," she said.

I patted her head. She pulled away and swung her arms excitedly, her red skirt billowed out as she danced. I watched her. The evening was fine. A cool, refreshing breeze blew from the sea, the autumn twilight sky deep blue with big, bonny white clouds. I felt the fineness of the day, and wanted to stay rooted to that spot a long while, but it was time to go.

When we were in the boat, I said to Marcus, "Where did you disappear to?"

Marcus shrugged and smiled. "Looking at storm damage from the last gale. There is some work to be done."

"I thought the pixies had taken you."

"Thank God you found Aedith. It would have been the end of her mother."

I breathed hard as I rowed. "What is their story?"

"Aedith's father went out to fish one day two years ago, when a sudden squall came over. He never came back, nor did his body. That was when Gwyn, Aedith, and Emer came and settled on the island. Aedith's mother stays in bed with a kind of madness. I didn't realize that Aedith…" He hesitated. "I found her apron on the beach."

"I see." We rowed in silence for some moments. "Is there anything we can do? Should we tell anyone?"

"No, let's not tell. But we'll pray, and God will tell us what to do."

A man stood in the water up to his waist as we approached Iona. It was Luke, praying in the frigid water, stock still with his arms outstretched. His sunken eyes were closed, and he was turning blue with the cold, swaying in the waves. The bell was struck for Vespers. Luke began to stumble forward, and I rushed into the water to help him as Marcus beached the boat.

"Is that the scribe?" Luke asked.

"Yes." I put my arm around Luke, who could hardly walk because of the numbness of his legs. He continued to lean heavily against me as we walked up from the beach to the church. I noticed for the first time how hard and uneven the path was, exposed rocks in the yellow soil bumpy underfoot. I limped, my uneven gait revealing to me that something was sore in my groin. A new lump.

After the chant we went together to Luke's cell. I wrapped him in his blanket and rubbed his legs. The cat jumped on him and settled on his chest. Luke stroked its white fur, a patch of light in the darkness. Because Luke never burned a lamp, the air in the room was clear and dry.

"You didn't strike me as having much to repent," I said, referring to his penance of standing in the cold sea.

Luke smiled. "Sometimes the hunger for salvation rips through me like a bitter wind, and I must quench it. The water felt burning hot to me, in my burning passion. Penance is the only relief."

I sat on the floor next to his cot.

"Do you understand salvation?" Luke asked.

"I think so." I hesitated before continuing. "Today I met a girl who I think is much in need of salvation. She was drowning, and we saved her, but I fear she was attempting to take her own life. God forgive me for saying so."

Luke gripped my hand and breathed deeply with his eyes closed. After a bit, I thought he had fallen asleep. But then he spoke. "Can you save her?"

"I'd like to."

"But *can* you? Do you understand salvation? I fear you don't."

I thought there was much I could teach the girl Aedith, but I thought it might not be enough. "I feel God is calling me to try."

A small smile passed over Luke's mouth. "I think you should try, then." After a pause he said, "At least the girl inspired you to mention God."

I came out from Luke's cell to a sharp, groaning wind. Purple clouds lowered in a threatening sky. I studied them, thinking of the inks and paints that would create these colors, the mulberry for mauve, easy to get, the white lead, the azure blue for the sky from crushed lapis lazuli, the only source far away in Arabia. Smoke rose from the great house, and I imagined the monks warm and dry inside, Nithard teaching the boys, the men reading, writing, or doing chores. It seemed distant from me as I stood outside in this barren landscape.

Cellach came out of the kitchen and went to the well, followed by a yellow dog. I joined him, taking a drink of the ice-cold water.

"Are you getting on?" I asked.

"Aye. I like it here."

"You don't miss Colonsay?"

Cellach shook his head. "I always felt a stranger there. Right away I felt I belonged here."

I nodded, and Cellach returned to the kitchen with a pail of water in each hand, his thin, hard shoulders straight as stretched cords. As I walked to the abbot's house, a light rain began to fall, scattered drops in the wind.

I knocked, and when I entered the abbot was dictating a letter to Jeremiah, his face and hands skeletal in the dim, green light. The abbot turned to me with a smile, which surprised me. I sank to my knees and the abbot motioned for me to rise. Jeremiah set down his stylus and wax tablet, making no move to leave us alone.

"What do you seek?" the abbot asked.

"I wish on certain Fridays to go to the other island. Some of the children could benefit from instruction."

Jeremiah clucked his tongue. "That is a very odd idea."

"Why?" the abbot asked.

"I'm concerned about someone there. Someone who needs spiritual guidance."

"A monk is not a pastoral guide. A monk does not go into the world," Jeremiah said, nodding.

The abbot sighed. "You seem to want to do everything but the one thing you are here for."

I would have said the one thing I was there for was to scribe, but I knew the abbot meant prayer. "I'd like to teach the children a bit of the Psalter. It would be good for their souls." I turned to Jeremiah. "Aedith, your niece, asked me to. She seems very bright."

Bresal sighed and tapped his desk. "That is a waste of your time. I see no need for such a scheme." Bresal made the gesture of permission to leave.

"Thank you. Bless you, Father."

Jeremiah picked up his stylus, and stared at me as I left. I could feel his sharp hawk eyes on me as I went out the door.

# CHAPTER TEN: TEACHING

Lent didn't increase my suffering. My belly was already always cold with hunger. When it was time for my confession with Luke, I spoke little, though my soul clamored for answers. My thoughts spun and it was too hard to speak. I wanted to know what sin I had committed, to leave my family and come this way, and not have my reward, the work of my dreams. Reward was not appropriate, but was punishment? I wanted to ask, and I wanted to expel all these sorrows, but I didn't talk to Luke, or tell him I might be dying.

As Easter approached and the cold ground eased its way from hard to yielding, Jeremiah crooked his finger at me and led me to the abbot's office. When I entered, the abbot smiled at me, but it was a strained smile, as if mixed with misgiving. I knelt.

Bresal said, "I have a job for you and you will be pleased by it. You wanted to teach. Brother Leo is going away on a journey to Lindisfarne. You will take over his teaching on Monday through Thursday. Bother Nithard has the boys on Friday and Saturday."

My eyes searched the room, at our shadows stretched across the floor, my shadow crouched below his.

"Are you pleased?"

"That might be interesting. Thank you, Father."

"Brother Leo will be leaving right after Easter. Before he goes, he'll introduce you to the boys."

There was still something wrong, I sensed it. Jeremiah cleared his throat and put his hand on the door, but I didn't move.

"Is there something wrong?" I asked. "I can't help but feel there is something."

"Nothing for now," Jeremiah said.

I waited.

Abbot Bresal bowed his head in thought. "Perhaps you should know." The abbot pulled a small sheet of curling vellum from his desk. It had been rolled up, a letter. "I received this from Lindisfarne a few days ago." He handed over the letter.

The writing was small; there were blotches of ink as if the writer's hand was shaking. "My Dear Father Bresal, bless you and pray for us. The room I write this in is half destroyed. White devils, a plague from hell in ships, have attacked and ravaged our holy home in horrific sacrilege. It is like end times have come upon us. I write in haste and beg you to send us help. I will return with your brothers to tell you more, if words can come. Yours in Christ, Brother Daric."

I read it several times. "White devils? What can this mean? This is all he wrote?"

Bresal nodded. "We're sending Brother Leo and some others as soon as we can. I haven't decided whether to make this known."

"Since we aren't certain what happened," Jeremiah said. "For now we'd like to keep this knowledge, such as it is, to the few of us."

I handed back the letter. "Thank you for taking me into your confidence. If only there were more information. Is it the end times? Is it possible?"

"We must pray and carry on our work. There is nothing else," Bresal said.

On Easter we made the procession around the island at dawn, with Bresal in front carrying aloft a Bible. We stopped at various points, such as the little stone hut Saint Columba would retreat to, chanting at each stop. We took communion. It was March 30, the stone floor of the church cold beneath our knees.

The next day I met the five boys who were taking instruction. Four of them were oblates, committed by their families to become monks at a tender age. The oldest, a big blond boy, was named Tarain. He was around twelve and not an oblate. I noted he wore a gold torque, perhaps a gift from an indulgent father.

Brother Leo, a hearty, bluff man whose beard grew heavy between the monthly tonsures, introduced me. They continued the *Ars Donatus.* One by one the boys stood and repeated the lesson. Brother Leo stood by, silent and watchful. As I looked down at the book to read the next section, I heard a muffled chortle and looked up.

"Stand, Raef!" said Brother Leo.

Raef stood, hanging his head and holding out his hands. Leo took a step next to him and quickly swatted the back of Raef's hands with a switch in four sharp blows. Dark red marks appeared across his pale skin.

"Thank you, Brother." Raef sat down.

A bead of sweat trickled down the back of my neck. I continued the lesson with the silent class. Afterward I walked outside with Leo.

"I don't know about punishing the boy," I said.

"Don't be foolish. Besides, they want it and they enjoy it."

"They want it? And enjoy it? "

Brother Leo raised his eyebrows and thought about it. As he thought he looked more intrigued. "Well. I've never thought to analyze it. You've had dogs, and observed them?"

"Yes."

"They seek their leader. Boys are much like dogs. Actually, just like dogs. They want to know someone is in charge."

I knew I had a doubtful look on my face.

The teacher continued. "Weren't you ever a boy? Look, have you ever patted a dog and said 'no!' at the same time? That's what women do. The dog doesn't know what to do. It makes the dog nervous not to know. The boys *want* to know you're in charge. The boys aren't happy if they don't know. It makes them happy to know who's who and what's what, and they'll obey. Yes, even if it means thrashing them, it makes them happy."

Though it wasn't impossible to understand, I still wanted to object. I looked up at Brother Leo's simple, confident face.

Brother Leo gave me a mocking but friendly smile. "It must be difficult to go through life having to *understand* everything."

I felt myself blush.

"Besides, I don't thrash them all that much. Two or three blows at the beginning settle it. I've never caused any permanent damage. When I was young, teachers were much more strict. I'm really very soft." He smiled. "My advice is, thrash someone the first day, or for God's sake at least threaten to, and that will be the end of it."

I swallowed back a reply, promising myself I would never hit the boys, and changed the subject. "Who is the bigger boy, Tarain? Not an oblate?"

"No, and he is the instigator of any trouble. He was the son of a king. When his parents died and there was a battle, his uncle sent him here for protection. He will probably return to his land at the head of an army. I hope in the meantime some discipline and holy learning will do him some good."

Within the week, Brother Leo and some other monks left on the journey to Lindisfarne. I felt determined to be a good teacher, as my one legacy.

On a typical day, young Tibald was squirming during the lesson.

"Stop fidgeting," I told him.

A few minutes passed and he squirmed again.

"Tibald."

It happened a third time, and Tibald whispered something under his breath.

"Stand up."

Tibald squeezed back tears and held out his hands.

"What's wrong with you?"

"Tarain keeps blowing in my ear."

"Tarian, stand up." Tarain stood. "Stay behind when the others go and copy noun declensions."

"Yes, Brother. Thank you."

I felt the eyes of the other monks, who were reading and taking notes nearby.

Later, Reuben took me aside. "You aren't severe enough with the boys," he said.

"I will teach as I see fit." I didn't feel the need to say I had vowed not to strike them. Perhaps if I had, he could have given me further advice, but I raised my chin in defiance. He looked at me, his expression surprised, affronted. I turned away.

The bell was struck for Tierce. Inside the church, the air was cool, dark in the winter afternoon. It refreshed me to chant after the tiring hours of the boys. As we left the church, Jeremiah crooked his finger in his usual way. I followed him to the abbot's office, though to my surprise, Bresal wasn't there.

Jeremiah cleared his throat. "Marcus is going to the other island Friday. He goes there from time to time to help the women. How well do you know Marcus?"

I paused. "Not very well. We were boys here together. He was attentive. A good scribe."

"I'd like you to watch over him."

"As an amchara?"

Jeremiah shrugged. "If he confesses to you, it would be a good thing. If he is in a state of sin, the abbot should know about it."

I looked at the one small window. Jeremiah was reflected in the glass, his bones outlined in green. "A confession is a confidential thing," I said.

"One's sins will be shouted from the roof tops. Or at least punished as is fit."

I was confused. "I doubt I'll find out anything the abbot would care about. He's a busy man."

"Our souls are his priority."

"I'm grateful for that." His face was imperious, and I thought how I had been accused of pride, but this was truly the face of pride. "Brother Jeremiah... what if the world is... ending...? What is important?"

Jeremiah's eyes narrowed, his face suddenly wrathful. "Yes, it could be, and for that reason we must be pure. We must be pure to the utmost. You will go with him and watch over him like a good brother and report to me." He made the gesture of *thank you,* the sign of the cross, and then, *you may leave.*

The night before I was to accompany Marcus to the other island, I sat in the refectory watching the other monks reading by lamplight. Gormgal sat at the center of his long, narrow table that partially blocked access to the book cupboards. To his right was a stack of books needing repair, their bindings loose and corners frayed. Beside the stack were his tools: a knife and sharpening stone, coil of gut, jar of glue, box of tacks, and a small hammer, all neatly arranged. To his left was his great ledger where he kept track of all the books lent to the monks and to other monasteries. He opened the ledger and scanned a page with his finger and made a note on his wax tablet, no doubt a reminder to send about returning a book.

The doors of the cupboards were covered in thin fretwork, the books like prisoners behind bars. The keys to the cupboards hung from his belt, black and well oiled with no rust at all.

I wanted to take a children's Psalter to the other island. I couldn't ask for it. Gormgal would question me. My students were onto *Ars Donatus,* not a beginning Psalter. I would not receive permission to take the book over there and teach.

The bell was struck for Compline, the last chant of the day. The monks rose and filed out, and I waited. Gormgal waited too, by his desk, clearly wanting to leave last. I took a few steps to the door, and Gormgal passed me, his head bowed under his hood.

I stopped and watched the monks go ahead, then turned and hurried back into the house. Gormgal had blown out the lamps, but the moonlight through the windows and open door was enough. The Psalter was at the end of a shelf near the hinge of the cupboard door. I took the hammer and tapped the pin out of its hinge. Gritting my teeth, I pulled gently on the edge of the door. I slipped my fingers inside and grasped the leather cover of the slim volume. Holding my breath, I traced my finger up the binding, hooking my finger on the thread of gut. I eased it out and slid the pin back into the hinge.

I put the book into my wide sleeve and stood for a moment leaning against the table, feeling lightheaded. It grew darker in the room. I thought for a moment I would faint, so nervous and so hungry. A shadow on the floor revealed the outline of a man. Jeremiah stood in the doorway, blocking the light, his bald head outlined in the moonlight. His gaunt face was stark, the triangle shadow of his hawk nose on his cheek, his long chin glittering with straw-colored stubble, his light eyes glinting with curiosity under a questioning brow.

I didn't know how long Jeremiah had been standing there watching. I waited for Jeremiah to speak and accuse me, as I held my arm bent by my side, the small book at my elbow inside the sleeve.

Jeremiah tossed his head impatiently and beckoned. I clasped my hands in prayer in front of my chest and walked toward the door.

Jeremiah stepped aside for me to pass, whispering, "Come along. What did you want to do, scribe in the dark like a ghost? It's Compline."

We both quick-stepped to the church, my hands in prayer under my chin, the little book tapping against my ribs.

## CHAPTER ELEVEN: SECRETS

The next day Marcus and I rowed to the other island. When we walked into the green, I approached Morgan, avoiding her lapis blue eyes.

"I thought I might teach the children the Psalter."

She looked surprised. "I suppose, if you think it's right."

I bent down and put my hand on Brion's shoulder, the boy who loved shells. "Would you like to learn the Psalter?"

The boy furrowed his brow and shrugged. "Maybe."

Aedith skipped up to us and put her arms around the boy from behind. "Are there shells in the Book?" she asked with a smile.

"There's a wondrous animal of the sea called the hillazon, which the Jews use to make their special blue dye," I said.

"You see?" she said to Brion.

Brion wriggled free. "We'll see about that."

I went toward the house, and Aedith immediately gathered the children and we sat outside.

"This is the Psalter." I held up the book, which was scribed in large letters for children. "These are prayers that we chant every day. I could tell you what the letters are, but they're in Latin. I'll read it out to you, and you repeat it back to me."

The children did as they were told and we read psalms awhile. Aedith recited with a look of concentration. She squeezed the hands of the children next to her and encouraged them.

"What does it mean?" asked Emer, the girl who'd given Brion the top shell.

"This one asks for God to give us strength when our enemies are against us."

"How do we know who the enemy is?"

A small boy of about four years grabbed her by the arm. "I'm your enemy!"

Aedith pulled him back. "Hush. You're no one's enemy. Only grown-ups have enemies. Isn't that right?"

I shook my head. "The enemy is the devil, only the devil."

Aedith's eyes widened. "Does he tempt us to... to lie and do bad things?"

"Aye."

Aedith looked down. She spoke haltingly. "There must be a great deal that is at war, all around us. Sometimes it seems all we have to do are our daily tasks, eat, sleep, and nothing more. As if we were dolls that could move and eat, but no more than dolls, or animals that see nothing. But there is something. There must be. God is something more, isn't He?"

"Yes, so He is."

"And prayer opens your heart to God. It opens up your soul when it's shut tight against God's word." She looked up at me. "We *must* be more than animals."

Brion made a dramatic wave of his arm and jumped up. "You are mad sometimes. Everything must be proved to you. I'm going out to look for shells before it's dark." He left, followed by Emer.

Aedith cocked her head. "It's happiness to love one thing and find it on the sand everyday. I shall love God, and I will find Him wherever I look."

"He will seem hidden at times."

"When he is hidden, I will pray. That will make the eyes of my soul keener for seeing Him."

"You are a wiser child of God than I am," I said.

She gave a little laugh and tugged on my sleeve, her green eyes sparkling at me; she had been holding back tears. "You seem awfully doubtful for a monk."

"Perhaps. You are right in everything. I only meant that sometimes the simplest goal requires the greatest exertion."

Aedith clasped her hands. "You must know all about the saints, of Brigid and Kevin, and Columba and Patrick."

"I know a bit. You know the breastplate of Saint Patrick is called the Deer's Cry."

"Why?"

"Well, it happened that when Patrick and his eight companions went to Tara to challenge the high king, they were turned into deer, so they could go through the forest undetected by his soldiers. This is the Deer's Cry." I stood up and spread my arms, and Aedith and the children did likewise. I taught them the prayer:

"Christ be with me, Christ be before me:
Christ be behind me, Christ be with me:
Christ be beneath me, Christ be above me:
Christ be at my right, Christ be at my left:
Christ be in the fort, Christ be in the chariot:
Christ be in the ship.
Christ be in the heart of everyone who thinks of me:
Christ be in the mouth of everyone who speaks of me:
Christ be in every eye that sees me;
Christ be in every ear that hears me. Amen."

Morgan approached us. "Aedith, you must get the bread."

Aedith left for the oven, leaving me alone with Morgan, who began weaving at the loom against the wall of the house. Her back was to me, straight as she leaned from her ankles. The wide neck of her garment revealed the bone of her neck curving into her muscular back. I saw every little muscle pulsing to her effort, diamond shaped muscles between her shoulder blades rising and flattening in rhythm. The shadows created by her muscles were blue, and the highlights of her skin glistened with a fine sweat. My sense of her motion was increased by the steady sound of the loom, drumming a beat to her swaying back. With the beat of the loom to measure time, she sang softly, the notes on the downbeat a little louder, some force on the exhale as she beat up the weft. Her voice was husky and high, the sound of it recalling to me the sound of fire, the way it breathed, her voice like fire singing. Pleasure vibrated within me.

Aedith returned with Marcus and Fiona, carrying the bread. Fiona carried a pot of meat.

"You see, I cooked as I was supposed to, Morgan. I do more than you think," Fiona said, setting the pot on the table.

Morgan put up the beater with a prayer to Saint Brigid. "It is a good thing to do more than what one is asked," she said when she turned around.

Fiona threw up her hands. "It is a good thing to be satisfied with someone's efforts. Really…"

Marcus patted Fiona's back. Fiona started to put her head on his shoulder, but he stepped away.

"When is a woman ever satisfied?" Marcus said. "Men are quickly satisfied, right, Connachtach?"

I started to agree when Fiona burst into a laugh. She smothered her face in her apron. "You are a naughty monk."

"It is easier to be among men," I said, embarrassed.

Morgan started to serve the meat as the children lined up with their bowls. Friday was a fast day for monks, and to keep it I only ate bread and some whey. Aedith, chewing her meat, saw this.

"Surely you must eat?" she asked.

"It is a fast day for me."

She whispered with a shy smile, "No one would know."

"I would."

She set aside her bowl and clasped her hands to join me in fasting. I gave her a gentle smile. "You must eat," I whispered. "It is right for you to eat."

"Can't I be like you?"

"First you have growing to do."

She gave a little nod and went back to her meal, handing some leftover bread to little Emer.

It was time to go. Morgan walked us to the boat on the rocks. She turned to me.

"The abbot permits you to teach her?"

"Yes, for a little while," I lied.

Morgan was looking straight into my eyes, as she had done before. I became a little short of breath. I wondered if staring deeply into each other's eyes gave her the same pleasure it gave me. I couldn't look away.

"Will it lead to anything useful?" she asked.

"I don't know. I worry about Aedith, and it seems to me it will help her soul."

"She is already too imaginative. She isn't rooted in practical matters."

"Is she lazy? Does she work?"

"Yes, she works well enough, but sometimes I don't know where her mind is. She has flights of fancy. I will allow this teaching if it brings her down to earth. That's what she needs."

"I'll do what I can."

"Very well." Morgan rolled her eyes and sighed, her hands on her hips. I realized how tall she was, how solid and strong. She could probably raise a house beam as well as learn to read if she chose.

"Would you like me to teach you also?" I suddenly asked.

"I have enough to do."

"Of course." I felt embarrassed because she needed nothing from me. But when she looked into my eyes again, her clear lapis blue eyes looking straight into mine, my chagrin melted away.

"Aedith has much to do also, but for now I'll allow it and we'll see."

"Of course. Thank you. Good night."

As we rowed back to Iona, the waves beat under the skin of the boat like a heart. I felt my blush must be visible in the moonlight.

I became resigned with the boys. One day, tired of their boredom, I raised my voice. "Don't you burn to know the language of God's holy word? This learning opens up for you all that humanity has achieved, all that we understand of God's grace. With these letters you can discover the turmoil of young Augustine, the miracles of the saints, the very words of the Apostles. This language is a direct road to all that is valuable in the world!"

One boy looked at me in wonder. The others only looked confused.

What legacy could I leave? I was starting to doubt everything: my desire, my mission. Perhaps everything had been a mistake. It was still my first year; I was still a penitent and hadn't taken the final vow. Perhaps I shouldn't. Perhaps I should return home and die with my people. The world might end or not, and my dream was only a delusion. The lump in my armpit had grown bigger, as had the new one in my groin. The leech had said it would end my life. What was I doing?

I didn't admit this to myself at the time, because I lived blindly, but I had caused suffering to come here. Others had suffered for this mission to scribe a great Gospel. To go back would mean all was for nothing. I was stuck, and all around me was failure.

One day on the other island, we heard the children calling from outside: "Bees! Bees!"

In the middle of the green, the children grabbed handfuls of sand and threw them on the bees to make them stay, chanting, "Sit down, sit down, Bee! Saint Mary commanded thee! You shall not leave; You shall not fly to the wood. You shall not escape me, nor go away from me. Sit very still, wait God's will!"

I joined in. I looked at Morgan, and we laughed together. If the bees remained, they could have honey on the island, something most of us had never tasted. By the next week, Morgan had woven a basket, and the hive hummed under the rowan tree at the edge of the hollow. The air around the houses quivered with their motion.

In the spring, it was strange to notice how lush with yellow and white wildflowers Iona was, in the meadow between the monastery and the sound, and yet right across that sound the Island of Women was so barren. The few purple wildflowers clung desperately to the rocky outcroppings, trying not to slide into the

sea, straining in the wind. Short grass grew in the hollow of the
island, nibbled by a few cows, and the bees had to fly over the
few yards of sea to Mull to find their nectar. There was no herb
garden, no fruit trees, no wood to hide in or flowers to braid in a
garland. The women, like the bees, had to search and find, travel
or import, and make do. But they stayed without question, simply
meant to be here, apart from the fertile land on Mull or Iona.
Iona was for the monks, and the Island of Women the gift of
Columba to them. There was a constant negotiation between the
monastery and their island for resources and goods, complicated
for both the women and the abbot.

Iona seemed a paradise of riches compared with its sister's
dry, rocky inheritance. But it drew the bees, it drew Marcus and
me. It had something else, a richness of voices, of calm amid the
buzzing of the children, of serenity born of tough-mindedness
and laughter.

For Aedith's—or anyone's—lessons, reading and writing were
two very different things to learn. The boys had tools, wax tablets
to practice on. I had nothing for Aedith. Sometimes we went to
the beach and she copied letters in the wet sand with a stick, the
tide washing them away. She was nimble in her copying, but I
would have liked a better way.

When we were about to leave one Friday, Marcus approached
me with something in his hand. "I have to think it is good to have
an apt pupil," he said. He handed over a small wax tablet made
of thin boards with a hinged cover.

I took it, surprised. "That's kind of you."

We pushed off the coracle and jumped in.

Marcus nodded to the tablet. "I take it this is a secret?"

I thought about lying. But Marcus's matter-of-fact gaze gave
me confidence. "Perhaps a little."

Marcus nodded. "We will keep each other's."

I didn't know what secret Marcus was referring to. I recalled
Jeremiah's accusations and decided not to ask questions.

Emer ran up and threw her little arms around my leg. "What
did you bring?"

I bent down and scooped her up. "Why did you expect me to bring something?"

"Because you have something in your hand." She kicked her feet.

"It is not for you. But if you'll hold this, I'll show you something you may give." I handed her the wax tablet and then opened my palm to show her a small shell.

She pressed the wax tablet against my chest, trying to give it back so that she could take the shell. "I want to give it to him."

Aedith had caught up to us, and Emer thrust the tablet toward her, almost knocking Aedith off balance. Emer snatched the shell from me and wriggled, trying to get down from my arms.

Aedith grabbed Emer's foot with her free hand. "You're being rude, Emer."

Emer stopped squirming and grew serious, twisting the shell in her hands. "May I?" She looked me in the eye, her face earnest.

"Yes, dear."

She scrambled down and ran off to find Brion.

Aedith started to hand the tablet back. "I'm sorry. She's still so very young."

I gently pushed the tablet back toward her. "Emer is giving out the presents today. That's for you."

"A book?" She stroked the wooden cover, opened it to examine the pale orange wax, and pulled the slim wooden stylus out of the leather thong on the side. "I write in it?"

"It is a practice tablet of wax."

She closed the cover and pressed it to her small bosom. "You're too generous, Brother Tach."

I looked around for Marcus, who had gone ahead and disappeared already. "It was really Brother Marcus who passed it along."

She crossed her arms over it. "Both of you, then."

She took my hand and walked to a bench outside the house, where we sat in the sun. From inside, there was soft singing, a child's song, a cooing sound from Gwyn in her bed.

Aedith opened the tablet and slid out the stylus. "Please dictate. Spell the words that are important."

I smiled. "Deus. D-E-U-S."

"I know that one." She scratched into the wax, wrinkling her nose.

"Saint. S-A-I-N-T."

Emer and Brion approached, their hands thoughtfully behind their backs. "What are you doing?" Emer asked.

"Shh, I'm writing," Aedith said.

Emer perched on the edge of the bench and watched while Brion folded his arms, standing by.

"Columba. C-O-L-U-M-B-A." Aedith pursed her lips with concentration while I added, "When you know more Latin, there are sentences that contain every letter of the alphabet. They're called abecedarian sentences."

Aedith laughed. "Abeced…?"

"For ABC. For example, 'Trans zephyrique globum scanduat tua facta per axem.'"

"What does that mean?" Aedith asked.

"'Your achievements rise across the earth and throughout the region of the zephyr.'"

Aedith laughed again and clapped. Then she tilted her head. "There was no W in that sentence."

I patted her head. "You are smart. But there is no W in Latin."

Brion took a step closer. "If I say something, can she write it?"

"If I spell it."

"So I can say whelk?"

I nodded. "W-H-E-L-K."

"There's my W," Aedith said with a giggle.

Emer hopped off the bench and ran inside. "Mama, Aedith is writing." The singing stopped and there was a muffled sound. "Come out, come out," Emer yelled.

Aedith slowly finished "whelk," and Gwyn appeared in the doorway with Emer. Gwyn was tall, like her brother. In the strong light her skin was transparent, blue veins on her forehead and hands. Her gown was loose and large around her frail body, hanging in folds from her sharp shoulders. She leaned against the door frame, her thick brown hair wild. She gazed off, squinting at the bright sky, not looking at us.

"Spell Mama," Emer said.

"M-A-M-A."

Emer tugged Gwyn's hand, but Gwyn only glanced down, a distant smile on her face.

"See Mama, look."

Aedith held up the tablet of words. Emer pulled Gwyn closer.

"Oh, this is devilish!" Gwyn said. Her eyes narrowed, and she reached to grab the tablet.

Aedith snatched the tablet back. "It is holy work. The monks would not do a devilish thing."

Gwyn's stern face crumpled in hurt. "Is it not?"

She leaned and started to fall. I jumped up and caught her.

"It is no harm," I said, holding her up. Her body was light as a bird in my arms.

Morgan approached carrying a milk pail. "Aedith, take this and start it," she said.

"But I'm writing."

Morgan put down the pail. Her strong mouth was set. "You *were* writing. Now you are starting the cheese."

Aedith laid the tablet on the bench. "Yes, Morgan." She rose and took the pail around the side of the house.

Emer took Gwyn's hand and led her back inside while Brion ran back to his shells. Morgan and I faced each other. I felt a little weakened by her grim expression.

"It is quite something, you got Gwyn out of bed," she said.

I cleared my throat. "I suppose so."

"I don't know the ways of the monks," she said, picking up another pail by the doorway. "I can't tell you your business or if this is a... productive thing to do."

"I mean no harm."

She motioned for me to follow, and we walked across the green and up the rise to the cows, where one red cow hurried up to us, eager to be milked. Morgan led the cow to her stool.

"Aedith is not a monk," she said, starting to milk.

I held the cow's head still. "Of course, but she needs something."

"She needs to stop dreaming. She has always dreamt. Her mother dreams in bed all day, and Aedith dreams while she's awake."

"She dreams of a bigger life."

"Life is big enough. What can you give her? What she needs is not going to come from the monastery. Soon she will need a husband, and I pray once she is settled she will find her way."

"I think it is peace she needs to find."

Morgan stopped milking and leaned back, stretching the tension from her shoulders. "Is peace found in writing words?"

"I find peace in it."

"I don't understand such things."

I looked at her intelligent face. "I think you can. I think perhaps you do."

Morgan went back to milking. "I don't feel right arguing with you. I only fear for her. She is not finding her way by learning the work of a monk."

The cow stamped its foot and snorted. Her milk was done. Morgan stood, and I took the pail. I struggled whether to tell her about the rocks that were in Aedith's apron the day I found her.

"Please don't ask me to stop so soon."

She shook out her arms and stretched to her full height. Her loose hood fell back, and she smoothed it over her black hair with a sigh. "I will not forbid it, but I will seek counsel, or ask you to."

My heart skipped. Bresal had already denied permission. Would Morgan find a way to ask him about it?

"Allow me to," I said.

She shrugged. "All right then."

We walked back to the house. Marcus had propped a ladder on the side and was on the roof while Fiona handed bundles of thatch up to him.

"There you are," Marcus said.

"There *you* are," I replied, climbing up the ladder to help. It was a relief just to work for a while, filling the gaps with reeds and bunches of herbs to ward off vermin. The warm roof smelled of the sweet cut thatch, the herbal blossoms, and the scent of peat coming up from below, the mingled scents heavy in the air under the glowing sun.

When we were finished, we sat looking at the green below. A few children ran among the cows, the women sitting outside drop-spinning wool. Aedith had finished her cheese, hanging it up to drain, and sat on the bench again studying her tablet.

I leaned back and stared up at the few scattered clouds while Marcus sat propped on his elbow. I closed my eyes as the island hummed around me.

"What do you mean?" Marcus asked.

"What?"

"You just asked what to do."

I didn't open my eyes. "I didn't know I spoke."

"Are you going to stay all day?" a woman's voice asked. Fiona had climbed the ladder and was standing with her head at roof level. Flowers were tucked behind her ear.

Marcus crawled over to the edge and as I looked, he gave her a kiss on the forehead. It was only a peck, it could have been a kiss of peace, but the way she smiled up at Marcus told me otherwise. Marcus had a wife.

Fiona stepped back down the ladder, and Marcus followed. I sat up and took a final gaze around. The bell was struck across the sound on Iona, and I could just make out the white robes of the monks gathering to enter the church. When I came down the ladder, Marcus was waiting, and we each took an end of the ladder to carry to the shed.

We lay the ladder on the floor. It was close and dark inside after the bright sunlight.

"Is Brion your son?" I asked.

Marcus's ironic smiled was visible in the dark. "Stepson, you could say."

"You don't fear the sin?"

"What about you and Morgan?" he asked.

"Don't be absurd. You know there is nothing there."

Marcus gave a little chuckle. "I suppose. Some of us are not as holy. Or as cold."

In the dark shed I tried to search out Marcus's face. "So I'm damned if I do and damned if I don't. If I sin, then, I'm sinning, but if I don't sin it's only because I'm cold and inhuman. You have me bound in your logic."

Marcus folded his arms and tilted his head with a gentler smile. "Perhaps I am unjust. I don't always sin, you know. Sometimes we just talk. It can be just as much a relief. You do confess, don't you?"

"Of course."

Marcus nodded. "Of course you do. But Connachtach, confession isn't just enumerating your sins. I think you need to talk. Unburden yourself. I don't think you do confess. You keep much hidden."

"God knows my sins. I hide nothing from Him."

"And from yourself?"

I paused, swallowing around a lump in my throat. "I cannot escape myself. That is my torment."

"Then unburden yourself. I feel your suffering whenever I see you."

I put my hands to my face, wiping my eyes. Marcus put his arm around me, but I stepped away. "I'm fine." I cleared my throat. "I appreciate your gesture. My only burden is my own sin. My unknown sin. Whatever it is."

"God loves you, Connachtach. It is in that, that you find solace. Let God know you." Marcus' eyes, always so penetrating, were soft with understanding.

"It's time to go back," I said.

"Yes. But please remember my words. We have a bond, keeping each other's secrets. I hope you know that."

I nodded, not sure of what to say. Then I gave Marcus the kiss of peace, and we went outside.

## CHAPTER TWELVE: A DEATH

I hated teaching the boys. One typical day there was a snort of laughter and I looked up, but the boys were still. I looked at my book again and heard another snort, looked back up quickly. Tarain's head was turned to the side, and he pushed the stylus beside his nose, appearing as if he were pushing the stylus up his nose as Raef snorted again.

"Tarain, this afternoon you will only have bread and a bowl of whey," I said.

Tarain set down the stylus and slumped. "Yes, Master."

Why didn't they love learning? When I was a boy, I lived for these lessons. Was I so peculiar? Did I never know what typical boys were like? Now teaching Aedith was my only solace.

Sometimes Cellach came with us to help with chores on the other island. As he chopped kindling, he began a light song about the birds of spring, with its rhythmic chorus. "Cuckoo, cuckoo," he sang.

Aedith and I were inside. She turned her head. "Cuckoo," she sang. "Cuckoo."

They sang together, looking at each other through the open door and smiling. I drew her attention back to her page.

She read the page aloud and said, "Done!" and leapt up with a dance step. "Oh—that was a good lesson. Thank you." She hurried outside.

I left, walking past Cellach and Aedith, who were engrossed in conversation, and went to the shed. I took the pruning hook and began to sharpen it when Morgan entered.

"Lesson over?" she asked.

"Very much so."

She smiled at me with a twinkle in her eye. "I saw them talking. Who is he?"

"Slave to the monastery. He was a masterless boy, and we gave him a place."

She nodded.

"No land, no cattle," I added.

She gave me an exasperated smile. "Yes. But we'll have the honey."

I continued to sharpen the hook. Yes, Aedith would have to marry. She was not a monk. And I was selfish not to want things to change. I still expected some reward, for waiting ten years and, now, for doing a job I hated.

At the monastery I prayed in Saint Columba's tomb until the muscles in my back knotted and I broke into a sweat. I prayed for peace, but peace was the furthest thing from my mind.

As I came out of the tomb, Jeremiah approached me. The day was gloomy, the sky heavy and gray. A breeze insinuated itself between my cowl and neck. Jeremiah's face looking down on me was pale yellow, his light eyes flashing in the gloom.

"What of Brother Marcus?" he asked. He tried to suppress an eager smile. I felt he would have liked the dirty details, an eyewitness.

"There is nothing to the rumor."

Jeremiah's tongue darted to the corner of his mouth. "He came here as on oblate, given to us by his parents. I am not sure of his sincerity; a healthy young man has needs."

"If he has needs, I don't know about them. I am not his amchara."

"And what of your needs?" Jeremiah's look turned wrathful.

"You are not my amchara either."

"I know you are alone sometimes with a woman there, Morgan."

I clenched my fists at the sound of her name in his raspy voice. "If I have been briefly alone with her, it has only been to give instruction on the souls of her children."

"You must be above reproach, Brother Connachtach. You must not allow for the possibility of a stained reputation. Of gossip."

"Gossip? Or did you force such words out of a young slave boy?" I could picture Jeremiah relentlessly twisting Cellach into talking. "And if you threatened or beat it out him, why question me?"

"I want to give you the chance to repent of it and reform, so that it doesn't go to the abbot."

I grabbed his arm, wanting to push him down. "What do you want?"

Jeremiah raised his eyebrows. "Whatever do you mean? I seek your best interest." He pulled away with an air of cold dignity.

A few raindrops fell on my tonsure. The cold of the day, the cold of the man, bore into me. "I've told you all I know. I'll take better care not to be alone with the woman. Is that all you want from me?"

Jeremiah smiled, his gray teeth in shadow. "I had almost forgotten. If you prove yourself, I could speak to the abbot about our need for more scribing. I have a certain influence. Perhaps more scribing, even a new Gospel is something we should have."

I looked at him in surprise.

"You would deserve some reward for doing your duty. I want the path to righteousness to be an easy one for you," Jeremiah said.

I pulled the hood over my head against the rain, looking up at the man's jaundiced face, and stood tall. "The path is a steep and narrow one," I said. "And one that I don't expect you to walk with me." I turned and left him.

It was July, the hungry gap when the bread was gone until the harvest. The children chewed blades of grass between their

teeth, distracting themselves with any game they could think of.
Morgan asked Aedith and me to row the few yards over to Mull
to forage for acorns. I carried the basket while Aedith picked
through the nuts on the ground.

"Morgan thinks my learning to write is useless," Aedith said as
she dropped a few nuts into the basket.

"Perhaps it is."

"Why is it that something can seem so important when it is
really so useless? It seems more, I don't know, a more real thing
than hoeing in the garden or gathering wood. Those things are
necessary for life, but life is… It has to be something more than
that. Am I mad? I feel I must be mad."

I set down the basket, and brushed the hair from her eyes.
"You are not mad. Perhaps, though, you should tell me now.
About what happened the day when you ran into the sea."

Aedith's eyes clouded. "It's all right now."

"But for how long will it be all right?"

Her eyes flew open wide, and she looked me in the face.

"I don't want to force you to talk, but I think it will help to find
the words."

She furrowed her brow. "Find the words… I can almost write
them now, slowly but surely. Some things can never be taken away
from you. And it is strange, the things that can be taken away."

"Like your father?"

She leaned against me. "When he was gone, for a very long
time I thought he was coming back. I expected him. Every day I
expected him to walk in the door. I must have been mad to think
that, but I did. Then one day I truly understood. It took me two
years. Perhaps I had to be older before I truly understood he was
gone. If only there was something: his boat, his net. Something."
She wiped her eyes. "That was the day I met you." She took a
deep breath, struggling to speak. "Anyway, it wasn't only that. We
moved here from Mull to be near my uncle. I told everyone on our
farm to be sure to tell my father where we were." Her voice broke.
"We moved to this tiny, remote place, and life seemed tiny, point-
less. I felt we were hardly above the animals, especially that day.

"But you've taught me that life is more. Even though it may be useless, but it isn't useless. It can't be. Oh, I must be mad." She suddenly laughed. "Yes, I am."

I put my arm around her shoulder. "I must be mad with you."

When the basket was full we rowed back to the island. Morgan met us on the rocky shore. "Go ahead and put them in the water to soak," she instructed Aedith.

I stood alone with Morgan while Aedith disappeared down the hill. It was a bright, hot day, the sea below us deep blue and the sky cloudless. The rust-colored boulders were warm underfoot.

"I suppose your lessons can distract from our hungry state," Morgan said. Her face was gaunt from lack of food.

"Man does not live by bread alone, but by the word of our Lord."

She folded her arms with a sigh. "What is it in books that makes them so important?"

It felt good to talk with her like this. "To be able to share the word, to express one's thoughts to the world, or privately to one person, and to make one's thoughts eternal. An author never dies. I can read the thoughts of someone long before me, respond to them, and pass that on to future generations."

She squinted disapprovingly. "Men are so wordy. Men think women talk, but I have rarely known a man who didn't talk and talk."

"Perhaps, but then I'm supposed to be on a vow of silence."

"And so you write, which is the same. So wordy that talk isn't enough, it must spill over to writing and into books. I think if something can't be talked out in a few minutes, it isn't worth going on about."

I smiled at her. "I think hunger has soured your mood."

She smiled back. "Perhaps."

"Is there nothing you would like to say, either to the world, or perhaps to your children's children in the distant, unknowable future?"

She rubbed her jaw and pondered it. "What is worth saying that lives up to your sense of eternity? And what might I say that

later I wouldn't wish to alter or take back? What can be said
that is eternally true? So fine and true it should outlive me and
all my kind?"

I waited, looking at her lapis blue eyes, bright in the sun. But
she didn't go on. "If you think of something, you'll tell me?"

She cocked her head. "All right. But I won't let you in-
fect me as you've infected Aedith. She must find her way in
this world, and she is not a monk. She must wed. The honey
comes at the perfect time. It's a true blessing. Aedith will have
a dowry. We can get a few head of cattle and buy Cellach's
freedom."

I looked away. "If he had cattle of his own, the monastery
would grant him his freedom, I'm sure. As long as he had a place."

"What's the matter? Your expression is pained."

I shrugged. "I didn't want things to change."

She blinked at me. "I thought Aedith would be hurt. I was
wrong. It isn't her."

My face grew hot. "Was it for nothing?"

"What is anything for? I'm sure you helped her. Besides, you
brought Cellach."

I understood everything she said was right, which only made
it harder.

"This scribing means much to you, doesn't it? It means the
world to you. Just forming letters?"

"There's more. Fanciful designs, Aedith never got to that. Laying out pages of brilliant colored pattern. All sorts of colors one
gets from plants, stones, even beetles."

"Really?"

I nodded enthusiastically. "Vermillion, scarlet from Spanish
beetles. Copper, iron." I paused and gazed into her eyes. "To
catch the color of your eyes, I'd need the rarest stone, lapis lazuli
from Arabia."

She returned my gaze, and her eyes widened in surprise, then
softened. The sun beat down on me.

I looked at her, unable to look away in shame. The wine stain
on her temple was bright, her eyes blue flames, the bones of her

face sharp. The look on her face was mild and understanding, and I did not want to be understood this way. I wanted to deny all that she was thinking, her assumption of my feeling, her tender sympathy. I liked her when she was hard and cool and strong. I didn't want this. I struggled to speak, the hot sun draining my mind of words.

She spoke kindly. "I had thought it easy for monks, because they did not love. It is one thing to give it up, to sacrifice for God. But it is a fine thing to find someone pleasing to wed, and Aedith is not a monk. And love is commanded by God."

Her frankness helped me speak. "We do love." I held her gaze, standing so close I could smell her sweat and see the pulse in her neck. "And we do sacrifice." I was dizzy with emotion and hunger. Perhaps it was the lack of food making me reckless. I took a deep breath and looked out over the slanted sea, which wavered in my lightheaded state. To the west Iona was close by, but to the north was the open sea. The tiny island felt unsteady, as if I were in a small boat. "And we should not demand others to sacrifice. You're right, it is good to find a pleasing husband. If one is free to marry." I looked at her again. "I can't help but think about my family. I have a niece who is blind. She will most likely have to sacrifice marriage. If one can marry, one should. And I have to wonder if by leaving her, I've condemned her to even greater solitude. Aedith often makes me think of her."

"I see, I see," Morgan said quietly. Her face was knowing and sad.

We stood quietly. In the silence, my feelings for her floated in with my breath, a tide expanding my chest, as wordless as the ocean. I would let her think a simple truth, that I was a monk and that was the end of any possibility. But the possibility that I could leave, that I could have a family, return home, that I had not taken the final vow yet, all that was made futile by the hard lump that ached under my arm. I could only make her a young widow. There was only now, this moment as we stood on the bare rock, sharing the harsh blue sky, listening to the cries of the gulls and the keening waves.

Suddenly a child's scream shrieked from across the island. It was not an ordinary, playful yell but a scream of terror.

"Emer!" Morgan cried.

We ran down the hill to the beehive under the rowan tree. Emer jumped up and down, screaming. "He was stung, and he fell, see!"

Brion lay on the ground, clutching his throat with his tiny hands.

Morgan and I knelt by the prone boy. His face was horribly swollen, barely recognizable, like a drowned man's.

"Carry him inside," Morgan said.

I lifted the boy and brought him in, laying him on a mattress. Emer's shrieks had stopped, and Marcus held her in the doorway. He was praying aloud quickly and quietly.

Fiona bathed her son's face with a damp cloth and tilted his head back.

"We must keep his throat open," I said.

Brion's eyelids fluttered. Morgan held his head and put her mouth over his to give him her breath.

"Hail Mary, full of Grace, the Lord is with thee," Marcus whispered. Fiona's low voice joined his. "Blessed art thou among women, and blessed is the fruit of thy womb, Jesus. Holy Mary, pray for us sinners, now and at the hour of our..."

I could barely hear the last word as Morgan breathed into the boy's mouth, Fiona cradling his head. It did not seem that Brion was returning her breath, and his eyelids stopped fluttering. They opened, still and staring, sightless. The room fell silent.

Morgan gently lay his head down. "I'm sorry," she said.

Fiona closed the boy's eyes with trembling fingers. Marcus, holding Emer, came forward and knelt beside him.

Emer gave a shriek, jumped out of Marcus' arms, and ran outside. I raced after her. She grabbed a stick and ran at the hive, her small legs so fast I couldn't keep up. She stopped and swung the stick at the hive. It lurched and swarmed. She flung the stick away and was about to leap onto the hive to crush it with her little body when I caught up and grabbed her. An angry cloud of bees spun around us.

"Let them sting me! Let them die! And let me die too!"

The only escape was to the water. I ran to the shore and pulled her under with me. Bees burrowed into the waves, some stinging us as they drowned. I plunged us in over and over as deep as I could, until the bees gave up.

Emer coughed violently, her retching displacing her tears for a while as we knelt on the rocks. Then she wailed. "Let them sting me and die!"

I held her in my arms as she shook and cried. "You should have prayed," she said, suddenly quieting. "You didn't pray. You didn't say the words."

From the green came the sound of children and women chanting: "For a thousand years in thy sight are but as yesterday, or as a watch in the night. As soon as thou scatterest them, they are even as a sleep, and fade away suddenly like the grass. In the morning it is green, and groweth up; but in the evening it is cut down, dried up, and withered…"

Marcus came down to the rocks and took Emer from my arms. "We will bury him with kings," he said.

Cold and wet, she shivered, her silent tears trembling on her face.

Marcus rowed to the monastery and, with few words, returned with the abbot to pray over Brion, who lay covered with a blanket where we had left him. Then we carried him back over the sound, where the monks had gathered on shore to pray for him, and we buried him in the cemetery among the kings of Scotia. Later Marcus came back and covered Brion's grave with his shells.

A few days later, Jeremiah was in the house while I taught the boys. He sat apart, unobtrusively observing. I had the boys sing Psalm 90. Something sounded amiss. One of the boys was singing the wrong words.

"Everyone sit but Tarain," I said. "Tarain, recite what you were singing."

Tarain beamed and could hardly contain his laughter as he let loose a stream of profanity in Latin. Not all the boys understood it, but they looked puzzled and frightened. My rage seethed and exploded—to profane the Psalm of God and to shame me in front of the abbot's assistant.

"Hold out your hands!" I had never done this over the months, but without a moment's hesitation I struck Tarain hard with the willow branch, four blows that left deep red marks. "And afterward go straight to the barn and spend the rest of the day shoveling manure, since filth is what you love."

Tarain sat, red-faced and trembling. We finished the lesson.

When the boys had gone outside, Jeremiah put his hand on my shoulder. "It was about time."

I shrank from his touch and turned away. Later Marcus found me in the crypt, and I cried in his arms.

## CHAPTER THIRTEEN: A BARGAIN

Aedith and Emer were staying in Fiona's house. She had asked that they sleep with her after her son's death. Fiona had quickly changed, the light of her former gaiety snuffed out. When we came to the island, she went off with Marcus to mourn with him.

As Aedith scratched letters into the wax, Emer rose from her nap in the corner. She rubbed her head and looked around the shadowy room.

"Is Brion outside?" she asked.

Aedith looked up at me with pleading eyes. I rose and sat on the mattress next to Emer and took her hand.

"You have forgotten. Our poor Brion died, two weeks ago."

Emer's look was disbelieving. "You're wrong."

"I'm sorry, my child."

"Not Brion. Not the bees. The bees. I dreamt it. It was a dream."

I pulled her to me. She was trembling and weak, not crying or struggling, but confused and lost.

"I must have dreamt it."

"He is with God."

Curled in my arms, a shaking delicate ball. "Why did God take him?"

"He is in heaven, and it is a joyous place. Full of shells and the sea and wonderful things. Remember, he received baptism at Easter. He is there."

Emer took hold of my robe and kneaded the wool in her tiny hands. "But he is taken. Why should God hurt us so? If he is happy, is it a sin for me to suffer? But I can't be happy. Why should I be happy? He is lost somewhere."

I didn't reply quickly, trying to think, trying to anticipate what she would say. "We must suffer. Heaven is all the sweeter for us, because we suffer here."

Emer sobbed in deep confusion. When she finished shaking, she wiped her face on my shoulder and sat up.

"Then I will not love. And I do not love God. God is wrong to hurt us. I hate God forever."

I stroked her downy hair. The room seemed very dark, as if there were only a small light shining just on us. All else receded into shadow.

"The world needs your love, Emer, because we suffer. You may be angry with God. And I know it is wrong that you suffer. It is wrong. I won't defend God. I can't. I don't know His ways or reasons. But you must love, and you will love better because you know suffering. Only those who suffer and grieve know how precious love is, and how precious our brief time is. Your mother needs your love. Aedith does. We suffer with you, and we love you and need you."

Emer lowered her eyelids and thought, making a small noise to speak several times, but no words came. Then she asked, "Do you need my love, Uncle Tach?"

I didn't know where this came from, calling me Uncle. Her wet green eyes were penetrating.

"Yes, I do, very much."

"And I do, too," Aedith said.

Emer turned to Aedith and kissed her. "I should go to Mama. She may need me."

"She's sleeping at home," Aedith said.

But just then Gwyn came to the door. She stood with clear eyes, her face pink, looking at them as if seeing them for the first time in months or years. "My girls, my girls," she said.

Emer ran to her, and Gwyn pulled her into her arms and lifted her up.

Emer turned her head toward Aedith. "Come, we must help Mama."

Aedith put down her pen and joined them. The three of them went outside. I went to the table and closed the lesson book.

Morgan had been sewing by the window. We were alone in the house now. She sewed with the fish bone needle rapidly, making tiny stitches. "Oh," she started. She had pricked herself.

I knelt beside her and pressed down on the puncture with my thumb.

"I only don't want to get a stain on the fabric. Emer loves this pale yellow."

We stayed in this position for awhile. Her finger felt so strong in my grasp. I could study her fine features. There was a little gray in her black hair. This might be the only time I would ever be so close to her. I was close enough to kiss her.

"Do you really want to be a monk?" she asked in a low voice.

I said nothing and didn't move.

"It's just that you do seem full of love," she said.

"What's love to a practical woman like yourself?"

She laughed, the sound like a spring bird. "Am I right in thinking this first year is a time for you to make the final decision?"

So she knew all that. "That's right."

"Do you ponder it?"

I pulled her hand to my lips. "There is nothing else for me but this vow." I closed my eyes, surprised at the softness of her hardworking hand. With my eyes closed I said, "I won't go into it, but I have a premonition of an early death. There's no point in my marrying. Even though it sometimes seems there's little point in my vow. Perhaps there is nothing that can make me happy. I once told my sister happiness wasn't the goal. Now I know I was lying."

"I think you can be happy." She turned and grazed my lips with hers.

I had never been kissed. It was only a touch, like the sigh of a cloud. I pulled away.

"I'm sorry," she said. "I don't want to lead you into sin."

I wrapped her hands in mine. "Don't be sorry. Perhaps... Perhaps I should consider it all very carefully."

Her smile back was cautious but sweet.

I hiked up to the top of the hill of Dun I, barefoot, the sharp stones bruising my feet, a few drops of blood wetting the light, dry soil. I turned my back to the monastery and sat, pulling off the white scapula and folding it beside me. It was cold through my thin tunic, and I felt my skin turning as cool as the rocks. The sun was dim. I looked at my pale hands and legs, grayish in the cloudy afternoon. I sat still and concentrated on the cold, trying to feel it with my whole being. Then I picked up the flail and struck it against my outstretched legs, which were already streaked with the red marks of days of this penance.

Afterward I went down to the beach and stood up to my thighs in the frigid water, the salt biting my wounds, my arms out-stretched in prayer, murmuring Psalms. The cold water burned. When the bell was struck for Nones, I put my robe back on and joined the swarm of monks, melting into the crowd, dissolving in the common voice of the chant.

I didn't notice how the abbot or anyone else reacted to this penance, which I observed every day between Sext and Nones, no longer remarking how anyone looked at me, or feeling judged. I didn't carry out this activity as a punishment, not to castigate or torture myself. It was not out of a belief that I had sinned against God and deserved pain. It was only that penance was the one opportunity for relief.

I was glad for the vow of silence, that I wasn't required to speak. My whole body felt like a vessel of secrets, of painful long-ings and sinful needs. I only wanted to need nothing, to cast all need out of myself, in icy waters and starved sleep, to burn up all need like burning a wasteland of weeds to clear new ground.

One day as I sat reading in the house, someone set a book in front of me.

Marcus squeezed my elbow. "Do you remember this?" he whispered.

I opened the book. It was a favorite from our youth, something forbidden, a comical verse. In a flash I remembered sneaking off with Marcus to read it when we were boys. I smiled as I turned the pages.

Marcus kissed my cheek. "Try it," he whispered in my ear.

When I had the boys the next day, I held up the slim volume. "I have something new. It is something only very advanced boys get to read. I've decided to reward you with this, if you are good."

The boys looked curious. I glanced at Tarain, who sat straight and attentive in his chair.

"It is called the *Hisperica Famina. The Western Orations*, about hungry scholars. It is about boys like you in a Latin contest, showing off their skill." I opened the book to show them. "Tarain, why don't you try reading this?"

Tarain cleared his throat. "Nam aequali plasmamine mellifluam populas ausonici faminis per guttural sparginem?"

The boys giggled at the flamboyant language.

I translated, "Do you produce with equal skill a mellifluous flow of Ausonian speech from your vocal chords?"

They laughed.

Tarain continued, "Uelet innumera apium concauis discurrant examina apiastris mnelchillentaque sorbillant flienta aleuriis, ae solidos scemicant rostris fauos."

Tarain broke into a smile.

"Can you translate?" I asked.

Tarain blushed. "As when countless swarms of bees run to and fro…"

Raef raised his hand. "In their hollow hives…"

He turned to Oswald, who said, "And swallow floods of honey…."

Tarain raised his hand and finished, "And make their solid combs with their probosces."

The boys laughed again, repeating "probesces" to each other. They spent an hour puzzling over the parodic verses.

When the bell was struck, Raef said, "Can we do this again tomorrow?"

"Only if you continue to be good."

The boys thanked me and started to leave. I caught Tarain's eye and motioned for him to sit back down. Tarain sat, looking nervous.

"I was better today," he said.

I didn't smile. "I think you are old enough that I can ask you: Why? Why do you incur my wrath? Are you completely a wretched sinner who can't control himself?"

Tarain flushed. "I am not wretched. Or I am. I am wretched. I want you to expel me. Send me home. Isn't it the only thing to be done with me?"

I sighed and shook my head. "You must stay until you prove yourself."

"I want to prove myself! I want to prove my ability to ride and to fight and to lead men and solve problems. Why can't I prove myself in that way?"

"In time you will. And in time you will go home. I think sooner rather than later. You can prove yourself by showing you can withstand a situation that isn't your choice. Be a man and bear up to it. There is manhood in facing unbearable situations."

Tarain rested his chin in his hand. "If I am good, can we look at this book every day until I may leave?"

I extended my hand, and we shook on it.

We continued with *Hisperica Famina*. One day I brought another book, the *Lorica of Laidcenn*.

"It begins with a long prayer of protection," I explained. "Tege spinam et costas cum artibus; terga dorsum et neruos cum ossibus; tege cutem sanginem cum renibus, cata crunes nates cum femuilbus."

I had them translating on their own, scratching into their tablets, until they had puzzled out: "Protect my spine and ribs with their joints, back, ridge, and sinews with their bones; protect my skin, blood and kidneys, the region of the buttocks, nates, and thighs." They laughed as the list of body parts went on for pages.

On Thursday evening before Compline, Jeremiah came into the house and tapped my shoulder. We went straight to the abbot's house. I knelt before the abbot's desk.

Bresal smiled. "Connachtach, I want to compliment you on your teaching. I know you have improved greatly."

"Thank you, Father, with God's help."

Bresal's smile broadened. "Brother Nithard is getting quite old, and his duties burden him. Now that you have found your way in teaching, you will teach Fridays as well and relieve our dear brother. You are up to the task."

It did not seem like a question. I knew there was no refusing. There would be no more Fridays spent with Aedith and Morgan. "Yes, Father, thank you."

Bresal patted my shoulder, and I left. Outside, I looked across the sound at the dark, quiet island, the water such a slender obstacle. A boat could easily cross, but there was no boat to cross circumstance and Rule. But it was my own pure selfishness that longed for such a boat. I was so far away. I thought of Aedith, then Deirdre, and my throat hurt.

As I went into the house and glanced at the library books, I remembered I had left behind the lesson book on the other island, the children's Psalter. I decided to let it stay there.

## CHAPTER FOURTEEN: THE PEN OF GOD

I went to Luke's cell and knocked. I had finally decided to unburden myself to him. That was what I was supposed to do. There was no answer, and I went into the dark cell. "Luke, are you asleep?"

The white cat brushed by my ankles and slipped outside. I closed the door, the room black. I fell to my knees. Unable to hold back anymore, tears overwhelmed me.

"Luke, I must know. There was something I wanted. To create a book that would stand as the word of God forever, as we are a religion of the Book. You've tried to show me there is more. But I wanted this, and I must know. Is it pride? Is it the sin of pride? Is it only pride that drives me? Only pride?"

I put my hands over my wet face.

There was no answer. I reached out for the monk in the bed and felt a cold hand. I found the lamp and lit the wick from an ember of the banked fire. Luke's head was turned strangely, his sightless eyes open and staring, unmoving, his mouth open. I put my hand on the monk's forehead. It was cold. He had been dead for some hours.

After Luke was buried, as the monks came out of the church, Gormgal stopped and stared at Luke's cell on the little hillock. "See the light," he said softly, and the monks stopped and nodded.

I looked but saw no light, just a cloud above that glowed with the moon behind it.

It didn't surprise me that I didn't see the light the others saw, because I knew I wasn't blessed. In the refectory I noticed kind glances from Gormgal, Reuben, and others. After the meal as we walked out, I felt a hand on my back. Bresal was comforting me.

I had thought myself lonely before Luke died, not appreciating what Luke meant to me. It was this unexpected sympathy that revealed the keen loss. It was the sympathy that opened my grief.

Bresal beckoned to me, and we went to the abbot's office. I knelt and the abbot motioned for me to sit on the low stool.

Bresal said, "I wondered who would be a good amchara for you."

The ledger was open on Bresal's desk. It was the chronicle of the monastery, and Luke's death was the last line recorded. "I don't know. I don't feel the need of one right now."

"We all need to unburden ourselves."

I couldn't imagine confessing to anyone else. "In time I will find another."

"Perhaps when Brother Leo returns?"

I felt myself flush at the thought of confessing to the blustery teacher. "I will find someone in a while."

Bresal's face was sympathetic as he leaned forward with his hands clasped on the desk, his head tilted, inviting me to speak. I had never seen this softness from Bresal. It was too painful. I thanked him and faltered out of the room.

It was a dark, heavy September, time to plough and sow the field on the west side of the island with winter wheat. We went out in the dawn after Prime. I had asked to help, and I joined Cellach and Oswald, who trained the four red oxen. The yoke and plough were under a shed by the oxen field, which was separated by a fence from the cow field where the calves trotted beside their mothers. In the oxen field the four castrated bulls lived apart, their lives dedicated to pulling the plough and hauling trees. As the men pulled out the implements, the oxen lifted their heads and stared. Oswald whistled and patted his chest. The oxen lumbered over.

"Back, gee, back," Oswald guided them into the harness. The oxen understood: "gee" was right and "haw" was left. Cellach tapped them with the goad on the side they were supposed to turn toward.

I held the plough by its two wide-set handles, taking long strides with the quick, jerky motion of the oxen as the dirt from the mould board sprayed beside me. I thought of water, of the sea, and how easy the boat ride seemed to the other island. The devil made it seem easy. The devil makes an easy path to sin, but under the rolling, buoyant waves there is a tide that pulls one down. I thought of this, and beneath my feet dark earth appeared like a thick line of ink on the cream-colored soil.

Earth was simple. God's work was hard. My spread arms were tense holding the bouncing, jumping plough; I felt it in my shoulders and back most but also my forearms and my clenched hands. Hard work led to the fruits of abundance, and the ease of the devil's path led to the nettles and bracken of sin that tore one's soul with remorse.

We came to the end of the furlong. Cellach tapped the goad.

"Gee, gee," Oswald commanded.

The plough leaned to the right. I leaned and lifted it slightly. We turned oxen and plough together, each doing a separate job in unison. Nothing existed but the pull of the oxen, the weight of the plough, the wavy line in the soil, my body shifting, Oswald's voice commanding them to turn, the goad rising and falling.

The sun came out from the clouds, and it was suddenly bright and warm. Sweat trickled down my forehead. In the cold dark of the morning, the devil felt very present to me, but now as I shook my head away from a cloud of midges, unable to let go of the plough for a moment, the work absorbed me. How simple it was to work, to keep going forward in this dark line of earth, following the team, each part doing its duty. We three men and the oxen were connected but unique in our own challenges, the oxen to strain together pulling, the ploughman to hold the plough, the slave to tap and goad them straight on, the leader to voice commands and encouragement and to set the pace in front. This was everywhere, every spring and autumn: no one lived without this. It was a common, universal activity I had done all my life. To avoid such work seemed to break the bonds I felt with men who everywhere did this, and break the bonds with the good work that supported life.

I forgot my thoughts because pain consumed me. My shoulders ached, my hands burned, my knees felt like pins were driven into them, the sun parched my throat, and flies teased my skin. There was nothing in life but this work and this pain. There were no thoughts, no philosophy, and no regret.

We ploughed through Tierce and stopped when a quarter acre was turned.

Oswald put his arm around my heaving shoulders. "We'll trade places now?"

I took the goad from Cellach and stepped around to the right side of the team. Walking without the plough, my legs felt spongy and light. I could look up now. We were on the west side of the island, on the other side of Dun I, and the monastery was out of sight. Some brothers were milking in the cow field. The season of milk was passing to the season of meat. Calves butted their heads against the milkmen. I was still breathless and saw these things without thought, just saw and felt love slowly displace the hot pain that gradually seeped out from my joints and muscles. It was not a love directed at anyone or anything, but something that spread in me as the sun spreads on hills when the clouds burn off. It was something I felt without words and without naming it, a physical presence.

We worked past Sext and Nones to finish the acre. I took another turn at the plough, and then Oswald took his turn again. The second time at the plough, the pain bathed me, held me like a blanket, and I immersed myself, pushing into the earth and pushing into the pain, the earth always giving way and the pain giving and rolling back like a wave. Again there was nothing but dirt, heat, and pain, and it spoke my name like a mother singing a lullaby.

And then we were done, and the end seemed sudden after a lifetime of ploughing. I took a staggering step back.

"Water," Cellach said.

We led the oxen to the trough and pulled off the yoke. The oxen stamped and flung their heads to the water. Cellach fetched a pail of water from the well, and we drank lustily. The sun was low, and I wanted to wash myself before Vespers. I helped put away the plough and yoke, and we went to the pond at the south end of Dun I.

I took off my scapula and tunic and waded into the water in my braes. It was cold, but not nearly so cold as the sea water I was used to. I stood up to my thighs and splashed myself all over. Cellach joined me, stripping nude.

Cellach swam and splashed like a merry boy and then floated on his back.

"You swim well," I said.

Cellach stood up to his waist. "Wouldn't it be wonderful if the water was warm, really hot?"

"The last time I was in water like this was almost a year ago when my sister and I cleaned the hides after slaughter. It's hard to believe it's only been a year."

The water darkened around us as the sun sank. The bell was struck for Vespers. I threw on my scapula and hurried ahead of Cellach to join the throng. I still felt weak and light from the day's effort, floating on the waves of the chant.

As we came from the church I looked up at Luke's cell. The golden moon was setting over it, and light gleamed along the edge of the roof. The light brightly washed over the thatch until the whole roof glowed. Perhaps I did see the light. Surely this was the blessed light. Someone stopped beside me. I turned to Reuben.

Our eyes met. What did my face reveal? I recalled Luke speaking of this, how wonderful it was to see faces and their emotions. Reuben had a smile, sad smile on his face, his eyes glittering and knowing.

My heart seemed to fill my chest with a slow beat. I had never loved my brothers. I saw my pride like a flail that had whipped me on. For some time I had been thinking much of the devil, instead of God. At that moment I felt there was no devil but pride. Because pride had kept me from love. Several monks gathered around us, looking at that light on Luke's cell, and all their faces were beautiful.

The next day, there was a call from Mull to send a boat. I caught my breath, thinking Brother Leo and the monks were back. I walked briskly to the beach where even the abbot was waiting. The boat returned with the monks, but when we saw their faces, our smiles disappeared. We could see immediately something was wrong. Now it was time to know the meaning of Daric's letter.

A strange monk was with Brother Leo and the others, a visitor. He was an old gray-haired man with hollow cheeks and dark, heavy brows. Brother Leo helped him out of the boat, putting his big arm around him. The abbot extended his hand to the stranger and introduced himself.

"I am Brother Daric, the Master Scribe of Lindisfarne," the stranger replied.

Something caught my eye. Handed from the boat was a red leather-covered box, bejeweled and bound with silver. It was the Gospel I had seen all those years ago, that I had ached to emulate and outdo. I had ached for it, and now it was before me.

"May we address the brethren?" asked Daric. "We have news, terrible news."

We walked up from the beach, the old scribe trudging heavily. We went into the refectory, and the abbot sent to have the bell struck. As the monks filed in, the abbot sent out two or three to gather all the monks from their chores around the island. The later the monks arrived, the more alert and curious their faces were as word of the visitor spread.

We stood around the tables, and Bresal led us in prayer as the monks pulled back their cowls to look up at the visitor, who stared off as if he didn't see us.

The abbot said, "This is Brother Daric, the Master Scribe of Lindisfarne. He asked to speak."

Daric frowned and bent forward, staring at the floor in front of the assembly. His voice was hoarse. "Lindisfarne has been met by a horrible calamity. Pagans from across the sea came in great ships, bringing fire and death. With a cataclysmic roar they swarmed onto our beach, overrunning our home like a tidal wave, swinging swords and axes, butchering our brothers. They burned the barns, burned the corn they couldn't carry, seeking only silver and plunder. They might have been men, but if they were, I know not what men they were. Giant spawn of the devil. They came as swift as the ravens of war, destroyed with terrible speed, and left us to bury our dead. We escaped and we saved our great, holy Gospel, which we bring with us for safe keeping here. We ask for your prayers." Tears fell over his mouth and chin. "We ask for your comfort and to beg God to deliver us from such evil ever befalling us again. I pray to God it isn't the end of the world." He put his hands over his face and trembled.

"It was a fine day. The pastures were green and rich, and the cattle nudged the grass and cropped the sweet clover, not knowing their fate, as we did not know our fate. The sky was clear, yet we heard a strange sound as of thunder. It came from the sea. We looked to each other in wonder, and gradually all came out to look over the waves. A dozen ships, huge and slender as knives, cut the waves, rowed with a bank of oars like a forest. They sang in a strange language to the beat of the oars. We saw the boats turn toward our beach, and then men the size of giants leapt ashore.

"They seemed ready for battle, in helmets and leather armor, they raced up the beach with drawn swords, screaming to their awful gods of battle. We thought it must be some mistake. We hardly had time to think. Surely these warriors mistakenly took our holy land as the field of some battle. But were they even men? They seemed to be the very spirits of war, demons. Their eyes glowed, their thick necks strained with their screaming.

"We raised our arms. 'Stop. We are monks, men of God!' we shouted. We raised our arms in supplication and fell to our knees to show them we would not fight. We held up our crosses and rosaries. Their swords passed through us as if we were only grass to be mown down. They used their swords like scythes, and our humble crosses flew in the air to be caught in their laughing grip. I was not in the front, I had time, though it was time measured in grains. At first I ran toward the church, but then I turned. I was going to beseech God there, but suddenly, in a flash of wordless understanding, I knew they were after treasure, that there was treasure in the church that I could not protect. It was men I had to save. The boys."

Daric stopped for a long pause, his eyes vacant as the shock and fear came back to him. "The schoolboys were still in the scriptorium, copying lessons. Their master, a strict man, had not let them rise to see what the noise was. I burst into the room, screaming for them to come with me to hide. By now the sound of the Morrigan was all around, and they knew a battle raged. Ink flew in the air and spattered us as they jumped away from their work. We ran to the barn, where several boys could hide in the threshing pit. The rest of us ran to the milking sheds beyond the fields. There I watched, and after a few minutes I smelled the smoke.

"I ran, choking on my own screams, toward the barn. It was engulfed in flame. I didn't give a thought anymore to the demons, who were carrying off their treasure. I tried to chant and screamed psalms at the flames. There were too many wounded and dying for us to try to put out the blaze, and it burned quickly. I raked and tore at the embers to get at the threshing pit. The boys were below the smoke in that pit and could breathe. Some of them had burns on their backs and arms, and their hair was scorched. But they lived, praise be to God and Holy Mary."

He took the Gospel out of the box and held it over his head. The abbot led us in prayer as we marched to the church and prayed more in a vigorous chant. Our voices were different, strange, louder than usual and quivering.

To honor Brother Daric, the abbot ordered a meal of meat, cheese, herbs, and fresh bread. But no one enjoyed the feast. The sounds of eating, even the sounds of our hand gestures, seemed to echo in a nervous clatter. The abbot read to us, but was dimly heard.

Sensing our distraction, Bresal stopped and said, "Perhaps you may make an extra confession to your amchara today, after the meal."

If this was permission to talk, the monks took it fully. The monks gathered in groups of two or three all over the island and

asked, "What of us? We too have silver and treasure for plunder."
There were whispers that we should cast the silver into the sea,
and some even suggested we should fashion weapons to defend
ourselves against attack. I heard snatches of these conversations.
I stayed to myself and then went into Columba's tomb to pray
in silence.

The next morning after the meal, Bresal stood before us with
Daric and the great Gospel that Daric had brought from Lindisfarne. "Though we honored our guest with a feast yesterday, now
with such a tragedy that has befallen our brothers, he asks to do
penance, and I agree."

We rose and followed Bresal and Daric out and marched
around the island, stopping at each holy spot to pray. We circled
the island three times and gathered together at the Bay of the
Dead.

"Let us remember on this shore where the dead land, those
who have been cut down. Let us do penance in faith that God
will have mercy."

All heads bowed in prayer, except mine, because I glanced
upward at the Gospel that Bresal held above. I felt a hand on my
elbow and turned to meet Gormgal's eyes. I thought I was being
rebuked, but Gormgal darted his eyes toward the great Gospel,
raising his white brows.

Bresal led us up the Road of the Dead to the cemetery, and we
chanted among the standing stones until it was time to file into
the church and chant more. For our penance there would be no
second meal. We would offer prayers in constant vigil.

I prayed in Columba's tomb. With my eyes closed and head
bowed, I again felt Gormgal squeeze my arm. Gormgal knelt
beside me, his thin face more hollow than ever, his eyes burning.

"We must do more. We must make a great offering. You know
what we must do," he said.

I didn't know. I wondered what more I could sacrifice. I felt I
had given up everything I possibly could.

Gormgal whispered his prayers in a long breath, which had
the sharp, sour odor of one who hadn't eaten. All the monks

smelled like that now. I rose to go, and Gormgal, still kneeling, grasped my hand.

"We must do more. We must go to Abbot Bresal."

I felt tired, lightheaded from lack of food. I didn't want to do more. I kissed Gormgal's hand and left him praying.

When I taught the boys, I could see in their faces and hear in their weak voices the pangs of hunger. I went to Bresal and asked to allow the boys to eat.

"They are growing and require more than we do. They can barely listen over the groans of their stomachs."

Bresal frowned, but he agreed. When I told the boys they would eat after Nones, they threw their arms around me.

Every day we paraded around the island with the great Gospel. Afterward, Gormgal locked it in the cabinet.

One day, Gormgal approached the class as they finished their lesson. "Would you like to see the glorious book?" he asked us. "I would like you to see it."

I wondered if hunger had maddened the old man. He had never been so carefree before about anything even half as valuable. Gormgal took out the Gospel and opened it on the table, turning the pages to their amazed eyes.

Colors danced before us, twining letters spiraling in dense dreaming patterns. I had seen this many years before, the last time Lindisfarne had lent it to Iona. Then it was like a dream, and it was loaned innocently, only for humble veneration. Now the book was our precious ward, for its protection. It had never seemed so valuable and sacred as now.

The boys sighed and exclaimed over page after vivid page, even their hunger forgotten.

"This was made for Saint Cuthbert," Gormgal said. "But our dear Saint Columba has nothing such as this." His weak voice trembled.

The boys quickly responded, bouncing in their chairs, talking at once, "We must make one, then. How will Saint Columba protect us without a great Gospel? We owe it to our saint."

Gormgal hushed them and put away the book as the bell was struck for Tierce.

As we headed out to the church, Gormgal slid his arm under mine. He was growing too weak to walk steadily. I didn't feel much stronger. I wondered at what Gormgal had said, which had utterly surprised me. But it made sense.

We chanted, all our voices weak from the penance. Afterward, Gormgal gestured toward Columba's tomb, and we went inside. A shaft of light came through the doorway, shining on the white stone box that held the saint's relics. Gormgal stroked the lid, which was carved with a cross and doves.

"We must honor our saint."

I swallowed and looked over at the box of scribing tools. I felt ashamed remembering the previous year when I had first arrived so full of excitement to do it, so full of pride. "I don't know," I said. The dark room was humid with our sour breath. I needed fresh air and light. This tomb had been a place I had come to often in despair, and now it felt heavy and cold, and I had no more answers now than I did before.

"Dearest Brother Connachtach, I need your strength. We must raise up our saint. You have come from pride to doubt, and now you must come to your simple faith. There is nothing but faith. There is no Connachtach, no Gormgal, there is only our work and our offering."

He fell into my arms, and I held the shaking old man. The feeling I had the day I plowed the field began to swell in me again.

"Yes, yes. Let us go into the light." Clinging to each other, we went outside.

It was strange that the day was so fine, the sun so bright and warm, the waving grasses golden in the autumn day. Soon it would be Martinmas again. If there were a Gospel to be made, there was much to arrange and hides to prepare.

Gormgal straightened up. He too seemed refreshed by the glorious day.

"Let me speak with some of the others," I said.

Gormgal made the sign of the cross over me and went into the house. I walked to Columba's Bay, where many of the monks had been building their piles of stone, a stone for each sin. Marcus and Reuben were there among them. Reuben was crouched on the stones, sifting through them with a distracted, vacant look, while Marcus threw stones onto his pile angrily. I tapped Marcus on the shoulder and motioned to Reuben, and the three of us walked a little way up the hill from the pebble beach.

"Brother Gormgal thinks we should create a great new Gospel for Saint Columba. I feel awkward suggesting it," I told them.

Marcus rubbed his dirty hands together. "I have always wanted to."

Reuben glanced sideways at him. "This is a sacred undertaking, and a great burden."

"It would be a glorious offering," Marcus said. "I think now is the time to take this action."

Reuben looked from me to Marcus. "Can the monastery afford to take this on? What will Abbot Bresal think?"

"There is only one question," Marcus said. "Are we ready?" He put his hands on each of our shoulders. "I say we are ready."

We climbed over the hill and down the road to the abbot's house. On the way, we stopped at the house, where I gestured for Gormgal to follow. At the abbot's house, Jeremiah answered our knock with a quizzical air. The visiting monk Daric was with the abbot, sitting on a low stool, his head bowed in contemplation. When we entered, he stood and bowed to us.

The abbot also stood. When we kneeled, he motioned for us to rise. Gormgal spoke first, his hand squeezing mine.

"Dear Father, we have been discussing our penance and our offerings to Columba. And we wondered, humbly, if it would be right and fitting to create a new Gospel, along the lines of the glorious book Brother Daric has brought. We would copy from theirs and use it as a model."

Jeremiah, standing next to the abbot's desk, cocked his head and furrowed his brow. "This would be a great undertaking," he said doubtfully.

Before the abbot could reply, Daric pounded his fist into the palm of his hand. "Yes, yes! This is the effort we need." His voice boomed, in surprising contrast to our quiet, weak voices.

Bresal smiled at Daric and looked at us, his eyes glittering from the fast. "I think perhaps this is an appropriate offering. Creating a new Gospel to offer to God would be a great gift of faith."

Marcus said, "I think Brother Connachtach should lead us."

I bowed my head. "I have the least seniority."

"It is more burden than honor and would be a great penance for you," Reuben said.

"You must do it," said Daric in his strange, echoing voice.

It was a queer feeling, after all, for this to be coming true, now that I had given it up, and under such circumstances. The terrible context, to do this as penance for the nightmare raid on our brother monks, made me unsure of how to proceed. I couldn't take pleasure in it, but it was a sacred duty. And perhaps that was the only true justification for this effort, not my pride or pleasure, but only sacred duty.

"Of course, if you ask this of me, I consider it an honor and a blessing to be asked."

The abbot took his wax tablet to write notes on. "First we must account for materials. How many hides will it take?"

"At least a hundred and fifty," Marcus said.

Reuben nodded, "We must send an envoy to the high chief at Dunadd to tell him our plan and ask for hides from all over the land of the Dál Riata."

"We've no time to lose then, to get this donation arranged before the autumn slaughter," Bresal said. "We must send men of rank to show our respect. I think Gormgal should go. His enthusiasm will sway the chief to our need."

"Let me go as well," Reuben said. "Gormgal is very old."

"I am not so frail," Gormgal said, his strained voice a croak.

"Very well. And a boy to serve you."

"Cellach," I said. I felt that curious Cellach would enjoy traveling such a distance.

Bresal nodded. "Go over your store of inks and paints and determine what we need. Now that Brother Leo has returned, you don't need to teach."

Gormgal slid to his knees. "Thank you, sweet Father, for blessing this labor."

The abbot stepped around his desk and gave Gormgal his hand to kiss. We all went down on our knees and kissed his hand as well. When it was my turn, the abbot patted the top of my head with tenderness.

Before Vespers, I took a coracle and rowed to the other island. I hadn't been there since July. The rocky shore glowed in the late afternoon light as I landed. I paused at the top of the hill above the green. The children were holding hands in a circle, singing. Emer was in the center, rushing at their arms in a game. She saw me first and darted out between their legs to run up the hill. I came down, being pulled along.

Aedith took the lead in quieting the group, lining them up to bow to me. Emer's hands were in little fists as she swayed in excitement.

"Where have you been, Uncle Tach?"

Aedith tried to shush her, saying, "He has important things to do."

Emer held her breath, her cheeks puffing out, her eyes big upon me.

I knelt before her. "I've missed you."

She threw her arms around my neck, and I held her. I was afraid she was crying, but she only breathed hard in my ear.

"He's had to teach on Fridays, Marcus explained." Aedith said. "Do you need your book back?"

I let go of Emer. Aedith looked at me with a pained expression, though trying to look brave. Her red hair blew in the wind, and I thought of Deirdre, of the cost of not saying goodbye, though this time I was not so far away.

She twisted her hands and said, "I could go in and get it for you." But I knew in her face she didn't want to give it up.

"You may keep it, if you take very good care of it."

Her face relaxed and she beamed at me.

Morgan had come out by then and stood with her arms folded. "We're glad to see you," she said. "But I have a feeling this isn't marking a return."

I stood up, surrounded by the children. I wanted to be able to talk to Morgan alone. I didn't know if she knew of the raid. Perhaps Marcus had told her. As the women's island held no treasure, I thought they were safe if the raiders came here. The raiders would seek the church and its silver.

Morgan's face was set, as if she already knew what I had come for.

"We're going to create a new Gospel. I will be very busy."

Morgan nodded.

Aedith grasped my hand, laughing in wonder. "Will we be able to see it?"

I didn't know, but I said, "Someday."

"You will be doing holy work."

"Yes. So I have come to say goodbye."

She stood back and put her arm around Emer, taking Morgan's hand with the other. Her face was serious, and she nodded slowly.

I looked at Morgan, longing to say more, longing perhaps to hold her. Her expression was the same as I first met her: firm, her mouth set. She looked as if none of this was a surprise, and I would never know how she felt.

"Goodbye, Brother Connachtach." She started to walk away with Aedith and Emer.

I stared after them, hoping she would turn around.

She turned. For a moment she paused, gazing at me, her face full of soft warmth in the setting sun. Then they were gone.

The next day after Prime, I walked across the causeway of the pond to the west pasture, where the calves trotted by their mothers. I stood by the fence and counted them, looked them over. Reuben joined me.

"Are you pleased?" Reuben asked.

"Not that our brothers were slaughtered."

"Of course." Reuben leaned against the rail, weakened by his penance. "Yes, it is done out of tragedy. We can only hope it will bless the work all the more."

"We must fill it with our love, rather than our grief," I said, putting my arm around him.

"Yes."

That is the story I wanted to tell you, my dear Aedith, now that such a time has passed: my confession. A calf, springing over the grass, bounded up to us. I recalled our friend Cellach's lovely words, on the boat on our way to Iona. I scratched the calf behind the ear, stroked his white and brown head, and said into his big brown eyes, "The pen of God will be written on your skin, and you shall live forever."

# PART TWO

OONA

# CHAPTER ONE: ULTAN'S RETURN

It's a miracle to meet you and tell you, after all this time in this strange land. Yes, I'm Oona. Where should I begin? It was Easter. That dark Easter morning.

I could see my breath, and the cold of the hard frost under my feet flowed up my body to my chest. I felt my heart struggle against the cold, pushing against the chill reaching through my clothes. I unclenched my fists; the blood eased into my fingertips.

I watched Dermott start the fire. It had to be a new fire, lit from scratch. He placed the small patch of char cloth on a nest of brush on the kindling. The crowd was silent; the only sound was of the flint hitting the file. I chanted the Lord's Prayer in my head to measure the time; it usually took about three times for the flames to rise. But the cloth didn't light. The crowd started shifting on their feet. I looked to the East, anxious the sun would rise before the fire was lit.

Dermott was breathing hard now, and striking faster, and the pitch of the sound it made rose like an alarmed birdcall. I glanced from side to side and saw others glancing at me. I looked down and closed my eyes.

Then a gasp from all startled my eyes open. Dermott's hand flew to his face; a fragment of the flint had hit him in the eye. In the moment that his hand went to his eye, a spark landed on his sleeve. It would make a hole.

Dermott faced the crowd and spread his arms out in prayer. "Our Father who art in heaven," he started, and we joined in quietly, uncertain, except for old Fiachrach, whose voice rose above the others with a loud, chiding edge. I shivered.

After the prayer he tried again. Now his striking wasn't so fast, but smooth and measured. I felt calmed by his confident air. This was the fourteenth Easter that I'd watched him end Lent with that spark, and when it flickered and I heard the approval from the congregation, joy lit me from within. He picked up the little glowing nest of brush, waved it in the air, and placed the fire ball on the kindling. The fire was blessed.

"Saint Patrick defied the druids and their pagan king by lighting the first Easter fire in Scotia. We call upon God to bless our fire at this dawn, in memory of our saints."

It was still dark, as if the sun had been paused in its rising, and the fire shone as a mighty beacon. The nephews hoisted up the straw man over their heads and threw it onto the holocaust. That the straw man ever meant something druidic we ignored; the straw man was winter, was Judas, was an old life before the resurrection. It was anything to destroy and turn away from, and its blaze sent sparks dancing into the dawn. The crowd exhaled and watched the fire with new eyes grown limpid with gratitude and relief below the creased brows of a people weary with winter.

Alan the Deacon slid the Book out of its leather bag and handed it to Dermott, who opened it and read aloud Latin that no one understood, magic sounds. Dermott held it up to show us the words. The script danced in the uncertain light, like the ripple of waves. Then he explained what he knew, telling us of the tomb and the Apostles who feared and were rewarded, and the resurrection of the Savior.

I prayed with the others before the tall wooden cross. Secretly, I prayed we would build a church. A place painted all colors, lit by candles and oil lamps, a jewel house for our souls. I thought of it especially now that it was Easter, and there was no special altar for receiving the host. Dermott blessed the bread I had baked. Alan held it up to him on a dish, and he carved it in half, then half again, in careful cuts while he prayed, until he had twenty-four little pieces.

Dermott went from one to the other in turns with the bread. I closed my eyes as he placed it on my tongue. Twice a year we received communion; it was a rare, glorious moment. My shoulders relaxed as the bread dissolved and communion spread down my throat like a warm balm. I felt eased in the knowledge that there was a perfect truth, and a perfect path to walk, and that life was possible only if one kept looking for that perfect path to God.

As Dermott chanted the last prayer, a fine rain began to fall. I spread my cloak around Deirdre, who put her arm around my waist. A lock of bright red hair slipped out from under her hood, and I tucked it back in. Only her blue eyes, milky with her blindness, marred her face.

We walked in one cloak down the hill. Dermott led the way, carrying the Book. I thought perhaps he should hold it in his sleeve to keep it dry, but then that would doubt the Lord's protection, and I understood Dermott was right to proceed as if the sky were clear.

Everyone had spent the cold night without a fire. We lit the peat again from a torch from the bonfire, and the air that had been so cold and fresh was now singed with that sharp, sweet smell. Dermott and Alan went from house to house blessing their hearths while Deirdre and I went inside.

I poured water and a measure of barley into the pot over the fire in the middle of the room. A few drops of rain from the opening in the thatch dripped into the pot.

"I'll stir," Deirdre said. "You rest a bit."

"I'm not tired, but I'll let you." I handed her the spoon, and we sat on the bench by the fire.

"What distressed the crowd?" Deirdre asked.

"It was nothing, only a spark."

The spoon scraped the pot for a while. I thought about taking up my drop spindle, but didn't move. I wouldn't admit it, but I was tired.

"I know how you hate when things go wrong," Deirdre said.

Dermott came in the door. "Blessings on you," Dermott said, and he kissed us both on the cheek. "It was a long wait until Easter this year."

The winter had seemed longer and darker than usual. I drew the bench up to the fire and filled a bowl with mash for him. "Warm yourself."

"No baptisms. How many years has it been since we've had an Easter with a babe to christen?" Dermott said.

I filled another bowl for Deirdre. I didn't answer; I was angry that he would ask that. The joy of the communion drained away. It had been four years since we'd christened a son who died a week later. I'd thought this Easter would be better, but the pain was fresh with Dermott's thoughtless question. Had he forgotten? The mash was hard to swallow, and I got up to have a cup of water. I stayed at the other end of the room in the dark shadows.

Dermott rose and set down his bowl. "Forgive me."

I turned around and held him, ashamed of my anger, warm in his arms. I ran my hands down his arms and held up one to the light. "There's a hole in your sleeve."

"From the spark," he said. "I didn't notice. I'm sorry." It was his new Easter tunic.

"It couldn't be helped," I replied. Now I almost felt cursed. Easter was the great day, the biggest and best day of the year, and it had to be perfect. Everything was conspiring to ruin it.

Deirdre said, "Don't be anxious. We can worry about it tomorrow."

I put my arm around her. "How big and wise you're growing."

"Every year, you seem more worried," Deirdre whispered, her head on my shoulder.

By late afternoon the air warmed and the sun, though pale, shone on the day like a weak smile. The communal table outdoors was spread with lamb, bread, butter, geese, and oatcakes, for the families hungry from a long winter's fast. The lamb was juicy and redolent of the garlic that had sprung up through snow, the first flavor of spring. The oatcakes and bread soaked up the juices, and the thick beer was strained into our shared mugs. Everyone was playing a game of knuckle bones when one of the children called out, "There's a stranger coming down the hill."

We all turned. The stranger was just passing by the cross, where he stopped and crossed himself. Then he waved his staff at the crowd, which had grown quiet and still, even the dogs. He was slightly bent and used his staff to make his way down the steep, rocky path. When he got down to the footbridge, he straightened up and quickened his pace. Now we could see he was old but not unfit, agile but careful. He was a tall, bony man with a gray head, his beard clipped close to his face.

Dermott rose and greeted him as he stepped off the footbridge. "A blessed Easter to you."

"Blessings on you. I am Ultan, coming from Meath. I came here once before, in the autumn."

"You were here?"

"For but an hour, and then I went on my way. I met Oona, her poor daughter, and the man who would be a monk."

Dermott turned to me, and I put my arm through his. "He came when you were droving the calves. It was he who said Deirdre has cataracts."

"Where is the poor girl?" Ultan asked. "Is she well?"

I sought Deirdre in the twilight. The children had gathered close to see the stranger, but Deirdre wasn't among them. For a moment, I hoped she had hidden herself, but Deirdre approached with a mug of ale.

"Here, you must be thirsty," Deirdre said, holding out the mug.

"I thank you." Ultan took a long drink.

"Have you any news from your travels?" Dermott asked. "Come, have something to eat."

We all sat around the table. Ultan prayed before he ate.

He seemed hesitant to speak. "There is some news I've heard, though it isn't happy, I'm afraid. I met a monk from Iona."

I crossed myself.

"The brother told me that the scribe at Iona had died recently. There was a great funeral."

I held my voice steady. "The new scribe, Brother Connachtach? Or the old scribe?"

Ultan scratched his beard. "I didn't realize there were two master scribes. I don't know."

"My brother isn't very old."

Ultan drew in his breath, as if unwilling to say it. "Your brother was ill when I met him. Perhaps he spared you the truth."

Dermott took my hand. "I'm sure it was the old scribe."

I squeezed his hand, my own turning cold.

"Where are you going now?" Deirdre asked.

He helped himself to another slice of bread. "At Armagh I heard that the bishop in Spain has discovered Saint James' bones. It is a fantastic find. I want to go and be blessed by them."

I poured him another cup of ale, calculating in my mind how much was being eaten and drunk. "So far?"

"If I have luck and the blessing of Our Saviour."

"Stay with us at least a night," Dermott said.

Dermott and the old man traded insights about the Apostles and the holy places. Dermott's book of psalms was the first book Ultan had seen in years, but as a boy he had learned some reading at Tara, and he lovingly read aloud from it with a tallow candle close by. We didn't know Latin, but the sound was as soothing as rocking waves.

"It's a fine hand," Ultan said when he was finished.

"Do you know any more news of Iona?" I asked. I took the book from him and held it to my chest.

He considered. "Just that miracles are being reported upon the death of the scribe. There's a well where the blind are given back their sight."

We sat in silence for a few moments.

"Speaking of the well, I should draw water," Deirdre said.

"It's no bother for me to go in the morning," I said.

She pulled her cloak around her shoulders. "I'll go."

Deirdre took the pails and left.

When she was gone, Ultan leaned forward confidentially, "This well at Iona is supposed to be a great cure."

Dermott took the book from me and put it back in its leather bag. "She doesn't seem to mind being blind," he said.

"But who will marry her?" Ultan asked. "Few men would take a blind wife. It's considered bad luck in many parts to even cross paths with a blind person."

I looked at Dermott, who looked away. It was something to consider. We would die, and there would be no one left to take care of her.

"I could take her there, before I go to Spain," Ultan said. "I could also be reassured that it's not your brother who passed on." His smooth voice was reassuring. There was a confident, familiar twinkle in his eye when he caught my gaze.

Deirdre returned with the water and soon we were all took to our pallets to sleep. I nudged Dermott.

"I'm awake."

"What do you think?"

He propped himself on his elbow. "I think I won't send my daughter off with some strange man."

"He seems saintly enough."

"Aye, too much so."

There was an edge in his voice, and I felt anxious not to cross him, but something pushed me forward. "I understand your views. But this well might be a miracle, and he's right that no one will marry her. I wouldn't send her with him alone. We would both go."

Dermott laid his head back on the pillow and slid his arm around me. "I think you have the wanderlust."

"It sounds like a grand thing, to see holy places. But it's Deirdre I'm thinking of." Reassured by his affection, I put my head on his chest, but I felt his deep sigh.

"There's work to be done. There's sowing and calving. We're needed here."

"We can go after that, in mid-summer during the wait for the corn."

"And the farm would have to sponsor this journey. It is up to them as much as me. Not to mention the king"

"Would their support encourage you to go?"

"If I said no, would you go without me?"

His voice was tired.

I slid my hand across his chest and up to his neck. "No, I wouldn't leave you." I waited, hoping he would come round. He didn't speak. "It would be nice to see my brother," I added.

He grasped my hand and held it tightly in his fist. I knew he was growing frustrated. "To be a monk is to be cut away from family. It is not so easy to go that long way. It is a mad idea."

I didn't say anything, afraid to anger him. I lay stiffly against him, squeezing back tears, because I hated to argue. His hand loosened its grip around mine, and he rolled over to face me in the dark. His lips found mine. I let a few tears fall in relief.

"Let me think about it," he said.

I kissed him and held him close, as if we might be parting.

The feast continued the next day. It would go on until the lamb bones were picked clean and the ale keg emptied. The sun was warmer and the damp almost felt like the humidity of summer; we could almost smell hay and clover.

As Maeve and I laid out the table, I looked about, suddenly missing my daughter. I went to the stream where Deirdre was washing the linens.

"Dearest, there's no need," I said.

"I wanted to have it done before you send me to Iona," Deirdre said.

"Did you think I would send you away?"

Deirdre wrung out the cloth. "The man's words are a temptation. A holy well of miracles."

"Do you doubt the Lord?"

"Not the Lord I doubt. God took my sight from me. He can restore it with a snap of His fingers... I don't want to leave you."

I helped her spread out the linen over the rocks.

"I would never send you away without me." I took Deirdre's cold, red hands and rubbed them. "I only thought we could go together, and I could see my brother. But not if the plan displeases you."

Deirdre squeezed my hand. "I think you would regret not trying, and I would live to regret that."

"Not if it displeases you."

"I am content."

But we knew it was not our decision or even Dermott's, but the clan's decision whether we could go. Our work would be missed.

At the feast I looked at Dermott, pleading with my face.

He sighed with exasperation, stood up, and said, "Perhaps Ultan can tell us more about this holy well."

Ultan's words were smooth and honeyed. He spoke of a bent man made straight, and of a lunatic made sane. In the name of the Lord, a blind woman was given sight. He did not seem to exaggerate, but spoke with both humility and assurance. "And I would be happy to take Deirdre there to be blessed."

Kevin and Enan asked to go and were hushed. Deirdre, meanwhile, kept her sightless eyes down. I grasped her hand under the table.

"What do you say?" old Fiachrach asked Dermott.

Dermott looked hard at me. "It isn't my decision alone. I know we all have to agree."

I felt myself blush, ashamed for being insistent, for forcing him. I almost wished he did say no. But something was pulling me along, and I felt as if it weren't my choice.

After the dinner, the men went up to the cross, which served as a meeting place. They spent the evening in debate. Down the hill, the older boys discussed which of them should also go. I sat outside the house in the last light of the afternoon and mended the tunic where the spark had made a hole. I wanted to leave nothing undone. Nearby, Ultan told more miracle stories to the girls and younger boys.

A squirrel's loud chatter came from the large oak tree by the wall. Deirdre came out of the house and listened.

"I've never heard Augustine carry on so," she said. She walked up to the tree and raised her hand, holding out a crust.

The other squirrel, at which Augustine sounded his alarm, moved a little closer, then a little farther from Augustine's nest. Its fluffy tail shook as Augustine's squeaky chatter rose in pitch. The strange squirrel leaped into Augustine. When the two squirrels fell at Deirdre's feet, they jumped onto her, climbing up her dress as if she were a tree. Unperturbed, my daughter held her arms outstretched with a chattering squirrel in each hand. Deirdre carefully turned around, smiling, like a saint blessing the animals. The last gleam of the afternoon sun lighted her red hair.

I cast aside my mending and started to go to her. "Dearest, you shouldn't."

Deirdre suddenly grimaced as the strange squirrel sunk its teeth into the base of her thumb. She jerked her arms to shake them off, and they chased each other over the wall. Deirdre held her wounded hand and turned away, hunched over and holding back tears.

"Foolish animals," I said. I put my arm around Deirdre and led her back to the house.

Ultan had seen this happen and broke off his story to follow us inside, where I washed Deirdre's wound.

"I have an ointment that will help," Ultan said. He took a small round wooden box from the pouch on his belt. "If I may?"

Deirdre held out her hand, tears slipping down her face.

When he smoothed the ointment over the wound, Deirdre murmured, "It is cold, tingling. I feel…" She stumbled forward into Ultan, who gently lifted her and lay her down on the cot.

"She's very sensitive to the medicine," he said. "She'll sleep a little while, perhaps through the night. Keep her covered and warm."

"Thank you," I said as we spread a blanket over the girl. Deirdre's lips moved, and she whispered something I couldn't make out, pushing the blanket off. I pulled it over her again and smoothed it across her shoulders.

Ultan put away the little box. "She trusts too much," he said. "Wild animals can't always be pets."

I took a stool by the fire and sat where I could watch Deirdre. It was growing dark. "Will you read to me again?" I asked. "Dermott won't mind." I took the book out of the bag.

"Certainly." He read to me the Latin that I didn't understand but soothed my mind. My head leaned forward and I dozed. The few words I knew—*Christi, sanctum, Deus*—stood out in the reading and echoed. I didn't remember going to bed later; didn't remember Dermott coming back or Ultan finishing the reading.

When I awoke, I sat up with a start and saw I was alone. I had overslept, and everyone had gotten up without disturbing me, as if I were the one under the spell of the herbal balm. The room was cool. No one had banked the fire the night before, so it was almost burned out. On my hands and knees I blew on the coals, and added peat, banking it down again until it glowed warmly, saying the prayer of Saint Brigid. The smoke smelled good and familiar in the house that seemed strange and empty. I took a swallow of water from the pail. Then, with a pang of fear, I felt the book bag to assure myself it was still in its place, and sighed in relief. I went outside.

The mending from the day before was still where I had left it beside the door. The women were already setting up the feast for the last day, and the children were running around in circles playing a game.

Dermott came toward me from the shed. "There you are," he said. "You were dead to the world." He kissed my cheek.

"Where are Deirdre and Ultan?" I asked.

He turned his head. "I see them." He pointed up the hill. They were on the other side of the cross, Deirdre leaning her back against it so that only her shoulders and arms were visible. Ultan faced her, listening intently. I felt weak in the stomach.

"You look pale," Dermott said. "You should eat something. It looks ready; let's strike the bell and get started." He went over to the bell, a flat triangle of solid iron hanging from a tree, and he struck it with a rod that leaned against the trunk. The children immediately stopped their game and ran to the table.

Ultan looked down the hill at the clan and gestured to Deirdre. She stepped out from behind the cross, and they walked slowly down the hill with Ultan's hand on the girl's elbow. Their bobbing pace was languid, and it felt as I watched them that Deirdre was floating down the hill, as if in a bubble that was tethered to the old man.

I met them at the footbridge. "Deirdre, what are you doing?" I asked.

Deirdre smiled. "I had such a strange dream last night, and Ultan was interpreting it for me."

I looked from one to the other. The old man continued to beam confidently.

"The saints are truly watching over this girl," he said.

"So am I," I said. I took Deirdre's hand and led her to the table.

Deirdre told her dream to everyone over dinner. Her face shone as she spoke, and her voice, usually low and serious, rose excitedly. "I do dream at night, but I don't see pictures usually, though there are images I remember. I hear words and songs. My mother was singing. Then it grew faint because a storm began to blow. Trees whipped wildly; I could hear the breaking branches. There was a terrible storm. Trees fell all around me, and the wind tore at me, but I was rooted to the spot. Then a white deer ran, jumping over the fallen trees, chased by a pack of snarling hounds. When the deer came to me, I took it by the horns, and the dogs fell back and ran away. I followed the deer far to the edge of the sea, and it stepped into the water and disappeared. I tried to follow, but the waves pushed me back. Over and over I hurled myself into the waves, but the sea wouldn't take me. I could see an island, and I knew it was Scotia; I could see our wee croft, but I couldn't get to it.

"Then a cloud came over the island, and I could see it no more. But around me things grew very bright. The sea pulled away and was gone. Everything was very dry and hot. I could hear my mother singing again, but I couldn't see her. I had a sense of great peace, that the storm was over now and I had come far through it. I could only see a sparkling white, not like snow or frost, but hot and burning. Then I awoke. Ultan knows what it means."

Ultan finished gnawing the last bone, then spoke. "The white deer was actually Deirdre herself, chased by demons and those who wish her ill. That she is a white deer is emblematic of her saintliness. She overcomes her enemies. She comes to the sea, which we will cross soon, and loses sight of her home. But she does see, and I'm sure her sight will be restored. The sea will not take her, as the storm did not take her; it's a sign of protection. The white hot place is the desert of Moses, where one finds salvation. She is at peace because she is redeemed. She hears her mother's voice, signifying she will return home, a new person, a woman and not a girl by then. I do think this means"—he turned to the men—"that she must be allowed to go and seek her redemption."

Fear rose in me as I looked to the men for their answer. I was afraid of either answer. I felt sure this trip must be accomplished. Yet perhaps this dream was a bad omen. Connachtach had once said that wise men believed there was no meaning to dreams. But it was so wondrously vivid, and Deidre's feelings about it so strong.

Lemar answered. "You can't leave now with the lambing and calving, or during the sowing. And for certain spring weather is not the best time to take a journey. We will decide if you may leave after sowing. A few less mouths to feed between sowing and harvest might be a benefit to us all. But we will know better then."

Ultan spoke up. "But surely such a prophetic dream would add some urgency to the journey."

Dermott frowned and opened his mouth to speak, but Flachrach cut in.

"A dream exists in its own time. It may mean something far in the future, or long in the past. We must decide what makes sense for the clan." He spoke with finality.

Deirdre, still glowing, turned to Ultan. "We can't keep you here for two or three months. You must go to Spain, and return to us perhaps to lead our way. We will be waiting for you."

Ultan smiled and his confident air returned. "I would be honored. I had no plans made for after my pilgrimage. I will leave tomorrow, then, and return after the spring sowing. Bless you, dear girl."

He took Deirdre's hand and kissed it. I was still holding her other hand, and I felt a tremor through it, but did not know if it was a trembling of pleasure or a shiver of fear.

## CHAPTER TWO: THE TWINS

We lost a cow that gave birth to twin calves, which also died. Dermott grew ever quieter with his bad luck.

"I must go to Tara and become a base-client," he said. "I will arrange to take on four calves in the fall."

The day after Dermott left, I was getting water when a man and a woman with a mule cart arrived over the hill by the cross. They stopped and prayed, then waved when they spied me. I waved back and they descended.

"Welcome, strangers. This is a farm of the Ui Neill family. My husband Dermott is the priest, but he has gone to Tara. Did you not see him on the road?"

They had not seen him, having come from the southwest. "I am Joseph and this is my wife Brigid. We are smiths offering our work."

"Come and have some water."

They tied the mule to a post and went inside, where Deirdre was spinning wool

"Tell us of your travels," Deirdre asked warmly when they were settled. "Have you ever traveled with a man named Ultan? He came this way, an old man traveling alone."

They shook their heads and then exchanged a look.

"He might have taken that name," Brigid said.

"Or his brother," said the Joseph.

I brought them a cup of water to share. "That sounds like something to be told," I said.

Brigid spoke. "From our way, two brothers have gone traveling on pilgrimage, going separate ways. One is a most holy man, Ewan, whom it's a blessing to know. He is generous and hardworking, and reads the scriptures. He has a brother, his twin. Yvain is his name. He is an evil man, luring young girls into his carnal schemes. He gains the trust of people with his twinkling eye and musical voice and then leaves them in shame."

I looked at Deirdre. She did not seem to react to this, but her voice was strained.

"And what became of them, and what did they look like?"

"Yvain was run out off the farm and wanders alone. Ewan, the holy man, decided to set out on pilgrimage to try to expiate his brother's sins. They are both tall and gray-haired, with a closely clipped beard."

"Would the holy man Ewan travel under some other name?" I asked.

Joseph answered. "He might, out of modesty, so great is his reputation."

"Is there not any difference between them?"

"Yes," said Brigid. "Yvain has a scar on his arm from a time when vengeance was taken on him. It is a deep gash below his right elbow."

What I thought was that Ultan had not lifted a finger to help us in our chores during the feast.

"I think the holy man was here," Deirdre said. "Is that what he looked like, mother?"

"A man as you described stopped on his way to Spain. He's returning soon, I noticed no scar, but his sleeves would cover his arms," I said.

"Of course it was Ewan," Deirdre said. "He was a wonderful man, who told us many saints' lives. The children adored him. The dogs didn't even bark at him."

"'Tis a blessing," Brigid said.

I gave them bread and meat with garlic. Afterward they went out and offered their iron work to the clan, and set up their tools. The smiths built a fire and worked, Brigid blowing the bellows to melt the iron, her arms bulging with muscles. They stayed a week, making new scythes and sharpening knives and tools, in exchange for food, ale, and linen. I kept an eye out for Dermott every day. I felt irritable that strangers seemed to be coming so much, and didn't want more guests without my husband nearby. I began to worry that Ultan would return before Dermott.

That night I slept with Deirdre curled beside me. Before we fell asleep, I whispered to her, "Best not to mention Ewan and Yvain to your father when he returns."

"As you say," Deirdre mumbled sleepily.

After Joseph and Brigid left, I was mending a gown late in the afternoon, outside by the door of the house, when I heard the cart. I jumped up and ran to the footbridge. On the hill in the long shadows were Dermott and three other men, the two he had left with and another. A tall, hooded shadow moved slowly behind the shorter shadows of my family. The thin shadow of a walking stick slanted across all four shadows like a yoke holding them together. When they arrived at the cross they stopped to pray; Dermott thanked the Lord for their uneventful journey.

I took a few steps back. Unconsciously my mouth worked to whisper the Pater Noster with Dermott, whose voice cut through the shadows, while I stared transfixed at Ultan. I wanted to hide from the ready beatific smile I knew would beam at me at any moment. There was nothing to hide behind, the trees too few and thin. The men and nephews came from the barn and fields, having heard Dermott's voice, and when they jostled and hurried to the bridge, I stepped back among the crowd of men. They waited in respectful silence until the returning party brought their outstretched arms together with an "Amen."

Dermott came straight to me and clasped my hands. "Dear wife," he said. I was glad he had come to me first.

The men plied the sojourners with questions, and the younger boys and girls ran up, followed by the other women. While Dermott tried vainly to answer the rain of questions, Ultan stepped out of the group and approached Deirdre. I watched as he bent down to pat the dog and greet Deirdre.

Dermott waved his arms to quiet the group. "We'll have dinner and light a bonfire and tell you all about it," he said.

"Come to the stream and wash yourself," I said to Ultan.

"Thank you, bless you, dear Oona. Are you in good health?"

"Go inside now, girl, and get a pail," I said.

Deirdre, still smiling, slipped inside. The dog, his tail wagging, remained as Ultan scratched his ears.

"Do you leave everything just so, so she can find it?" Ultan asked.

"Yes. She does well."

Deirdre returned to give me the pail and a cloth.

"Come then," I said, beckoning to Ultan. But as we headed for the stream, I thought that it might be too dark anyway to see what I was looking for.

Ultan cleared his throat. "Are you sure nothing's wrong?" he asked.

"Only that good men were gone when there was much work," I said.

"Tomorrow I'm glad to help. I'm not so old," Ultan replied with a chuckle.

We were at the stream, and as I dipped the pail, he sat down on the large flat rock and took off his shoes. I knelt and started washing his feet. Now it really was dark, and there was no moon. The bonfire started to glow from the green.

"Would you like a full bath?" I asked. "There's a tub on the other side of the shed."

I could barely see his face, but his smiling teeth glinted white "Perhaps tomorrow after our work," he said.

I dried his feet and he slipped his shoes back on.

"It feels so fine to be here again. This does feel like a home to me," he said.

"Have you been long in traveling? And have you no home?" I asked.

"When my wife died, her brothers drove me out to take the land. I had no sons to defend me."

I tried to hear in his voice whether this was true, and he sounded sincere, but I couldn't know.

"And where was this, nearby or far off?"

"Far off, north. I've prayed for God's help, but it is not His will. Now I suppose I will join a monastery. It's unlikely I'll find another wife," he added thoughtfully. Then he came to himself abruptly. "Not one as my Aiefe was like."

We went to the bonfire, where everyone had assembled, waiting to hear stories of Tara and their travels. When Dermott was through, they clamored for Ultan to speak of his travels to Spain. He started by announcing that the high king at Tara gave his permission for their journey to Iona. I didn't look at Dermott.

Ultan sat on a stool with his back to the fire. The light sparkled in his silver hair, and he seemed, rather than tired by his journey, to gain strength at our attention. He was in fine form.

"I came to the coast and walked along the cliff where the gulls dove amid the foam. It was gray, and a storm threatened from the sea. At dusk, I came to a family of fishermen, four tidy houses held fast against the wind, and a collection of coracles tied up. There were four burly brothers, who welcomed me with beer and fried bream. Bread was scarce for them; the sea was all they had. We ate dried seaweed for breakfast the next day, there were also two sisters, and their old great-uncle, a widower who lived in his wee cabin alone and preferred not to keep company with other men. He stayed in his dark room and prayed constantly, and they usually left him fish and what else they had every morning outside his door. The four brothers fished, the two sisters planted what they could, gathered berries and seaweed, and when they could they went to other homesteads to trade dried fish or the occasional seal meat for oats or wool.

"What the old man prayed for everyday was for wives for the brothers and husbands for the two sisters, to bring them land and children. It was a spare life they led, and lonely, but God kept them in harmony with each other, so that there were no quarrels between them.

"The weather was bad for sailing to Spain, where they were willing to take me when the wind turned. I stayed four days with them. After the first night, I stayed with the old uncle, and we prayed mightily together. The third night, I awoke to hear him crying and moaning in his sleep. I shook him and commanded that he tell me what troubled his soul. He confessed then that he had a secret sin that stained his conscience, and he knew that God was punishing his family for that, and that was why their existence was so mean and lonely.

"I reassured him that it was a blessing that the family dwelt in peace together, and I bade him come on pilgrimage with me to ease his soul. He was content at that idea. The next day two of the brothers took us to sea and we left for Spain. The sea was calm, and the wind was strong in the right direction. The men caught several fine big fish on the way, to present to the Moors when we docked. We arrived at the largest city I have ever seen, at least a score of houses glistening white in the sun, with clay tiles for roofs. The sun at this place was bright and hot, and it hurt our eyes.

"We were quickly surrounded by Moors and we said, 'Saint James, Saint James,' to them and gave them our fish. They made sure we had no weapons, but that wasn't enough for them. They took one brother as a hostage to ensure we would return in peace from the chapel at Compostela, while a Moor was sent to accompany us. We didn't speak any common language, and he rode a fine black horse beside us as we walked the few miles to the chapel, the one brother, the old man, and I.

"The chapel was a holy sight to see, so white and spacious, with two windows made of glass. When we entered, the air inside was thick with incense. A stone in front of the altar marked the place underneath where the bones of Saint James conferred their blessing on the church. We fell to our knees and prayed all the rest of the day until sunset. Then, as the setting sun made a streak of red-gold light across his face, the old man suddenly gasped and clutched his chest. He collapsed across the stones. His nephew ran outside to try to tell the Moor we needed a priest. The Moor understood something dire had happened, and he came to the door and saw the prostrate man. He went back out, and I heard his horse gallop away.

"The old man was gasping, and his eyelids fluttered. Since his breathing was difficult, we thought to take him outside, away from the smoke of the incense. We carried him out, laid him on a bench beside the chapel, and prayed over him. Very soon, the Moor was back with a man on another horse, but it was not a priest, but another Moor with a large cloth bag.

"The other Moor, an older man with black hair and a gray beard, came up to us with his bag and knelt beside him, opening our dying companion's shirt. He took small glass flasks from his bag and held one to the lips of the dying man, who drank, hardly aware of what was happening. The Moor was a doctor of some sort, and he took the old man's pulse. He shook his head and took out a jar of ointment, which he rubbed on the man's chest. The old man began to whisper, and the Moor bent his ear to his lips. I knew he was confessing his secret sin to the Moor in a language this Moor would not understand. The Moor kept hold of his wrist as he listened, and the man gasped out his final confession. The Moor looked very thoughtful, as if these unknowable words had some meaning to him. There was a final sigh from the old man, and when the Moor lay his hand back down on his chest, I knew our sorrowful companion had expired.

"Now no Christian would ever know his secret, and I was both angry and frightened that he would die without a priest, but instead with a useless doctor who could not save his soul. But at least he had made this pilgrimage and encountered the bones of Saint James. I prayed this would be blessing enough. Other Moors arrived with shovels and picks, and we buried him in that holy place.

"It was dawn when we walked back into the city by the water. I was in a daze of sorts. We had come to help this man, and now he was dead and buried in a faraway land. I heard the high cry of a man calling forth a sinuous song, and the multitude knelt everywhere they stood, bowed very low, and prayed to the rising sun. It did feel like an evil thing, that his soul was fastened to this foreign place that worshipped the blazing sun.

"The Moor who had come with us invited us into his home, where in a shaded courtyard he gave us olives and meat for breakfast. He invited us with gestures, and seemed to understand our mourning. He spoke a little in his tongue as if we could understand, and I replied likewise. He gave us a bag of olives and dried fish for the journey. Then there was nothing more to do, and we found our boat at the dock.

"We sailed in silence, and the sea was rough. The two brothers worked hard in concentration to keep us afloat and in the right direction. Then I wondered if I had done the wrong thing to take us on this pilgrimage. But it had to be God's will. The beach was a welcome sight, and when we arrived and dragged the boat ashore, the two young men collapsed with exhaustion. I made a fire for us from driftwood, and we sat, still stunned in quietude.

"It was a cloudless night, and the moon on the water looked like a silver high road. I thought it could be the path for the old man's soul gliding up to heaven. I stayed awake all night, watching over the two men, so like boys in their sleep. In the morning, the brother who had been held hostage took a small wax brick from his pouch and showed us something amazing that I'll show you when I am done.

"I stayed while they sent for a priest, and we held a prayer service for their uncle's soul. I wanted to discover if the old man's wish would be answered, if wives and husbands would now be found. But in that time I saw no answer. All in good time with the Lord."

Ultan finished his story, and there were many questions about the Moors, the foreign land, the chapel, the miracles of Saint James, and the olives, which no one had ever tasted. All of the night was spent in this discussion, and no one minded.

"Ah, and something interesting indeed," he said. He put his hand into the pouch on his belt and took out a small waxen brick. "Bring me a pail of water and a sooty stick." The children ran to do so.

Ultan pushed his sleeves up his elbows. I stepped up close beside him. He smeared the soot on his right arm. Then he took the wax brick and dipped it in the water and swished it around. He rubbed the brick on his arm. It foamed on his skin. He dipped his arm in the water and rinsed it off. His arm had come very clean very quickly. "This is soap," he said. "They use it in Spain. I've asked fellow travelers I met since then, on my way to Tara. It was known in old Rome and is common in the heathen lands. It cleans by melting itself on the skin, pulling off the dirt. I'll show you how to make it."

The crowd was awed by the foreign wonder. I stared hard at Ultan's arms in the sunrise, with his sleeves pushed up around his elbows. There was no scar on his naked, hairless arms.

We feasted the next day, as well as we could for the time of year, when grain was becoming scarce. Lemar drained his wooden cup and leaned sideways until he almost slid off the bench.

Dermott grabbed him and Lemar straightened himself with a jerk, saying, "You are going. It does seem to be God's will, and we are decided. Good journey to you! You have much to prepare."

I reached across the table, and Dermott took my hand. I tried to search his face, but his eyes were downcast. When I squeezed his hand, he looked at me. His face was bewildered, uncertain, and I grieved to see my steady husband look like a lost boy. His expression would haunt me.

Maeve walked Lemar to his house, the place that used to be Connachtach's, to tend to him. After the other women and I finished clearing up, Maeve came to me by the stream. The sun was just beginning to rise. Maeve's frightened eyes glowed in her shadowed face.

"I must tell you something," she whispered.

I shivered with the fear this could not be good. "What is it?"

"In his drunken state, Lemar told me plainly that he plans to steal your cattle when you go. He says you will never return anyway. He will take it, and if you do return, he will put you off your land."

I took Maeve's hand. "Thank you for telling me."

"You mustn't go."

Maeve's strong grip was cold, hanging onto me like the grip of death, but I stopped shivering. Calm descended on me. "I must go. It is God's will. I'm sure of it. But I will tell Dermott. Somehow…" I breathed the last word in a whisper to myself.

In the house, behind the curtain in the dawn, I kissed Dermott, traced my fingertips along his neck, and we knew each other with a lost passion, both knowing the inevitable fate. I fought back tears.

Afterward, the words I had to speak were like shards of ice in my throat. "Maeve told me that Lemar plans to steal our cattle when we go."

He was lying on his back, and he turned to me, his face peaceful, a note of relief in his voice. "Then we cannot go."

"You cannot go. Someone else can go with us. One of the older boys."

Dermott's brows knitted, the peaceful look gone. "You are stubborn, like your brother."

"I feel called by God to do this."

"So he said, too."

"I can't explain. I don't feel there's a choice."

He turned and tossed his head back on the pillow, looking upward into the dark. "I would not be surprised to get word you've left me for a convent. Go if you will. I will not have you thinking I own you like a slave. Go. But if you don't return, I will have a wife. I will marry Maeve if you don't return."

I trembled at the cold distance in his voice, put my arms around him and cried quietly against his chest. "You parted from my brother in anger. Don't do the same with me. Please, I cannot bear it."

He didn't reply for a while but held me, stiffly at first. Then he pulled me tightly into his arms. "Don't cry. You are grieving for my anger. But I am grieving, too, for your madness." He kissed my face, and we lay in silence until the sun was high.

A week later, Deirdre, Ultan, the young man Ferdich, and I set off. We packed a mule with some bedding, dried meat and oats, and skins of milk. We rose well before dawn, and the stars glittered like hopeful eyes in the sky. It was warm and damp. I rolled up bedding and our cloaks, and there were conferences on the best way to pack. Deirdre held the mule's rope and stroked its nose while this went on. I felt Dermott was prolonging the packing, and my throat ached.

At last there were no more knots to tie, and we stood by the footbridge. Dermott held Deirdre close and kissed the top of her head. Then he embraced me so that my breath was tight in my chest.

"Take care, my dearest," he whispered. "I fear we may be parted very long."

"Don't say so, it's bad luck," I said with a kiss.

We went up the hill and past the cross. I looked back down and saw him, his arms outstretched in prayer. His lips were moving in words that were to God, but his eyes, shining in the darkness, stayed on me. For a moment, I almost halted the group, almost called off the trip, almost ran back into his arms. I took a few steps forward, and when I looked around again, I could no longer see the light of his eyes nor the movement of his lips, and then he was gone behind the hill as we descended the far side. The farm was gone and we continued through the fields, and when the sun had risen, I was in fields I didn't know, bordered by a dark wood I had never entered before.

## CHAPTER THREE: THE ROPE

We could see the wood from a long way off beyond a deserted plain. The plain was criss-crossed with low stone walls, but there was no house as far as we could see. Ahead there were the white blossoms of an apple tree beside a circular wall that might indicate a well, and we headed for it. We had not stopped to rest yet, and it was midday. The sky was hazy and bright, casting greenish shadows.

The apple blossoms perfumed the air when we arrived at the tree, and I tossed a pebble down the well. We heard the splash and smiled, unloading the tired mule in order to use the twine. We'd brought a small pail and a cup, and after we pulled up the pail of water, we passed the cup many times and drank our fill. We sat down under the tree and sparingly ate some dried meat.

"Do you know this well?" I asked Ultan.

"When I came before, I stayed to the edge of the wood rather than cross the plain," he replied. I didn't ask why he avoided the open plain, but he must have seen the question in my face. "It was stormy and the wood sheltered me," he explained.

So far, Ferdich had hardly spoken, and he stretched out on his back. He was a big, strong lad with broad shoulders and large hands, and his lip and chin were lightly covered with pale brown hair. He kept his golden brown hair short, and it curled gaily on top of his head. He was humming quietly.

"Sing us a song," Deirdre said, flopping down beside him.

"Only if you sing with me."

They sang rounds and their voices echoed in the bright, still air. I was looking at Ultan, who watched the singers, particularly Deirdre.

"You have a fine voice—both of you," he said.

"Thank you," the girl said, turning her head as if to look away, or to hide a blush.

They stopped singing. A crow landed on a nearby wall beyond the apple tree and started fluttering between the top of the wall and something just on the other side of it. Ferdich noticed and got up to investigate.

"Fresh meat," he called. "A deer has died here."

"No!" Deirdre cried.

He laughed. "You are too tender. Animals don't die in their beds."

"But we can't stay here long enough to make use of it," I said.

"Why not?" Ferdich asked.

"Because we should continue, even now."

He shrugged. "Seems a waste."

Without speaking further, we packed up.

When we entered the woods, Deirdre asked, "Could the deer have been poisoned by the well?"

"And how could the little deer have reached the water?" Ferdich replied. "The water was down a few feet. It tripped on the wall and broke its leg."

We slipped into the woods, from the bright afternoon into green darkness, and the air was cool. Hawthorns bloomed among the hemlocks and oaks. Ultan knew his way through the wood, quicker, he said, than keeping to the field, and knew a cave by a spring where we could spend the night. The deeper in we went, the colder the air felt. At first a flock of crows flew with us from tree to tree, but after a while the flock turned off.

"We are a sorry lot," Ferdich suddenly said, breaking the silence. "We should be passing the time in merriment, stories and song. Why are we somber as a funeral? Nay, I've been to merrier funerals!"

We laughed.

"Then you start," I said to the boy.

"I see I am in charge of the entertainment," he replied. He started asking riddles: "I am below and above the water. I glide like a swan, but I steal her eggs."

"An otter," said Deirdre. "That was too easy."

"I live in packs of my kind, yet all men admire my solitude."

"The wolf," Ultan said.

"I can be seen, but I cannot be held. I can be felt but not touched. I can be heard, yet I have no voice."

"Fire," I said.

"I cannot be stood upon, but I bear great weight. I can be drunk but never quench your thirst."

"The sea," Deirdre said.

He went on riddling as the trees grew thicker and more tangled. A chorus of birdsong and insects arose as it became dusk.

Ultan stopped and looked about. "I think we've come to it," he said. He led us off to the left and suddenly there was a large outcropping of rock and a cave opening in the earth, big enough for all of us. There were the remains of a fire, and it seemed like a commonly used place. Ferdich struck a fire from the flint and char cloth, and I gathered plentiful dead wood while Ultan sat with Deirdre and told her a story. Then Ferdich went off to see if he could catch a squirrel or a rabbit.

The three of us sat by the fire; we could hear Ferdich tramping in the wood but lost sight of him.

"Won't you sing again?" Ultan asked Deirdre.

She smiled shyly. "All right." Her sweet voice trembled on the air.

The song ended. It was dark, and Ferdich did not return. I realized I couldn't hear his footfalls anymore.

"Do you think Ferdich is lost?" I asked.

Ultan smiled. His teeth were big in the shadows of his face. "Of course not."

"He doesn't know the woods."

"He's a clever lad."

Deirdre leaned her head on my shoulder, and I wrapped my cloak around her. Suddenly there was a crashing sound of wings through the brush, a loud cackle, and then Ferdich's step. He emerged from the trees carrying a large, round brown bird by its feet.

"I've snared a grouse. It will do," he said. He gutted the bird and boiled it in the pail.

After eating, we spread out to sleep. When I awoke, the woods were dark but with the gray glow of dawn. Ultan was feeding the fire.

"I'm glad you're up first," he whispered. His hoarse whisper blended with the hiss of the fire.

"Why is that?"

"I want to talk with you. Come." He led me away by where the spring bubbled from the ground. He rubbed his hands. "When Deirdre is old enough, I'd like to marry her," he said.

I sighed. I'd half-expected this. "You're very old. And you have no property."

"She is blind. Her expectations are low. I spoke with the high king at Tara. This summer, he will enforce my land rights with his men, for a share."

I wasn't sure I had ever believed his story. "It's up to Dermott. We'll see when we return. And we'll see when you get your land back."

He nodded with a slight bow. "That is fair."

We set out again and walked until mid-day. We came to a clearing in the woods, where the sun dazzled out from under the dark trees. We spread our bedding to doze in the warmth and then boiled some oats in some of the milk.

Ultan took a small pair of scissors from his belongings and turned to me. "I keep my hair very short, and it itches me when it grows. Would you mind trimming it?"

He loosened his robe, pulling the wide opening down to his thin chest. He knelt on the ground and I stood behind him. As I bent over him and started to clip his hair, I saw something that stopped my breath. Just under his left shoulder was the red scar of a deep gash. I felt dizzy, swaying in the heat.

"Are you all right?"

"It's just the sun." I clipped his gray hair and handed the scissors back to him.

"We're almost through the wood," Ultan said. "By nightfall we'll be in the open again. Then we'll make better time, and be at the coast within days."

I nodded dumbly. He startled me by seeming to read my thoughts.

"Those who took my land gashed my arm as a warning," he said.

"I'm sorry. It's a terrible wound."

"I'll have my revenge soon." He tied his tunic at the neck.

In the clearing as we packed, I thought how to escape with Deirdre, but as we entered into the dark wood again, I reflected. *Could the visitors have mistaken a gash below the left shoulder for one below the right elbow? They were so precise about it. Certainly he is Yvain, and an evil man. I have done the wrong thing. I didn't trust my misgivings. Still, Ferdich is with us, and he has done no harm by us. By now he may be repentant.*

We did not exit the woods before nightfall, and we stopped where a stream wound snake-like around small hills.

"Now we follow the stream, in the morning," Ultan said. "It will take us into the fields of a man I know. He will shelter us tomorrow night."

Ferdich slapped him on the back. "That will be a pleasant change. Are there fish in this brook?"

"Aye."

Ferdich set up a line as he whistled a tune.

I took Deirdre's hand and led her to the edge of the stream. We dipped the cup and drank. "Why don't you gather wood?" I called to Ultan. *At least now he may lift a finger, to please me for Deirdre's sake*, I thought.

Ferdich strung the line across the brook and joined Ultan, and soon we had a lively fire and four trout to fry. While we ate, Ultan told us the life of Saint Brendan, who sailed to strange islands. I had always loved when my brother told of it.

When we scraped the last morsel from the bowl, Deirdre said, "You like the stories of those who travel to far lands."

Ultan smiled. "Yes. I am a wanderer, but I won't wander forever. I long to settle down again."

The fire lighted Deirdre's face, so sweet and bright. "When we come to Iona, it is such a holy place, I'm sure the monks will pray for you and your brother, and all will be well."

His smile froze, and then he furrowed his brow in exaggerated puzzlement. "My brother?"

Ferdich was sitting between Deirdre and me, and I couldn't squeeze her arm or nudge her without Ultan seeing.

"Oh, I think I know your secret. We're friends, you can tell us. Are you not the holy man called Ewan? We heard the tale."

Ultan glanced aside, considering, and he frowned in thought. "I am no more or less than what I say I am." He turned and took her hand, pressing it hard. "Have no illusions about me, or fears. I have nothing, but a reputation is more a burden than any possession, I'm sure for the holy man as well as his brother."

There was something in this that made Deirdre shrink back and pull her hand from his.

I caught Ultan's eye and said, to dismiss it, "The girl is too fanciful."

But in that moment I felt that he saw in my eyes the look that betrayed everything, and in his eyes I saw a harsh and angry gleam. He smiled strangely.

"You must grow up, dear child," he said to Deirdre, but he didn't take his eyes off me.

"I have no choice but to grow up," Deirdre said with directness that did seem mature.

"There are always choices," Ultan said softly, almost warningly.

Deirdre stood up and turned awkwardly, her blindness apparent in a way that was rare for her. I jumped up and put her arms around her. Deirdre was shaking, and I held myself still for her sake. I looked down at Ultan, but he was staring at the fire now, absorbed in his own thoughts.

Ferdich did not seem to notice any of our discomfort. He looked up in surprise at Ultan. "Choices? All is God's will, is it not? The only thing is to choose God's will."

Ultan didn't answer for a while, as if he didn't hear. Then he asked, "How do you know God's will?"

"But everything just is."

Ultan smiled a little. "Everything just is," he repeated.

I stroked Deirdre's hair and grew calmer. "All will be well," I murmured in Deirdre's ear.

Ultan stood up and said, "I'm tired. I'm going to sleep." His jovial, genial, saintly air was replaced by the demeanor of a tough, tired old man. He walked a little way from the clearing to sleep beside a rocky outcropping.

I banked the fire and then started to pack, leaving by the fire a bag of oats and a skin of milk. When Ultan was snoring, I began to pack the mule.

"What are you doing?" Ferdich asked.

I told him quietly about Ewan, Yvain, and the scar.

Ferdich looked flabbergasted. "And just go back?"

"No, go on."

Ferdich looked even more stunned. "How will we know the way? Why?"

"He said to follow the stream."

He grabbed my arm as I tried to tie our things onto the mule. "He's a kindly old man and no more. We can't leave him."

"He's tough and has been travelling alone. He knows the way. He'll expect us to go back, so we'll go ahead." I tied the knot.

"You are mad."

"Then we'll go ahead without you."

He made a fist and raised it over his head in an impotent gesture. "I won't let you go on alone. Let's only think about this."

I untied the mule from the tree. "It's the best time to go, while he's sleeping. We must hurry." I handed him the end of the rope and went to Deirdre who drowsed by the banked fire. "We're going on," I whispered.

Deidre's sightless eyes rose upward. "Going now?"

"I don't want to frighten you. But I saw his scar."

"I'm sure it's a mistake. He is kind."

"We must go. Don't argue." I put my hand under Deirdre's arm and helped her up.

The stream wound in great bends, and I felt it was likely taking us twice as long to leave the woods this way. We came out just as the sun broke over misty fields, and there were houses in the distance. The mule stopped here and wouldn't go further, almost kicking Ferdich while it hungrily browsed.

"We should find hospitality here," he said with a mixture of uncertain hope and impatience at the turn of events.

"But can they be trusted?" I asked.

He gave me a stony look. "We must replenish and rest, and get directions to the coast, if we must go." He looked down and kicked a rock. "He was just an old man, only an old man."

We sat in silence at the edge of the fields. The mist only grew heavier, and the sun didn't seem to rise any higher. I closed my eyes and nodded off, exhausted from walking all night.

I awoke to voices. A boy and girl in their teens had come and were already talking with Ferdich. I nudged Deirdre, who was asleep beside me. The boy and girl saw us rising and quickly turned to greet us.

"We are Heive and Liam," the girl said. She was a short, slight girl with blond hair flowing over her shoulders. She wore a necklace of river pearls and beads, and her dress was fine.

The boy smiled. He was also slight, with long brown hair. He was holding a flute. Liam said, "Come to the house. My wife will give you porridge."

Heive laughed shyly. "He does like to say 'my wife.'"

"You are newly wedded?" I asked. We started to walk across the field.

"Aye, the feast ended last night. It was all gaiety. You will be our first guests."

As we walked, Liam played his flute. I looked about. The fields had been sown. There were five houses and a barn. No one was about.

"Where is your family?" I asked.

"Sleeping it off," Liam said. "Before the feast, we worked hard to get in the sowing."

192 A M Y   C R I D E R

We went into a very small house that was newly built. It had two rooms, a table with two stools by the fire. Deirdre and I sat on the stools, and Ferdich leaned against the wall. Heive put a pot on the fire to boil the porridge.

"You are going to the coast?" Liam asked.

"To the island of Iona, the monastery," I said. "My brother is there. How far is it?"

"I've never been, but my father fished on the coast when he was young."

Heive was in the shadows fetching the water and barley. After measuring the barley into the boiling water, she appeared with a skin that had been hanging on a peg. She poured milk from it into the pot. It caught my eye, and I looked at the skin in Heive's hands. It was exactly the skin I had left for Ultan.

"We are your first guests?" I asked.

"Oh yes," Heive said. She gave Liam a quick look. "No one comes through the wood, and no one comes from the sea in winter. I hope it's late enough in the season for you to travel by boat."

There was silence. I drew in my breath. "Do you know an old man named Ultan?" I asked.

Liam smiled easily and furrowed his brow to consider it. "That name isn't familiar to me. He might have known my father, but my father died over the winter."

"I'm very sorry to hear it."

Heive gave a bowl of porridge to Ferdich and a bowl to Deirdre and me to share and gave us each a piece of bread. We ate hungrily without talking, while Liam played his flute.

"We've walked all night and are very tired," I said. "Is there some place we could rest for today?"

"Come to the barn," Liam said.

Heive took up a lamp and we went out. It was a warm, humid day, and rain was coming. The barn was close by, a small, dark building with no windows. We went inside, and in the dark I could half-see and half-sense the men-folk gathered inside, who surrounded us and stood in front of the door. The small light from the lamp created a haze through which shadows moved.

"What's this?" Ferdich asked.

"You mean harm to our kin Ultan," a man said. "And you're to stay in here until we know what to do."

Deirdre grabbed me around the waist.

"Don't be foolish!" I snapped at them. "If we meant him harm, we wouldn't have run away from him." I told what I knew about Yvain and the scar.

The man who had spoken folded his arms implacably. "I don't know any Yvain. I know you chased the old man Ultan through the woods all night."

Heive spoke. "He is my uncle. His late wife was my mother's sister. Her brothers took his land, and we are too small to fight for it back from him."

I wrung my hands. "Then it was a mistake, and I was wrong. Surely you understand my confusion."

"Some folk create confusion for their own ends," the man said.

"What would I want from him?" I asked.

"Perhaps, to please the cousins who took his land, for some reward you would kill him. Shut up now. Our king is away, and when he comes back, we'll ask for his judgment."

They filed out and barred the door behind, leaving us in almost complete darkness; Heive left the lamp for us on a shelf by the door. Ferdich flopped down in the straw and sighed loudly, but said nothing. I took Deirdre's hand, and we sat down together.

"He does mean mischief. Why else would he deceive them into thinking we meant him harm?" I asked.

Ferdich sighed again, and I knew to stop talking. There was nothing to do but try to sleep, so we stretched out and closed our eyes. I felt the rhythm of walking still vibrating in me. The straw was fresh, sweet smelling, and slightly intoxicating. My head spun. Exhausted, I fell into a deep sleep.

Through my sleep I heard the storm. A cold draft passed over me, and I curled up tighter. If there was anything to hear or sense, it was swallowed by the thunder and rain. When I awoke, I knew hours had passed. The lamp had blown out. I lay still and heard

Ferdich's light snoring. Something seemed missing. I didn't hear Deirdre's breathing.

I stretched my arms and felt around. Deirdre wasn't beside me. I got on my hands and knees and crawled, unable to see in the pitch black, feeling for her.

"Deirdre?" I whispered. "Deirdre?"

Ferdich awoke with a snort. "What is it?"

"Deirdre!" I called. I stumbled through the straw, pushing through it. "He's taken her. That was what he wanted."

We rushed to the door and hurled ourselves against it. It was no longer barred, and we crashed out of the barn into the night. We had slept all day, and now it was dark and raining heavily.

We could just make out the white stone foundation of Liam and Heive's cottage, and we ran to their door, pounding on it and shouting, not much louder than the storm. After a time that seemed forever, Heive came to the door with a candle.

"What are you doing here?"

"He's taken her. He wanted her, and he took her while we slept."

Heive went inside, and Ferdich and I followed. Heive went to the house's other room and knocked on the door, calling Ultan; then she opened it. The room was empty.

Liam took the candle, put it on the table, and looked wrathfully at us. "I don't know what trickery you practice, but if it's true and her spell on him has deceived him to this, there's nothing to do now."

"We have to find them!" A clap of thunder shuddered through the house.

"You're mad. There's no way to follow anyone in this storm."

I turned and ran outside, leaving Ferdich in the house with Liam and Heive. I bolted across the fields toward the woods from which we had come. Flashes of lightning made the woods jump toward me as I ran.

"Deirdre! Deirdre!" I shouted, and the wind pushed back my voice. I heard something, a cry tossed in the wind; I couldn't tell which direction it came from.

Branches shook wildly in flashes of light; the trees bent in the wind. Through the booming thunder came the crashing sound of boughs breaking and falling. The wind whipped off my hood and blew wet hair across my eyes as I ran, slipping across the drowned field.

I arrived where the stream came out of the woods. The rushing water shone in the dark, and what had been a quiet stream that morning now roared with fury. I shouted for Deirdre again. I was sure I heard a voice. I stood still, trying to concentrate on the direction it came from. The voice of my daughter seemed to come from just within the wood, and I followed the stream into the trees. A branch crashed in front of me, and I slid and stumbled over it.

"I'm here!" Deirdre called.

"I'm coming!" I scrambled down the bank and into the water, which was up to my knees, and tripped over the slippery stones, cutting my ankles and hands as I stumbled ahead. My foot got wedged between two rocks, the water and mud sucking it down. I pulled my foot out of one shoe, then the other. I pulled myself up the other bank toward the voice of my daughter. The clouds were lifting now, the moon peeking out, and I could just see Deirdre sitting below an oak. I crawled up the slope, tearing off hunks of moss.

"I'm here," I said at last, falling onto my daughter and throwing my arms around her.

"I don't know where he's gone," Deirdre said. "I'm not hurt."

I clutched Deirdre close and stifled a sob. "You aren't hurt?" I asked.

Deirdre put her hand on my face. "No. He carried me off and dragged me here. Then he ran his hands over my body and cried out that he had nothing, nothing left in the world. Then he disappeared."

Lightning flashed, and I pulled Deirdre away from the tree, looking upward. Then I saw it, and mouthed a prayer, my breath still coming in pants. Above us, Ultan was hanging from the tree.

"He's killed himself. Pray to God for his soul," I said.

We trudged back to Liam and Heive's cottage. Heive stirred porridge over the fire, and Liam was sitting up in the bed, whittling a stick. Ferdich was on the bed beside him, his feet and hands tied together.

"I see you found her," Liam said in an uninterested voice.

"He hanged himself in a tree, to prevent his sinning," I said.

Liam stopped and sharpened his knife on a small stone. "Then it's a bad business, and you should be on your way. You can have a bowl of porridge first and then leave. It's not hard to find the sea from here. Go west."

Liam untied Ferdich. We ate the porridge in silence. Then Liam spoke again as he set down his bowl.

"We'll keep the mule as your payment for Ultan's life," he said.

Ferdich glared at me. "As you say," was all he answered.

"Your things are in the barn. Take them and go."

We each carried what we could in bundles on our backs. The rope Ultan had hanged himself with was the rope that had held our things onto the mule's back and made a lead for the animal.

"Perhaps we should get our rope," I said.

Ferdich's eyes popped. "The rope? With a curse of the most mortal sin on it?"

"We might be able to trade it for food later."

"There's no food I can't catch. I won't hand on this sin to an unsuspecting Christian."

"We might need it," I said. This was the beginning of a long time when I could only feel a great coldness and stiffness in my belly.

Ferdich regarded me, glanced at Deirdre, who was biting her lip. "What am I doing taking this mad woman and her ill-omened daughter on this mad errand?" he said to the floor. He looked up again. "We should go back and quit this."

Just then voices and treading feet headed toward the barn. Liam and some men entered carrying Ultan's body on a board. They set it down.

"You're still here?" Liam asked with exasperation. The rope was hanging over his shoulder. "The path that leads west from the barn connects with another. Follow it to a small lake. That will take you until nightfall. Perhaps someone there will take you in and guide you further to the coast."

I reached out and grasped the rope in my fingers. It slid off his shoulder. "I only was waiting for my rope," I said.

The group of men stepped back in horror.

CHAPTER FOUR: THE SEA

I led the way out the door, and we marched west. The sun was getting high in the sky now, and the mud from the storm was quickly drying in the bright day. After setting a brisk pace, I slowed for a bit and put my arm around Deirdre, pulling her close to whisper in her ear.

"Everything happens for a reason," I said, and repeated, "everything happens for a reason."

Deirdre had not spoken since leaving the woods that morning. With one hand she held my arm, and with the other hand she rubbed tears out of her eyes. "It's my fault. It's all my fault," she said.

I clutched her tightly but didn't stop walking. "No, my dearest. Nothing is your fault."

"If I weren't blind, we wouldn't even be on this journey."

"And did you make yourself blind? No, God did. It's God's will, everything is. God gives us no choice. The man had nothing left, he had come to the end of his rope. And didn't we, in a way bring him back to his kin? What else might have happened to him if we hadn't brought him this far? He might have been killed by thieves or wolves, or his enemies who took his land. It's impossible to say."

The path went uphill. Liam's fields were behind us, and bracken bit at our feet. I was still barefoot from losing my shoes in the stream. To be barefoot in summer is common, and I paid it no mind; my feet were tough.

"Where are we?" Deirdre asked. "Aren't we going back? We didn't come this way."

"We're headed for the sea, as we intended."

"Why?"

"Because we started and we'll finish. It's in God's plan."

Ferdich was behind us, and he caught up as we reached the top of the hill. We stopped.

"Smell the breeze," Deirdre said, for a moment forgetting her misery. "I smell water and lavender."

"Yes." I gave her a hug. I peered down the hill, at the bottom of which was a lake and a settlement.

"I hear voices," Deirdre said.

The lake farm was bustling with activity. In the lake itself, men were building a crannog, hauling stones into the middle to build a rocky, man-made island. On the shore craftsmen were carving a huge stone cross. Some women daubed a house with mud while another stood at a loom outside and others spun wool on drop spindles. It was a great contrast to the strangely idle, empty place we had just left. Voices rose, women singing and children playing. I felt happy and at peace; I felt I could stay here, if it weren't that we had to keep to the journey.

"It's a busy, God-fearing place," I said to Deirdre, and I recounted all that I saw. Even Ferdich smiled for the first time since we had left the woods. We went down the hill and were greeted by a man who oversaw the carving of the cross.

He was a slight man with blond hair and a shaven face. His eyebrows were dark and heavy over deep brown eyes. "I am Aidan, the priest," he said.

I wondered if Ferdich would tell him of our unlucky adventure, but he was reticent. We were quickly surrounded by children begging for tales, and one by one the women rose from their chores to greet us also.

"We're from Connacht, on our way to Iona to see my brother who is master scribe there, and to visit the miraculous well we have heard of," I told them.

"You're close to the sea now. If you spend the night here, you will be at the coast tomorrow afternoon," Aidan said. "Of course, you are welcome to stay longer."

"Yes, stay," a young woman spoke up from the crowd. She was looking intently at Ferdich, who looked away.

"It's a fine cross," he said, and we went over to inspect it more closely. It was about seven feet tall, of gray-green stone. The carvings depicted lambs, grapevines, and scenes from life of Christ: the raising of Lazarus and the last supper.

Aidan gave us a tour of its carvings and explained he had just become the priest and all were eager to have a cross for their masses. Two men were digging a hole for it close by, and after a brief pause to welcome us, they finished it. No one wanted to delay its mounting. Ferdich helped them haul stout beams for tipping it up. A rope was tied to the circle that connected the cross's arms.

Aidan walked out to test the rope's length. "We need more," he said.

Some of the men wore belts that they untied and fixed to the rope, but it still needed to be longer. I handed Aidan my rope. He smiled and tied my rope to the line, and it was now long enough.

Some of the men joined together to pull, while others with Ferdich piled the beams behind the cross to keep it up, and the rest guided the base into the hole. It rose, inch by tentative inch, but it was bound to rise; by the collective will of all who watched, it had no choice but to rise, and I felt our prayers instilling the cross with its own will. With a sudden thud, the base slid into the hole fast, the last moment of its rising beyond their effort, released into its secure footing like a soul suddenly slipping away from death into paradise.

The children cheered and the men slapped each other on their backs. The women hugged each other. Aidan gathered them round and offered a prayer. I squeezed Deirdre's hand. Aidan's voice reminded me of Dermott, and I longed to tell my husband of everything that had happened.

The ropes were untied and returned to their owners. "Your coming here was lucky," Aidan said as he gave me back the rope.

It was mid-afternoon and dinner was laid out. We ate our fill of lamb and spring onions and mash. The children, who had been silenced for a while by their mothers, began again to ask for stories. Ferdich told them about Tara. He spoke well, and I was grateful he had thought of something to tell them.

The women continued their chores while the men took Ferdich out to the crannog and showed him all about it. I went to the loom where Ives, the girl who seemed to admire Ferdich, was weaving. Deirdre ran her hand over the cloth.

"It's very fine," Deirdre said. The cloth was white, undyed linen.

"We have good flax along the lake," Ives replied. "This began as a shirt for my baby brother, but he died this winter, so I continued to make it larger for my father, and then he died of the sweat. Now no one wants the shirt it will make, for it seems cursed. But I don't fear such chances. I will marry a man in this cloth someday, for I know the cloth carries no blame for chance misfortune."

I too ran my hand over the fine weave. "Those are brave words, well spoken," I said.

"There must be some plan for my labor; I only need to find it. I pray over my weaving every night, that it will be redeemed of its ill luck."

We helped her by beating the weft, and we talked more and more gaily; as the time passed, a burden lifted off our shoulders.

"Is Ferdich your son?" Ives asked after a while.

"No, my cousin."

"He seems a fine, upright man."

"He is that." I paused. Ferdich had still seemed a boy when we left a few days earlier, but now it seemed true that he was suddenly a man.

The light was fading, and Ferdich and the men returned and built a bonfire. After such an exciting day, a quiet calm descended over the croft. Everyone sat by the fire; there was a quiet murmur of voices mingled with the fire's crackle. The children, huddled at their parent's feet, closed their eyes and drowsed.

Suddenly a loud voice shouted from the edge of the wood, and a man, naked and muddy, burst from the trees. He ran straight for the fire.

"I am Lugh, hear my rebuke!" he shouted, and he shouted other incoherent things.

Three men jumped up and ran toward him. He got to the fire, pulled a burning branch out of it, and waved it at his pursuers.

I could see by the reaction of the crowd, anxious but exasperated, that this was not planned but yet something they had seen before. I turned to Aidan.

"He is partially mad, our friend Adam. Twice a year he goes berserk, ranting, singing, and sleepless, thinking he is some pagan god. It lasts a week, and then he is calm again. It started when he was a young man. For a long while we lived with it and accepted it, but last year he burned down his house."

Adam swung the burning branch in the air, and a shower of sparks fell on his matted hair, which caught fire. He dropped the branch and sank to his knees. One of his pursuers grabbed a leather bag to smother the flames, closing it over his head. I tossed my rope to Aidan, and the men quickly tied his hands and feet.

As soon as he was tied with my rope, his shouting stopped. His chest heaved with deep breaths. The bag was still over his head. He trembled slightly, and then he was very still. The crowd watched in silence.

"Hello?" he asked meekly from within the bag.

Aidan stepped up to him and pulled the bag off his head. Adam's face was no longer contorted with madness, but mild and peaceful.

"What am I doing here?" he asked.

"You were mad again," Aidan said.

He swallowed and looked around. "So I was. God preserve me. It's gone now. I'm thirsty."

Aidan put a cup of water to his lips. "We'll leave you restrained a little longer."

"Aye, all right. As soon as I felt the rope, I felt the madness leave me."

Aidan looked to me and then looked over the crowd. "This is a blessed cord, then, with power to heal."

Aidan and some men, with Ferdich, volunteered to stay with the tied-up Adam all night to make sure of his cure. Deirdre and I were invited to stay with Ives. We rose early the next morning and went outside just as Aidan was untying Adam. I approached them.

"Thank you," Adam said. "Your rope has healed me."

I took the rope and tied it around my waist. "I think because it was used to raise the cross," I said. I looked at Ferdich for reassurance, but he only looked away.

We ate mash in high spirits and joined in the day's chores, deciding to stay for a few days at Aidan's invitation. Though Deirdre was unfamiliar with the house and grounds and could do less than she had been able to at home, she was able to spin wool while Ives continued to weave. I made myself busy. I cleaned the house, chopped wood, and when Ferdich and some of the men returned with fish from the lake, I rendered the oil for the lamps. Ferdich gave all the fish he caught to Ives and made some needles for her from the fish bones.

The third morning of this pleasant respite, I said over breakfast that it was time we continued our journey. Ferdich nodded with resignation, and after eating went to talk with Aidan.

Ives cut the cloth from the loom and draped it over herself. The women gathered to admire it.

"Yes, I shall be handfasted in this gown," Ives said. She and all the women worked on it, and by midday the dress was finished, a simple, long-sleeved tunic. She girded it with a red leather belt, and the women decked her with flowers.

Ferdich and Aidan approached as they were finished. Ferdich took Ives by the hand and kissed her cheek. Ives shone in her gown, her blue eyes sparkling, flower petals falling all around her.

"Let us be joined," Ferdich said.

The women went and gathered everyone together. The couple was handfasted by Aidan with a small length of cord cut from my rope. There had been no time to prepare a true feast, but a fine meal was scraped together and draughts of ale flowed through the sieve.

Somehow it was generally known that the couple did not want to consummate the marriage until Ferdich's return from the journey. Instead the couple and the whole company sang and danced all the night through, and Ferdich and Ives beamed as happily as ever any couple did. At dawn, after a short sleep, we rose and the whole company walked with us partway around the lake, and Ives said goodbye to Ferdich where the path turned away to the west, with a kiss. A little piece of cord was still wound around her hand when she waved goodbye.

After we turned up the path, we didn't talk for a while. We followed the way that Aidan had instructed us as the fastest way to the sea.

Then I asked, "Will you stay there or bring your bride to our farm? I fear you will leave us, and we will miss you very much."

"Yes, I think I will stay with her people. It's very pleasant and busy there. I like it very well."

We came up a hill, and at the top I drew in my breath. There was the wide ocean, bronze as a shield, streaked in red below the setting sun. Ferdich gave a shout.

"What is it?" Deirdre asked.

"The sea is as endless as the sky," I said. "The sun is sinking into it, sending out streams of bloody red. The vast ocean fills the horizon. We have come to the end of the world."

Clustered at the edge of a low bluff were seven dark fisherman's houses. Not a sound arose from them. Slowly we picked our way down to them. No one came out to greet us. We stood outside the first house and knocked, calling "Good day." No one answered.

Ferdich looked at me with a frown. "Could they all be fishing? Or gone to some market?"

Deirdre pressed my hand. "Do you smell that?" A strange and rank odor filled the air.

"It's probably their fish drying," I said.

"It smells worse than that," said Ferdich.

I turned away from Ferdich and led Deirdre around to the yard in the center of the houses. I stopped short and put my hand to my mouth, about to vomit. Five men lay dead in the yard, rotting and covered in blood.

Ferdich came up behind me and stopped. He tugged my arm. "Let's go back," he said.

I breathed through my fingers. "We have to see if there are survivors. We might be of some help."

"It's clear none of these are living," he said.

"Dead men?" Deirdre asked.

"Yes," I replied. Ferdich was right. Their bones were sticking out of their leathery flesh.

I hurried into the nearest house. The humid room had a musty odor from the half-eaten food: four bowls of pottage on the table, a cup of milk next to a full jug turning thick. The cauldron of pottage still hung over the cold hearth in the center of the room, its contents dried and hard. I walked around the room. A chest was tipped over and linens strewn on the floor. I rocked the chest back in place and started to stuff the linens back in. A small, hard object came into my hand: a wooden comb. A few long, red hairs trailed out of it. The bodies in the yard were all men. Where were the women and children? Next to the chest was a crib, and a bulky sheet was stained in blood. I was afraid to pull back the sheet, afraid of what was under it. I took one of the clean sheets from the chest and draped it over the bloody bulk in the crib.

"There's no one here," Ferdich called from outside.

I went back out.

"Some battle has been waged here," he said.

I didn't want to discuss why a king would raid fisherman's houses, or why Aidan knew nothing of a battle.

"Let's go back," Ferdich said, leading us out of the yard.

I looked down at the ocean. I did not want to leave the ocean behind, after coming so far.

"There are boats," I said.

"So?" asked Ferdich.

"We have been walking so far. Let us take a boat and go around the coast to the next place."

He stared at me.

"It might be dangerous to go on the road, if the brigands who were here are out. We can float to the next fishing croft."

"It's too dark to go out on the sea."

"It's also too dark to go back."

In the twilight, Ferdich's face looked as hard as Dermott's. Ferdich seemed much older than when we had left.

"Let us stay in one of the houses tonight, if we can stand it," I said. "We might as well sleep in beds, and tomorrow we can see."

Ferdich rubbed his face and shrugged tiredly. "It is a place of no good here. But I am tired and ready to sleep. Perhaps there is some food."

We went into the house farthest from the yard. It too had old food in bowls on the table, but there was a wheel of cheese that was still good, and we ate. Deirdre and I huddled in a bed and Ferdich took one by the door. I tried to ignore the smells creeping inside. Deirdre shivered in my arms.

In the night, I woke and sensed by her breathing that Deirdre was awake too. I whispered her name.

"Are we going?" she asked.

I went cold at the thought that I had not asked her her own mind, and whether she wanted to go on or turn back.

"Do you want to go back?" I asked.

There was a long pause, as Deirdre's throat made a small sound. She was struggling to answer.

"You can tell me your true heart," I said.

She pressed herself against me. "Are we very close to getting there?"

"I think so. It's just over the sea a bit." I wasn't really sure. I didn't know if I was lying.

"We may as well finish our journey, don't you think?" she sounded uncertain.

My heart ached, because I felt she wanted to please me, and that I might never know her true mind.

"I think so," I said.

We settled in, the house as quiet as a tomb, to sleep fitfully. The next morning we rose early and finished the cheese. Ferdich pressed his hands on the table, tired and exasperated.

"The only thing to do is go back." His voice was hoarse with exhaustion and frustration.

I stared at the room, the half-eaten meal, another chest broken open, a torn apron on the floor. Not even the pounding ocean waves from below could fill the void of silent death.

"If we take one of the boats, we could go farther, and find a place where people could help us get on our way. Going back means never getting to Iona. And we have come so far." My voice felt dry in my throat. I wanted to cry, but no tears came. "When we have completed our journey, I will ask Dermott to give over to you some of the cattle, to start your new life with Ives."

"That isn't important," he said.

I wrung my hands in my lap. We had to go on. I felt no choice about it. There was no convincing Ferdich, but we had to go on. "Can we at least walk down to the beach, so that I may see first-hand the vast ocean?"

Ferdich heaved a sigh. "All right."

I took Deirdre's hand, and we found the path down to the beach, walking in the bluff's long shadow until we stepped onto the white sand. Slowly we walked over the slipping, uneven surface, my arm tight around Deirdre. We walked toward the little boats, some coracles and a curragh. The dark body of a seal lay among them. A harpoon stuck out of it. Ferdich pulled the harpoon out and studied it.

"I've never seen carvings like this," he said. The shaft was carved with something like letters, all straight lines at different angles. He rinsed it in the water and held it up. The ivory tip gleamed in the dawn.

I gingerly stepped toward the water and put my bare foot into it. It was cold and prickly. The wet sand yielded underneath. Deirdre stepped in beside me. We stood in the water to our ankles. The ocean was dark, glinting with sharp-edged silver waves.

"This is what forever looks like," I said. An incoming wave turned to foam around our feet, pulling out again, pulling some of the sand out from under me. I swayed slightly. This was the tide. This was what people meant by it. I wanted to be on it. And forever meant never again to see my brother. Never again to have this chance. I started to cry.

"Shall we go?' Ferdich asked from the shore.

I turned, but stayed where I was. Tears ran down my face. "Please. Please, let me see my brother again. This one time. This is my only chance. We're almost there."

Ferdich put his hands on his hips and bent over, the patience sucked out of him as if he had been punched. "All right!" he cried. "But I have no more to say."

He turned over a coracle. Two oars were underneath. He slid it into the water and over to where we stood. "Get in."

I helped Deirdre in, and we sat in the small boat. Ferdich got in and pushed the oars into the sand, moving them out with the tide. The waves swelled, and I felt the rocking in my body, bouncing forward and back. We were soon away from shore. Ferdich and I each took an oar and tried to guide the boat along the coast.

"This is mad. We will land again at the first chance," Ferdich said.

I trembled in fear. He was right. We should land as soon as we could. Rowing was hard, and my hands were soon raw, stung with the salt spray. Perhaps when we landed, we would find sailors who knew what they were doing, who could take us the rest of the way. As the tide took us farther out, I became more frightened and prayed silently. God was with us, this was God's plan, I told myself.

Deirdre was sitting between my feet. I looked down at her as we bumped in the water. Deidre hadn't spoken most of the morning.

"Deirdre? Will you give us a song?" I gasped as I rowed.

Deirdre's face was tense. "Will we be on shore again soon?" she asked.

"Yes, my love, yes."

Deirdre began to sing, her voice thin above the sound of the wind and waves. An island came into view.

"I see cattle," I said. "Behind you, Ferdich."

Ferdich twisted around to look. "There must be people, then," he said.

Relieved, I rowed harder. The tide pulled us toward the island. Suddenly the sun disappeared as a thick fog enveloped us. We could only see a few feet around us. We could hear cattle lowing and a bell being struck.

"What do we do?" I asked.

"Just try to follow the bell," Ferdich replied.

"What is it?" Deirdre asked.

"Just some fog, love. It will rise again soon. And the tide will take us to shore."

The sound of the bell seemed to move, first ahead, then behind us, nearer, then farther. Then it stopped, and the cattle lowing also stopped. We started to shout greetings toward where we had seen the island, but there was no response. The waves spun the boat around, and the mist drew closer; in our little cloud we drifted. I knew we were beyond the island now. I closed my eyes. The water grew very still and barely lapped the sides of the boat. I prayed the angels would guide the boat to shore.

I thought I heard men singing and opened my eyes, expecting to see the shore and monks chanting psalms, but before I even opened my eyes, I was disturbed by the song. Its words were strange. It wasn't Scots, and I was fairly sure it wasn't Latin. I turned toward the singing, which was not coming from the land but was close by on the opposite side of the boat, and getting closer.

Then I saw it.

A ship larger than any fishing boat was bearing towards us, with a prow carved like the head of a serpent. A forest of oars extended out the sides, beating the waves. Shields glittered on the sides of the ship like shining scales. I thought I must be dreaming. Ferdich waved at the ship, and I wanted to grab him and keep him still, to hide. But there was no hiding. The singing stopped and turned into shouting. Men in leather with long white hair and beards ran to the side of the ship. Ferdich called to them, and they called back, laughing. The ship pulled up beside us. Ferdich had my rope, and he tossed an end of it to the men, who pulled our little boat closer.

The men were huge, giants. Surely I was dreaming. Two big men reached down and pulled Ferdich onto the deck of the ship. Before Ferdich could speak, they ran their swords through him.

# PART THREE

CELLACH

CHAPTER ONE: DUNADD

I have decided to set down this story of my journey years ago,
when I was sent by the monastery to aid the monks in gathering
materials. We had to go to Dunadd to ask for hides, and little did
I know how far I would travel from there. I wasn't pleased to be
sent, at first. But Connachtach took my hand and said, "Cellach,
you can be my eyes and ears and tell me of the new places you
will see, people whose hearts feel differently than ours, who look
for different things in the world than we do. You will be interested.
You are curious, and I think before the end, you will wish to keep
traveling always." I don't know how he knew me so well.

The monks who would go on this journey were Brother Daric,
our leader and representative of Bresal, the pale old man Brother
Nithard, a round-faced smiling brother named Reuben whom I
did not know well, and Brother Gormgal. The captain of the
boat was Brother Cole, whose beard always grew very heavy between the monthly tonsures, and to help sail was Anthony, not a
brother but a worker at the monastery. Brother Cole had been to
Dunadd before and knew the way.

It was a fine morning in early autumn when we stood on shore
about to push off. All the monks were there, and Bresal asked
Gormgal to make a prayer for their journey.

He said, "Almighty God, keep us in your hand as we brave
these treacherous seas in our humble boat. Columba, for your
sake we journey, for your sake we take on this cross, to honor you
in the creation of a great Gospel. We venture forth and risk our
lives for you, knowing that you would not let us down, you would
not turn away, because you are a mighty and powerful saint, our

treasure. We expect you to guide us, for if you abandon us, we would doubt your power and will, and we would wonder whether to spurn you for some other more attentive saint in our desperate hours of hopelessness.

"Never would we challenge your might, O Columba, never would we say of you, you were not a saint of furious blessing and subtle understanding, and we expect that never would you give us, your humble, prostrate servants, to doubt the beneficence of your love and wrathful vengeance against any who would thwart our just cause in your name. In the name of the Lord, amen."

As we turned toward the boat I heard Brother Reuben murmur, "If I were Columba, I would not get on Brother Gormgal's bad side." I would soon get to know Reuben's asides, and learn that monks were not all identical in holiness and humility, but each was different as any farmer or master was different from the other.

I looked back at Iona from the boat and thought how I loved it there, the good work and serenity of it, and I realized my irritation to go was really a fear—the question of whether I would return, or what I would find when I did. Then God drew a veil of mist over the little island, and I did not gaze upon it again for a very long time.

But I was quickly distracted by the captain Brother Cole, who put me to work at sailing, which I had never done before. I had thought I would have nothing to do but row, but there was much to do, and I found myself feeling happy as we flew over the water. I was stronger than I thought and met the challenge.

It was not just labor as I was used to. To sail is to master the wind, and I had never experienced this kind of power over nature. Gormgal had prayed for the saints to give us this wind, but we used it with cunning, with mastery, with quick-wittedness. We slipped through the air with the grace of an angel. I felt that though we were merely human, we had a power I didn't know before, that we had possibilities, that man was not just a laboring beast, but that God loved us for a reason, and this was the reason, that we could move like angels with the use of our minds. I started to understand that man can choose to be a beast or something more like an angel.

The monks maintained their monastic silence for a while, and the only voice was Cole giving orders and instructions. He was a patient teacher with the expectation that I would learn quickly, and I did.

Gormgal (to spare ink and the weariness of the reader's eye, I will forego saying "Brother" at every name) was writing on a wax tablet. When he was finished, he tapped Reuben on the shoulder and showed him the hymn he'd written.

Reuben quoted it aloud. "Mary, mother of pearl, grace of tears—why mother of pearl?" Reuben stopped to ask. "She is the pearl."

Gormgal tapped the tablet with his stylus. "Mother of pearl. Jesus is the pearl."

"I wouldn't call Jesus a pearl."

"Of course Jesus is the pearl! Why wouldn't he be?"

Nithard extended his hands in pacification, his soft high voice meekly pleading, "I think Mary can be both pearl and mother of pearl, depending on what you are writing. And Jesus can be the pearl of wisdom."

Reuben would not give up. "I can't see Jesus as a pearl."

"Why not?" Gormgal asked with a glare.

Nithard shook his trembling gray head. "Now, now. It's a small matter."

Reuben was unruffled by Gormgal's emotion. "A pearl is feminine. A pearl is white and smooth and curved. A man would not be a pearl."

They stopped arguing and grew quiet. I found myself thinking of soft white, curving women, but I'm sure that thought was not why they cast their eyes down and ceased talking.

Nearby, Daric was listening, but with a different frame of mind. He had kept to himself and seemed to be brooding. I was too young to be considerate, to think how the terror on Lindisfarne affected his mind.

With a concentrated look he said, more to himself than to them, "Holy Mary, tears like pearls…"

The others looked up, their reverie broken, and Gormgal started rubbing out the line on his wax tablet and jotting down the new words.

We would sail near Colonsay, my former home, but Cole was headed to land on the east coast of Jura to spend the night. To get there, we would have to pass through the heavy chop of the Gray Dogs, through the strait between the islands of Scarba and Luing, and around the Corryvreckan whirlpool. I had heard of the whirlpool all my life, but had never sailed around it.

The boat rose and fell hard in the waves, quickly pulled by the tidal waters. Cole worked hard at the steering oar to keep the boat into the waves, and not to be rolled over if we were parallel to them. I wondered that his oar didn't snap. The brown, rocky hill of Scarba seemed to leap up and down beside us, and I felt sick. We were all silent, and if we had talked, we would have been drowned out by the crash of the waves.

We shot into the strait at last. The sun was setting, the sea glazed in red. A louder roar rose above the crash, a roar like the clashing of swords and shields. The Morrigan, raven spirits of battle, could not have cried more fiercely or have caused more fear in my heart. We rounded Scarba, deep in shadow. Ahead, a shaft of light flashed between Scarba and Jura, the narrow strait from which the sea's roar came. I had thought I wanted to see the whirlpool, but now I wished we were not headed closer and closer, at full speed. The strait cut through the rock of Scarba and Jura. Waves crashed, the foam red in the setting sun, a warfare of waves: the Corryvreckan whirlpool, spinning near the shore, spouting a wild spray, the din clashing to the sky.

"Cailleach Bheur washes her plaid," Anthony shouted to me.

If the hag of winter laundered her blanket there, surely it was to rinse out the blood of unlucky sailors. I stared enchanted by the leaping waves. A higher sound arose, just barely, a high rasp above the din, coming from close to me. Daric's hands were clutched over his ears, his eyes squeezed tight. He emitted a keening wail, ghostly and shrill. His face was white in his bony hands. He shook, beyond the quaking of the boat.

The sailors ignored him, intent on controlling the boat in the fast tide. I touched Reuben's arm and pointed. Reuben slid his arm around Daric and pulled him close. Daric buried his face in Reuben's shoulder like a child. They held each other until Jura loomed beside us, and the roar dimmed, though still audible, rushing like the blood in my heart.

We pulled ashore and carried the boat up the beach in the twilight. Anthony started a fire. I gathered driftwood and, when the fire was lit, sank to my knees in exhaustion.

Cole leaned down and patted my shoulder. "Hard part's over," he said.

We ate dried meat and bread and told the legends we knew of the whirlpool. Bhreacon the prince of Norway sought the hand of an island princess. The king challenged him to anchor three days at the edge of the maelstrom. He went home to make three ropes: one of wool, one of hemp, but the third, to work a blessing, woven of the hair of pure maidens. The first day, the woolen rope broke. The second day, the hemp couldn't hold. He was almost to his goal, but at the end of the third day, the maiden's hair rope snapped, because one of the maidens had not been pure. He was drowned under the sea and washed ashore, where his dog dragged him to the cave on the beach.

"Pagan nonsense," Gormgal muttered.

*The whirlpool is real enough,* I thought.

Nithard held out a hand, in the placating manner I would come to know. "There is some wisdom in old stories. The danger is real."

Gormgal, tired and impatient, said, "Stories are for children."

Reuben rubbed his face and spoke through a yawn. "Not everyone gets to see the origin of such a tale. And pass through the danger unscathed. Were you excited?" he asked me.

I was surprised. He gave me an easy smile.

"I was more frightened than I expected to be. One hears the stories and forgets the danger."

"Now you have a story to tell," Reuben replied.

Daric sat nearby, staring into the fire with a haunted face. He seemed to ignore us, until he said, "Let there be no more to tell. The unspeakable. All is unspeakable." Reuben and Nithard each put a hand on his shoulder, but he only stared blankly at the low flames.

We stretched out. I was exhausted and fell into a deep sleep, dreaming of whales wearing strings of pearls with dogs riding on their backs.

The next morning, Anthony and I made a fire to cook some cured pork in a pot of milk. Gormgal protested that meat should not be boiled in milk, as prohibited in the Holy Book.

Reuben looked at him dumbfounded. "Surely Paul answered that question, that we are not bound by Jewish law."

Gormgal set his jaw. "We still shouldn't completely flout the law our Savior lived by."

"If you feel that way, you shouldn't eat the pork at all."

I waited with the bag of pork, hesitating to add it to the pot while they argued.

Nithard shook his head from side to side and held out his arms. "Now, now, brothers, it is not a great matter."

Gormgal was trembling with his self-made irritation. "Then for that fact we should not eat any meat at all!"

"I thought you hated the Céli Dé," Reuben retorted.

Gormgal took his wooden cup, dipped a mug of milk from the pot and stormed off to drink. I asked Reuben who the Céli Dé were.

"They are a contingent of monks who seek a stricter rule, who pray more often, eat even less, and preach that we are all grown soft. But some of us feel they are too proud in their strict worship. Pride is the most terrible sin." He glanced over at Gormgal who crouched a little away from us drinking his milk. "And some people are often guilty of what they most condemn."

After we'd eaten, Gormgal came back, and with an eerie friendliness put an arm about my shoulders and told the familiar story of Saint Kevin fed salmon by the otter. He seemed to be mollified by his own discipline of only drinking the milk.

When we were back at sea, Gormgal took a rod and began to fish for himself. He was surely hungry by now. He laughed suddenly, a choking, wrathful laugh, as his pole bent. He jerked it up and dangling in the air was a bright dancing fish. He bobbed it up and down a moment, laughing.

Suddenly, from nowhere a golden eagle swept down and grabbed it, neatly pulling the fish off the line and flying off with it in her feet. Gormgal stared open-mouthed.

"Doubtless the eagle is taking it to feed some hungry saint waiting patiently by his cell on shore," Reuben said with a satisfied smile.

We crossed the sound of Jura and passed into Loch Crinan, surrounded by purple hills, and entered the broad estuary of the River Add, almost level with the green boggy plain that stretched to the hills that circled the horizon. In the distance was a single tall mound, the hill fort known as Dunadd, an oddity, the only hill at all rising in the center of the broad, flat plain. We could have walked straight to it, but for the bog, and we had no course but to follow the sharply winding river, coiling through the plain like an adder, for which it was named, and its black color increased the comparison.

The monks had been quiet for a while when Gormgal turned to Daric. "How are we going to approach Donnchaire?" he asked.

Daric, until then staring with a fixed gaze at the sky, turned to him. "What do you mean?"

"Will you anoint him first, or ask for the hides first?"

Daric looked at him, and then started staring at the sky again.

Reuben sat up, saying, "We can't make those two things related."

Gormgal glared at him. "We can't anoint him and then be refused."

"Of course we won't be refused. Why would he refuse?" asked Reuben in an annoyed voice.

Nithard lifted his arms and beckoned for peace. "Now, now. God will provide."

Daric suddenly looked back at the group with a darkened, furious face, and we all took in our breaths. But then he spoke mildly.

"We will allow him to offer. He knows the will of God cannot be avoided." He stared at the sky again and repeated, "God's will cannot be avoided."

After a bit, I noticed flashes of light on the black water. A school of dead fish floated around our boat. I didn't want to speak of it, but looked round. Daric's gaze was fixed on the water.

"This place has a sickness," he said.

I felt queasy, but I rowed hard and steady, and the work settled my stomach. Daric started a chant to set our pace, and after a verse or two was repeated, Anthony and I joined in. I had never chanted like that before. I felt the power of our joined voices, and the beauty of the sound echoing over the plain.

Ahead of us a gate blocked the river next to a fort on the bank. This was the guard post of Dunadd, the hill fort still beyond. We heard voices, and a group of soldiers came out of the guard house. Knowing the monks' white robes, they did not present arms to us. Their leader stood in front, a tall, slim man with curly brown hair and a mustache. He had a serious, dignified air. When I caught sight of him, I immediately wondered if he saw my skill in rowing as we pulled up to the quay. Anthony threw a rope to one of the soldiers, who tied up our boat.

"Welcome, I am Giric," said the leader of the men. He stood at attention, his legs like sapling trunks wound about with leather braes. His blond mustache was clean and well-trimmed, and his eyes had a direct, clear look to them. It was Giric's command that encouraged such respect from his men. He quickly stepped up to the boat as we docked at the gate, and helped Daric off first, putting his long arm around him, understanding at first glance the fragility of the old monk.

As I tied up the boat, I again wondered if he noticed me. I wanted to make a good impression.

The gatehouse stood on piers on the boggy bank, and inside it smelled of new wood that seemed to glow as the sun shone through the doorway. We all stood as Gormgal offered the prayer of thanks. I felt unsteady on my feet after the boat journey, my knees slack, but I stood as straight as I could muster.

When Giric showed the monks to their seats, I hung back, ready to serve. But he waved me over and seated me like an equal with himself and the monks. I shared soft wheaten bread with them, dipped in salt, and drank sweet ale, a slave of no status served like a guest. I rested in a momentary sense of security. Giric asked one of the servers, a boy, to sing hymns while we ate, so that we would be refreshed before answering any questions about why we had come.

When we had eaten, Giric said, "We are blessed to be visited by such holy men. What is the cause of your long journey?" He addressed himself to Daric, who hunched his shoulders and looked away.

Gormgal answered, "We have undertaken the holy task of creating a new Gospel, to glorify God and Saint Columba. We need many hides, and we wish to humbly beg your king for a contribution."

Giric's face looked grim. "King Donnchaire died last winter, God rest his soul."

The soldiers echoed in unison, "God rest his soul." The room fell silent.

Daric suddenly spoke in a loud, shaking voice. "This is a poor beginning, and a punishment. We are on trial!" He started to choke, turning red.

Reuben reached to slap his back, and Giric himself rose and knelt by him, letting the old monk lean against his shoulder until he was able to breathe again.

"You have come when we are at turmoil," said Giric, "but I know you are here for a reason, and you will help us. We will help each other with God's blessing."

"What is the turmoil?" Reuben asked.

Giric took his seat again and explained. "There are two now who claim the kingship of the Dál Riada: Donnchaire's son Rhun and Eochaid, who is married to Rhun's sister. Donnchaire was half-Pict, and in the Pict-land, inheritance goes through the daughter. So Eochaid claims he is heir through his wife."

"Is it war, then?" Reuben asked.

"It hasn't come to blows, but it threatens to. The men are divided as we've struggled to settle the matter peacefully."

Somewhere behind me a voice murmured, "Eochaid the Venomous," and a shiver went up my spine.

Daric clapped his hands together. "God will decide. We will pray on it."

Giric looked to Daric with an encouraging and soothing gaze. "If you aren't too tired, we can go now to meet with them. The court has gone to Kilmartin, on the other side of the fortress, to enjoy the sweetness of the weather. You will be interested in the monuments there, erected by druids in forgotten times. I'd like to take you."

Daric stared back at him, light coming to his clouded eyes. "Yes, we will go."

Giric took Daric with him in his own boat, and we followed in ours. I longed to be with them, though was also relieved to be free of Daric's grief. What I longed was to be one of Giric's men, and as we rowed, I thought of my future, how I would likely become a sencleithe, an "old housepost," as the old slaves are called. I would go from boyhood to old age and never be a man because I had no land.

When the banks became good, hard land and we were beyond the bog, we dragged the boats on shore and walked along the edge of a wheat field, the tall grass blocking some of my view. Singing and the voices of playing children let me know we were almost at Kilmartin. The warm wheat brushed my shoulder. When we rounded the field, spread before us was a plain edged by woods, and sheep frolicked among huge gray stones standing upright all over the plain, so strange and haunting that at first I didn't notice the members of court playing among the sheep and stones.

As Reuben and Gormgal hurried up to join Giric and Daric, no one seemed concerned with me, so I wandered off by myself. I leaned back against a monument, measuring its height against mine—it was roughly twice as tall as I. There were more than a dozen of them. Who had erected them? Giric had said the druids. They were religious monuments. It started to dawn on me, the power of a church. It took power to raise these stones. And now our monks might be called upon to decide who would be king, anointing the chosen one in the name of the abbot. All power is God's, and the church is the doer of God's work. The mighty stones, taciturn and holy, were testimony to the power of faith.

As I stood there feeling the cold, hard stone, guessing at the weight on the backs of the faithful who erected them, a low chuckle came from behind me. I was near the edge of the wood, and a man on horseback had just ridden up nearby. His gaze directed mine toward a fawn and doe stepping out of the wood, tan harts dotted with white spots.

I looked back at the man, who put an arrow in his bow. I couldn't avert my eyes. He shot. The arrow struck the fawn through the neck. It fell at once, bleeding profusely. The doe bleated in a loud groan and pawed the ground. The horseman bore down upon them as the doe reared, jumped, and only at the last moment as the horse galloped upon her did she turn and run into the woods. There was no question of the horseman's aim. It was for the fawn.

The fawn's legs jerked a few times, and then it was dead.

The horseman dismounted, turned his cold eye upon me, evaluating me as a slave, as no one important, and said, "Boy, take it up."

I stroked the dead thing's neck and worked out the arrow. Its blood was warm on my hands. The horseman handed me a cloth to bind it, to keep blood from spilling on him, and I hoisted it onto the horse, which snorted and tried to rear. The horseman held firm and had him under control.

The warm day turned cold. I wanted to walk away, but as a slave I had to do what I was willed.

In a bored voice he asked, "So who are you?"

"I am Cellach, slave of the monastery of Iona."

"Iona? What are you doing here?" He looked more interested, curious now. He was not tall, and he looked down on me slightly, a pale man close shaven. His teeth were gleaming white, perfectly straight. He would have been handsome had he not reeked of evil.

"I have come with monks who have business with the king. With the court." I corrected myself, since I knew there was no king.

"That is my business," he said. "What is it?"

"They seek hides for a Gospel."

His face relaxed into a smile. "That is good. Is there a particular reason for this endeavor?"

I didn't feel it my place to explain everything, but I had no right to refuse him, and I told him of the terrible raid. His face seemed to brighten the more I told him.

"And Brother Daric, you say, witnessed the whole thing?"

"Yes."

"And who does he chiefly pray to?"

It seemed an odd question. "He seems to love the Holy Mother best of all," I said, feeling vexed.

He looked away in thought, then brusquely dismissed me with a wave of his hand, never bothering to tell me who he was, but I guessed. He dismounted, gave me the reins to lead his horse, and strode ahead toward the monks, whose white robes could be seen in the middle of the field.

The monks were speaking with a lean man whose thin hair had the appearance of a tonsure, with a worried crease in his forehead.

"That is truly a horrific tale. God save us," he was saying. The monks had just told him of the raid.

Giric said, "A good army is more a force than any savages."

They turned to us, and the man I followed introduced himself. "God bless you. I am Eochaid the Fourth. You must be Brother Daric, a holy man. And Brothers Reuben and Gormgal. I have heard of your arrival and pledge any help I can. Along with my brother Rhun."

"Yes, we are bound to help you," the gaunt man, Rhun, said. "Tomorrow we will have a prayer service."

Daric was ashen and trembling from having told his terrible story. Eochaid put his arm around him.

"We will pray to Holy Mary," Daric said. Daric buried his face in Eochaid's shoulder. Gormgal and Reuben reached for each other and held hands, making peace in their mutual desire to alleviate the old monk's torment.

"We will ask for guidance in how best to aid you," Eochaid said.

"Holy Mary will tell us," Daric said, muffled by Eochaid's steady shoulder.

"Perhaps some of our men could help build a stout wall around the monastery," Rhun said.

Eochaid stroked Daric's shoulder. "I think it would be wondrous to create a new Gospel, for Saint Columba's blessing," he said.

My heart went cold in my chest.

Gormgal said, "Yes, that is our mission."

"We have begun to plan it," Reuben said.

"And we will give all we can," Eochaid continued. "How many hides would it require?"

Reuben and Gormgal looked embarrassed before Reuben replied, "One hundred and fifty."

Rhun started. "Of course we will help, but I don't want to promise more than we can give and disappoint you."

Eochaid waved his hand. "Of course all is possible with the Lord."

The coldness I'd felt was matched by oncoming clouds, and a light rain began to fall. The stones turned dark. The world darkened for me from that day.

Eochaid didn't stop there. "I will personally make sure you will be supplied. But I have a favor to ask, if I may, a favor to seek Mary's blessing. This Gospel, will it be filled with beautiful ornament and illustrations?"

"Yes," Gormgal said. "We call them illuminations."

Eochaid's face took on an exaggerated, beatific look. "Then if you would include an illumination depicting the Holy Mother, I would feel doubly blessed."

Daric straightened up and kissed his cheek. "Of course, broth-er, of course."

Rhun cleared his throat and looked at a loss for words. The situation had slipped from his grasp, if he ever looked at things in such a way, which I think he did not. "Yes, we will secure the blessing of Holy Mary and Columba. And let's pray to Saint Patrick as well. Yes, all the saints."

Gormgal turned beet red. Even I knew from having lived on Iona that Gormgal hated Saint Patrick. Or, I should say, loved Columba and felt a hot jealousy at the ascending star of Patrick. It was not the right thing to have said. I tried to quell my fear that Rhun had already lost the support of the monks.

"Let's go back to the court, now that the weather has turned," Eochaid said. "We will feast in your honor, if you've a mind for some refreshment."

The women were gathering the children from all their hiding places around the stones. Two women caught my eye especially, a pale blond woman who I learned was Eochaid's Pictish wife, and another one, dark and tall, her brown hair in a braid around her head, wearing yellow all embroidered with silver, gleaming in the mist of rain. I stared at her, noticing she walked alone behind all the others.

Giric went back to his guard house while we climbed the steep hill up to the fortress. It was ringed with several walls along the way, the path becoming increasingly narrow between rocky, heather-covered outcroppings. At the top, I caught my breath at the view. The distant hills blended with the storm clouds in a mass of gray and blue, and the bog was golden green in shafts of waning light.

Eochaid nudged me. "To the kitchens."

"Yes, sir."

A boy led me the back way, so that I didn't see the smiths and stalls or the front of the great king's house. The kitchen perched on the edge of the hill, smoky, hot, and dark in the corners. A huge black cauldron bubbled on the enormous fire. At the far end, the fawn was hanging. I tried not to look at

it. Eochaid may have said some message to the master of the
kitchen, because I was not allowed to even serve my monks, but
stayed in the kitchen tending the fire until I sweated and my
throat was dry. The feast seemed to last hours, until at last we
servants could eat and slake our thirst. No one was temperate
in their drink at the end of the long night, and the ale started
to loosen my tongue.

"A great chief must have raised those stones at Kilmartin, and
we will have a great chief again," someone said. "If only Eochaid
would let us fight."

"It was the druids, their priests who raised the stones," I said.
"It is the church of any people that makes them strong. Like those
who raised the stones, our monks will anoint your king. Eochaid
the Venomous serves himself, and we will anoint Rhun as is fitting." I spoke as if I were equal to the monks, my masters.

They laughed. "Are you a monk, then?" someone asked.

"If I could, I would be. For there the true power lies."

A big burly man named Berach clapped me on the shoulder.
"If you are to become a monk, you must know a woman first. You
must know what you're leaving behind." He held my gaze, and
in his nearness I smelled his yeasty breath. "Bina is for that. You
saw her, I'm sure, with her long brown hair."

I had glimpsed her at Kilmartin.

Berach continued. "You must go to her house on the other
side of the fort. She is waiting. She will be your guide. Go to her,
go and unwrap the mystery of a woman's treasure, and then you
can take the white robe and become chaste, but not chaste in
ignorance."

All the rest quickly added their encouragement. I was drunk,
and a spell came over me, compelled by their certainty. So I rose
and pitched out into the night. It was dead night, now, the moon
had set and all was dark as I staggered out. Somehow I knew my
way to the little house, because it was apart from the others.

There was a sliver of light spilling out of her doorway. The
door opened silently, and suddenly, in the light of a candle, I saw
her lying there. Her brown hair was arrayed across the pillow, she

was naked, and I saw the whole of her. Her breasts were poised upward, her gleaming legs were slightly apart. There was a small patch of black curls crowning her womanly mound and a thin line that marked the forbidden opening.

I crept up and kissed her rosy mouth.

She opened her eyes, and seeing me, she sprang away and grabbed the sheet over her. She did not look horrified, but more impatient, and her face darkened in anger. "What the devil are you doing? Do you want to be killed?" Her throat muscles rippled with her fierce whisper.

"They told me—"

Her arm swung out and she boxed my ear. "Don't you know not to listen to fools?"

Behind me, a man chuckled. It was the same chuckle I heard when the fawn came out of the wood, and my blood went cold. I turned around. Eochaid stood there, half-dressed, but a dagger by his side.

"What does the boy think, that he can share my bed? I knew when I first saw him he was far bolder than his height should allow." Eochaid reached across the bed, pulled me off, and pushed me to the ground at his feet. "You lust above your station. There are servant girls aplenty, maybe even a virgin like yourself among them." With a rapid punch he hit my chin and sent me reeling back.

"Let him go," Riua said tiredly without emotion.

I sat on the ground and rubbed my face. He looked like the pleasure it gave him to be able to beat someone outweighed his anger at finding me there.

"Crawl away then, little bug," he said.

I crawled all the way out of the house and part of the way back before I stood. I was no longer drunk or dazed. The blood pounded in my ears. I marched back to the kitchen, still under my innocent delusions, as even that scene was not enough to make me wise.

The servants were still sitting and leaning by their fire. I felt as if I'd been gone an hour, but it was only a few minutes. As I walked in they stared at me, some in surprise, others covering their smiling mouths.

"The Venomous keeps Bina as his concubine!" I exclaimed as if that would shock them.

They burst into roaring laughter. My face burned in shame. Of course they knew.

"You're alive!" Berach cried. "We had a bet on whether he would kill you. Now I owe Senna a brass buckle. You are troublesome."

I started to back away when he grabbed me and forced me down by the fire. The house grew silent.

"The Venomous is our chief," he said between gritted teeth. "Eochaid is strong, clever, and knows how to command men. We don't take kindly to those who think they have the balls to say otherwise. You are still a virgin, but maybe now you will be more a man. Drink." He pushed a cup at me and ruffled my hair, saying, "It was a good laugh."

I drank and said nothing. The group returned to their joking and laughter. I slipped outside.

I slept outside their kitchen on the cold, hard ground. I was a man now, not because I lay with a woman, but because I slept alone.

Early the next morning, stiff and uncomfortable on the ground, I awoke to the sound of my name. A servant named Dairmait was kneeling beside me.

"You're wanted," he said softly, with an embarrassed look.

"Where?"

"At Bina's house. It has nothing to do with last night. It's your fingernails."

I sat up and rubbed my face, feeling for the first time a trace of hair above my lip. "I'm too old for that."

"You know you aren't. I'm sorry. Come and wash your hands."

He led me to a cistern of water and scrubbed my hands for me. I gathered he had been told to make me ready. He polished my nails and even cleaned under them with a little file.

"You're like a procuress," I said.

"Shut up. You should feel happy they have some use for you after all."

A few people were stirring at fires and fetching water. The door to Bina's house was shut and I knocked loudly. It swung open to an old man.

"Don't make such a racket," he said.

Inside Eochaid stood with his mocking smile behind the table. When my eyes adjusted I saw Bina curled up in a corner of the bed, ignoring us and combing her hair. Nearby sat Sicga, who I learned was Giric's brother.

Without waiting to be told I sat at the table, and the old druid sat opposite me. He beckoned and I spread my hands on the table. He took them in his own knotted old hands and gazed at my polished fingernails. I had heard of this form of prophecy-making, to gaze into the fingernails of virgin boys, but I had not been used for this before. He gazed a long time, humming softly. His humming and the sound of the comb hushing through Bina's hair were like a rhythmic chant.

Finally he spoke. "I see clarity. How they shine. If there is to be bloodshed, it will not be great. More like a single sacrifice."

"But who wins?" Eochaid asked.

The old magician held my hands so close to his face, I could feel his breath on my fingers. "I see brothers. I see Cain and Abel."

He stopped. Eochaid started to pace. Then he sat down next to the old man. "Who is the monks' leader?" He was addressing me.

My stomach sank to have to answer, but I knew I was not in a position to resist anything. "At the monastery it's the Abbot Bresal."

"But who here is in charge? I don't mean just officially. Who carries the most weight?"

"Brother Daric is our leader."

"Daric is mad."

That was the first time I'd been given such an idea, but immediately I realized it was true.

"Tell me about these monks, their characters, what they value."

It sickened me to have to answer, but I had no choice. "It's hard to say because they're so different. Brother Reuben is mocking and educated. Brother Nithard tries to make peace between him and Brother Gormgal. Brother Gormgal is a choleric, angry old man who loves Columba beyond any other saint."

Eochaid's eyes lighted up. "That's good. What about Daric? You said he prays chiefly to the Holy Mother?"

"Yes."

Eochaid nodded and lapsed into thought. "And they want hides."

I nodded. Eochaid smiled to himself, the only sincere smile I had seen from him. I looked over at Sicga, who was watching Bina brush her hair. He glanced and saw me watching him, and he glared. "It sounds like there's no need for war."

The druid set down my hands at last. "No, but a sacrifice. Cain and Abel."

Sicga ignored the old man even though he had, without realizing it, absorbed the man's prophecies. "We need to do something about Rhun."

Eochaid was staring in thought, and I knew he was listening to all intently, though he appeared not to be. I could see his mind at work.

I felt fearful for Rhun and dared to say, "Rhun seems a holy man."

Eochaid's eyes darted to me and furrowed his brow as if a new idea started him. Then he chuckled, the chuckle that made my blood run cold. "Yes, of course he is. He is a holy man indeed." He slapped the table. "We're through with you. Go away."

I left, feeling that everyone about in the fort could see the shame on my face. There was a great buzz of activity now, and as I headed toward the work sheds that lined the interior of the wall, I caught sight of Giric, who was handling a new sword at one of the smiths'. I hung about and watched the shining sword flash in the morning sun. He saw me and looked puzzled for a moment, then he remembered who I was and nodded. He lay down the sword, as the hilt was still to be decorated.

"This must be quite a journey for a young pup," he said.

"I'm Cellach. I'm not so young."

He regarded me and touched the new down on my chin. "So I see. I'm sure you'll grow tall soon enough. Come along, I'll show you around." We walked from shed to shed, lingering to watch the various craftsmen. There were silversmiths fashioning jewelry and cups, potters, leather workers, wood carvers, glass blowers. I had never seen so many men working without being engaged in raising cattle or growing crops. Some of this work is done at Iona, but always as an adjunct to the farming. Even the scribes did some farming. I was fascinated by the craft work and wanted to do all that I saw, to be a silver smith or a leather tooler.

We stopped by the cistern for water, and I wanted to tell Giric of my recent shames, but didn't know which one at first. I was far more embarrassed by the previous night, so I told him about it. Later I regretted not telling him of the morning prophecies.

He laughed at my tale. "That's a great story. Don't be ashamed. Not many men can say they survived such wrath from Eochaid."

"How is it a king hasn't been decided on?"

He hesitated, then shrugged as if it didn't matter to tell me. "I am the leader of half the men, and I am for Rhun. My brother Sicqa leads the other half of the men, and he is for Eochaid. The men are divided, but as brothers we have held back from coming to blows."

"Will you let the monks decide and anoint the chief?"

He cocked his head. "We would have preferred a larger delegation of monks for that, with your Abbot Bresal to lead them."

I cast my eyes down. It was true we were not a good assortment of men to decide this. I thought again to tell him of that morning's conversation, but still I did not. I resolved I would tell him later. A bell was struck.

"It's time for the prayer service that your monks are holding for Donnchaire."

"I will pray for you!" I blurted out. I had no idea why I said this.

He gave an ironic smile. "Thank you. I must return to my fort." He held out his hand and shook mine as if I were a friend. Then he disappeared through the crowd.

I passed the work stalls where swords were being sharpened, wondering if they would soon be used. The monks were just coming out of the guest house when I found them, and I asked Reuben to speak alone with me for a moment.

"Are you going to be the ones to decide who should be king?" I asked.

"Yes. We are praying on it. We are on our way to the church now."

"I think you must pick Rhun. Eochaid is an evil man."

"Why do you say that?"

"He killed a fawn in front of the doe yesterday."

Reuben looked grim. "That is the prerogative of a king."

"He keeps a concubine."

"That is commonly done."

My throat felt tight. It was a losing battle. "You aren't going to pick him?"

He sighed and shook his head. "It is a good thing to be friends with a powerful man. We must go now."

The church adjoined the great house, and inside it seemed dusty and neglected. We prayed and sang hymns. As we came out, a group of men coming up the hill hailed us. They had just arrived by boat with a splendid gift from the king at Tara and needed help carrying it up the hill. We went down.

Lying in the boat was a pillar of shining black stone. It was carved all over with something like letters—little pictures of hawks, fish, eyes, and other designs. It was about a foot on each side and ten feet long.

"This is splendid," Eochaid said.

"They call it the Stone of Destiny," one of the visitors said. "It is a most ancient stone, and no one knows its origin."

We would erect it at the top of the hill. It was a heavy burden, carried on our shoulders. By "we" I do not mean Eochaid or the court, but myself and other slaves. To Eochaid it was a splendid signifier of the power of kings. To those of us who strained to hoist it up the narrow, rocky path, it was a folly of vanity.

At the top of the hill, a hole was quickly dug, and pulling on ropes, we raised the black emblem of power.

"From now on this spot will mark our meeting place for assembly," Eochaid said.

Exhausted, I leaned back and gazed at it. It was a striking sight as it gleamed in the sun. I only wished it were a cross.

"We will treat it as a cross, and consecrate it to holiness," Rhun announced, echoing my thoughts. He crossed himself and asked the monks to sing a hymn.

I looked around for Giric, surprised not to see him among us. As the monks finished their hymn, a group of soldiers came up the hill, Giric's men, carrying a flag. The crowd gave way. A soldier raised the flag over his head.

"It is with the pain of a great loss we must tell you news. A few minutes ago, our beloved thegn Giric accidentally fell to his death from the top of the fort."

The crowd groaned. My eyes stung with tears. I thought he must have died the moment we raised that awful black pillar.

"We will go back to the church and honor him with a great funeral," Rhun said.

Eochaid took hold of the flag and led us, but I felt he could hardly contain his glee. It was Giric who had been in his way. I was sure his death was no accident. Cain and Abel, as the druid had said.

After all the prayers, I went to the well to drink and try to quell my grief. Daric came to my side and also drank.

"We must get lapis lazuli for the Holy Mother," he said.

Summoning my strength, I said to him. "Please, you cannot choose Eochaid to be king."

He turned to me with an awful glare. His throat bulged red and a rage came into his eyes. He took a big dipper of water and poured it over my head, pushing me by the shoulder to the ground. "Cast the devil out of this boy! Cast out the devil, I say!"

He prayed and I crouched by his feet.

After praying he calmed himself. "We must get the lapis," he said, and walked away.

That night we all met around the pillar with torches, and Gormgal anointed Eochaid as king, and I went off by myself to cry.

The next day at the feast, Eochaid rose amid the toasts and announced that Rhun would retire to the monastery.

Eochaid then beckoned me over, to my surprise, and put his hand on my shoulder. "I have also decided to begin with an act of generosity. To buy this boy's freedom and make him one of my men, with a few cattle and grant of land."

His face was triumphant. He was buying me. He divined all that I understood about him, and he couldn't stand for that, lowly and unimportant as I was. So he would buy my favor.

I turned to my companions. "If you please, though your offer is gracious and well beyond generosity, I have a different end in mind. That I would like to join my brothers, and become a monk at the monastery."

The monks beamed at me. Eochaid gave a surprised smile and then raised his cup in a toast to my cleverness. I had beaten him. Resisted him. I would ponder and pray a long while whether it is a sin to have made this decision for such a reason.

Daric stood and said, "We must obtain the lapis for Holy Mary. She must be depicted in blue, the color of purity. We must press on."

Eochaid knocked on the table in agreement. "Yes, you must. We will send you wherever you must go to obtain it."

That night I joined the monks in the guest house. I was treated as a penitent, welcomed with kisses. But the joy was brief, because the matter of obtaining the lapis was a point of argument.

"We must go to Frisia. There is a market there where they have all we need," Daric said.

Reuben and Gormgal were in a delicate position. Daric was our leader, as if he were our abbot. It would have been sinful to disobey him. But he bordered on madness.

I wanted to go. I wanted to be the devil on his shoulder, whispering, "Press on, press on!" I wanted to see the world and fill my yearning to understand how it worked.

"But, dear Brother, we must take Rhun back to Iona," Reuben said gently.

"The sailors who brought us here can take him back without us," Daric replied.

"It would be dangerous to stray so far," Gormgal said.

"We have Eochaid's power of protection," Daric said. He smiled like a willful child.

"It is beyond our mission," Reuben said.

"We must go. It is God's will. We have promised to paint the Holy Mother, and we have a duty to our benefactor King Eochaid, and to God. We must go."

Reuben sighed and looked at Gormgal. They sat silently, having run out of arguments.

And so, we were going to Frisia.

## CHAPTER TWO: FRISIA

It took us some while to arrive at Frisia, having walked across Alba from west to east and north to south. We were detained for months in Kent during the civil war between Eardbert and Cenwulf. It was a harrowing time of heads hanging from walls and burnt houses and fields. Once more, I had a hope for the victor to be a godly man, in this case Eardbert. When Cenwulf arrived with his victorious army and called him out, I thought they would capture him and send him to a monastery. I was there when Eardbert came out, and instead of tonsuring him, they cut off his hands and gouged his eyes, making sport of him until he died. So are the Saxons entertained. The next day, the bishop of Kent, with whom we had been staying, anointed Cenwulf king. I am disgusted he received blessings from the church after his display of cruelty—cruelty is too light a word. Why is the church a handmaiden to such evil? I don't understand.

We finally arrived, sea sick and exhausted from a choppy sail on the North Sea, at Frisia in the spring. It is unpleasant to come to Frisia when sick, because the whole town stinks of drying fish, which they live on. Our legs quaking, we staggered into an inn, which had a cheerful look with two bright glass windows lit from within. Inside it was just as promising. Bundles of lavender and sage sweetened the air from the rafters, and there was a tidy fire. The place was cleaner than its occupants, fisherman throwing dice, red-faced and weathered in the firelight, their clothes exuding salt and the damp of the sea. But if there was hope of their getting warm and dry, it was here.

They all cheered the ale wife as she came to strain ale into their cups. Taking one look at us, she spoke in perfect

Scots, her accent softening the roughness of our tongue. She
had the brown eyes of a doe, and her uncovered hair was
bound in a thick blond braid around her head. What struck
me most about her was her hand holding the strainer—large,
strong-fingered, the hands of someone who could take care
of herself.

"Good monks, we have bread and cheese, God bless you."

The captain of our ship spoke to her in Saxon and she replied
likewise. I caught her name as Liutgard. She left to fetch the dinner, returning with meat for the captain and our bread, cheese,
and ale. The ale was thin but sweet, and I was thirsty. Gormgal
led us in prayer over our dinner, and the gamblers and drinkers
became much louder as if to drown us out. When she came by
to refill our cups, the captain asked her about merchants for our
quest.

"The *negociator* of the great Karl Rex is the man you want. Seek
him at the docks tomorrow. We have two empty beds upstairs if
you would like to stay."

Gormgal put his arm around Daric and helped him to his feet.

I caught Reuben's hand. "I'd like to sit up a while."

Reuben shrugged and patted my shoulder. The three went
upstairs to share the beds. I drank my ale and watched Liutgard
serve the other traders and sailors, who were drowsing and growing quiet. She saw me watching her and came to me. She brought
me a bowl of stewed onions and turnips

"You're thin as a reed. Have it. The innkeeper is away." She
sat across from me.

The few patrons still up were drowsing by the fire, sometimes
singing but trailing off at forgotten words. Sitting across from me,
she looked younger than I'd thought at first.

"You aren't the innkeeper's wife? His daughter, then?"

She shook her head. "I made my own way and work for a
mattress by the kitchen fire and sometimes a coin."

"Where are you from?"

"I ran away from the gynaeceum outside of Mainz."

I asked what a gynaeceum was.

"It's a big hall where girls and women weave all day for the benefit of the estate. The boredom is maddening. We weave the wool from the sheep and we are like sheep ourselves. But I am no sheep. One day I realized—the door isn't locked. I could just leave. It's unheard of. But why not? I took the length of wool that I wove that day—it was my work, after all—and I left. I traded it for bread and a wheel of cheese.

"There were days I didn't eat. Once, I met a priest on the road who guarded me a while. Other days, I hid from the soldiers coming north from Aix. I made my way here and found this place, filthy and mouse-infested with bad food. I offered my services and proved myself. I scrubbed. I got him a better deal on salt and pepper. I strained the ale. Now the sailors and traders prefer it here, and the word spread it is a good place."

"How old are you?"

"I don't know. Seventeen or eighteen. What about you? Are you a full-fledged monk, so young?"

"I'm fifteen. An oblate. That means I haven't taken final vows and this is a trial period."

"You probably can't talk with me."

I pointed to the other patrons. "We aren't alone together. And my companions won't know."

"But you will give up your independence."

"Every man must have a master. You have the innkeeper. I will have the abbot."

She looked down thoughtfully. "But still, no one is making you. It's your decision."

"I chose it, in a way, to maintain my freedom." I told her the whole story of Eochaid the Venomous and how I felt he wanted to buy my loyalty. She opened her mouth in a smile of delight as I concluded with my decision to join the monastery.

"That was clever. I'm glad you resisted him. But you have made a serious choice for the rest of your life."

"It's an interesting world. Eochaid thought he was all-powerful. But all power resides in the Lord, and the Church."

"You're drawn to power." She said this with an approving nod.

I blushed at her frankness, feeling exposed. "I don't know."

She looked at me with wide, earnest eyes. "Will you go to Aix and visit Karl's court? He is truly the most powerful man in Frankland, in the whole world maybe. I long to go there."

Even then, Karl had been the most powerful man on the continent, aside from the pope, since before I was born, but I knew little else about him.

"It's a grand place for someone like you," she continued. "For Karl is a reverent and Christian king. His father was blessed by Pope Stephen, and Karl is great friends of Pope Hadrian. He's converting all the pagans between us and the Romans of Constantinople, like a tide of faith rolling over the hills." She tapped her fingers excitedly. "He lives in the greatest palace in a city filled with all manner of people—noblemen and soldiers and merchants. Surely the lapis you seek would be for sale there. They have everything from all over the world. And Karl has a menagerie of animals from as far away as Africa. I would like to see a peacock. And his church, it's three stories high! With colored glass and gold altar pieces. You must see it."

"Daric said it is a great center of learning."

"Yes, of course! There is a school and hundreds of books. I would like to learn to read like a monk, and even write. Can you write?"

"A little. We spent the winter in Kent and I started to learn."

She was caught up in enthusiasm. "The whole family of the king is learned, both the girls and boys. Learning is very important at the palace. That's another reason you should go."

The more she spoke about it, the more I shared her longing to see such a place. Again I wanted to be the devil on Daric's shoulder, whispering "Press on, press on further still!" If he wanted to go, we surely would, for it seemed nothing would stop him from dragging us on his journey.

I asked Liutgard to tell me all she knew about Karl, King of the Franks. She told me of his hunchback son Pepin, sent to a monastery for trying to overthrow him, his string of wives, and how his latest wife Fastrada was called the iron lady. She had clearly gathered all the information she could from her patrons, the sailors and traders. Her words lit the fire of my curiosity.

We talked deep into the night. The men who were left slid to the floor and slept. The one candle burning between us went out.

"I'll have to pay the innkeeper for the candle," she said, but with a happy, glowing face. Moonlight from the window outlined her pale hair. The tips of her eyelashes were blond, little sparks around her dark brown eyes.

"I'll owe you for it," I said.

She took my hand to lead me to the stairs and said good night. She did not squeeze my hand, but dropped it modestly. I felt my way up the stairs to the loft. A drop of moonlight in the one small window showed me Daric's sleeping white head.

I crawled in beside him. "Press on," I whispered in the dark. "Press on."

The next morning we returned to the docks, inquiring for Isaac the *negociator*. We found him directing the loading of a ship, a wiry man dressed in fine clothes, with long black curls and a black beard.

Our common language was Latin, which I had spent the winter learning in Kent. Daric greeted him and asked about the lapis after the appropriate courtesies. I held my breath.

He shook his head. "I have no lapis now, as I have not been to Arabia in some while. I'm on my way to Aix, in Frankland, and there may be some there, but I won't be returning north again from there."

We were all afraid to speak, staring at Daric, waiting for his reaction. At first his face blanched and he closed his eyes.

When he opened them he said, "Then we must go to Aix."

Reuben and Gormgal sputtered, saying we could not go further.

Gormgal asked if there were any other traders.

Isaac shrugged and said, "There are the Easterlings, the Northmen." He pointed to another ship.

Daric cried out and fell against me. "The white devils!" He clutched me, almost pulling me over. "The white devils! The monsters, here!"

He pointed to a long, narrow ship along the dock that was just casting off as we watched, being rowed by gigantic white-haired men. It was a huge boat by our standards, with thirty rowers. The prow was shaped like a serpent and colorfully painted. Dried fish hung along the sides, and the smell of death wafted over to us. Manacled slaves sat on deck, Scots.

These were the race of men—if men they were—who had burnt Lindisfarne and butchered his fellow monks. We all stared, speechless. The captain came to our rescue by putting his big burly arm around Daric and holding him upright while he flailed in terror. Isaac asked what Daric was about, and Reuben explained.

"They are ruthless men for sure, and pagan," Isaac said, "but I didn't know of this savagery."

"What hell is this place? Where is your bishop?" Gormgal asked.

"We have no bishop, but there is a missionary, Udger. I'll take you to his house," our captain said.

Daric crouched against the captain, and trembling like a puppy, he walked with an uncomprehending face. We turned down the winding alleys to a small wooden house with a cross nailed over the door. The captain knocked and called for Udger.

The door opened, and Udger welcomed us in, a small man with red hair, blue veins running through the sheer white skin of his forearms, head, and sandaled feet. His high voice in a singsong, he took Daric's hand immediately and entreated him to sit. Without asking who we were, he carved a cheese and bread and filled a cup of barley water, which he held to Daric's lips. Daric closed his eyes and drank, then heaved a deep sigh and slumped forward, keeping his eyes closed, holding himself. Udger put a blanket over his shoulders.

Reuben explained who we were. Udger gasped with pleasure to meet with, as he put it, "such holy men."

"How often I have prayed for a good Christian company in my home among these poor, derelict pagans."

Gormgal asked if the Frisians had not become Christians since Saint Boniface.

"It was a true heinous act when the Frisians slaughtered our dear Boniface for his treasure chest, thinking it contained gold and not the Golden Word, his precious books. And that only a generation ago. Now, we poor missionaries continue his work, and have made inroads, but there is still ignorance and superstition, and still many pagans, so that I can't say the Frisians are yet a Christian nation. Karl has sent me among the wolves, but Karl has many cares on all sides, and though he rules the Frisians in name, his hold over the land is light and tenuous, and his support of our humble work is…" Udger blushed, searching for the word. "He is a great king and lord, and leading by example, we must all be soldiers of the lord."

Udger filled another cup, and we passed it between us. The captain, seeing we were settled, took his leave to return to the dock.

Udger said, "You must stay for our catechism class this evening. I have a good company of humble men and women thirsty for the Good News who take instruction from me. They in turn spread the Word. This is our work. They will be overjoyed to meet you."

Of course we agreed to stay, and we spent the day seeing the little church attached to his house, with its simple altar and brass service pieces and candelabra. He showed us his few books and, most holy of all, the very book Boniface held up against the mortal blow that the pagan sword struck and cleaved.

I stared at the book. The red leather over the wooden cover was split, exposing the deep scar from the sword, a palpable wound. I looked at Reuben, raising my eyebrows in question, and he nodded. I traced my finger down the scar. I imagined Boniface on that beach, raising the Bible over his head, the pagan sword coming down across it, down through his skull, the gash across his face continuing the gash on this very book. Chills shook me between the shoulder blades. It was not Saint Boniface's death I was thinking of, but our mission. Our journey was to get materials to make a great new Gospel, as protection against the terrifying demons who sacked Lindisfarne. Yet this Book did not protect Boniface at all, and the very demons were here, accepted as traders.

In this strange place, it stayed light far into the evening, so that I could not tell what hour it was. Gradually a small group of Udger's pagan students assembled at his house, a few men, some children, mostly women. They were all very dirty and impoverished. But last, to my surprise, Liutgard arrived, a fresh wrap around her hair and a new candle in her hand to donate to the church. She saw me and allowed a quick smile to me before lowering her eyes in reverence and taking a seat right beside Udger.

While Udger spoke, Liutgard leaned forward and listened intently, nodding and sometimes offering her own explanation when someone had a question, as if she were Udger's assistant. She was his star pupil.

The talk was about the Incarnation. A big, hirsute man with a tangle of filthy hair spread his hands across his chest and asked, "And so our Lord and God had his way with the girl Mary and fathered our Savior?"

"Oh no, no," said Udger with a stammer.

Liutgard broke in. "God created our Savior in her womb by His thoughts, not with carnal relations. Our Savior was born of a virgin."

"He didn't disguise himself as Joseph and take his form?"

"God has no form," said Liutgard. She turned to Udger, "That is right? God is formless."

The folk looked puzzled. Udger held up his hand parallel to the floor, his index finger extended. "The nature of God is beyond definition."

The big man addressed Liutgard. "You have taught us an idol is only wood that can burn or iron that can melt. That is wise. But God must take forms, must enter into beings. For how does God see without eyes or hear without ears?"

Liutgard looked at Udger, nodding again with encouragement, looking like she expected him to say something brilliant.

Udger's hand was still in the air, paused as if holding onto a thought. He looked at her bright face. "Our eyes see because we have the sense of sight, our ears hear because we have the sense of hearing. God has the sense of sight and the sense of hearing without the physical accessories, in the way that the tree has the sense of sunlight and grows toward it, though it cannot see sunlight."

"The Christians chopped down our great tree!" said one of the children.

His mother put her arms around him and shushed him.

"God is not a tree," Udger said. A thin film of sweat covered his face.

The big man continued. "You taught us that casting spells with ashes and pebbles and herbs is false and superstitious because there is no magic in a stone or a twig. But to pray will bring a greater sort of magic. So it is the sense behind the prayer that is the magic of it, and not the sounds of it? That God hears the sense of it?"

Udger slowly nodded. Liutgard beamed. The children looked baffled and a little angry.

"You taught us the special prayer. I memorized it," said one.

Liutgard scooted over and put her arm around the girl. "It's a good prayer and powerful. The more you understand the words, the more power there is in the sense of it."

The big man turned to us, and I wondered if at that moment the others were as nervous as I was, wondering what he was going to ask. "And all the monks chanting scripture together, there is much sense in your combined voices?"

Reuben rubbed his apple-cheek and smiled. "Much sense."

They were clearly taken with this new concept of "sense," though I'm not sure if anyone in the room truly understood it.

Daric suddenly made a loud clap with his hands and bent forward. "It would be a mistake to think there is more of God in a large congregation than in one word of prayer. For God is infinite. There is as much of God in a single drop as in the mighty ocean, as much of God in an acorn seed as in a forest of oaks. For being formless, God is without bounds. Without beginning, without end, nothing can limit His power."

The group looked at Daric with thoughtful, surprised expressions.

He continued. "If God entered the form of a feline to see in darkness, still His eyes would be limited. If He entered the form of an eagle to see from a great height, still He would be limited. Any form, wolf or bear, lion or ox, is still limited. But God's senses are without limit."

The group nodded.

The outspoken girl who was squeezed beside Liutgard said, "And if my brother is not saved, he will go to hell, won't he?"

Reuben said, "Your brother will be saved."

The girl screwed up her face. "I want him to go to hell. He hits me."

Her mother gave her a little shake and hushed her.

A boy hopped down from his mother's lap. "I want to be a soldier for Karl and kill the Saxon unbelievers."

Udger smoothed the boy's hair. "Salvation is best spread through education, peace, and love."

The boy twisted back and forth where he stood. "This is boring. Odin is a warrior. Is Christ a great warrior or not?"

Gormgal reached over and pulled the boy toward him. "He is the greatest of warriors. Even now, he is fighting for your soul. Even now, the saints are fighting against the devil. Does Odin fight for anyone but himself? Does he fight for you, your mother, and your father? To Christ, even a little boy is as important as a great king."

The boy sighed and looked unhappy. "I will fight," he murmured.

Udger spread his arms. "Let us sing a psalm."

As the group left, I walked outside with Liutgard. "You are a model student."

She beamed. "Karl has made Christendom all-powerful, and he expects his court to be one of reverence."

"Is that self-serving?"

She cocked her head. "What about you? Last night you spoke with great heat about the power of the church, which you want to share in."

I felt my face turn red. "I didn't mean it that way. The church should be all-powerful. I didn't mean I wanted the power."

"I think there is something you do want."

"Do I?"

We gazed at each other in the twilight.

"Do you think you know me so well?" I asked. But I knew I had been very forthcoming in our previous talk.

"The secret to knowing people is to listen well. Knowing what people want makes you strong. That's a secret I don't share with anybody. But you know what I want, too. Isaac the merchant is returning to Aix soon. That's Karl's seat of power. I have some money, but no escort. If only some nice Christian pilgrims would accompany me." She tilted her head and batted her eyelashes in self-mockery.

I laughed. "It's not my decision. I am the least of the group to have a say."

"But I think the old man would follow you, and the others follow him?"

"You have a high opinion of my powers."

"The last secret is that anyone can have power if they only dare take it." In the setting sun her eyes shone like bronze. Her hood slipped off her hair, braided in a crown around her head.

"It's up to God," I said.

"Of course. But I do believe God helps those who help themselves."

"And why should I want to go to Aix? You assume I want the same as you."

"I think so. I think you long to see the great Karl's court, because you're curious."

"And I think you have been planting the idea in my head from the start."

She smiled, radiant in the rosy light. "We shall always be open and honest with one another, for I think we are too alike to keep secrets from each other."

She held out her hand, thin and strong, and I took it, and she grasped my pinkie in hers. As she tugged on my pinkie, she tilted her head back and looked at me hard with a knowing look of approval.

"Trust, then," I said.

"Trust."

With that she turned and left, though nothing was decided and we knew I could promise nothing. I only knew somewhere in the world I had a friend, a sister, who dispelled a loneliness heavier than I had realized before.

The next morning after prayers, a visitor knocked loudly on Udger's door. A man stepped in whom I recognized as one of the soldiers who had accompanied us from Kent to the sea, but had not crossed the sea with us. It was a surprise to see him now.

"There you are. Messengers have been trying to catch up with you all the way from Iona, from monastery to monastery to Kent, and it was a hard sail to get here. Bless me, father, I have a letter for your guests," he said to Udger, and he flopped down on a bench. He slid a rolled up scroll from his belt and handed it to Daric, who read it and passed it with shaking hands to Reuben.

Reuben said, "Our Abbot Bresal is dead. Brother Connachtach is the new abbot. Work has commenced on the Book. We have been gone too long and must return."

Tears slipped from Gormgal's heavily wrinkled eyes. "My dear friend Bresal. We missed his last days. We missed his funeral, God forgive us. This has been a foolish mission."

"Our abbot sends for us, so it's decided," Reuben said. He looked grim, as if expecting trouble, which he was right to expect.

Daric smashed his fist against the table. "Connachtach is not my abbot. I am from Lindisfarne, not Iona. My abbot commands me to make the great Book, and it will be perfect. We will have the lapis!"

Gormgal's grief flew into rage. "The lapis is the devil's! The devil has driven us this way on a fool's quest! We've come far enough, too far, and my dear Father, my dear friend——" he started to sob.

Nithard put his arm around him.

Reuben sighed and waited.

Daric bit his lower lip, shaking. Quietly he said to the air, "I will go. If I have to go alone, I shall go and serve my Lord."

Reuben narrowed his eyes, and I felt there was a gleam of malice in them. "Then perhaps that is for the best. We will return at our abbot's pleasure, and you will go on to obtain the lapis."

I stifled a gasp. It seemed cruel to abandon the old man, far from home, and he so ill. It was impossible to say what could become of him.

But Daric nodded his head triumphantly. "Yes, I shall go."

"Go!" Gormgal croaked through his tears. "Yes, go!"

I looked around in a daze. Then I turned to Reuben, who had now become the leader because he was willing to lead. "What about me?"

Reuben looked at me in surprise, having forgotten about me. He studied my face and seemed to divine my desire. "Perhaps... you should go too, with Brother Daric."

Daric stood and took the pouch off his belt. "Then we should divide the silver for both our journeys."

The others busied themselves with that and Reuben took me aside. "I don't think I can dissuade you and Daric. You will go together and God keep you from harm. But remember, you are the old monk's responsibility, and you must take care of him."

I looked in his eyes, knowing I had a solemn responsibility. "Yes, Brother."

Reuben gazed back. "You weren't as tall as I at the beginning."

I realized he was right. He was not a tall man, but I had grown much. He pointed at his cheek and I felt my own. I had whiskers.

"I feel this is your journey and God's will. But you must take care of him," he said. Then he put his hands around my shoulders and embraced me.

It was decided I would go to Isaac with some of the money and tell him of our decision. I found him at his warehouse. He was happy to hear the news. He took a silver coin from me and said I would need the rest to buy our food, which I should do right away, bring back to him, and he would have it stowed for us.

"And, also…" I said, not sure of how to go on.

"Speak, don't waste my time."

"Liutgard, the ale wife. She wants to go too. She has some money."

His manner instantly changed. He smiled. "Does she? Well, if you are her escort, I suppose it's not impossible. But I leave tomorrow and won't wait if she isn't ready."

I left to buy our fish and cheese and ran into Liutgard at the fishmonger's. I wondered if she would actually go, or be afraid to now that she had the opportunity. But she was resolved.

"Of course I can be ready. Nothing weighs me down."

I gave her a copper. "For the candle," I said. "So that you leave nothing unfinished."

She smiled and took the coin. "You know how I think. Now I will owe nothing."

"Will you be leaving friends behind?" I asked. I was already feeling some pangs to be parting from Reuben, Gormgal, and Nithard.

"One doesn't have friends in Frisia. One has useful acquaintances."

I looked at her, wondering if I was in that category. She must have seen it in my face.

"But there will be room for friends in my new life," she said, and she grasped my pinkie in hers.

## CHAPTER THREE: AIX

The last of our ship was loaded. It was a much larger boat than I had ever seen before, with a deck and stores below. Most of the merchandise consisted of casks of wine, furs from the North, quernstones, and woolen cloth. The last item to be brought aboard was a falcon in a wicker cage.

Liutgard was immediately taken with the falcon and stayed by its cage. She sat on a bundle of purple cloth like a queen on a throne, resting her elbow next to the cage with her hand on her cheek. "I am going to marry a rich lord and hunt with falcons."

Isaac saw Liutgard dreamily contemplating the falcon. He smiled.

"You like the hunter," he said to her.

"Yes. It does seem a shame, though, that this noble bird should be enslaved."

His eyes narrowed in irritation. "It is no slave. The falcon and the hunter are equal partners. You think too much." He turned and walked away with Daric following, his hands clasped behind his back, continuing their conversation about the East.

We passed the vineyards and a deep forest darkened the hills around us, in a narrower passage. The river twisted, and Isaac stayed at the prow with the captain to watch the turns for sudden rocks.

The sky was overcast and Liutgard's face had a clouded look as well when I sat down beside her. She wouldn't meet my gaze.

"What's the matter?" I asked.

She clenched her lips in hesitation, but then shrugged her shoulders to gird her courage. "Isaac asked me to marry him."

I started in surprise. "What did you say?"

AMY CRIDER

"I didn't say anything."

"That's unlike you."

She gazed out at the dark hills, and I poked her with the corner of my book.

"He's very rich," she said.

Her words disturbed me less than the fact that she wouldn't look at me. "You're considering it?"

She shrugged.

"It's not like you not to know your own mind."

"I wish someone would make it up for me."

I wanted to say, "Then don't marry him," because I felt she truly didn't want to, but I held back. "Why are you unsure?"

"I've been lucky so far, and I fear my luck will run out."

"You've made your own luck."

"Perhaps you overestimate me."

"Why doubt yourself now?"

She sighed. "In his gentle way, he has been reminding me of all I risk and the difficulty I face, a woman alone, headed to a strange place with no people or prospects. I can't just dance my way into the king's court. I must be mad to think I could."

"I don't like that he undermines your courage."

She smiled grimly. "Thank you, but I have to face facts. What will become of me?"

I couldn't answer. I struggled for words, knowing I had no easy answer to give. "The choice is between certainty and uncertainty. He offers you security. And there's certainty in being secure. You don't know what lies ahead. In freedom there is uncertainty. There is fear."

She slowly turned to me, her eyes wide in surprise, almost in fear. "Yes."

We sat in silence awhile, until Daric came up to me and asked to be read to from a psalter we had brought on the journey. We moved away, and I glanced about as I read. Isaac approached Liutgard to talk. I watched intently. I could see by his face—startled, disappointed, dark—that she refused him. She held out her hand in friendship. He took it briefly and dropped it.

One afternoon, we were talking about Karl's court when Isaac sat beside me. I was asking Daric about the palace school, by reputation the most learned in Christendom.

"There must be great power in knowledge," I said, just as Isaac sat beside me, and for some reason I was embarrassed he overheard me.

"Such knowledge I have brought you—a little knowledge is a dangerous thing," he said. This was cryptic at first, then I realized Isaac was the source of most of Liutgard's information about Karl and his court. Isaac had brought her this knowledge, fueling her ambitions, and with it the seeds of his own unhappiness.

"Knowledge that informs choice is indeed liberating," she said casually.

He turned to her with a dark look. "If you seek all power, knowledge, freedom, and security, then I wonder why you don't enter a convent. You could become an abbess and rule vast estates, your ambition could be limitless." With that he rose, returned to the prow, and hardly spoke a word to us for the remainder of the voyage.

When we arrived at the river port a few miles from Aix, Isaac was in a better mood. After the boat was unloaded, he was solicitous toward us, making sure our few things did not go astray, safeguarding our money, and offering to hire a horse for Liutgard. She preferred to walk as it was not a long distance. I think she didn't want to be in his debt. She thanked him, and he sighed with a clearing of the throat, a slight reprimanding sound, as if to say, "another bad decision I must accept." But he looked softly on her and bowed.

There was a good road through the woods to Aix and then, out of the woods we passed vineyards with tiny blossoms, fields of grain in all their golden glory. We were all cheered by the fine spring day. Even Daric seemed to be aware of his surroundings.

Late in the afternoon, the road ahead came to an end at the largest stone wall I had ever seen. The wall stretched across our horizon like a dragon in our path; smoke rose from within it. The wall was a dark, dark shadow breaking the golden fields and flow-er-dotted meadows.

Liutgard's mouth was open in wonder. She turned to me with a broad smile, her brown eyes shining.

"What beast is this, smoking from below?" Daric asked.

"We've come to Aix," Isaac said.

"Ah yes." Like Liutgard, Daric's face brightened with possibil-ities. "It will be here."

Liutgard quickened her pace, and I had to take her hand to keep her from running. She laughed at me but slowed down.

We stopped before the gate for Isaac to put his cargo in order, and he led the way after a quick exchange with the guards. We entered through the shadowed gate.

Aix-la-Chapelle, swarming with visitors, craftsmen, petition-ers, teeming with people whose business I couldn't fathom, idle folk who found ways to busy themselves in this bedlam of a city. This was a city. A city was something I'd heard of in Bible stories, but I could not have imagined this Babel.

It was built of stone and was still being built, its stout walls crowned by towers, within which workmen hoisted blocks on mechanical pulleys, masons chipped with hammers and chisels, carpenters pulled on their saws, smiths pounded out nails. The great city was being raised before our eyes. I had thought it noisy when we first arrived at Dunadd, and then Frisia, but they were nothing like this pounding and echoing toil. The workmen shout-ed above the noise in tongues I didn't know, that formed words from deep in the throat.

The streets were paved with smooth stones and a beggar was sweeping them in exchange for alms. Suddenly an approaching horse shied at him, the horseman yelling oaths at the industrious beggar. Idle children ran like dogs, stopping to watch a man jug-gling apples, who called to a passing woman holding a basket of laundry on her head. A woman dressed like a princess walked slowly past, and when I saw her wink at the juggler, I knew she was a whore. A girl pushed a cart of bread to sell to the workmen and the petitioners.

Yet with all this confusion and activity, it was a sense of idleness that bore upon me. Most of those I saw should have been at work, in fields or at looms, and were instead here on God knows what business. The children most of all brought out my pity for their idle lives, with no one shepherding them.

The air was still but seemed to move, heavily, with the stench of sulfur that wafted over the city, almost visible, so that around each corner I expected to see spraying pits of fire, the hellish source of the smell, but I learned later it was not fire that singed the air with this odor, but water people drank and bathed in. The water was considered healing and wholesome. I thought it foul, and it cast over the city, squirming with so many moving arms and legs, a sensation that this was the stew pot of hell. I was not afraid or repelled; truly I was impressed with the wealth, the nerve, the pulsation of the place, but the air rising from underneath, rising from sulfur springs, underpinned all with a sinister color.

Beggars waved like thin reeds drifting in a current here and there. The men they begged from, in shining silk tunics edged in bright embroidery, were stout. I had never seen so many overfed men, and such variety of sizes of men, the thinness of the beggars and the fat. I stared at the fat men at the market stalls and then realized everywhere their hands were giving and taking coin. Money was everywhere. The idle, deprived of honest work, begged for it, the other idle, the fat who somehow gained money without honest work, exchanged it for every good. It seemed to me this item, the coin, was the cause of all the peculiar sights around me, both the fat and the thin, the frenzy of activity and idleness. For the rest of my life, I would associate silver coin with that sulfur smell and chaos.

Shortly inside the walls we entered a market of dark wooden stalls lining the streets. Some were open to the sky, some tented, and others had a house built above that extended over the street. There were river eels for sale, chickens and rabbits hanging from beams, smiths hammering, a great oven for molten glass. We walked together slowly, separately stunned, and I lingered to watch the puff-cheeked glassblower. A boy ran into me.

"Excuse me!" I assume he said.

"No matter," I replied with a smile, and he ran off.

As he disappeared, my belt felt lighter. He had cut off my little purse. I had given the silver to Isaac to keep safe, and it was empty but for my lock of Aedith's hair. Now I would never stroke it again.

The city was roughly a circle, and everywhere I felt it was closing in on us. We couldn't walk straight through the market, but had to wind down the twisting streets. The idea of getting lost in an enclosed place—not large, not a forest—seemed strange, but as the streets wound it seemed as if the interior of the city was larger than the circumference of its walls.

Isaac knew the way, leading us cheerily, smiling at his acquaintances in their stalls. Finally, something stopped the cacophonous route like a breakfront in the sea. There was a long, whitewashed wall cutting across the center of the city, with large ruddy stone building complexes at each end and a gatehouse in the center. Isaac went straight to the massive wooden doors of the gatehouse. The guard, bearded, yawning, suddenly perked up on seeing Isaac with us. He said something guttural in a friendly voice. Isaac responded and motioned at us. We passed through to a huge courtyard, and I could see the sky again.

The wall that broke our journey was one side of a covered walk that connected two complexes of buildings. Another such walkway extended on the opposite side of the courtyard. The complex to our left was a rectangular palace with a square tower on one side. On our right the church rose an extraordinary four stories above the world, perhaps the tallest building in Christendom, domed on top, and a striking shape: it had eight sides. Another walled courtyard at right angles to the one we were in made the front portico of the church, and a few buildings were attached to it, the palace school, library, and scriptorium I saw later.

"We should offer a prayer of thanksgiving," Daric said.

"I'll send someone after you who speaks Scots as I take in my cargo," Isaac replied. Isaac took his things and turned toward the palace while we headed for the church. A crowd of people were entering ahead of us, for a service was just starting.

I would be constantly amazed those first hours, discovering the church and the palace. The inside of the church was staggering. The dome rose high above, painted with Christ blessing us. Marble columns held up arches that were ribboned in red and white brick. Windows admitted colored light, and the floor was marble. Prayers echoed harmoniously through the vaults. Surrounding me were nobles in bright silk clothes. I gazed straight up again, and as my eye descended to the second story, I saw him.

Karl sat upon a simple throne made of stone, looking down on us like God himself. A shaft of golden light lit his pale, almost white hair and beard. His furrowed brow was concentrated in prayer, but the concentration reminded me, for some reason, of a boy trying to work out a sum. His face was round and ruddy. A plain blue mantle stretched over his broad shoulders, fastened by a golden broach near his thick red neck. In his intent prayer he looked apart, as if he felt himself to be alone.

His family was by him, in shadow, a large group of children and youths. Suddenly I noticed a severe-faced woman behind the king.

"There's the queen!" Liutgard said, poking me, for she was especially looking for her.

The Queen Fastrada was rotund, her face round and pale. When she faced us, her fierce expression transfixed me. Her eyes glowed darkly beneath her black brows. She had a feline air, not cat-like in the sense of sleek grace, but as a round, fat, and baleful spitting cat that has its run of the house. This is bold to say as a first impression, but such was the ferocity of her look.

I understood some of the Latin, and I prayed what I was able to. I thanked God for delivering us safely. When it ended, the king stood and made the sign of the cross over us all.

Outside, a boy was waiting who greeted us in Scots. "The king will receive you after you refresh yourselves. Come with me." He took us to guest quarters where even the latrine was nice. I washed my tired feet.

When we were refreshed, the boy returned. Along the covered walkway, the sunlight picked out the straight columns, making a pleasing rhythm of light and shadow. As I passed each bright column, I felt I heard a note plucked on a harp.

When we entered the hall, we saw Isaac, who motioned for us to join him. In the flickering torch light, I tried to learn and distinguish who was important at the feast. The stream of children surrounding the king resolved to his two sons and five daughters, children of different mothers.

Karl was playfully arguing with his bright-eyed daughter Gisela. Her eyes danced in the fiery light as she asked if she could play the harp for the diners, and Karl was insisting she eat.

"Rotrude can eat mine."

Rotrude, like her brother Louis, was solemn and serious. "No, I'll do as the king says, as you should."

The eldest, Bertha, was the most beautiful. She was holding a baby, though I saw no husband near. "Stop pestering," she said to Gisela. "If you don't feel like eating, you can hold Nithard for me."

Gisela took the baby Nithard, and Karl leaned over to stroke the infant's face.

Near me was a man of fifty who I could soon tell was a favorite of the king's. He was Alcuin, sometimes called Flaccus, because, as I quickly divined, the close-knit men had pet names for one another. Alcuin seemed especially enamored of using those pet names. Karl was David, the warrior-king. This name was reserved for his closest friends. The other nobles addressed him as "Your Security" or "Your Clemency." I could tell from his accent Alcuin was an Englishman, and I asked in Saxon why the king called him Flaccus.

"He flatters me. That is the family name of Horace, a poet of antiquity. I scribble verse."

"Are you the court poet?"

He beamed at me. "No, I am the headmaster of the palace school. Poetry is not so important to our David, except the poetry of the psalms. We'll hear them read later, or perhaps we'll hear Augustine's *City of God*. That's the king's favorite."

"Are you a monk, then?"

"No, neither monk nor priest, but a deacon and an outsider from York. I am a lamb among lions here, but I soak it up."

More than once he turned to me privately to explain some detail of Karl's leadership that came up in conversation. Karl was using his power to make sweeping improvements in Frankland.

"False scales are an abomination to the Lord, but a full weight is his delight," Alcuin quoted Proverbs. Karl was reforming the weights and measures of the land, reforming the coinage too. He even renamed the months to rid them of their pagan origins.

I never thought about this before: the use of power. At Dunadd, Eochaid's power was only for its own sake, to lord over men, to take away, to control. But Karl was using his position of power to lead change, to reform and better his kingdom in ways sweeping and fundamental. To think he would rename the twelve months! That was audacity, ambition governed by beneficence. It was hard not to stare at him, but he seemed so accustomed to it, he didn't notice.

"We must ensure these schools are established. Flaccus, is there some way our missi could gather a measurement of how well the schools are teaching the boys? Could you devise an examination that could be given for their understanding of Latin? Right speech leads to right thinking, and I want no child left behind."

His jester rolled his round eyes, raised his red eyebrows, and said, "How you take the measure of a man was a lesson to the Northmen. That's the sort of lesson we like."

The table laughed, though the holy men present only gave smothered smiles. I asked Alcuin what he meant.

Alcuin winced. "At the most recent battle against invaders from the North, our warrior David took their measure by measuring the men against the height of a sword. Those that were taller than a sword were shortened by a head." Alcuin put his hand to his mouth and quickly said, "He is a just man who acts as is necessary for a king. It is not one's favorite aspect of the rule of a king, but he is a great man and often spares his enemies."

He said this last in a whisper so that others around him might . not hear his apology, and I knew he was ashamed of having to defend Karl.

We were interrupted by a change of subject, when someone asked about a certain man nicknamed the Eagle.

Alcuin's soft face glowed. "Oh! I received a letter from him today! It filled my heart with gladness to hear from my sweet friend. He must have had enough of my chiding, as I send him three letters for each one I receive." Alcuin recounted the letter with childlike enthusiasm.

I was not interested and stopped listening, instead becoming aware of the food. I was delighted at the bread and roast meat, dripping with juice and fat. But I was increasingly astonished at the stream of dishes that were continually brought out to us. There was beef, venison, and pork, roasted, stewed, and in pies. There were leeks, cheeses, pottages, sausages, fruits, and walnuts boiled in honey. To drink there was ale, wine, and mead, each dish and drink sweeter than the last.

I had taken a few bites when Daric slapped my hand.

"Penance!"

I was not to eat the roast meat and stewed fruits. As an oblate, my first year had to be one of penance and denial. I took a crust of bread, dipped it in a bowl of milk, and sucked at it through clenched jaws. The aroma of the juicy meal, the spice-soaked apples and pears, teased me until I nearly had tears in my eyes. Beside me Alcuin relished mouthfuls of saucy dishes and sipped the Rhenish wine until he glowed. I noticed at a certain point he stopped drinking wine and switched to the barley water. He was not dissolute.

The king preferred roast meat, saying with a chagrined smile that his doctor had told him often to give it up, because he was thick in the waist, but he would not. He did not otherwise over-indulge. When someone at the end of the table laughed loudly from an excess of wine, Karl gave him a dark look and told a servant to give him permission to leave the table. "I loathe drunk-enness," he said to us. "I trust you are continent."

"It is a fine vintage and not to be guzzled," Alcuin said, admitting his enjoyment of luxury in his temperate words. He denied himself nothing of the fine meal. Alcuin was not exactly corpulent, but he was soft and paunchy. His face was full and gleamed with good eating. He had very good teeth and licked his lips habitually. He had a graceful way of gesturing, leaning right and left and dipping the air with a cupped hand and lifting it up, as if pulling his words from an imaginary pool.

One man at the table, Paulinus, ate like a penitent. He broke some bread into his pottage and nibbled lettuce, but avoided the dripping meat and purple wine. He never laughed and only rarely spoke, in low tones, to agree with some observation of Alcuin's or to whisper "let me not hear, O Jesus," when the laughter rose at a barbed witticism or bawdy joke. At such moments Alcuin deftly changed the subject, and the king shrugged indulgently at the offender.

"What has Ingeld to do with Christ?" Alcuin asked. "Some kings listen to legends of Beowulf as they feast. Our David has none of that. Timotheus," he turned to Paulinus, calling him by a nickname, "let us hear Christian truth that puts trivial legends to shame."

Paulinus rose and walked to a lectern. The entire room, a moment before buzzing in conversation, quieted. He opened a Gospel and read of the wedding at Cannae. Karl chewed and swallowed intently, nodding. Beside him Fastrada looked grave, but her sideways glance was on her husband.

When Paulinus finished reading, Gisela put her hand on her father's arm and raised her eyebrows at him. He touched her cheek and smiled with a nod. She rose and took up the lute, playing a lilting song. She was a skillful musician.

When she stopped, Isaac at last introduced us, in Saxon for our benefit, most of which I understood. Saxon would be a common language between us and much of the court. I sensed awkwardness when Karl was told we were Scots. Farther down the table, I saw a nobleman nudge his companion, put his thumb to his mouth, and tilt his head back.

Isaac personally recommended Liutgard to the queen as someone who would be of great help with the children.

Karl said, "You are welcome and must stay in our kingdom as long as you are able, after your long journey. You must see my city. Come with me and you will see something grand. You must like water, I hope."

He rose and dismissed the nobility and his family. Fastrada took Liutgard with her, and only the men went with Karl. Less serious now, he strode out, beckoning us. We followed him outside, through the gate opposite the one we had originally entered.

"Welcome to Aqua Granum," the king said with a flourish. We passed through the gate to an extraordinary sight. Within was a courtyard taken up almost entirely by a huge bath, a man-made pond with straight sides, lined with tiles. It was a hundred feet long and steam rose from the clean blue water. Karl quickly threw off his mantle and tunic. We hesitated, and he waved at us, laughing. We stripped and splashed in after him.

The water was hot. I had never stepped into hot water before. It was fantastically pleasing and soothing. The king bounded back and forth across the pool, and we imitated him. Then after a bit we all sat at one end and felt our cares melt away in the liquid silkiness of the water.

Karl was growing sleepy, but he wanted to talk. "Did you hear of Widikund on your journey?"

We said no.

"It has been many years since I defeated him, my old relentless enemy. But I fear the people in the forests still make a legend of him. It was a long battle, searching for him and destroying his followers. I spent years after my enemy Widikund. But I defeated him in the end, as was God's will." He chuckled. "They worshipped a tree and called it Irminsul. They thought the tree was the center of the world, of the universe! But my good soldiers found it and chopped it to bits. No one will hug trees in my kingdom. There will be no more ignorance and superstition. If they talk of Widikund, it's not to extol him. They see even their greatest leader is no match for a Christian king. Loyalty is all I ask. I give much in return for it. Three hundred Saxons hanged. They would swear no loyalty to me. So they hanged. I spared Widikund, and that is an example of my just dealings, because he swore his oath to me. But I suspect there are those who secretly praise him. My missi go out to the countryside and listen. They will find out what people are saying. So, you heard nothing of Widikund?"

We said no. Karl caught me staring at him, for I was studying him.

He smiled. "You don't have a care in the world, do you?"

"I'm not sure."

"You're lucky to be a monk. You'll never have a wife."

"Wives give you children."

Karl opened his mouth wide and grinned. "You see into my heart! You know how I love to have my children with me."

I felt badly because I had begun to think about him in a dark way.

"You have many. You are well blessed."

"You haven't seen all of them. I have a son elsewhere, my beloved Carloman. But you see my darling daughters. They are my precious treasure. I won't let them go. King Offa of Mercia wanted Gisela for his son. Perhaps I should have allowed it. But no, they cannot leave me. Never."

After Pepin's conspiracy, Karl had decided to impose an oath on all men and boys over thirteen, to swear allegiance to him. Messengers—his missi—would ride over the land to administer the oath.

"If my enemies bow down to me, if Widikund himself could take such an oath, how much more should my own kinsmen pledge to me?"

Alcuin said, "Of course they will be persuaded by your own reputation for justice. It is better to lead people by reason than by threat, for fear may dissipate but reason lasts. The lion has only to roar to be obeyed, for reputation is enough."

"The lion must be seen to strike from time to time, to put the fear of God in his subjects." At times, the king grudgingly agreed with Alcuin when in his presence. But later in the evening as we bathed in the delicious hot pool, his mind turned to his enemies, real and imagined.

"There were seven conspirators, in a court of, say, a hundred, that's seven per cent. If seven per cent of my people are disloyal, how many missi must I send out to find them all? If I send two missi for every dozen counties in Frankland..." His lips moved as he worked out the sum, his voice trailing off into a drowsy buzz echoing and absorbed by the warm water. He often mentioned Widikund, and retold the story of felling their sacred tree, and his round blue eyes would gaze into the distance, into the blazing bonfire his generals made of that mighty oak.

The next day after the morning service, the boy—whose name was Fredigus and who was Alcuin's secretary—brought us to the library and scriptorium, where Alcuin met us and gave us a tour. The number of books was staggering: there were hundreds. A team of men scribed from dictation, and the musical sing-song of the Latin led their pens in a subtle dance. We watched briefly and then, not to disturb them, we went into Alcuin's office.

The office was in a corner of the building and was lit by two large windows of leaded glass. The windows and brightness of the large, airy room seemed as significant of power to me as the king's throne room. It was quite a clean room, with a carpet on the polished floor instead of rushes. A cupboard brimmed with yet more books, and on the desk was a neat array: a leather box of quills, a bound notebook, a stack of fresh vellum, chalk and ink bottles and a straight edge. Alcuin opened a book to show us their scribing.

"This is an odd script," Daric said. I didn't know what the difference was, but I observed the script was small, square and compact-looking.

Alcuin beamed. "This is our script which we developed. It's efficient and easy to read."

Daric sniffed. "I don't know about efficiency. With labor comes grace."

"We have so much to write, charters and the like," Alcuin said in an apologetic tone.

Daric said, "Yes, I see, for charters of course, but not for Holy Scripture."

Alcuin was mild in the face of this criticism. He had an open, pleasing face, the lines of which indicated that he smiled much. Though he was old, he was not as ancient as Daric, and he said, "I defer to the wisdom of my elders."

"May I learn to write here?" I asked. I saw Daric frown at me. Daric immediately thought I meant that I particularly desired to learn their Frankish way of scribing, which I didn't mean. I only took the opportunity to ask because the subject was at hand.

Alcuin gave me a regretful smile. "The older you are, the more difficult it is to achieve. Our David, though he can read beautifully, has never attained writing." The regret in his eyes softened and his smile turned further up. "Still, you are not so very old. It is quite possible. I'm sure the question is up to your masters more than me."

Daric put his hand on my shoulder. "It would be a great opportunity, but we don't know yet how long we are staying. If we are able to obtain lapis quickly, we can return before autumn," Daric said.

I hoped we would stay the winter. Though not obtaining the lapis would seem to make this long trip senseless, it was no waste to me. I wanted to see all I could, for its own sake, for the sake of my understanding.

Daric continued, "It was my belief you would have lapis to donate to our holy mission, dear brother."

Alcuin licked a corner of his mouth as he thought. "I'm afraid we haven't had lapis for some months. We have other paints, many colors to donate, but not lapis now."

Daric's face turned white, and he stared for some moments. Alcuin's gentle smile faded as his eyes opened wider in concern. My heart beat hard until Daric spoke.

"Ah then, that is too bad."

He turned suddenly and walked out of the room, and I hurried to keep up. We marched back to our guest room. Once inside, I was terrified by his show of rage.

His cries were like a wounded hound as he grabbed the desk, turned it over, pulled the cloths off the bed, and struggled to tear them with hands and teeth, tangling himself in them. Swaddled in the bedding, he grabbed the legs of the bed and slammed it up and down. An ink bottle just missed the window. Our silver coins scattered like debris across the floor. "What is silver, but the devil's bribe?" he bellowed along with incoherent howls. His face twisted into a living, moving mask, working into horrible expressions, as one might imagine in knotted tree trunks at night when one is lost and frightened.

I crouched in a corner, speechless.

When he was thoroughly entangled in the bedding and all was devastated, he rocked the bed back on its feet and fell into it with a sob. He squeezed his eyes shut in his red face and stopped howling, his breath deep and hoarse.

In the contrast of the sudden stillness, my own breath was loud and fast. Coins glittered on the floor like broken glass. A puddle of ink spread from one corner like the blood of a calf. He lay in a precarious equilibrium, prone but tense, at any moment liable to go off again, but for now still as a quivering rabbit in a frozen pose.

I slipped out and hurried back to Alcuin, who was still in his office dictating a letter to Fredigus. I entered with no announcement or courtesy, but as he looked up startled, he saw my urgency. He listened to my story with all concern. When I finished I saw a firm determination in him more decisive than I expected from him. He was no ditherer.

"I will send you Saint John's wort from the infirmary. Fredigus, if you would—"

Fredigus quickly went to get it.

"Add it to his barley water or ale every night before sleep, and in the morning too if necessary," Alcuin went on. "It will soothe him. You must be very calm and quiet with him and not show your fear. Most important, don't ask him questions or correct anything he says. You must not argue, but instead, by nodding and repeating his words, show that you are listening." Alcuin sighed and smoothed the page before him. "I do wish we had lapis, as I know in his state nothing will substitute for it. But we don't and that's all there is to it."

Fredigus returned with the cloth bag of powdered Saint John's wort.

Alcuin patted my shoulder. "Come to me any time."

I realized now it was up to me to deal with the situation, and that no one was coming with me. I left and went to the kitchen to beg a cup of ale. The scullery girls snickered because of the Scots' reputation for drink, but I didn't try to explain.

When I returned, Daric was asleep, though his body was still stiff and tense. I straightened the room and set the ale on the desk. I sprinkled some of the green powder into it. I sat for the day beside him, until the bell rang for evening service. He opened his eyes and fixed them on me.

"I had a vision."

"Tell me your vision."

"A white stag crossed the frozen stream. The ice broke with a mighty crack. The current rushed him past the sharp rocks that tore his flesh. He was pulled to the sea, and on the shore the Holy Mother gathered shells and blue seaweed. He landed fainting on the sand. She reined him in with the seaweed binding. Healed, he rose and she climbed on his back, and they rode through the gate."

"A blessed vision," I said with a nod.

I took a chance and touched his arm. He trembled.

"I've brought you a cooling drink."

I gave him the ale and he gulped it down.

"I thought, my eyes are blue, and I can pluck them out to make blue ink. Would that do?"

I trembled to realize his madness. "There is no need. I promise you, we will get the lapis. Let us go to the church and pray."

Daric grew sleepy during the service and leaned heavily on me. Afterward, to my gladness, Fredigus offered to take him to the infirmary for the night. Daric nodded absently and accepted his supporting arm. I needed to talk to Alcuin and sought him out.

"He is in pain because others died and he did not," Alcuin said.

"Shouldn't it be a relief, shouldn't he be happy in some way to have survived?" I asked.

"That is not how the soul works."

"He rarely speaks of the raid. Most of the time it doesn't seem to be in his thoughts. He seems only to care about obtaining the lapis lazuli."

Alcuin looked far off and sighed. "It is a token of his faith, and his restitution. The soul seeks to atone. You are his protector, the protector of his dream. You have a grave responsibility. I don't think you understand what you have taken on."

"No, I don't. I'm not ready," I said.

He replied, "We are never ready. Not for our burdens, not even for our faith at times that leaps into our hearts like a thunderbolt. Not for death though it means everlasting life." He smiled. "If I were young I would go, as you go, and as you will have to go, into this journey. If you want to save him, you may indeed go to the ends of the earth to obtain this boon."

"It is only a small blue pebble," I said.

"It is a flint that ignites the soul."

We parted. Alone in my room, I dropped a pinch of the Saint John's wort in a cup of water for myself, a taste like burnt spinach, and fell into an exhausted sleep.

## CHAPTER FOUR: A GOODBYE

I had been accepted as a pupil of Alcuin with a small class of older boys. Alcuin appointed Daric as a teacher, and resuming such duties seemed to steady him, though he often paused and stared. But no merchants came with lapis. An early winter came, with sleet and frost. Because it was not fit to travel, we remained.

The lessons were about words. Alcuin loved to speak and write with correctness and precision as well as with playful abandon. He wrote poems of wordplay. His nicknames for people, such as his beloved friend Arno "the Eagle," were sometimes teasing interpretations of their given names. His Latin was expert and he had a fair command of Greek and a bit of Hebrew. In our first lesson he had me write the following from dictation:

"Correctness in language is evidence of correctness in thought. Heresy arises from wrong words. Words are the voices of ideas. The word carries the idea like an eggshell containing its yolk. Language can be fragile. Language can be shattered by misquoting or mistranslating. Language can be shattered, and in turn shatters sound logic which gives rise to the breaking off of heresies that divide the true Church. Right intellect, well educated, must protect our use of words as carefully as a nest protects the egg, and we must be like the good mother robin who makes a strong nest protected in the boughs. For the wind of heresy blows strong, and the branches shake, but our education is strong and fixes our understanding."

One of Alcuin's enjoyable teaching methods is to ask riddles, and we made up riddles, too. Our group of boys was delighted by sessions that went along these lines:

"What is a year?"

"A cart with four wheels."

"What horses pull it?"

"The sun and the moon."

"How many palaces has it?"

"Twelve."

"I have seen a woman with an iron head, a wooden body, and a feathered tail carrying death."

"The woman is a soldier's arrow."

"Of what does man never tire?"

"Profit."

Sometimes when I was alone with him, I tried out my own inventions:

"What are three things that roar?"

"The lion, the wind, and fire."

"Three things that fell a tree."

"Wind, fire, and an ax."

"A dull tool."

"A hammer."

I thought the last very clever. I was calling Karl's grandfather, Karl "the Hammer" Martel, a dull tool. I mingled in innocent ones: "Two sharp things that cause food to be brought."

"A scythe, and hunger."

"Cause of man's death, it renews its life."

"A snake."

"Two dangerous beauties."

"A rose and..." He put his finger to his cheek. His gleaming hazel eyes crinkled with amusement. He let out his breath in surprise, and said with an expression of merriment and disbelief, "... a queen?"

I smiled back at him and nodded.

He shook his head but the smile didn't die on his lips until I asked, "A lion in the sky?"

He looked puzzled, and more troubled than I expected. "A lion in the sky?" he repeated. He licked his lower lip. "I can't think."

"An eagle!" I was proud to have stumped him.

His cheeks flushed and there was a choking sound in his throat. I asked if he was all right, and his eyes hardened. "Of course." He then dismissed me. There was something to it, but I didn't know what.

My head filled with new ways of thinking: about words, about language, about ideas themselves. That everything that is began as an idea in the mind of God. And that everything we know, we know first as an idea. Everything begins as a thought. A flicker of understanding caught flame in my mind and grew brighter each day.

Liutgard would find me in the inner courtyard by the fountain, with the three dogs, such poor guards, curled at my feet. I told her all I learned, babbling in a rush of enthusiasm, getting myself twisted up and confused in my newness, because my thoughts were like a bowl of ingredients not yet stirred by experience.

She held her hand up to stop me and raised her sharp chin. "You seem to be saying words are as powerful as kings."

"The king rules by law, and laws are words!"

"The king *makes* the law. He is the speaker of those words."

I was not a good debater, and in my newness her questions confused and disturbed me. I wanted her to be excited with me. I replied, "Before there was a king, there was an idea of a king. A king is merely a man, and people don't bow to him as a man, but because he bears the aura, he bears the idea of kingship."

She smiled. "He bears arms, and an army of men in chain mail bearing swords. These things are real. They are tangible. The body of a hanged enemy is not an idea, but a tangible fact."

I struggled to respond, frustrated, but she sensed my disappointment and put her cool hand on mine. I looked at her confident face and felt the warmth of our friendship.

I said, "Your point is valid. There's so much I don't know. You only raise more questions I must ask."

I was often curious about how Alcuin really felt about Karl. For some reason I despised Karl more every day. I tried to question Alcuin, though my own ideas were inarticulate. I asked Alcuin what would happen to those men and boys who refused to swear allegiance to the king. Would they be measured against a sword?

He raised his eyebrows in surprise. "Of course not. They will lose the protection of the king and be outside the law. That is all."

"Isn't the oath for the king's protection?"

"Yes, but it works both ways. The king is the protector of the people."

"And who protects the people from the king? If he abuses his power?"

Alcuin looked at me sternly. "As long as the king is just, as Karl is, beyond any king in Christendom, the people are loyal. You have already seen what happens when a king is unjust, as in Kent. He is quickly deposed. And you saw the horror of civil war there. There is nothing more terrible than the scourge of civil war." He cocked his head and became mild again. "The blessings of a strong, just ruler cannot be overstated. What alternative do you propose? What alternative is there? There is no peace without strength of leadership. It is the nature of men to engage in conflict, and a dispenser of justice is a good and necessary thing. What is it you seek?"

I lowered my head, my thoughts confused. "I don't know. At Dunadd I met a man who should have been king, a wise and gentle spirit. He was banished to the monastery. I long for such modesty and godliness in a king."

"The meek shall inherit the earth. But they do not rule it."

I met his gaze. "Do you ever feel you are compromising something of your ideals to be here?"

"Of course not!" He turned a bit pink. Then he sighed and shook his head. "It is my greatest honor to serve. I will stay at the king's pleasure. Of course, I would like to retire from my cares and become an abbot. I make that request frequently. I'm sure the time will come soon."

I felt some satisfaction to know that Alcuin's real desire was to leave the court.

But Liutgard and I continued to argue. Her voice seemed harder, slightly metallic as she enunciated her words with an increasing accent of the Frankish tongue, her vowels short and her consonants heavy.

"That Alcuin is quite rude, isn't he?" she asked.

"How so?"

"Presuming to tell the king what to do. Criticizing his stern, strong ways on converting the Saxons. If Karl is stern with his own people, how much more strict should he be with the pagan enemy? I was rather insulted for him. The king puts up with it out of his generosity."

"He is the king's own teacher," I said.

"The king is not a boy at school."

"Alcuin quotes Proverbs: 'For lack of guidance a people falls; security lies in many counselors.'"

She rolled her eyes. "Alcuin says, Alcuin says. Listen to you." A cloud moved across the sun, and her eyes darkened in the change of light.

"Surely at least you agree with Alcuin's point about the conversions. Force is not the way to convert pagans or control a people," I said.

"Power must be exerted. The king must take control. Otherwise he won't stay king for long. He rules by the number of battles he has won, and by dispensing justice. Justice must be enforced, ultimately by the power of life and death. I can quote Proverbs, too: 'Where there are no oxen, the crib remains empty; but large crops come through the strength of the bull.'"

I replied, "That is only what seems to be. Karl is exerting his rule in other ways, more important ways. He reforms the money and taxes, he reforms weights and measures, builds roads, develops crops, or encourages their development. He builds schools and sends them books. His real power is through the scholarship of his administration. Education is the source of his power—his own education, through which he has learned how to make these reforms, and the education that he advances throughout the kingdom, that's the lasting source of power. And he doesn't do this alone. He isn't a lone soldier with a shield and sword burning pagan temples. He has a government and a school of leadership, books by past leaders like Cicero that instruct him. He isn't doing it by himself."

Liutgard's lip curled as if tasting vinegar. "Alcuin."

Now my anger did rise. "What have you got against him?"

"He presumes much. And his false humility. And his little mottos and nicknames, and his goading. Fastrada doesn't care for him, and neither do I."

So she was looking through the eyes of her mistress. A drop of icy water fell on my heart. I tried to look into her face, but her eyes were fixed on the trembling trees. She would not look at me. Because I was young, anger rose in me rather than sadness.

"I thought you of all people would think for yourself!" I said.

"I thought the same of you." She stood, taking away from me the angry pleasure of being the one to break off the conversation. "We should not talk of these things anymore."

Now my heart pumped a river of cold water, because I took this as a rejection of all my thoughts and feelings. Only later did I understand she meant that as a form of kindness, to end our argument, but anger is not hot and burning, but cold and freezing, and I turned cold against my only friend.

Autumn slid by in drizzly days, and the breath of winter frosted the grass. Liutgard and I met less frequently and briefly when we did meet. Though my anger quickly cooled, I didn't know how to renew our warmth, until this occurrence.

I was alone with Alcuin in his office, when there was a rapid, urgent knock on the door, and without waiting for a response, Fredigus stepped in. He glanced at me with hardly a nod. His face was grave, and he turned to Alcuin, standing close.

"I have terrible news about Paulinus."

Alcuin gestured for him to continue.

"He has, God help him, tried to take his own life."

Alcuin raised his hands and then settled them on Fredigus' shoulders. "Does he ask for me?"

"He is in such a terrible state, he isn't coherent, changing his mind moment to moment. I was able to get him to the infirmary, and we bandaged his arms. He's in bed now, restless, trying to pray and crying in turns."

Alcuin put on his cloak. "I'll come now."

Uninvited, I followed. They had forgotten about me and didn't notice. The infirmary was dark with just a lamp burning on the wall, which lit up Paulinus' tear-stained face and left all else in shadow. I stood near the door with Fredigus, and Alcuin went to the bed and pulled a stool close to Paulinus, who shifted restlessly, stroking his bandaged arms.

"Tell me why you've done this to a creature of God," Alcuin asked.

Paulinus's breath shook as he spoke in broken fragments. "For some time now, the burden of my sins has weighed on me. Something in me... gave way."

"You are hardly scarred by sin. To me you always glow with righteousness. You deny yourself much, perhaps even too much."

"I can control my actions. I can control what enters my mouth. I can control the diligence of my work and the steadiness of my effort. But my *thoughts*. My mind is black with the tar of sin. My thoughts! I can't control the vile deeds my mind imagines, my pride, my arrogance, my shameless lust. I disgust myself."

He cried, shrinking into his tears, his face screwed up and contorted with pain.

Alcuin waited, then asked, "Do you know what Augustine says on the question of whether one should kill oneself in order to stop sinning?"

His breath shook. "He said it was wrong."

"It is the greatest sin, to destroy the gift of life."

"But how can I bear it?" Paulinus choked on a stifled sob.

"You are a Christian. I fear you know little of what that means."

"I love Christ with all my heart," Paulinus said.

"But are you redeemed?"

"I pray for my salvation." He gave a shudder and silent tears spilled down his face.

"Tell me, what do you think it feels like, to be redeemed? What does redemption *feel* like? Imagine it, with all your might."

"It must feel like a cloud lifting on the horizon. A sun breaking brightly through the storm."

"More."

"As if I were on top of the water, instead of under its heavy surface."

"More. Feel the redemption inside you."

"I would feel as if a yoke were lifted off me. As if I were riding the oxen instead of pulling the plough myself."

"Then tell me, you who are a Christian, redeemed in the Church. Do you feel redeemed?" Alcuin asked.

"I have never felt it."

"But you *are* redeemed. You are redeemed, but you deny yourself the wonderful gift."

"My sins—" He flushed, and more tears silenced him.

"You are redeemed, now. You always have been, and yet you close your heart to the gift of this light, wallowing in guilt. Christ who loves you has lifted the guilt from your shoulders. Open your eyes, open your heart, and feel the redemption of Christ's love for you."

Paulinus shuddered so that the bed rattled, and then suddenly he was still. I felt the relaxation of his body as if the room suddenly warmed, as if the fire had been stoked. His face, red, then white, took on a pink glow. His eyes opened wide. His mouth fell open and slowly dawned into a blissful smile.

"I feel it. I feel it." He straightened up, seeming slightly to rise in the air. He took Alcuin's hand. Paulinus's face beamed forth in transfiguration.

Alcuin began to recite Pater Noster, and we all joined in, our voices hushed but strong, filling the little room.

"I am ready," he said. "I am ready. To live."

"Yes, live and find eternal life."

We crept out in silence and went separate ways, Alcuin to return to his office, and I in wonder saw the moon bright overhead, the stars blazing in glory, and the wonder of God filled my soul.

I, too, had not thought about redemption, for all my arguments about the power of the Church, had not thought of this, its greatest power and reason for existence.

I didn't have the chance to speak with Alcuin, but I had no quarrel with Liutgard now. I knew I loved her as a sister and my anger was vain and trivial. It was nothing. The next night, we met as usual and I was eager to forgive and renew our friendship. When she sat beside me, I took her hand at once and said, "Our quarrel must end. I've discovered the simple and glorious truth of our faith. I want only your friendship."

She looked at me with her frank gaze, but only smiled weakly and looked down with a sigh.

"What is it?"

She lifted her head and looked hard in the distance. "Fastrada is gravely ill."

To my shame, I didn't immediately regret that. I blamed Fastrada for our fight, for all my troubles, because Fastrada had turned her against Alcuin.

"Are you sure?"

"Yes, there's no mistaking it. She grows weaker day by day."

I didn't respond, but waited to be inspired. Liutgard was very troubled, and I didn't want to be insensitive. I merely said, "This saddens you very much."

She pursed her lips grimly and hesitated also, finally saying, "Fastrada has been the mother I never had."

Then I understood, and remorse filled me. She leaned over and put her head on my chest. I put my arms around her.

"Without her I'll be lost. I don't know what I'll do. And what will be my place?"

I knew Karl acquired wives the way some men acquired horses. Fastrada was at least his third. "He'll find a new wife quickly, and you will serve her. Certainly you won't be turned out."

"It will be strange. And I was just growing complacent and used to things here as they were. I wish things wouldn't change."

I held her tight. "You have my friendship, and that will not change."

She wiped away a few tears and straightened up. "Thank you, it has been hard."

I felt stricken, understanding my own fault in our argument. "I have been hard and I grieve that I haven't been a friend these last few weeks. I can only beg your forgiveness."

"I forgive you, of course, dear little brother."

A few tears slipped down my cheek. She wiped them away with a wan smile and said, "I must return to her. She needs my comfort often, and I try to do what I can to give her ease. She is in much pain."

"Does Karl know?"

"So far we've kept it a close secret. Please tell no one. She can't bear her weakness."

"I won't tell."

She stood and we parted. I went to the church, finding Daric and Paulinus praying together, and I stood beside them and prayed that nothing further would break the bond between me and my dear sister.

Karl's daughter Rotrude is a serious, studious girl who loves to look to the sky at night and learn of the stars and planets. On the dark winter nights when the sun set early, we—my classmates and I, and Rotrude and I—would go out to gaze at the heavens. We learned of the five planets and the zodiac. Alcuin knew much of the pagan myths about constellations, about Venus who plays such a prominent role in his favorite poem, the *Aeneid*.

Alcuin struggles with his love of pagan literature. He doesn't forbid it. We studied the graceful Latin of Virgil and Cicero and read how Saint Augustine at first considered their eloquence a sign of superiority over Christian writing, before he accepted the Bible. Yet, Alcuin isn't comfortable with his enjoyment of these writings. He apologized for it.

I looked at the planets named after the pagan gods and considered. I wondered if Karl would seek to rename them. Karl has renamed the twelve months of the year, to rid them of their pagan names. Instead he names them after the work activities of each month—"Hay-making," "wine-pressing," etc. He is ever the reformer, but eventually I was not impressed.

Still, I am not enamored of changing everything to make it modern and reject the past. Then, I felt the fullness of time as we gazed at the stars. The world is six thousand years old, and there are many Christians who believe this is the last age of man, though Scots in general don't agree with that. I felt close to these men of past ages, studying the night sky, and I wondered if there might be future ages we can't imagine, before Christ's destiny for us is fulfilled.

In recent times, due to the scholarship of the Venerable Bede, we have come to date time by the years since Christ's life on earth. We call the present *anno Domini*, which means in the year of our Lord, and the previous years B.C., before Christ. There might be a day when, just as we are forgetting our pagan ancestors, scholars of the future might even date time some other way, and forget A.D. and B.C. I think that would be a terrible shame, not only to forget our Savior, if that is possible, but to forget those who believed in Him, to forget all of us, the generations who lived for His grace and for the blessings of faith. I will not forget the pagan men who named the red planet Mars or beautiful Venus, or the month of Julius for a long dead emperor, and I long not to be forgotten, though I have done no great thing and am only the humblest novice. I don't have any idea what I would want to be remembered for. Just that I was here.

One cold, dark night in Lent, we stood on a hill outside the city wall where Rotrude loved to go to view the sky. Venus and Jupiter shone enormously. Suddenly a shooting star streaked across the space between the two planets. It broke in half, two blazing flares, before flashing away.

The next day, Fastrada died. The grim days of Lent were mournful. And just as Liutgard lost her mother figure, so I soon lost my father figure. My beloved teacher Alcuin was given the post of abbot, in faraway Tours, his desire fulfilled.

And then a final loss, and I didn't know how final it was when I sat with Liutgard by the fountain and she spoke these words:

"Karl would like to marry me."

I held her hand, which was so cool and soft. I felt aware of her purple sleeves, the gold embroidery at her wrists, the fur trim on her blue mantle. I realized she had slowly been becoming this, a queen, all along.

She could not disappear into the tapestried rooms of the court, into royal duties and protocols, into hunts and travels, into furs and jewels, into dangers and intrigues, spying and secrets. And into motherhood of his children, into his bed. And into the nurturing of his outsized worldly ambitions.

"You can't. You can't possibly," I said.

"You are perverse!" she said with a catch in her voice. "You know all I wanted was to marry into the court. This is the highest honor any woman in the wide world could ever be granted. I am humbled by it. I can only hope to be worthy of the trust of the greatest man in Christendom, the greatest man in history."

"He is not worth your little finger," I exclaimed.

She smiled her rueful, ironic smile. "I don't know what's more bizarre, how well you think of me or how little you think of him."

"You can't do it. You can't go through with it."

"How can I refuse the will of the king, even if I wanted to?" she asked.

"Then I ask that do what you wish, what you truly wish. Forget his armies and his absurd power. You have a will. Is it your will to disappear into the court?"

"I won't disappear."

"I fear you will."

"It is my will, my wish, my heart's desire to marry him."

"This is goodbye, then," I said.

"I hope not."

"You know it is."

She squeezed my hand. Then she leaned against me and put her head on my shoulder.

"I will make sure you aren't forgotten," she said.

"I think you may as well forget me. I wish you were angry with me. That would be easier."

"I am angry!" she exclaimed. She lifted her face and tears fell down her cheeks. "I am most angry."

I took her by the shoulders and held her in front of me. We gazed at each other. Her tear-filled eyes blazed in the sunshine. Then I simply rose and walked away from her, and she made no attempt to follow me.

At the wedding banquet, Liutgard was presented with the falcon from our river journey. She was delighted. This inspired me. That night, I wrote her a letter, knowing she had been learning to read. It was a poem:

> My partner the hunter is a noble bird
> Soaring like a queen and yet is never proud
> Treats me as an equal, though has all skills I lack,
> Returns to me upon my calling word
> And knows me among the motley crowd.
> Never our friendship for any spite detract.
> Like a queen but never a proud word
> Would ever wound or need to be called back,
> Despite her cares and daily hard concerns,
> My inmost heart is always clearly heard,
> And every day I feel my heart's sore lack
> Until her grace on soaring wings returns.

I gave it to Fredigus to give to her. I didn't get a reply, she was so busy with many cares, and sudden news from Rome threw the court into upheaval. Pope Hadrian had died, and the new Pope Leo had been attacked by enemies and thrown into a prison. He asked for Karl's help.

They blinded Leo and injured his tongue, but he made an incredible recovery and made a daring escape from his chains. All the school boys acted it out, playing the great hero Pope Leo. The court went to meet him so that Karl could hear his case. I was vexed that Karl was powerful enough to judge a pope.

From the meeting with Leo they went on to Tours. I wasn't with them, as Daric was too frail to go or for me to leave him. He was balanced on the very edge of sanity, perched there, ever precarious, but holding on. I wondered how to broach to him the possibility of returning to Iona. It had been a year since we parted from the other monks.

In June a strange frost made a bitter landscape over Frankland. Within this cold time, I received a letter from Alcuin at Tours that drove the bitterness deep into my heart.

Dear Little Sparrow,

Let this letter kiss you with peace, and let me utter with ink-stained fingers what I would utter with my lips if you were here. I was going to write to you recommending you travel here, but time has passed too quickly, before I could do so. The queen arrived three weeks ago, and today the king is preparing to return to Aix, alas on his own—though surrounded by loved ones. The queen will not be returning with him, for her soul has returned to its true home. I have heard about the frosts biting our crops and vineyards, and this cold cruelty is a sign. She passed of the sweating sickness, burning amid this cold grip as if God himself were trying to cool her fever. But nothing could be done. My sorrow is great, and I know the news must grieve you, for I noted you and the queen were special friends—I do notice things, old and feeble as I am. Know that God has taken her to his soft bosom, and you will see her again in the hereafter. We will all pray with vigorous and holy energy. I hope time will lessen the sorrow of this day. My heart goes out to you.

Yours in love and friendship, Alcuin

This was the first letter I ever received in my life. The words were fixed in eternal ink, and nothing would ever change them. I sat silently in my room, next to Daric, who was sleeping like a gray ghost by my side. The cold, damp air hurt my throat. I thought there was no one to talk to as I sat staring at the shadows for an hour. Then a soft rap on the door. Isaac entered.

"I heard." He put his arms around me. I couldn't weep, but I shivered, my teeth chattering.

Daric woke and lifted his head. "Where are we going?" he asked absently, from a dream.

"We're going to Rome," Isaac said.

CHAPTER FIVE: ROME

The journey over the Alps gave me some distraction. The mighty hills never end, covered in broad meadows and silver streams, crested with dense, spirit-filled woods, until they rise to sheer rocky, snowy heights above where trees can grow. As we ascended, a cloud enveloped us. Yes, we had walked into the clouds. At one height, when there should have been a magnificent view, the water droplets coated us, and the view came in fragments as the cloud parted here and there, here a meadow below, there a grove of trees by a stream. I thought that is the human view of things, to see only in fragments. We do not have God's view.

It was only on our descent that the clouds did part, and suddenly a forest of mountains broke through to the sky in all directions in dizzying splendor. I tried to forget my sadness, but it can never be entirely healed.

There was some amusement on this journey, when we stayed at inns run by the estates of grand bishops, before we reached the Alps.

Isaac nudged me and said, "Pretend you are my secretary. You'll see some fun."

I followed Isaac to the antechamber of the bishop's room, where the bishop sat on a velvet throne surrounded by men who could have been deacons or courtiers. Isaac made a simple bow and gestured to me to bring him a small box he'd set on a table. He took a few steps toward the bishop, knelt, and opened the box. I expected him to take out a gold ring or an amulet of ivory. Slowly he held up a dead mouse, preserved with spices and painted with red dye.

"I have come from the Orient with this rare object," he said with a voice to inspire wonder. "It is a mummy, a rare specimen, preserved with exotic spices. This rare pet belonged to the most ancient emperor of Egypt, who preserved their bodies and pets in this way. This rare animal led a pampered life and in death is dusted with the powder of crushed rubies. It is an amulet against betrayal and jealousy. Its owner will be blessed with the serenity of kings."

The bishop's eyes were wide. He licked his lower lip and stretched his fingers toward the dangling mouse. Isaac held it just out of his reach.

"I will give you a pound of silver for it," the bishop said breathlessly.

Isaac's eyes popped in his face. "A pound! That doesn't even pay for my trouble! I have traveled five hundred miles!"

I could hear the bishop swallow a big gulp of greedy saliva. "Six pounds of silver."

"Six pounds! I should throw it into the sea rather than let it go at such a price!"

The bishop winced. His breath came in short gasps. The loss of such a prize was too painful to bear. "A measure of silver. A full measure."

Isaac relaxed into a smile. "Truly, that is a bargain, but you are a powerful man of your church, and I am humbly glad to offer you such a bargain." He dropped the mouse back into the box and closed it. Then he stood, walked to the bishop, and presented him the box with a deep bow.

That night at dinner, another feast, Karl tapped his knife against his silver cup and got the attention of the room.

"I understand our great host has acquired a fabulous token, to show all the world his prestige. His vow of poverty didn't prevent him from paying a measure of silver for this wondrous object." The king had the silver box beside him, and he stood, dangling the stuffed mouse from his fingers. The table roared with laughter, and the bishop's face burned red in shame.

We stopped several nights on our journey at bishops' estates, and Isaac and the king played the mouse trick every time. The court laughed harder each time and never tired of it as we made our way to Rome.

Rome is a dark city, smoky, a city falling in on itself. Though it is a large city, larger than Aix, it has clearly been larger in the past, and its depopulation has turned its grand, mighty buildings into crumbling shells. Gorgeous fountains no longer flow with water. Marble columns hold up roofless temples. Walls repaired with rough brick are stained with the soot of open fires. I saw a man tear the arms off the lovely white statue of a pagan goddess and cast them into the lime furnace. Everywhere something was being burned or melted, and whereas Aix is a city in a state of construction, Rome is in a state of demolition. How far the mighty have fallen.

It was sickly warmish, though winter was coming. There was a prodigious amount of rats. The lack of a bracing winter means the city can't be rid of a certain pestilence. Bishop Arno, the friend of Alcuin he nicknamed the Eagle, tried to point out to me the newly restored churches, paid for by recent popes and especially Karl, but I saw only the poor remains of its former glory.

But when we arrived at mighty Saint Peter's, it did give me hope for the power of the church. A fifth of Rome's population can fit inside, and there are as many golden and red marble pillars as there are monks on Iona. The pillars made me think of the standing stones at Kilmartin, stones raised by the faithful for their God. In the vast hall, the monks' choir voices echoed like a thousand reeds of a marsh on a summer's night.

There was one distraction for me. A great mosaic over the altar showed Constantine and Saint Peter presenting a model of this church to Christ. And I thought, in that model is a mosaic of the saints presenting a model to Christ, and in *that* model is the same mosaic, and on and on, and I didn't know how it could end. I pondered it a while until I felt too stupid to think about it anymore.

The Romans who had behaved treacherously to Pope Leo cowered in their homes at our arrival, but Karl's soldiers forced them out. They were frightened at the Pope's recovery. A kind of trial was assembled, and the Pope defended himself against the charges of corruption that had led to his overthrow. Some of his accusers were stricken mad at the awesome sight of Karl holding court in the church, others were arrested for treason against the church, and Pope Leo was restored. Most of Rome pretended they had never conspired against him, and in the end there was a general celebration.

When we entered Italy we had stopped at the monastery of Bobbio, where we picked up two monks who became my companions. Lantfrid and Sigimund wanted to bring back relics from Rome, so we searched about for a dealer in such things. We explored the city while Daric prayed all day. Isaac was very busy with his trade and left us to find what we needed for ourselves. I was still looking for the lapis as well.

My companions' innocent enthusiasm only reminded me of the world's deceitfulness. We found our way to a little church that we heard had relics to trade. I was not encouraged by the dark, dirty street we walked down. Across the street a woman leaned out of a window and waved to us. My companions didn't notice, but I noticed every broken window, dirty child, and hungry dog that followed us.

The priest met us at the back door of his humble room adjoining the church. From the dark street, it was a little velvet-lined jewel box. There was a couch with deep cushions, a gleaming table and an inlaid chest. Red curtains hung over the passage to the church. We sat on a bench, feeling too humble for the couch, and he took a silver box from the chest.

He waved his pudgy hand over the box to reveal a bone with a nail through it. "This is the crucified wrist of Saint James."

The monks beamed. "How glorious. May we touch it?" They picked it up and looked at it, enraptured.

I had my suspicions. The bone looked too thick to be a wrist bone. This looked like an ox bone. The priest caught my eye and must have read my face.

"We Christians must have faith and trust each other," he said. "I am putting my trust in you by inviting you in."

"Of course," said Brother Sigimund. "How much is it?"

I knew I would not dissuade them. I wish he had offered a small amount rather than ask how much.

"It is very precious. Because you are holy men, I ask only eight deniers."

The monks looked at each other. I knew we each had three deniers, and I didn't offer them mine.

"We were hoping to get more than one relic," said Brother Lantfrid.

"Ah. Well, we might be able to strike a bargain. Don't be anxious."

I interrupted. I didn't want to watch. "Do you know where I might be able to obtain lapis, for painting?"

The priest put a pudgy finger to his badly shaved chin. "I have none, but I believe there is a woman named Felicia across the street who trades in minerals from time to time. I'll send my boy to take you."

He picked up a little bell and rang it. In a moment a boy stepped through the curtains.

"Take the good Brother over to Felicia."

The boy bowed and led me down the alley to a staircase, and we went up. He knocked what seemed like a special knock, two quick taps, a pause, and another tap. The door opened.

Inside, four men sat around a table throwing dice. A woman stood over them, pouring wine into their cups. She was young but worn-out, looking older than her years, I could tell, thin, with lines around her large brown eyes. She wore a blue silk dress and a clean white veil.

The boy said, "This is Brother Cellach from Scotia, seeking lapis, Madame Felicia."

I didn't know how the boy knew everything about me, but I was not entirely surprised. It was the business of the priest, the dealers of Roman relics, the purveyors of wanted items, to know all, for their advantage.

She gave me a small, modest smile that had a touch of mourning to it. She set down her jug. "I'm sorry. I don't have lapis, but I expect it soon. Is there anything else I can provide you with? Vermillion, orpiment?" She opened the drawer of a high chest. Minerals were neatly arrayed, some in glass jars, some in clay, most still in rock form.

"The lapis is all I require."

"If you were to give me a down payment, I could make sure you were the first to get it."

"How much would it be, in total?"

"Five deniers."

"It's too much. Especially as my companions are spending what they have on your friend's relic of a nail through an ox bone."

She smiled mournfully again. "Friend is a strong word. I understand. He makes us honest traders look bad, and he annoys me because of it. I can see you're irritated. Sit down and take a little wine."

I felt a little ashamed for my attitude, so I sat away from the gamblers and had a cup. She sat on a low stool beside me, and I looked down on her. She seemed so small and young, though also old beyond her years.

"If your friends are cheated, I will arrange a trade for an honest relic," she said.

"Why?"

"Some things should not be trivialized that way. I am a Christian, too."

I drank and felt a little cheered for the first time since arriving in Rome.

"Have you seen the sights yet?" she asked.

"I've seen a filthy, grasping city."

"Meet me tomorrow after the mass at Saint Peter's. I'll give you and your companions a tour. You can't come all this way and miss the holy places."

I finished my drink. "You are very kind. I must return to my friends now. Perhaps we will see you tomorrow."

"I hope so."

She rang her own little bell, and the boy returned to accompany me to the priest, and we returned to our lodgings. I was further cheered to see the brothers were as yet empty-handed.

The next day was sunny and my mood continued to lift. We spent the day touring the sites with Felicia. I had to admit that in this dirty and crumbling city, there were monumental sites and beautiful carvings and statues. It was a bit strange, the former glory of the city visible through its sooty surface like a ghost or a dream.

My favorite place and source of astonishment was the Pantheon. It was one of the few ancient buildings mostly intact. I stood under the bright oculus of the dome, staring up in wonder. The coffered ceiling was so uniform and stunning in its simplicity, leading to that circle opening to the sky. I sometimes went and stayed all day just to watch the sun move and the shadows change around the interior. Other times, if it rained, I stood under it and let the shower cleanse me of sin. For I was soon a terrible sinner.

At times Daric joined us. He had spent some time acquiring knowledge of the proper Roman chant, to teach our brothers on our return. The monks of Scotia and Britain were eager to learn the proper way. On our outings, Daric stared hard at any carving of the Madonna and child, lost in his concentration. He spoke little; he was our shadow, and he felt to me like the shadowy spirit of Rome's former might.

Felicia took us to the prison where Saint Paul was martyred, and the Coliseum, where so many good Christians met their terrible deaths. She asked me about the saints of Scotia and listened attentively about Brigid and Kevin, Brendan, and others. Once in a while, Daric muttered a saint's name, a few words about their story, trailing off, his voice melting in the smoky air.

I accompanied Felicia back to her dwelling after a tour we took alone one day. I told her I was in a quandary about the fact that a monk was not to be alone with a woman.

"We're in public. We are certainly not alone together. And you strike me as independent and not one to fuss over small rules," she said. "Surely a Christian man would not allow me to walk the streets alone?"

She had a point, and we made our way in the lengthening shadows of the short winter's day, chatting about Rome's history. We were chuckling over some witticism I had pleased her with when we stepped inside. She gave a little cry.

The furniture was up-ended, and the drawers of the chest hung open, empty. She ran around the room and looked in every drawer and box. All her treasures were gone. She sat on the edge of her bed and cried unto her hands.

"These are only things. Things aren't so important. Money is not so important," I said, thinking to comfort her.

She wiped her cheeks and spoke in a dry voice. "This isn't the country, where women can grow their food. This is the city. In the city money is a necessity. I've lost all my trade. How will I live? How will I eat?"

I took out my three deniers and pressed them into her hand.

"I can't take it," she said. "You are kind, but I won't beg."

Felicia leaned over and put her head on my shoulder. I put my arm around her. She pressed herself against me.

"It's frightening to be a woman alone."

Her face was close to mine. "Don't be afraid," I said, feeling that she saw me as a man, a protective man.

I kissed her cheek. She pressed her cheek into mine. I could smell roses. I held her in my arms, and then, to my shame, I kissed her lips. To my shame we fell across the bed, and I did shameful things, and it wasn't even dark yet. I could see her rosy face, and somehow it was all less secret and more shameful for that.

Afterward we lay in each other's arms, and she told me of her dead husband and her difficult struggle until she had established her trade. She was ashamed of some of her life, and she had made a vow to be a good Christian. I listened and fell in love. She was so sweet and strong. I thought of my dear Liutgard, who was so like a sister to me and whom I grieved. I thought she would approve of this determined woman, making her way independently and alone in the world.

There was a pause, and I wanted to ask her many questions that I dared not ask. Then she said, "There is a way I can recover. When I started out, I would have gambling—as you saw, men still like to come here to gamble. They trust me. They'll trust you." Then she unveiled her scheme to use my innocent face to lure men to gamble, and to take a percentage of what I would win by cheating. She knew all the ways to cheat at gambling. "It's not moral, but it would be better than, than—than—" and a tear fell down her cheek.

I held her closely. "All right. I'll do it, just for a few days."

She gave me her mournful smile again. "We have an expression here: When in Rome, do as the Romans do."

to see the great king of Christendom receive the host. Some-where behind the altar a small bell was struck, a delicate tinkle that managed to sound above the rest. And somehow, by some sleight of hand, the Pope was no longer holding up the host. In his hands was a golden crown.

"I bless you, Holy Emperor of the Romans," he said in Latin. He placed the crown on Karl's head.

The music swelled to a crescendo as a dull roar rose from the crowd. Karl stood and stiffly walked back through the crowd. Everyone wanted to touch him as he passed.

I left in wonder. What did it mean? With my companions later we discussed this turn of events. We thought it spoke of the great power of Pope Leo, that he could declare a man an emperor. This cemented his place as being above a mere king or earthly ruler. I went to bed satisfied with this thought. We also heard that Karl was telling people he never would have gone to the service if he'd known what Leo had planned.

The next morning my head ached, as the ale had flowed the night before. I was about to go out to a bath when Isaac surprised me at my door.

"I was supposed to give you this today. I was to save it. I'm sorry, as I have a feeling it will be bittersweet for you."

It was a letter with a red seal. I invited him in while I read it. Small, careful letters greeted me, only the second letter I had ever received.

My dearest Brother Cellach,

If you read this now, then I am passed on to the glory of Heaven, yet live a while longer in this letter. How wondrous learning is, that our words can defy death. This token must mean more than a lock of hair or a ring, which cannot speak. I have your poem, which speaks to me so beautifully, and I have Gisela read it to me every day.

You were right, I didn't anticipate my daily cares and duties that have kept me from you. I had hoped there would be time. But time is slipping away.

I hope you are in Rome, and I instructed this to be given to you there. On the day of our Lord's birth, our great king has been crowned emperor. It will seem a great surprise, and a triumph of both men, but especially of papal power that can declare a man king of the world, over the Greeks of Constantinople, over any dukes and nobles that rival him in Frankland or Italy, over as yet unconquered pagans in the wilderness between East and West. And thus the Church holds that power over him, to be able to grant him that power as an instrument of God. Karl is doubtless complaining, and assuming modesty, and saying he didn't want this high and possibly dubious honor.

You should know the truth. It was all arranged at Paderborn. Karl required this of the pope, in return for his support. Karl has placed Leo in the Holy See, and both men have spurned permission from Constantinople for anything. Both men are the highest of the high, but it was Karl's will that he should be declared emperor, and his might that makes Pope Leo.

Perhaps I tell you this out of spite. But no, for I know truth is your highest value, and as you search out the world looking for the truth of how things work, you must know this. I know wherever this truth leads you, however it hurts, it's better than not knowing.

I think of I regret our arguments, which began in enjoyable debate. I never meant our sparring to divide us. The debate soured as wine turns into vinegar. No one should hold a philosophy above friendship.

Know that I love you, dear little brother, teacher, confessor and confidante. I will not live to see your smiling face or hear your teasing words. I forgive you anything, if any forgiveness is required, and I pray you forgive me as well.

Pray for my soul. God keep you and bless you on your long journey. There is no more to say.

With love in my heart,

Liutgard, Queen of the Franks.

Isaac put his arm around me. I leaned against him, my head pounding. "Why is a letter always such a terrible thing?" I asked.

"Still, it is a wonderful thing to have her voice again."

I nodded while silent tears slipped from my eyes.

By day I learned the arts of dice and knucklebones, by night gambled with vagabonds and pilgrims. I lost some of the time, enough that no one noticed that I won more than I lost. Slowly we accumulated coins, and on days that I wasn't with her, my brothers and I shopped in the city for more relics. I didn't rush to buy, for I wanted us to find something truly special.

At night after gambling, Felicia and I ate feasts of roast chicken with olives and lemons, which I grew very fond of. Felicia didn't always have me come to gamble. She said she didn't want to arouse suspicions. As the weeks wore on, her putting me off became more frequent, and I wondered jealously what she might be doing. I still lay with her many nights, to my shame. But in time she started to pick quarrels with me, and I was puzzled by her change.

One morning, early, when it was still dark out, Brother Lantfrid arrived at our room at the Scots Inn. I wasn't aware he had been slipping out at night because, after my own prowls, I slept heavily. He whispered my name, and I was wide awake. I sat up and he sat beside me.

"I need advice." His voice was heavy. He had been drinking; the drink was wearing off but he was tired and sluggish.

"What is it?"

"This poor woman, a dear friend I've met. You remember her, she showed us around that day. She has been robbed of her carefully gathered treasures. She is a shopkeeper, dealing in various things including inks and paints. I sought to surprise you by getting the lapis. We returned from praying in the church, and her place was ransacked. The intruder must have just left."

I went cold. "Go on."

"Now she has asked me a favor. No, favor is too kind a word. She has asked me, begged me, to help her cheat people in order to win back the money to replace her merchandise. She says my innocent face and monks' robes will fool people. I do feel for her, but it would be a crime and a sin. She cried piteously. What shall I do?"

He slumped over and lay across my bed. I pulled him up and doused him with a pitcher of water.

"You will do nothing, and never see this sinful woman again."

I threw on my shoes and robe and ran outside. By then I knew the dark, damp streets well. A thin black cat ran by with a rat in its maw. The dirty windows leaked soot through their cracks. A sick man groaned in pain from behind a door. The brick and crumbling marble of the city was cold and frosted.

I got to her door and stood before it. I could leave without seeing her, never see her again. My use was over. And what use was she to me? Why had I let her seduce me? But it was not she that seduced me. She was not to blame for my sin. I should leave and make confession, expiate my wrongs and sin no more. There was forgiveness for me, and for her, too, if she cared.

But still I was angry. Perhaps in pride I had felt that it should be my decision to break it off, when I felt like it, and here she was, set to replace me without a word. Did I think I was special? I must have felt something like that. I felt the anger of wounded pride. And despite what she was, I cared for her, in my lonely state. Rome especially was lonely in its decay, in the bareness of its past glory now stripped and moldered and empty. And she was all Rome had to offer me.

When I entered her house, she was straightening the place from its ransacked condition, pushing in drawers and righting chests. She looked displeased to see me and concentrated on her tasks.

"I know about Lantfrid. He is my friend."

"I don't know what you mean."

I took her by the shoulders, and she knew better than to oppose me. When she gazed in my eyes, hers were hard and cold.

"I won't let you corrupt him, too. He truly is innocent."

"More than you," she said, and I knew to my relief she hadn't lain with him. She shook her head and a small, cruel smile formed at the corners of her mouth. "What did you think? What did you really think?" she asked.

"That you cared for me."

There was a short laugh, but on seeing my face she stopped herself. "I can't afford to care. This is Rome. This isn't a backwater farm or monastery. Why? Did you think we were going to be married? You, a child monk?"

I let go of her and sat down on the chest. "Of course not. I only wanted to believe you cared. Nothing more, or less."

Her face softened for a moment. For a moment, there was a look that was affectionate and a little rueful, and I thought she allowed herself a moment of regret for living as she did. She poured us each a cup of wine, and we drank in silence. The silence and the way we shared it mattered more to me than any words she could have said.

"It's time for you to go," she said when the wine was gone.

"Thank you," I said, not sure of what I was thanking her for, and I left.

I was through with Rome.

## CHAPTER SIX: UNMOORED

We did find a proper relic for my two companions, a finger bone that could have been from Saint Clement. At least it was from a human being. I still had not found lapis. Daric had acquired a notebook in which he spent time drawing pictures of the monuments and carvings of the city. He was very talented and Einhard, Karl's dwarf secretary, assigned him to continue these drawings for Karl himself. The work seemed to absorb him, which was a relief to me. But I didn't know what he would do when it would be time to return without the object of our quest.

As Karl started to make plans to leave Rome and return to Aix, Isaac joined me in a bath. There were not many functioning baths in the city, but I had found one that was crumbling less than the others. The water was not particularly hot, but it was better than nothing. I leaned back and stared up at the mosaics of cupids and Venus.

"I have a surprise for you," Isaac said.

"I don't think I can take another surprise."

Isaac waved his hand. "Karl Rex is sending me on a mission to Arabia, to tell their king Harun about his elevation to emperor."

I closed my eyes. "Will you write to me afterward and tell me what it was like?"

Water trickled past my ears. He had cupped some water in his hand and poured it over my head. I rubbed my scalp where it tickled and turned to him. In the gloom his smile beamed.

"Why don't you and the old man come with me?"

I choked a little. "All that way? I don't know if Daric could make it."

"He is as strong as a leather cord."

I thought about it a moment, then laughed.

Karl was sending gifts to the great king of Arabia, to try to impress him. There were bolts of fine wool, some silver things, wine, and a brace of hunting dogs. I was to watch the dogs, which I enjoyed. We set off in a caravan south to Napoli. Along the way, Daric picked up a small brown bird, which he kept in his sleeve and fed berries that he gathered.

We wound among steep hills that changed often. Some had evergreens, some olive groves. The plains were green, the air was rather dry compared to home, and the light was strong. Now that we were out of Rome, I liked Italy.

We took ship from Napoli, a stone city clinging to cliffs above the sea. This was a proper ship, even bigger than the one from Frisia, and its motion through the water was smooth. As we cast off and sailed the sapphire blue water, I wanted to laugh again as the wind buffeted my face. This was madness! What was I doing? What must they think at Iona, that I had still not returned? Before we left Rome, I asked Bishop Arno to send a letter to Abbot Connachtach about my continuing journey. When I told Daric we were going to Arabia to get the lapis, his eyes lit up with joy, though he only made a small sound like a whispering ghost. Was I so different from the maddened old monk? He was driven on, to obtain the lapis. And I was driven on. I was drunk with a kind of freedom to wander, but I was driven by my own kind of madness, the craving to know the wide world, to drink it in like an intoxicating elixir. To think my purpose was for the old monk would be lying to myself. I felt during this part of the journey quite disconnected from my own past and the life before this wandering. I was unmoored from land, from all, from myself.

We sailed by islands dark with trees, not like the smooth bare islands of home. When we landed at night to take on food and water and walk a bit, the houses and walls on shore were all white, bright as stars. It grew warmer each day.

Among the Greek islands we picked up Christopher, a doctor who was traveling to Baghdad to learn of their surgery and medicine. He was a learned man, bald as if tonsured but‚still young, with an eager intellect. He quickly observed how Daric sat muttering prayers to himself with vacant eyes, and I told him of the tragedy. He spoke gently with the old monk, telling him of the islands we passed by and Greek legends.

On one shore where we stopped for provisions, there were mighty bones along a cliff that the Greeks say belong to the skeleton of Achilles. Christopher examined them.

"They are not human, but a great reptile from before the flood," he told me.

We discussed these ancient beasts, and I told him of Columba's encounter with the ancient sea monster in Loch Ness.

But what was even more strange: we climbed the mountain at Delphi to see the ruins, and there stood a statue that our guide told us represented the navel of the world, as the Greeks believe Delphi to be. Isn't Jerusalem the navel of the world, the very center? It gave me pause.


On a glorious, sunny morning onboard the ship, I heard something bump. A piece of wood knocked against our hull. There were more. They were charred. The sea was thick with debris.

Then the first body floated toward us. His neck was slashed, and his head angled away from his shoulders. He was not very bloated, had not been long in the sea. Other men rolled by in the debris of charred wood, broken pots and vessels, rent sails, loaves of bread, and other broken things. Gulls swarmed the carnage like the Morrigan. I felt I must be dreaming.

One man lay on a board staring up. Our eyes met and he blinked. His mouth trembled.

"Here's one alive!" I shouted.

Some of the crew and the doctor ran to the side. We threw him a line, but he was half-dead and couldn't grasp it. I decided quickly, and stripped to my linens and dove in. I grabbed the line and swam with it, wrapped it around the man, and knotted it. They pulled and I pushed until we hauled him aboard.

The man's breath came out like air from a bladder, creaking, crackling. The doctor pushed hard against his stomach, and he vomited some water. His wet clothes were pulled off and the doctor checked his wounds, which were light, now pink and puffy from the sea water. Salve was brought and linen dressing. We wrapped him in my wool scapula.

The crew kept their eyes on the sea for more signs of life, but he was the only survivor. We took turns watching over him as he slipped in and out of awareness, not speaking, his breath gasping and labored.

After a day and night, he sat up and took some wine. Daric came over and showed him his little bird, which still lived in his sleeve. The man's eyes grew misty and he held the little bird close to his mouth awhile before giving it back. Then he told his story in a hoarse groaning voice, which Isaac translated.

"We were a trading vessel, going from Marseilles to Alexandria. Devils, devils…" He had to stop and breathe. "Pirates from the heathen land. They held our ship with grappling hooks and leaped aboard with swords, long, thin curved blades, sharp as razors. It was all so fast, so fast, though it seemed like hours and days too." He had to rest. We prayed together, and he mouthed the words with us.

Later as he slept, I interrupted Isaac at his ledger. He kept busy as if nothing had passed.

"Is this common?" I asked.

He shrugged. "Not as much as it once was. Karl has made progress combating the pirates."

His casual attitude added a sense of disorientation to my growing terror. "We are in danger."

He pointed up at the mast. "I fly the banner of their people. We are under Harun's protection."

"They don't sound so discriminating as to respect a flag."

"I can't offer you comfort. It's a dangerous world."

I didn't sleep that night. Whenever I dozed off, I saw the bodies again. I strained to listen for unfamiliar sounds. By day I found myself jumping at the familiar. There was nowhere I could go, I was trapped on the boat. The sun crept across the sky torturously slow as I waited for landfall.

There was something else too. I felt rage and hatred for these godless heathens. Unable to contain it, I asked Isaac for a weapon that I could kill these devils with if they attacked.

"Did you feel this way when the raiders from the North attacked Lindisfarne monastery?"

"I wasn't there."

"As a monk, you are forbidden to fight."

"There must be retribution. There must be blood."

"Such a feeling can never be quenched," he said. "Your religion is supposed to give you the answers you seek. I cannot teach it to you." He fixed his eye on me. "You surprise me."

I was surprised at myself. I hardly knew myself, and I told him so.

"You have confessors in your church? Find one, then. I'm a realistic man, and my trade involves risk. I'm not one who can help you."

I paced on the deck. When we had set off, I felt free and unattached on the boat in the sea, so apart from the world. Now it was fearsome, to be cut off from the world, naked and vulnerable on our tiny boat in the great sea. Where were we going? We were sailing into the unknown. It was impossible to know what might happen, and somehow my fearful ignorance of my fate was internally being isolated on the sea, cut off from my brothers in mankind.

After pacing about on the deck, I went to Christopher, who was writing in a little notebook. He set it down and gave me a tired smile. I told him my violent feelings.

"Death comes to all," he said. "It could come in the way you fear, at the hands of the heathen, or in a raid from the white men of the North. It could come in illness or in a sudden bursting of the heart. But it will come. One must have faith and be prepared."

By saying these things aloud, I understood my own feelings better. "It's not that I'm afraid to die. But to die in surprise, unarmed and vulnerable, in an unjust way. I can accept a just death, but not to be cut down in a senseless act of brutality."

"God is never unjust."

"But men are."

He thought about this and rubbed the graying hair of his beard. He looked out at the sea, blue as a sapphire, the sky above a brighter lapis blue, with some great white clouds, mighty and majestic. He said, "The important thing isn't to avoid one's fate, whatever it is—though in the end one's fate is always death. The important thing is to die knowing you always did your duty to man and God. Then you will die with grace."

These were wise words, but they did little to calm my simmering blood. Suddenly he grabbed my arm and squeezed it, and pointed out to the sea. "The important thing is to know death comes, perhaps on that ocean, and to still *see* it, to see God's creation. To imagine nothing about what is before you, to look and not see the possibilities you fear, but to see it as it is *now*, *these* blue waves, *that* blue sky."

I stared out at the deep water and felt the fresh sting of the sea on my cheeks.

We anchored at Caesarea on the coast of the Arab lands and changed our rags of wool for smooth, light cotton clothing as their people wear. Isaac busied himself arranging for a camel caravan while Christopher, who knew their language, stayed with us to be our guide.

I had heard of camels from the Bible. I had no idea they were so ugly and smelled so bad. They were astounding.

The night before we were to cross the desert, Daric held my hands and said, "I had a vision: that I will die in this land. But God will keep his promise to me, and I will keep my promise, that we will find the lapis and honor Mary. We will go to the very womb of our religion, and God is pleased." His face was shadowed and creased with pain. His soft, weak voice reminded me of the wind in a seashell.

The sky over the desert was the kind of sky that creates prophets. Of course people founded religions here. The blazing stars seemed to roar in the inky blackness, a kind of silent roar, if that makes sense, for the silence swallowed all of us, small figures in the vast rolling landscape.

One night something woke me. I sat up, sensing something was wrong. Somehow I could see a shadow stirring away from the camp. I recognized that shadow. I hurried up to Daric.

"Where are you going?" I put my hand on his shoulder, but he didn't stop.

"I asked Isaac if we are going to stop in Jerusalem and he said no. We must go to Jerusalem. It will be a blessing."

"I'm sure we are going to Jerusalem. Come, we must go back."

But he wouldn't stop, walking quickly. I had to keep up, but we were getting further from our camp. I was afraid to tackle him and carry him back, if I even could have.

"Let me lead," I said, thinking I could pretend to take him to Jerusalem and lead him back to camp.

But he didn't reply or stop. I was frightened but helpless. I couldn't leave him to die in the desert.

"We don't know the way. We must trust our guides." I grasped him firmly by the shoulders.

He threw me off with surprising force, so that I fell at his feet. He stood over me. "I trust in God!" he shouted.

"We can try together to persuade Isaac to take us."

"We don't need to bother with him." Daric began to walk away again, quickly. I bounded after him.

"God sent us Isaac for us to put our faith in," I said. All the while Daric continued to march away. I had to trot to keep up. "Please, Brother Daric. We will die here."

"I do not question God's protection." That was his last statement as I continued to plead, and it was not long before I knew I'd lost a sense of where our camp was.

Still he went on, with me following, my pleas dying in my throat because it was so soon too late. I was being led by a madman.

We walked north, guided by the stars, until sunrise flamed the red cliffs. We were in a valley. The place was desolate, and I knew no one would come after us. We had no water. We stopped as the rising sun pressed on us. At last he was tired enough to sleep, and we lay down in the shadow of a cliff. As he slept I tried to think, but my head pounded in the blazing sun. I had driven him on this journey with the promise of lapis. With desperate tears I thought how it was I who had led him, because I wanted to see the wide world. He was not the madman. I was not his victim. In reality I had used him, and it was I who was mad. It was my fault. My mad desire to find some kind of secret knowledge of the world might kill us both. I was to blame and I deserved this punishment.

We rose and as I stretched and looked up, I saw a shadow heading up the side of the cliff that looked like it could be a track. We followed it until I had to stop and retch.

"We should wait until night, when it's cool," Daric said.

"We'll lose the track if we do."

We walked on and found some camel feces. But how old were they? They would be preserved forever here.

As the sun set I saw what made my heart leap: a village of mud-brick buildings. I started to run, but Daric couldn't keep up. We hurried together as best we could. An hour passed, then another. The sun set.

"We'll be there tomorrow," Daric said.

We slept by the track, but the next morning the village had disappeared. It was a delusion.

My breath rasped in my dry, aching throat. I couldn't speak anymore and didn't want to. I prayed silently. I begged. *Let us come to a house, let us be found, let Isaac have sent someone after us. Let us find a well, just a well, Lord, just a pool to drink. Nothing more. No riches, no powers, no fine meals or fresh clothes, but a pool of water to drink, and enough besides to soak my cracked feet. Nothing more.*

"We are like Moses," Daric said with a small smile. I wanted to kill him, not only for leading me to my death, but because he was happy and made no apology. But later he started retching, too.

I held him and we stood up, leaning against each other. His breath stunk. We both were rank, the smell of life melting into death. I thought perhaps someone could find us, following this smell.

When I looked up from his shoulder, my heart stopped. On the horizon blowing up from the orange sand was a cloud like a vision of the end of the world. It filled the horizon, a brown and tan, slow moving creature coming toward us. At first it was eerily silent, like a dream as it rolled over the waves of desert. Then the wind came. We heard it before we felt it, like the ocean. Daric turned to look.

He took a few steps forward and raised his arms level with his shoulders like a cross, in prayer. I let him go, moving back and cowering by a hill. The cloud continued slowly, relentlessly. It only seemed slow; it was actually moving quickly.

Circling clouds of grit threw the desert into our mouths and eyes. The world shifted all around us. I thought we were dying now, and that this wind would sail us up to heaven, if we deserved it. Or that this sandstorm was purgatory and we would spend lifetimes crouched in the heat, sand sticking to our sweaty faces.

When it came, I didn't expect it to blot out the sun, but we were locked in darkness. The air was pitch black, and I lost sight of Daric. I didn't call because I didn't want a mouthful of sand. I could only crouch, aching to hold my stiff position. I only knew I was alive because my body hurt.

When it subsided, the sun had set, a different darkness, bright with starlight.

Daric sat with his legs crossed, still as a stone, his eyes closed. I didn't know if he slept. The moon rose, like a great dove, its light spilling like a path over the desert. I wanted to walk up it. I couldn't hide from the moon and stars that knew all. It was my fault, and neither my hatred nor my shame made any difference. I felt ready to die and face God. I recalled Christopher saying *now* and *this*. The world was mad and beautiful, I was mad and small.

Nothing mattered except perhaps I had failed to obtain the lapis, my only mission and excuse for this mad journey. That alone resolved me to live, not to die yet or let the old man die.

When the sun rose he opened his eyes, nodded with a beaming smile, his face sunburned and wind burned as mine was. I didn't smile and I didn't know what to say. The sandstorm had covered the track we were following. We started walking in a direction that was perhaps northeast, the sun pounding on us.

Since I am telling you my story, you know I survived. That afternoon towards sunset we heard tramping feet and camel hooves. A shadow appeared, kicking up dust. I couldn't run to it or cry for help. I didn't know if it was another dream. But they came, and we met. There were six men with their camels. We didn't have to tell them our desperate state. Saying little, they gave us a skin of water to drink, and without shame I sucked like a baby.

They spoke among themselves, and one man motioned to us to follow. The rest of the group went on in the direction they were headed, and the one man led us in the direction from where they came. By sunset we came to a village with a few green trees and wells.

At first, as we entered the man's cool, dark house, and sat on soft cushions, and had our feet washed by a sweet girl child, I forgot to thank God. I was still angry with Daric. I wanted him to apologize. To say *something*.

He turned to me as our feet were washed and took the bird out of his sleeve. The bird lived. And then tears came to me and I remembered God, and it was I who wanted to apologize to Daric, I wasn't sure for what—for hating him—and I shook and cried.

The girl finished washing our feet, ignoring my tears, and she reached for the bird on Daric's finger. It hopped onto hers, and she held it to her cheek with a smile. Her father entered and said something to the child, a rebuke. She cast down her eyes and held the bird out for Daric to take.

Daric looked up at the father and gestured with a flourish to the girl and with both hands placed the bird in her hands, presenting it to her. She looked up at her father with an expression of

question and pleading. The father shrugged, smiled, and spoke to
Daric with seeming thanks. The girl spoke too, a rush of grateful
words to both of them, and she left the room cradling her prize.

We ate a meal, joined by a large group of men. Heavily veiled
women served the platters but didn't eat with us.

Daric said to the man, "Jerusalem? Can we go to *Jerusalem?*"
emphasizing it in the hopes that the man would know this name.
The man held his hands palm downward and lowered them, to
indicate there was nothing to worry about.

We rested, sometimes glimpsing the girl with her bird. Mostly
we sat in a courtyard by a decorative pool. I was still shaken, but
I gradually composed myself.

As I recovered from the horror of our lost days, I became more
aware of my surroundings. Now that I had water, the dry sun was
pleasing. The house with its thick walls and deep windows was
peaceful. What I noticed most were the wonderful smells. The
main smell I remembered from long ago was the tang of peat.
These were different spice scents that made my mouth water.
The warm taste of the food, coated brown in these ground seeds,
inexplicably cooled me. When I was finally past my trauma, I
felt I could live there and perhaps not miss the cold rain and
insinuating fog of home. I couldn't depend on being taken in by
strangers here. When Daric said, "Jerusalem," the man nodded
and gestured as if to say, "yes." This man might take us to Jerusalem, but then what? We were still without our guides. At least,
though, there were Christians there and possibly people we could
communicate with in Latin. And I knew even here there were
monasteries, the Nestorians. I wondered if Daric and I could be
accepted by them. It would mean never going home, but at this
point, the fact that we were alive and had met with such kindness
was all that mattered. The generosity of these people, their smiling acceptance of taking us in, strangers who must have seemed
like some kind of ghostly spirits in the desert, is something I'll
never forget or neglect to be grateful for.

The next day we set out, though we didn't know where we
were being taken. He did seem to recognize the word "Jerusalem,"

and I could only trust he was taking us there. From Jerusalem, then what? The same man led us, in silence. We traveled lightly, with one camel packed with blankets, bread and water. Daric seemed happy, appearing even justified with his mad journey, taking jaunty steps.

We were marching where religions were born. The burning sun's rays were like a chorus of voices preaching of a jealous, furious god. Here is where hardened anchorites turn into bone and sinew. What else was there to do here? Our old pagan religions were rich with gods, myriad spirits, stories of selkies and swan maidens, magic wells and green men. But here this desert only gives us a burning bush to look into, among rocks and dry shrubs, under the single burning fire of the sun. It did seem like this was Daric's land, suiting his obsession.

Then suddenly, we crested the hill of Zion, and Jerusalem glowed below us in the twilight, made of golden stone under a purple sky. I caught my breath at the Bible made real, this compact city between two ravines, mighty in history but modest after all. It is a city of staircases, making me think of Jacob's ladder and the many metaphors of stairs to the stars of heaven.

As we descended the hill, I heard dogs barking. I was sure they were the dogs Karl had sent Harun. We came to an inn and there was Isaac, sitting outside with Christopher and our guides, drinking dark brown liquor from tiny cups. He laughed when he saw us.

"Marvelous! You've found us! We didn't know where you had gone, and we had no idea in what direction to look."

"You told Daric we weren't going to Jerusalem."

"I wanted to surprise you."

I laughed like a madman until I sank to the ground.

We toured the holy places over the ensuing days, visiting the Church of the Nativity. There are not that many Christians left in Jerusalem, and its adjoining monastery has only a few monks. It was felled by an earthquake thirty years ago, but Karl, his reach seemingly endless, had sent funds to rebuild it, Karl's mighty cranes standing tall even here.

Outside Jerusalem we stayed in a Nestorian monastery, where the monks had been spending their days in copying ancient manuscripts for Harun's great library in Baghdad. These manuscripts were even older than Augustine or Jerome. They copied the pages not onto vellum, but onto paper made from wood pulp, telling us the Arabs learned about it from the Far East. It is durable and light, a little rough, and it does burn easily. But it can be made in great quantities. They let me have some, and I made some notes about my journey so far. I wished I could write a letter to Connachtach on it, to share it with him, but I didn't think it would get all the way back to Iona.

It was time for the last push of our journey, on to Baghdad.

## CHAPTER SEVEN: BAGHDAD

On the horizon was something white that I mistook for a bright cloud. It was the curving wall of Baghdad.

The call of their wailing prayer rang out, and we stopped for it. I sensed the stillness inside the wall as the whole city bowed, facing in one direction. When the wail ceased and there was a kind of hum rising again from within, we continued. The wall curved as if scribed by a compass, encircling the round city.

Baghdad is a new city. It sparkles white, clean as a bleached bone. The roads spiral like a shell, and in its center are towers with tops like onions. Fountains sparkle, raining over blue and green tiles. Boys and men smiled at us as they played or went about their business. There were few women on the street.

All seemed peaceful and serene. It was crowded, but the city was organized with a place for the market and places of other business and crafts, so that there wasn't the pageant of chaotic activity like in Aix. In the air was the sense of patience and civility. It was hot, blazing hot, and there was a slowness, a languor to the men who ambled from one place to another. I had the sense that here my purse would not be clipped from my belt.

I was feeling warmly toward it all until we came to a crowd gathered in front of a stage. There was a wooden block and a man with a black hood, his hands bound. Another man in neat robes had a large curving sword by his side. When the sword came down, I closed my eyes. When I opened them, the severed head's eyes were staring, it seemed straight at me, with accusation. What crime had he committed? Later I learned he had profaned their god and practiced some pagan ritual. It was a very strange thing in this peaceful, clean white city, this bloodshed—no different, I was realizing, from any other place with power behind its name. I thought of Karl executing the three hundred Saxons, cutting their heads measured by the length of a sword. It seems there is no escape from this use of power, and I pray my people on our little islands never come to this. For an executed pagan cannot then be saved.

When the crowd dispersed, the street gave way to a gleaming white palace with marble steps. Two guards came down to us, and at their command, boys appeared and unloaded our camels. We were shown into the courtyard. Its thick walls shut out the noise of the streets and reflected the bright sun. Deep archways covered with wooden screens led into the dark, cool interior.

Ali, a steward of Harun, entered and gave us a tour of the garden where jasmine scented the air. Peacocks glided across our path. I recalled Liutgard's first speech to me, longing to see peacocks, and my ears filled with the peacocks' strange, lonely cries, echoing my lonely loss.

At the end of the garden, past splashing marble fountains and through a long, shady archway, we came to a great pen, within which two elephants ate leaves side by side, a mother and her infant. I was not entirely surprised because so much strangeness had already greeted me, but I was awed nonetheless.

Ali made a whirring call, and the two elephants approached the fence. They seemed contented animals, and the baby stretched her trunk toward us for Ali to stroke. It was adorable.

I heard voices, and three men in flowing white robes approached us. Isaac introduced the three Musa brothers, whom he told us were brilliant inventors. Ali chatted with them, and they laughed, sharing a joke. Isaac looked displeased, but I didn't find out why until later. Isaac was right to be displeased, I learned.

We strolled away from the elephants to a bower hanging with blooming vine roses. Tucked amid the foliage was a silver birdcage with a little silver bird in it. By silver I mean the bird was literally made of silver. One of the Musa brothers turned a key in the cage, and the mechanical bird opened its beak and sang a charming tune. There was also a pond filled with mercury with golden boats floating upon it. And there were games. I poured water in a vessel by a small, curtained theater. The curtains parted and dancing dolls appeared. There was a water clock that rang a bell at each hour. The Musa brothers devised all these wonders. I felt content in this garden. I could enjoy its warmth and scented flowers for a long time.

A movement caught my eye. A woman crossed a path at the other end of the garden carrying a pail. Ali, with a little bow to us, hurried over to her and stopped her with what seemed to be a sharp reprimand. The woman's headdress slipped back for a moment as she looked up at him boldly. I glimpsed black hair that caught the light, but a pale face not like those around me. She seemed familiar.

Ali shortly returned to us, briefly explaining that the kitchen slaves weren't supposed to cross the garden.

We ambled back inside the cool hall, and Ali showed us to an indoor fountain room where we washed ourselves, and then we followed him to dinner.

For a long while, since after our arrival in Frankland, Daric had ceased to notice whether I obeyed my penance, so I ate a delightful feast of exotic dishes with light fluffy bread. The spices warmed my mouth, and we drank a sweet beverage made of limes.

As we ate dates and nuts, a girl was brought into the room. She was apparently blind. She stood in the middle of the room, rather stiffly, and she sang. To my shock she sang in my own language. She was in her teens, tall and willowy. She sang a long, lovely mournful ballad that I knew, and her flute-like haunting voice cast a spell on us. When she finished, her veil slipped back a little, revealing bright red hair. All the men gasped in admiration. Then she was led out again.

The youngest Musa brother shook Ali's arm, talking eagerly. Isaac translated to me that this was a slave sold to the court in recent months, and prized for her voice.

Strangely, Ali added with contempt, "But to me she is only a squeaking mouse."

Musa looked as if transported to another world. "What is her name?"

"Deirdre."

He repeated the name, softly rolling the r in a low voice. Then I remembered why she and the slave in the garden were familiar. I was sure I had seen them on the slave boat in Frisia.

Dancers came in next, who began a wild romp unlike anything I had seen before, but Isaac, knowing us to be holy men, rose and excused us, asking Ali to take us to our rooms, so that I only got a glimpse of the excitement.

In the hallway, Daric asked Isaac about the market, and he promised to take us soon, when his business was settled. We lingered as guests in the palace, and such was the largesse of the place that no one seemed concerned about us; there was plenty of food and space, in the sunny gardens and shaded halls. Isaac was busy, and we didn't see him for a while, but Christopher was with us, translating when needed and keeping us company. I was eager to see the House of Wisdom, and Christopher took us there.

The House of Wisdom adjoined the palace on one side, another massive white building with high windows with decorative screens. Within, the front was a large high room with tables and chairs, where men read and made notes. Dividing the room was a screen with a gate, beyond which rose shelves and shelves of scrolls, for three stories. The librarian guarded the gate at his desk.

"Harun is amassing all the literature of the world here. Your friends the Nestorians are copying and translating some of it for him."

I bent back and stared at the scroll-laden shelves, my mouth hanging open. Not even Alcuin had such a library.

"Of the writing of books, there is no end," Daric murmured.

Christopher led us to a far table where the three Musa brothers were standing, bent over a scroll, seeming to be disputing something, but in soft friendly voices. They straightened as we approached and grasped Isaac's hand, squeezing his arm. On the scroll before them was a drawing of an orb.

Daric passed his finger over it. "Is this the world as God sees it?" he asked.

Christopher translated. The brothers said it was. The youngest, with a shy, sweet face and round cheeks above his neat black beard, explained through Isaac, "I have measured it. It is twenty-four thousand miles around."

Daric raised an eyebrow. "You are confident, to measure the vast earth."

"I am a scientist. I am more curious than confident."

"But to place a figure on God's world. As easily as that."

"It wasn't so easy."

My brow wrinkled at the thought of it. Twenty-four thousand miles, a thousand miles for each hour of the day and night. How many had I come? How much more of the world was there? No man could see it all.

At last later we had an audience with their great king, Harun al-Rashid. Harun sat cross-legged on a cushion, his left hand resting lightly on his knee, and his right hand turned up, his middle finger touching his thumb. His copper-colored skin shone. He had a mustache, but no beard covered his sharp chin. He was about thirty years old. His eyes were intense and alert. Isaac interpreted for us. His voice was high and nasal, a bit like Karl's. He is a man of sharpness: sharp eyes, sharp nose. He complimented us on Karl's gifts, though they could not have impressed him. He did seem sincere in his appreciation of the hunting dogs. He intended to reciprocate in grand style.

He was curious about the world, sincerely questioning us. "What is the difference between Constantinople and Rome? Which is greater?" he asked.

Christopher answered, "Both consider themselves greater. Constantinople has been far richer, for its history and location. But don't discount Rome, nor Frankland under the Emperor Karl."

He smothered a smile. "And then, who is this pope I hear about? What sort of kingdom does he rule?"

Daric was sitting next to me. At that moment he lunged and prostrated himself. Speaking through Isaac, he said, "Kind sir, ruler of this empire. We beg you. I beg you. I have come this way on a mission, for only one thing. We need lapis lazuli to make blue ink, for a glorious work of art honoring our Saint Columba. If I may ask you, do you have lapis we can buy? We seek nothing else."

Harun listened. He smiled kindly on Daric and gestured to a servant to help the monk straighten himself up. He spoke to another servant who bowed and left.

"Please don't concern yourself," he said to Daric. "What your emperor and your pope could not give you, is easy for us. It will be sent to you."

Daric made a choking sound, trembling. "I have been promised often," he whispered, but only I heard, and I prayed that at last it would be fulfilled, because I was the one who had promised, over and over.

We returned to the palace to dine, and the Musa brothers joined us. Once again, after we ate, the girl from my country sang a ballad that filled my eyes with the green of my land, filled my ears with storms and Morrigan cries, filled my heart with the lonely hills, dark dappled forests, and pearlescent skies.

O if my love
Were like the swallow
That flies, up in the sky—
Then with my love
I would now follow,
And kiss my love, or I will die…

After she finished to scattered applause, the young Musa stood and bowed to her. She didn't acknowledge it as she was led out.

"She can't see," Christopher reminded him. "From the looks of her eyes, I think she has cataracts. I came here to watch your doctors perform that surgery."

The elder Musa brothers were laughing and teasing their sibling. An earnest look crossed the young man's face. "If it can be done, why should it not be, Allah willing?"

I had hoped to speak to her. It seemed right to inquire of Ali, the steward, but he was not with us that evening.

I arose early the next morning, wandered out to the garden, and took the path between white blossoms to the elephant pen. I tried making that whirring call Ali had made, and the baby came up to me. To my surprise, I heard the call echoed in a feminine voice behind me, and I turned. The slave that I'd seen Ali rebuke that first day approached, encumbered by a large basket of lettuces. When she saw me, she stopped and bowed, then approached the pen. She unlatched a low gate and slid the basket through it into the pen. Both elephants hastened to eat. She lingered to watch, holding her veil across her face.

"Where are you from?" I asked in Scots.

She turned and let go of the veil, looking me full in the face. Her mouth was set in stoic reserve. Her eyes shone hard; though they were dark, they flashed like moonlight on a dark lake. The reserve fell like her veil, and it seemed in her eyes I saw months of terror, bone-exhausting work, and a tremble of hope.

"I'm from Connacht." Her voice contained fear and doubt. She looked as if afraid to believe I could be a friend.

I was going to say I was from Colonsay, but for some reason I thought to say the monastery. "I'm from Iona."

Her lip trembled. "My brother is master scribe there. Connachtach. Does he live?"

My heart thudded in my ears. How could this be? Was I delirious? "Yes, as far as I know. He is now the abbot. Who are you?"

Her eyes filled with tears. She put her hand to her mouth and between her fingers said, "I was Oona. Who are you? Are you angel or devil?"

"I've probably been both in my time, but I can promise to be neither, only a child of God's mysterious plan. My name is Cellach. I travelled with your brother to the monastery."

She held out her shaking hands and I took them. We were too overcome to speak for a few moments.

"Please, tell me everything," I said when I could speak.

## CHAPTER EIGHT: OONA'S STORY

"It was in darkness we left, the dark morning with few stars in the cloudy sky and no moon. We left because a man, a terrible man, told us the scribe had died. I thought it could not be my brother. But that there was a well sure blessed by that scribe that would cure Deirdre's blindness. Deirdre, my daughter, my darling. She is here as well. I thought it was a sign, to obtain this saintly blessing. What choice did I have? If I could cure my darling babe, who is so good and hardworking and faithful, I would have no choice but to try. It was God's will, it must be. We left in the dark morning with the man Ultan, a stranger who brought this tale, and our own young Ferdich. We passed north to the sea, but on the way the devil made Ultan mad, and he tried to take my daughter, who was not yet a woman and not of age. He hanged himself from an oak in the storm-shattered night.

"We were so close, there was no choice but to keep on to Iona, to see my brother and drink from the well. We found a boat and we floated, our fate in the hands of God on the vast sea. In the mist came a ship, a ship from hell. Giant men—they were not men, gigantic white-haired devils—took us and slew the dear Ferdich. I don't know who or what these beings were or are now, it seemed I had dreamt them in a nightmare.

"They shackled us, and there were other Scots shackled aboard their hell-boat. They shouted at each other, and I think they argued over who owned us. I was sold five times on this journey all told, the first time on this boat.

"We ate dried fish but once a day. One of the Scots, a man, jabbered in an endless stream of talk and prayer. Fear had made him mad. We rolled on the sea, and when we arrived, it was night.

We pulled onto a beach with the other hell-boats. We came out into the darkness into a village. We were thrust into a barn. It was dark, and the earth floor was damp. There was one window and after a while wavered the red light of flames. There was only darkness and that fire, and hell was out there.

"In the dim morning we came out. There was a large group of us, perhaps a hundred, and mostly foreign tongues around me. I was shackled to strangers, and Deirdre was a few lines ahead. I glimpsed her red hair from time to time, and I followed it, trying not to lose sight of her. She was out of reach, and those who called out were whipped so that I could not comfort her with my voice. We were herded onto the boats again, prodded roughly, the children crying. I began the Lord's prayer and a few countrymen joined in until we were slapped into silence.

"The boat took us to a village on the water in a flat marshy land. I heard the name Frisia. There we were penned like cattle, and that was the second time I was sold. Before the journey continued, I shared a pen with a countryman, and we comforted each other, talking of our homes and our dear Savior. But we were separated the next day.

"Onto another boat, to another market where I was sold the third time. All the while Deirdre was near me, just beyond my reach. At this last market before the great river, we were separated so that women were shackled together in groups of five, and men apart, and children. It was to my great relief that Deirdre was put with the children and went unmolested.

"We were then put onto the great river. I did not know of any such river before, but it seemed to split the world. All along I was trying to imagine where I was, to keep some kind of map in my head. I had heard of Frisia before, and I knew we were east of there, and by the sun—though it was often dark and cloudy—I knew we were heading southeast. But what this river was, or these giant forests, I knew not.

"My fellow captive men were made to row, forced to take themselves to their fate. Most of us were not Scots, but of some pagan race with black hair and dark slanted eyes, long necks and jutting cheeks. The women I was chained to spoke an unfamiliar tongue, thick and strange, a heavy tongue.

"There was a child who was sick, and I was chained to her mother. Her mother, Rosa, called 'Natalya! Natalya!' to the girl, who was chained to Deirdre. Deirdre comforted her by singing, to soothe the child, who coughed hard and whose breath was a loud rasp. She was thin with great eyes and skin like the moon. She closed her eyes and stopped responding to her mother's calls, 'Natalya! Natalya!' I'll hear it until I die. The girl's loud breathing fell to a rasp, and then she stopped breathing. The beasts, our masters, cut her from her shackles and threw her into the river. I'll hear it until I die, the moaning. 'Natalya! Natalya!'

"The men, not men but the monstrous white-haired beasts who kept us captive, molested us, and the pain was like water surging in my lungs. I prayed and prayed. The other women I was chained to spoke in choked whispers one night. They were of the same race, and Rosa, though sick with grief, seemed to command them, as she was tall and broad and even in her grief seemed inordinately strong. They rose one night and dragged me over the side of the boat into the black river. I knew it was not to escape, but to seek the refuge of death. The monsters followed us quickly and with great struggles and fighting and heaving got us back onto the boat. But after that they quit molesting us.

"The river came out of the forest and into a grassy plain. I don't know how long we floated. It seemed this river could circle the world and we could never leave it, but I knew there was an end in mind for us, to be sold again.

"I prayed. One woman sobbed endlessly, and I felt annoyed by it. I knew I had no choice as to what would become of me, of where I was at that moment, but I knew I could choose to despair or choose to have faith. I chose not to despair, and that I would be rewarded with a miracle. Later the woman collapsed and died and was cut from the shackles and thrown overboard. I prayed for her pagan soul.

"At last we came from the river into a lake or a sea. There was no end of water, and the sight of this new sea did give me some despair. I thought of my dear husband and prayed he should know that I yet lived. I prayed over the water, for the water to tell the grass, to tell the birds that flew over the wide world, to fly to my home and tell my dear Dermott his wife was living and loved him still. My heart was sick.

"The land around us changed. It was dry and rocky. The grassy plains became a desert before my eyes. Surely this was the end of the world.

"At last we came to a village built of stone on the shore. Instead of pulling the boats ashore, there were posts and platforms to tie them to. The boat was boarded by men like those of this city, black and wearing gowns of silk. They counted us and divided us. Deirdre was in the line ahead of me. I called her name, and she called to me to have faith. She sang as we marched to her sweet, sad songs, and it filled my heart to hear her.

"From there we marched through the desert, south and west, past mud-brick villages and in a caravan with their strange, ugly pack animals. It felt good to walk at last. When we arrived at this city, I was able to grasp Deirdre and hold her. I tried to tell our guards she was my daughter, that they could see we were alike. At the gate the heathens in silk looked to reject Deirdre, but the monster men tapped her and gave her leave to sing. Our new masters seemed satisfied. They took her away, and I didn't see her as I spent the day scrubbing the tile floors. But that night we slept together, and she told me that she was taken to a hall where she could hear men eating and enjoying themselves. There was music. She was prodded forward, and they tapped her throat, and she understood they wanted her to sing, so she sang. She heard them sigh and utter grunts of approval. Every night she sings at their dinner, and they seem content with her, and every night after I scrub the endless tile, we are together. They dress her in silk like one of their women.

"I don't know how long we have been here. We've lived here long enough to know their language somewhat, and their language is our common tongue among the slaves. Rosa learnt it fastest, and she commands the kitchen slaves now. Deirdre eats and sleeps with us. She gives Deirdre the smallest portion to eat because, as Rosa says, she doesn't work.

"All along I felt my faith would be rewarded with a miracle, and I prayed and I asked God when the miracle would be. Now I know that time is eternal to our God, and no amount of time is long to Him, and that my fears are over and my faith is rewarded, for surely it is a miracle to find a friend of my brother's at the end of this endless journey."

She put her hands to her face and choked back a sob. I thought she would collapse into a storm of tears. But she straightened up and looked into my face. Her eyes held a ferocity I had never seen. I felt in this mad journey she had become another kind of being; she was no longer completely human. I wanted to reach out to her, but I felt afraid. I was shaking at the wonder of her story.

"Now my miracle has come, because I obeyed God's choice for me," she said. Her mouth trembled, and she rubbed her lips to still them, never taking her fierce eyes off me. My heart pounded. "Who are you?" she asked.

Steps approached. A woman who must have been Rosa was upon her, grabbing her by the ear. I couldn't follow her quick, accented speech, but she started to pull Oona away. I pulled Rosa's hand off The ear and put my other arm around Oona.

"She is from my homeland," I said. "I was asking her questions."

Rosa bowed to me, and when she straightened up, she towered over both of us so that I felt her commanding presence. She said, "We must keep our place. It is my duty to correct her."

"I will take responsibility."

"It is not yours to take, honored monk."

Oona slunk out of my arm and slipped away to the kitchen with no glance at either of us. Rosa gave me a shrug, another small bow, and followed after her.

I knew that men from the palace would be travelling west to trade with Jerusalem. I asked for some paper to write my very

first letter. I would write to Connachtach and send the letter with
them, in the hope that it would be taken to Aix and from there all
the way home. It was only a possibility it could get that far, but a
letter seemed a magical thing, and I wanted him to know of this
extraordinary news. And so I learned my first lesson of writing
letters: sometimes you regret writing them.

Afterward, Isaac and Christopher came across the garden and
joined me by the elephants. I told them Oona's extraordinary
story.

"We will ask Harun to allow us to buy her freedom," Isaac said.

Christopher patted my back excitedly. "Not only that, but the
blind singer is her daughter, and plans are being arranged for the
surgery I came here to witness."

"We will have an audience with Harun al-Rashid soon," Isaac
said. "He has gifts to present that we must take back to Karl."

The baby elephant, through eating, came over to us by the
fence and stretched out its trunk, which I stroked.

"Do you still think Karl an impressive king?" Isaac asked me.

I felt chagrined, but I wanted to answer intelligently. "There
are more grades of greatness than I thought. He seemed the
greatest of kings. Now Harun seems the greatest. Perhaps there
is a greater one still."

"There is a vast empire farther east, even beyond India, where
silk and other luxuries come from. But I wonder now how you
see mighty Christendom. You told me once that because Christendom ruled the world, ruled the prosperous nations, that that
was a sign of its superiority. What do you think of its superiority now? If the true religion belongs to the greatest kingdom,
does not the religion of these heathens surpass the religion of
your Christ?"

I didn't answer. This troubled me. Suddenly I knew that my
real quest was to find the greatest power there was, and perhaps
I had found it. My sense of the powerful had expanded. On
Iona, the abbot was the greatest power I knew. Then I met Karl,
king and emperor, a man who dared change the very names
of the months. In Rome I encountered the great pope with

his cathedral dripping in gold. Now even the pope seemed less mighty than Harun, and who knew what power lay in this empire to the east?

We soon had another audience with Harun, in the cool tent-like room. Daric trembled beside me.

"I think you wanted this." Harun indicated for his servant to come forward and place a pouch in Daric's hand.

Daric emptied it into his palm. Two blue stones clicked together: the lapis. Daric clutched it to his heart. A great light shone on his face. How strange and sudden it was at last.

"Thank you, kind lord," he said. His voice sounded stronger than it had in many months.

"I am sending back silks, a clock, other things, and a great surprise. Oh, I did like the hunting dogs. I tested them today. They are good animals. I thank your honorable king for them." He rubbed his fingers together. "I have heard you know one of my servants. A good worker, as I have been told. You are a friend of her brother's? I am pleased to grant her freedom to return with you."

I bowed deeply, and Harun raised his hand. "It is a pleasure to restore what is lost."

"Th... you. Her daughter is Deirdre, the singing girl." I meant this to imply her freedom should come, too.

Harun shrugged, and I should have paid attention to this. He replied, "When you are well-rested, you will return with my regards to my dear brother Karl. Please enjoy our city as long as you like." He made a little bow from the waist at his seat, and the servants led us out.

We went back out to the garden. Ali joined us with slaves carrying a sedan chair. "Ah, I was hoping I'd find you here. I have a treat for you. How would you like to ride the elephant?"

He saw my beaming face reply and admitted me into the enclosure. The slaves gave commands to the mother elephant, prodding her a bit with slender goads, and she knelt. They saddled her with the sedan.

I climbed in and the elephant stood. I had never been so high off the ground. Ali led the animal around in the pen. I swayed back and forth and kept feeling that I would fall.

"It's most disorienting. I am on top of the world but without security," I called to my companions.

"Let that be your first lesson about power," Daric called back. He was cured, and it was as if all that we had been through became known to him at once.

# CHAPTER NINE: LOST IN THE DESERT

Our huge camel train assembled outside the palace, much bigger than the humble cargo we had arrived with. Isaac walked down the line with his list of the treasures of silk, tapestries, pepper, spices, silver, and the carefully packed clock. Then there was the surprise. The baby elephant. Harun insisted on presenting Karl with it; we couldn't refuse. That was the joke Isaac had frowned over on my first day there. I was in charge of the elephant. How were we to travel with this beast? The farther we had to herd this intransigent beast, the more I felt he was somehow a punishment, and later I felt more keenly it was a punishment I deserved.

They blew horns to announce our farewell. A crowd had turned out to see this parade, and I wasn't even sure where our train ended and the onlookers began. Ali came out to send us off. Oona was with him, walking in a crouch like a dog used to being beaten.

Ali seemed irritated by her presence. "Now you are hereby free," he said abruptly and gave her a little push toward me.

"Where is Deirdre?" Oona asked, her eyes darting from Ali to me.

Ali shook his head and waved for the camels to set off. "She is still resting and recovering from her surgery. She will follow you tomorrow."

Oona fell to her knees. "Then I will stay with her, and we will both go tomorrow."

Ali rolled his eyes and pulled at her. "It is time to go. Your train will be slow, and it will be easy for one of our men to catch up tomorrow with Deirdre. Don't delay."

"But my daughter—"

"Your daughter is very well. Farewell to you, I said."

Oona started to tear at her clothes. "I can't leave my daughter!"

Ali grabbed Oona by the shoulder and pulled her up. "Be at peace, woman!" He let go of her. "Be still. You are being foolish; there is nothing to worry about. It would be easier to bring one woman tomorrow. Two women might as well be an army. You are only causing delay. May Allah be with you and farewell."

He waved his arms, and the servants prodded the camels and the great beast, and we headed out of the city.

Oona stumbled with us, in a daze, looking back, turning right and left wildly, looking everywhere for a glimpse of the missing girl. Onward we moved, and her feet went forward with us as her head and body jerked like a fish being pulled on a line.

I was distracted by too much at first to give her the comfort I should have. Somehow we would have to take the beast onto a ship over the sea. I was not happy about that. I thought we should have followed the Frisian trade route northerly, instead of to the west coast, but our travel papers and instructions were rigid, directing us the shortest way. Once we passed the gate of the city, the road was a secret in the sand that only our guides knew, and we had no choice but to follow, twenty camels and drivers, slaves, an elephant, a woman, and a thin black dog that ran out of the gate after us who barked and danced at our heels.

The first night, we stopped at an oasis. I dreamed of Rosa calling, "Natalya! Natalya!" I awoke to hear Oona's muffled crying.

When we started to set off, she asked, "Shouldn't we stay here and wait for Deirdre?"

Isaac only said, "She will catch up. We are slow, and they will be swift."

We lumbered across the desert to the next oasis. The closer we drew to it as night came, more soft noises came from Oona's throat. When we were settled, there was the sound of hoof beats. Oona jumped up, peering into the twilight over the purple desert. Two men arrived on camels and handed Isaac a scroll, speaking a few words. They did not dismount and rode quickly back into the night.

AMY CRIDER

the previous night and shushed me while he spoke a few words to them. They nodded and rode off.

"They will look for her. We must go."

That was all. As we rolled off, I realized the black dog was also gone. I'd thought that I would be able to write of Oona's happy return to our native land and complete the tale of her harrowing journey. But whatever happened to her, her story will not be written.

We could see the old wall of Jaffa from a long way off. I turned and scanned the horizon for a sign of Oona, but I knew we would leave her behind. I should have offered the men a reward for bringing her back to us. I could only pray for her.

As we approached Jaffa, we passed by farms of date palms, and we stopped at one. They gave us a hero's welcome and quickly spread the table with bread and meat and little cups of sweet date liquor. I drank too much in the hot sun and felt weary. Surrounded by the lush farm with its fountain, at which the great beast drank its fill and sprayed its back from its trunk, my legs felt very heavy and my head light, as if they were pulling apart.

A young man approached me, his eyes wide with concern, hesitating. "Are you well?"

I shook my head and found my whole body shaking. I felt I was going to burst into sobs. He brought me a cup of water and sat close. Finally I told him about Oona.

"The desert people will find her. They are good people."

"But I will not know. And what will I tell her brother?"

He put his arm around me. "No matter how awful her story seems, she has lived an adventure few could know. And she chose this."

"But she chose to run away in the moment, and then what? If she regrets it, there is no place for her to turn. And what of the will of God?"

"God's will is to bring us peace in our hearts. She will fulfill her destiny. People's choices arise, sometimes strong and good, and sometimes wrong and mad. And they choose because they are not at peace. Some find peace only in death. She will fulfill her destiny when she finds peace, or dies. But she will find peace."

"And what shall I tell her brother?"

A few tears fell from my eyes as he deliberated into his cup. He put his hand on mine and said, "Say that she has the heart of a lion and the will of a wild horse. She rides the storm like a soldier of thunder. She will survive."

I gazed at the bronze ring on my finger, with its incised cross. I wished she had kept it as an amulet, to keep Christ with her. She was alone now. But I felt she had a soul that was stronger than despair.

## CHAPTER TEN: BURDENS

Arriving at the port, a difficulty arose. We had to get the elephant onto a ship. There was no ship in port that could hold its weight. There was much debate over what to do. We could wait for a great ship to be built, which would take many months (first word had to be sent to Harun for permission and money to do it, then lumber from Lebanon had to be obtained, etc., etc.). Isaac decided we would continue around the coast of Africa to Carthage, where he knew they had great ships.

I felt my shoulders slump in resigned exhaustion. Since Oona had left, the elephant had become a vexation.

We set our pace to the great beast, the burden of our journey. At times it stopped for no reason, and we pushed against its leathery hide to no avail. At other times it took off at a trot, and the handlers ran shouting to keep up with it. At such times Daric turned to me and said, "Behold the caprice of power." The beast required twenty gallons of water a day, and it rarely slept, so we too barely slept and kept moving day and night.

Isaac spoke little to me after Oona left. I think he felt some shame that we had lost her and didn't try to find her. And now that Daric was lucid and speaking to me of our Lord, Isaac kept more of a distance from both of us.

So we passed through the vast desert, and I focused a strong dislike for the elephant as if it were the cause of any delay—which, at any rate, it often was. The more slowly we went, the more I desired for this journey simply to be over, my wanderlust finally surfeited, or the fact that now that something was making my getting home more difficult contrarily made me long only more to get home, and the length of the journey was the

elephant's fault. I hated its gait, its tiny twitching tail, its unpleas-
antly wrinkled gray skin, and its sickly smell. And it was growing.
It was no longer an adorable baby, but a hulking adolescent with
a voracious appetite.

Daric divined my feelings. "He is worth some pity, being
marched far from his garden home. His power controls us, but he
too is controlled and without choice. His only recourse is caprice
because he has no choice. Learn this lesson about the mighty."

Daric was trying to address things he had overheard me discussing all along. I only dimly perceived his subtle words.

At night when we camped—for our too-short periods of
rest—I thought about the desert. It is always the desert that exile
is compared with, that the white martyrdom is likened to. Our
ancestors in the anchorite ideal fled to the Egyptian desert to
sit on poles for years, to live in caves and sit in prayer until their
arms rotted and fell off. Where is Egypt? It must have been connected to this desert we now traveled. This sun, this glaring horizon, this thirst, was their penance for us all. What did they seek
in exile? Now I have seen both the kind of cities they fled and
this barren landscape they escaped to, where they sought this one
thing: to forget. To forget noisy markets and bitter wives, to forget
wily landlords and greedy councilmen, to forget anxious mothers
and demanding fathers, to forget crops and livestock, money, and
books—even books! To forget everything but God.

I wondered if there was any place left of real exile. The desert was well traveled and dotted with oases; cities thrived where I
never knew they existed. Everywhere men had marked territory,
mapped roads, and planted their crops. The islands around Iona,
too, were filling up with monks seeking isolation. The old days of
living off the wilderness were over.

The stars hung as big as lakes of fire in the sky. Under that sky,
as we quieted down and watched the last of the glowing embers,
I thought, I could not forget this sweet sad world.

And we did get to Egypt. I saw papyrus growing on the banks
of the Nile. Daric told me of the anchorites, such as Simon Stylites, and here was where they had fled to. Egypt was once ruled by

pharaohs, then by Rome, and now by Baghdad. Unlike the new cities of Aix or Baghdad, Alexandria is a thousand years old. But it wasn't dirty like Rome. Its gypsum-faced buildings still gleam white, a pearl on the Mediterranean. We stayed some weeks there; Daric and I visited holy places where the early bishops and church fathers had lived. He noted some of the swirling designs on the buildings, inspiration for designs in the great Book that must have been begun by now.

"It is no longer ruled by Christian Rome…" I said to Daric regretfully.

"You are too absorbed in these questions. We are not concerned with the power struggles of the proud and mighty, who think they control everything. They control nothing! We are children of God. Simon Stylites didn't think about who believed themselves to be lord over Egypt. He had but one Lord!"

There were miles to go from Egypt to Carthage. I tried to talk to Isaac about the point of view Daric was introducing to my mind.

He turned to me at night as we were retiring and said, "Now you are a monk, and I can't draw you out as I did. You are shut up in the monastery now."

"Not at all. We are still friends," I said.

But he shook his head.

Daric was especially pleased to go to Carthage, birthplace of Saint Augustine. We found his house, and stood in the very garden in which his conversion took place. We prayed together there in joyful solemnity.

One afternoon we stopped to see how the elephant was doing, in a pen that had been quickly built for it adjoining an old stone wall. Something darted at our feet and the elephant reared with a trumpet call. It was a mouse.

"See, see how the mighty must fear the small," Daric said. He knelt down and held out his hand. With a bent gait the mouse approached him, took a slow step onto his hand, and bit him. The way the mouse lurched away, I knew something was wrong with it. We sat together and soon Daric drowsed.

"I must rest longer," he said.

I swallowed a lump in my throat. We stayed. He shivered violently, and I lay him down with my cloak folded under his head. The others saw what had happened, too, and took turns giving him sips of water. His thirst was great. He motioned for me to bend my ear to his lips.

"The only power is salvation, and I am prepared. There is only one thing in life, to be ready for death. You should care for nothing else. See how the small overcome the mighty. Even Harun should fear a little mouse. But fear of death consumes the powerful. There is more glory in fearing the Lord, and not fearing death. Cellach, do you not know, it is death that makes us all equal. No man is lord, for death comes to all and levels the field."

He breathed heavily and the seizures began. I tried to hold him still, and we rocked. The saliva foamed between his lips. The others began to pray, the heathen in their tongue and Isaac in his. I held him fast, and he went limp and died in my arms.

I cleaned his body, and we wrapped him in his cloak and put him on the cart, to take him to be buried at the nearby monastery. The monks there gave him a good burial and chanted well, and I chanted through my tears.

I hated the elephant more than ever as it was goaded onto the great ship. The sea passed before me. I remembered how I felt when I first was on the sea leaving Napoli, that I was leaving myself behind. I had a feeling on the shore I would find a shell of myself that I would step into and reinhabit. Yet I knew this could not be. Would that former Cellach even recognize himself now?

Perhaps I had changed, as Isaac said, because on our return I was not interested in fooling proud bishops with the gilded mouse, as we had done on our initial journey. At any rate, we stayed less with bishops and more in monasteries, which suited my frame of mind. The monks were interested in learning Roman-style chants, and I taught them what I had heard. We told them of Baghdad, the Nestorian brothers, the great bones on the Grecian coast. I did not really want to hear news of Karl, who was now being called "the Great," or Charlemagne, since he was crowned emperor. I only knew he had not taken yet another wife, which pleased me. Some of the monasteries had received letters from Alcuin, and they shared those with us, which was a comfort to me also.

On this journey through the great forests and along fields and vineyards, I felt my whole life was only travel, and I couldn't tell anymore if I were on my way to or from, whether I was arriving or leaving behind. I had shed companions along the way, shed something of my youth, so that I was leaving behind a past that was already fading in memory. Yet I had to remind myself I was returning to my only home, and that I had to be ready to resume my life, or take on my new life as a monk, and that my travels would somehow, someday be over—though that seemed all but impossible.

We continued to Aix. We arrived in a light rain on a warm day. The elephant attracted a parade to the palace. We entered the courtyard and made circuits around it. Karl and all his laughing children came out to the clamor. We stopped, and the handlers managed to get the elephant to kneel before the king. Isaac spread before him the silks and spices and showed him the water clock

"I am well pleased with the gifts of my brother the emperor Harun," Karl said, beaming. To my mind, Karl was not nearly astonished enough at this incredible beast, and at our having taken it on this incredible journey over desert and sea. This was the moment I hated Karl most; how much he seemed like a spoiled boy who accepts such extravagant gifts as if he deserved them, as if this happened every day.

The children climbed on the elephant's back while it docilely knelt. It was taken to its new home in the zoo, and after a wash-up and rest, we joined the court for a feast.

We feasted, but I took no notice of what I ate. I felt the absence of Alcuin, who was still living in Tours, and my dear Liutgard. As the feast ended, Karl rose and extended his hand toward me to rise.

"Our young monk soon returns to his home far away on that remote holy island. He will not go empty handed. On this journey he had as his companion a venerable monk who died, having survived the terrible raid on Lindisfarne. Much treasure was lost to the Northmen that day years ago. So we ask that Brother Cellach take with him silver from our smiths to Lindisfarne to restore their loss."

I bowed, not entirely happy. Lindisfarne, on the east coast and somewhat north, was not exactly on my way home. But there was no turning down the king, of course.

I lingered for two weeks while the journey was prepared. Four horses were to carry the silver treasure of chalices, cups, plate, and crosses, as well as our supplies. Soldiers were to accompany me. We would travel west to the coast of Frankland.

The night before we left, I sought Isaac in the courtyard to say goodbye, and sat by him on the bench where I had often sat with Liutgard. Once again it was late summer. Once again the flowers were going to seed, and a few leaves had turned and fallen into the fountain, which was mossy and seemed dim compared to the sparkling fountains of Baghdad.

Without hesitation I put my arms around Isaac and pressed my cheek to his. "Farewell, my friend."

He gave my back a firm, friendly slap. "You will do well wherever you go."

The next day we set off through the deep woods. The soldiers sang marching songs. Sometimes we made camp in the woods, and other nights we were welcomed on an estate

After two or three weeks, there was a storm in the night. We huddled in our tents against the wind and slashing rain. When we rose, we found our path indistinct for the fallen leaves and branches. The solders acted confident about the way, but after we had walked the better part of the day it was clear we were lost. The woods loomed silently all around us. We stopped, for a few moments just as silent, looking at each other. A fine mist rose with a shiver in the air. The men began to argue about which way to go, whether to go forward or try to retrace our steps. They seemed about to come to blows when we heard a noise approaching, of horses and voices.

A band of men, women, and children appeared through the trees. The men, with long hair and beards, were riding, and the women and children walked alongside. They seemed to be a group of two or three families.

"What tribe are you?" one of the men asked as they stopped their horses.

"We are soldiers of the emperor Karl, and a monk going to Lindisfarne," said our leader, a bluff duke named Antony.

The other soldiers posed to reveal their weapons.

The man waved his hand. "We are not armed. We can take you to where the road is visible. You are well off the path. It will be night when we get there."

The soldiers looked to Antony. We had no choice. I was happy to join them. We pressed on together, the children singing. The soldiers smiled at their songs. When we stopped for the night and gathered around the fire, a good road now beside us, I remembered the people of the desert who had welcomed us with music and dancing. We shared food and beer and made merry. Then we slept soundly in our tents, perhaps all the more soundly for the beer.

The next morning, I heard a cry and came out of my tent. The band was gone and so were our horses. Antony swore and pulled the tents down onto the sleeping soldiers amid confusion.

"Fools! Shit! Shit! Get up, you bastard idiots! Oh, those bastards! I should have known, I had my suspicions! I let you decide. Look what you have done!"

The men scrambled out and lined up while he shouted and blamed them.

"Look to see what is missing!"

They made an account, and a thin young soldier, quivering with fear, said with hesitant optimism, "They left the silver, sir! Only the horses, nothing else is lost."

Antony took a deep breath and calmed himself. "All right, then. We have the silver. We'll carry it."

I was not so mollified. Carrying the heavy silver and all our gear would be nearly impossible. "Can't we just leave the silver?" I asked.

Antony shook his head, surprised. "Of course we can't leave the silver."

"We can't carry all this," I said.

"We'll leave the tents and the keg of beer."

We all hoisted the loads on our backs. It was miserable. I didn't curse the band that stole our horses, but cursed the king who had put so much store in those riches we were forced to carry.

We thought that at least we would soon arrive at some great estate from which we could requisition horses. He had that authority. But this road was a military road, built to make straight for the coast first by the Romans. It did not lead to any great estate, just a few outposts fallen into ruin. We marched the whole way to the coast, sleeping exposed to the nights, with no marching songs or humor, in quiet misery.

When we arrived at the coast, at a village at last, we hired a boat to get to the monastery, which was on the sea. Most of the soldiers would stay and wait, and four of them would accompany me.

I was exhausted and took little note of the voyage. The soldiers were mostly sickened by the chop of the waves. It was yet more burden, but I willed myself not to become ill.

The monastery was perched on an outcropping off the coast, a few buildings of wood and stone. Damage from the heathen raid was still visible on the blackened walls, while some new construction stood out. When we beached on the rocky inlet, a bell was sounded, and monks ran from the inn facility into the monastery. It seemed this was a precaution in case of attack. Two monks came to look at us from over the low cliff, and Antony called up to them.

"We come not to take your treasure, but restore it. We are from Karl Rex."

The monks quickly came down and helped us carry the treasure to the monastery. We were shown the guest house. The abbot himself, rather than greet us in his office, came to the guest house to thank us. The cellarer came and took the soldiers to the kitchen to eat while I remained with the abbot.

Because so many monks had been killed during the heathen raid, the abbot was young, perhaps only a little older than me.

He was square-shouldered, broad, freckled, his big hands hairy. He had an uncertain look about him, having been thrust into this office. I knelt before him, and he put his hands on my shoulders. His hands smelled like milk.

"I have terrible news. Your Master Scribe Daric accompanied me on a long journey, but he died before he could return. He died in Christ."

He bade me rise and we prayed.

"We will have a mass for him." There were tears in his eyes. "He was like a father to me. He saved my life."

We held each other as I realized how young he really was. He had only been a boy during the raid.

"Thank you for bringing us such treasure from Karl Rex. It will go a long way toward replacing what was lost. If only it could bring back our good brothers."

"It is a great loss that nothing can restore."

"You have had a long journey. Won't you stay some weeks and rest before going on?"

I thanked him and said I would. I added, "I'd like to take a bath."

He gave me a puzzled smile. "We bathe the last Thursday of the month, when we renew our tonsure."

I was disappointed. I was used to lovely, frequent baths in Arabia.

"Can you scribe?" he asked. When I nodded, he said, "Would you serve as my secretary while you're here? There is so much I need to do."

"Certainly."

"After you've eaten, if you would, go to the scriptorium and copy a few lines so that I may judge your hand."

This seemed unnecessary, but I assented. The bell was struck, and we went to the refectory for a meager meal of whey, cheese, bread, and vegetables. After all my fine feasts, it was hard to swallow the dry bread and mushy greens.

The abbot himself showed me to a desk and chose a psalm for me to copy, which I did while the brothers chanted in the church.

Their voices wafted to me, a rolling sound, lending rhythm to my work. I spent the afternoon at it, working as patiently and neatly as I could.

Before Compline I returned to the abbot with the page. He frowned over it.

"What sort of script is this?"

"The script of the court of Karl Rex. It is compact and efficient."

His shoulders twitched. "It may do for a secular court. Did you notice the script you were copying from? Could you not imitate it?"

"I could try. Perhaps, though, for your correspondence, this would be the right form. It is small and spares vellum."

His frown deepened. I felt he knew I was right but didn't want to agree. But he said, "Very well. But while you are here, I'd like you to be instructed in the proper way."

I thanked him. The next day a monk named Brother Edgar, a bony, emaciated man with a wrinkled scalp, stood over me as I began to copy the psalm again.

"Why do you use your left hand?" he whispered.

"Because I'm left-handed," I said rather lightly.

Suddenly the straight edge cracked against my knuckles. "Not here you aren't."

Perhaps he thought I was disrespectful in the way I answered. Perhaps I was, but the stick hurt, I struggled to use the quill with my right hand. Eventually I learned to use the Aix court script with my left and the Scots script with my right. I should have been grateful for the instruction. But who ever is grateful for instruction?

I returned to the abbot after several days of this practice. He was satisfied. He had a wax tablet with a letter written on it to the Abbot of Bobbio, which he asked me to copy onto vellum. I took it back to the scriptorium and spent the day on it.

When I started to write, I found a mistake in his Latin. I stopped and read it over. There were a few more mistakes. I corrected them as I scribed the new letter. At the end of the day I

brought it to him to sign and seal. He glanced at it, then stopped
and perused it.

"You have made mistakes," he said.

I felt my heart beat faster. I didn't think about having to tell
him the mistakes were his.

"Dear father, I corrected some minor errors. You are very busy
and wrote hurriedly. In my leisure I was able to correct them."

He sucked in his lips and stared at me, drew in his breath
to speak, and didn't. He dropped the letter on the desk. "You
have not confessed yet. You require an amchara. Brother Edgar
will serve. Please speak with him. I will tell him to make sure he
doesn't forget."

Now it was my turn to stare. My first knowledge of Brother
Edgar was the blow to my knuckles.

"You may go."

I bowed and left. There was no more scribing for me. I spent
the next day bored, feeling confined. After our meal Brother
Edgar approached me. We went to the edge of the bluff that
overlooks the sea.

The sun was bright on the water, green the color of Frankish
glass. The rest of the world seemed far away over the sea. And I,
on this journey, would be going farther and farther away from the
world, to an even more remote place.

I had been mostly silent in my week there. I longed to talk
about all I had seen and done. Brother Edgar looked at me
through narrow eyes. Could I tell him of snow-clad mountains
that disappeared into the clouds? Of cities dark and teeming with
rats and urchins? Of bright marble mosaics of flowers and vines,
and real flowers that smelled like paradise?

"Well, brother?" he said, his thin lips almost smiling a cruel
smile. He expected to hear my sins.

"It was the elephant's fault that Brother Daric died. But I'm
glad I knew him the short time he was well."

"Elephant?"

"I took an elephant from Baghdad to Aix. It was startled by a
rabid mouse, which bit Daric."

"I don't understand."

"Never mind. It was only a strange dream."

Brother Edgar's eyes closed. "That is well. But, your confession?"

I gazed again at the sea. The sun beckoned me back to the desert where I ate sweet brown dates and almonds. I tried to think of my sins. A golden eagle launched from a nearby tree and swept into view, soaring across the waves. And then something flooded me, and it was my sin—I hadn't expected it, to know the sin in my heart. My mouth filled with spit; the tears came suddenly. I felt hot and wet.

"I love the world. I love this world too much." I could say no more. Every emotion choked me.

Brother Edgar put his hand over mine, which was shaking.

"You are punished enough," he said.

I felt ready to speak and tell him everything, but he turned and walked away, leaving me alone on the shore, wiping away my tears in the bright sun of the day.

It turned out my scribing there wasn't quite done. The next day the abbot sent for me. He cleared his throat and motioned for me to stand, saying, "Your beloved Abbot Bresal has died on Iona. I have just received a letter from Brother Connachtach. It was long delayed."

I crossed myself and bowed my head.

"I'd like you to carry my response to your brothers there. If you would be so kind—" He dictated a letter of loving sorrow, and I scribed it, wondering as I did so at the thought that that they would receive this letter written by my own hand. I was careful to alter nothing.

The abbot was eager for me to return to Iona with his message. I would take about three days to walk to the coast, stopping on the way to spend a night with the local king.

Imagine my surprise when I arrived at the strong-farm, to find an acquaintance of mine. The king's son was Tarain, who had been a student at Iona. I only knew him slightly, and it had been four years, but we rejoiced in becoming reacquainted, and I had arrived in time for his wedding feast.

The ale flowed, and the meat was plentiful. Tarain had me sit right by his side, his lovely bride on the other. We sang, and he clapped me on the back ever with a joke in my ear.

As the night grew late and the singing died down, I rested in the hall of the great house. Some of the guests shook noise-makers and beat drums to drown out the sounds of the wedding night's consummation. The rattles and drums beat into my head. As I tried to sleep after my wearying journey, I couldn't help but think of all I was giving up. It would be fine to be a chief and live in a fine home with rugs and gold plate.

After we had all feasted for another day, Tarain took me to his stable. "Isn't he fine?" he asked, slapping a beautiful black steed on the rump. I agreed it was. "They're my pride, nothing finer than a great horse. You will ride him to the coast with some of my thegns."

I tried to protest, but he wouldn't hear of it. He loved his horses, and he loved to be generous. I had never seen a man so happy.

At the west coast, the thegns left me once a fishing boat had been secured, thanks to Tarain's silver, to take me to Mull. It took all day to cross the sea, and a fine rain mingled with the spray. I huddled under a blanket, rocking as the speedy boat made good time.

There was a monastery where I could spend the night on Mull, a bare, hard place with dry food and watery ale, a hard bed and thin monks chanting in a soft, pleading moan for deliverance. I thought of the feast I had just come from and the riot of singing. The monks sang of joy, but it did not seem to be a joyful place.

But the monks did their best, and two of them walked me to the last coast. The two were silent, except for chanting when the hour seemed right, and I felt lonely in their company.

And then we arrived on the beach across from Iona. After four years, it was strange to see it lying in the water, such a small place, so still and ageless. Only a few yards offshore to my right was the Island of Women, where by now Aedith must be wed and perhaps even gone to some new place. There was no lump in my throat at the thought. It didn't seem I was meant to marry her. I had decided long ago that I am prone to fall in love with every woman I meet, and for that reason perhaps I should never wed. Yet still, perhaps I could, and perhaps I could find a way to have land and be like Tarain with his horses and merry bride.

But I was landless, lordless, I had no cattle and no opportunity.

I thought of all this in a few seconds, only repeating thoughts I had been having some while. I called over to Iona for a boat. I heard an answering call. In about half an hour, two monks rowed onto the beach to fetch me across, and I was home on Iona.

# PART FOUR

## ILLUMINATION

CHAPTER ONE: RETURN

My dearest brother Dermott,

Last year I sent you a letter, which with a heavy heart I hope you did not receive. I don't know whether the many hands between us were able to deliver it, and now I hope not. I must either replace or amend this news. I wrote to you the extraordinary tale of how your wife and daughter were captured and sold into slavery in Arabia, and were on their way to return to you.

I write again with great pain that they are not returning. Cellach, the oblate who found her, has returned, without our dear ones.

As he stepped from the boat, I barely recognized him after his four years' absence. He was grown tall, with the stride of a man. A beard darkened his tanned face, and his voice had changed from reedy and questioning to deep and sagacious. Yet no matter how he had changed, my heart overflowed with joy at his return, but my joy immediately turned to fear and bewilderment when I saw he was alone. As he took the seat in my office, he stammered, hesitant to tell me the truth when I asked after Oona and Deirdre.

He told me of the death of the old monk who was with him, and of an elephant they brought to the great Emperor Karl which hindered their journey. Again, I asked, "Where are our dear ones?"

From the pouch on his belt, he removed two blue stones, round, smooth as eyes. They gleamed in the dark room like the portentous eyes of fate.

"I brought these back, instead of Oona and Deirdre. Two stones, for two women. The lapis."

My body went cold. "What does this mean?"

He told me that a man in Arabia who loved Deirdre bid her stay and marry him. Cellach is sure his love is noble. They learned this after they had already begun their journey. Oona, unable to leave your daughter, ran away in the night to go back, swallowed by the desert. She might be safe, found by the desert people—she may certainly survive. We cannot know, but I trust God is holding her in His hands.

Cellach took a ring from his pouch. Oona had put it on his finger in the night. She had asked me to take it when I left you. I wear it now.

Again, I asked Cellach what it could all mean, though none of us can understand God's plan.

Cellach said, "I asked a man in Jaffa what to say to Oona's brother. He said, 'Tell him that she has the heart of a lion and the will of a wild horse. She rides the storm like a soldier of thunder. She will survive.'"

We sat in silence and then prayed together.

I don't know what ruin I have wrought, what part I have played in this mad, inexplicable tale. I beg you to forgive me. I long to put this off, onto God, to say we cannot know His will. Yet I know we make decisions, we make choices, and my choice is part of this chain of events. I do believe Oona is well, not only because I have faith on God, but because I have faith in her, the being who has the strength of a willow branch and the stout heart of a stag. Let peace come to you in praying. As for your life, God will understand if you go on as a widower. As for me, I will believe her fierce will goes on."

With deepest love in Christ, your brother, Connachtach, Abbot of Iona

## CHAPTER TWO: AEDITH'S INTENT

My Dear Sister in Christ,

For years I have been writing the confession, the story of my decision to return as a monk, and the consequences it wrought. I had no object in doing this, only thinking to leave behind a story like the Confession of the great Saint Augustine. But this is not a humble goal, and I don't long for generations to know my tale, nor do I know if I have a lesson on faith to offer the wide world of Christendom.

Yet, I want to share this story with someone for whom I share some special bond. I've decided when the time is right, to send it to you at the convent, for you to read and wonder at your leisure. If I don't live to send it, I will leave instructions for it to be sent.

So from here I am writing more directly to you, dear girl. I will always think of your youth and quickness, your will so like that of my missing sister, your visage so reminiscent of my niece. When you stepped from the boat to speak with me, from so nearby, I thought you were my niece and had crossed oceans, mountains, deserts, and forests to return. My heart rose, and it rose no less than when I realized it was you.

You gave me a firm look, and I knew you wanted something from me, something serious. But suddenly we both were struck that the moment was too serious and we laughed.

"Aedith. Come to my office."

When we entered, I remained standing as a gentleman does, and you bade me to please sit when you had settled yourself. Did you know I was ill? I ached and was grateful to sit.

You hesitated to speak. "You were never shy before," I said.

"I was a child, so of course I said whatever was on my mind then."

"Still, when in doubt, that's the best thing to do."

A determined look replaced your diffidence when you said, "I would like to join my aunt at the convent at Kildare. You'll remember Aunt Fiona went there after my little cousin…was stung…"

It was not too long to have forgotten the death of Brion and the grief of his mother who left the next year to become a nun. "You seek my permission. As head of the women, what does Morgan say?"

You smiled with some embarrassment. "She said, 'Tell him he must judge according to what is best and useful, and not to romanticize.'" You blushed. "She is direct, as usual."

I smiled back and thought, *Some man is missing an interesting wife in Morgan.* "You were caught between us, you know. She did not want those lessons filling your mind with impracticality. And I don't feel a need to win in some way. I don't count it as a victory. What matters is what's in your heart. It is a hard life. To give up a husband, to give up children?" I might have been lying. I did feel it a victory, but I felt it must be your own decision. I didn't want you to decide based upon what either Morgan or I wanted.

You were prepared for my questions, confident of your answer. "This world is mortal. A husband's love can fade. A child can die as often as not. I want what lasts forever."

"But my fear…" I considered my words. "My fear is that you might be running away from life. When I found you… I never told, about the stones knotted up in your apron. Not even Morgan, and I should have told her."

"Why didn't you?" You looked away and stared at the ledger on the desk.

"I didn't want to shame you. I thought it would make everything worse."

"I'm grateful you didn't tell. I was ashamed. And it is a mortal sin."

I started to reach for your hand, but you wiped your eyes. I wanted to do more, but waited. I could not hold and soothe you;

I thought you might as well know you were giving that up. Your eyes cleared and you raised your chin.

"Leaving the sin aside," I continued. "I want to be sure that the convent isn't just a form of escape. It is compared to death, at times, the white martyrdom. You would be separated from your family forever, breaking the bonds of their closeness. Your family loves you very much. Could you sever that tie, to pray and fast, to work and study, with a life unsweetened by the honey of familial love, ordinary and wonderful love?"

You looked straight ahead, and spoke as if you had carefully planned this speech. "I have loved my family, but it does not sustain me. All this while, I have been sustained by the thought that there is another life, and I have been living a shadow life. All the day as I work at my tasks, there has been another me doing other things. I milk, I chop wood, I cut thatch. I hear the bell here and another me is praying, chanting words I long to understand, reading sacred and soothing verses, putting quill to parchment. A shadow of myself has been living this life always, since I first knew of it, and I long to join my shadow self and be whole. I ask you to let me be whole." You didn't demand or plead in the way you spoke. Your face was as I remembered, frank and open.

The sadness of another memory cast a shadow over me. "I wish I had such words for my sister when she asked me why I was leaving. You are driven to it. But I must say, from my experience, that your life may be different from what you expect, from what you are dreaming of."

You took my hand, unexpectedly, your hand so typically strong, as women's hands are. "Do you regret? Forgive my asking, but do you?"

I squeezed your hand and smiled. "Often at the moment that I might start to feel regret, the bell rings and it is time to pray. That is my answer."

Your expression asked me to go on.

I raised the index finger of my free hand, gesturing like a teacher. "And in true prayer there is no ambivalence, no questioning or self-doubt. There is no room for it. My lungs are full, my life is my breath, and the breathing, the chant that is God's breath, carries away the uncertain and petty thoughts. Those are born of idle moments. Time to regret means there is too much time on your hands. I have sometimes been frustrated, unsatisfied, and doubtful if my effort was worth anything. But regret—regret is a luxury. It is the luxury of believing one's choice was free, the luxury of being idle enough to think of oneself."

"Is our choice not free?"

"Perhaps I meant, without cost. Regret is the belief that one can gain without paying any price. I would pay that price again, and again. I pay it every day. And it is with a full heart. I wouldn't trade what fills my heart for anything."

You considered this, glancing around the room, taking inventory. I thought, *She is planning her office for when she is abbess.* Your gaze came back to me, more certain than ever. "I am settled. May I go to the convent? I am surer than ever."

"I know your decision isn't from caprice. Yes, you may go."

Then you slid a surprise out of your sleeve. "This belongs to you. I kept it all this while." It was the Psalter I had taught you from. I took it with a smile and wondered, *Would you have kept it if I had said no to joining the convent?*

You said, "I have sometimes tried to teach the little ones, when it's raining or there aren't many chores."

The little ones. "What became of Emer?" I asked.

You looked surprised, then the sad memory came, but you rallied with a brave face. "She is still young, not old enough to have married and left. She is quiet and hardworking, and will be a model wife."

"What is her disposition? Is she hard?"

"No, very tender and watches over the younger children with great care. They love her very much."

We bowed our heads and I recited the breastplate of Saint Patrick, the Deer's Cry, my niece Deirdre's favorite. Then I offered for you to spend the night in the guest house.

You pulled your cloak closer. "Thank you, but I'll go back and prepare for my journey."

"Do you have someone to go with you?"

"Brother Sedda will ask your permission to take me. I wanted to ask you for myself first."

"Very well."

We stood and went to the open door.

"Goodbye, dear Father Tach."

"Goodbye, dear Daughter Aedith."

Brother Sedda was waiting outside the door and I watched you slip away with him down the path. The bell was struck for Nones, and a crowd of monks appeared between me and my view of the young woman leaving.

I don't know if you knew the news about Cellach. I'm sure you knew of his remarkable journey across the world. Did you see him again to say goodbye? Did he tell you of the new and unexpected decision he has now to make? While he was away, his old master Congall arrived at the monastery from Colonsay with a story that didn't quite astonish me.

Cellach's mother was a widow who had come to Colonsay to seek work as a masterless slave and Congall took her in. When Cellach was born, his mother claimed she was pregnant when she'd arrived, not being sure of this until later.

Congall came to Iona to tell the truth. He is Cellach's father. His wife would have no concubines in the house, so Cellach's mother decided to keep the peace by lying. Now, Congall issn't happy with his sons. He'd always admired Cellach's intelligence and hard work, and came to offer Cellach the chance to be his heir. If he returned to Colonsay, Cellach Mac Congall could be a strong-farmer and king. Cellach was still yet wandering the world when I had this news, and Congall left without an answer.

When Cellach returned to Iona, I explained this, to his astonishment. He'd had some thought to become a monk. Now he has a decision to make. I don't yet know what that decision will be.

All along, we have been working on the great Book, the Gospel of Columba.

Once a week, after Tierce, the Gospel committee meets. Marcus, Gormgal, and Reuben come to my office. Gormgal is always early, coming straight from the chant, to try to decide any matter before the others arrived. I always say, "We'll see, as God wills," to Gormgal's eager suggestions.

After you left with my permission to join the convent, there was a knock, and I expected Gormgal as usual, but Marcus entered and knelt. I indicated the chair for him to sit. His crisp, handsome features had hardened, and his eyes that were always so frank and knowing now seemed closed off from sharing, hidden behind their dark, opaque brown from his secret mourning for Brion. He sat informally. Though he paid his respects to me, he didn't make much obeisance to the man he'd been at school with. I was glad.

"I saw Aedith," Marcus said.

"Yes, she is joining Sister Fiona."

His eyes narrowed. "Yes, I suppose she is my sister now." He shook himself. "As it should be."

"I know Brother Reuben is your amchara, but if you'd ever like to talk, please come to me."

Marcus nodded, spreading his legs, his elbows on his thighs. "Just give me work. I lose myself in it."

"There's plenty." I cleared my throat and tried to sound as if the next matter weren't important. "I am not able to do so many pages now."

He straightened and looked me in the face. As always, he looked as if no secret could be kept from him. "Are you not well?"

I waved my hand. "Only very busy. My office has many cares."

Marcus glanced at the hearth. The day had warmed, but a fire was burning, and he rubbed the perspiration from his neck. He looked at me again. I felt the monk didn't believe me, and I nervously stiffened, waiting to be questioned further. But Marcus didn't pursue it. "Do we need another scribe?"

I nodded. "I wanted to ask you how Cellach's letters are."

"They're very... advanced." Marcus seemed to surprise himself in realizing it. "Yes, very advanced. And ambidextrous as well."

"I'd like him to contribute some pages."

He didn't answer at first, a look of concern on his face. He glanced at the fire again. "He hasn't taken final vows."

"Perhaps this will inspire him to."

There was a knock, and Reuben and Gormgal entered, knelt, and took their seats. We discussed how many pages were completed, the state of each Gospel of the new Book, what paints and inks were running low. Luke was finished and Matthew in good progress. We discussed where to have full-page illuminations. The portrait of Mary and baby Jesus that Eochaid had requested on Dunadd long ago was done. It was the first page we'd finished, long before Cellach returned with the lapis, Mary's gown colored in royal purple, the lapis now unnecessary for that.

Such was the ending of that extraordinary journey, because Gormgal, filled with the objective of pleasing the nefarious Eochaid, insisted as soon as his group returned that they complete this page before any other.

I could tell Gormgal had been waiting with an anxious look for a pause to say something. With a sigh I asked, "Is something wrong, Brother Gormgal?"

Gormgal coughed, his thin chest shaking, one finger poised in the air. Reuben reached over and patted his back. Gormgal heaved a breath.

"I was looking over some of the pages and found something that disturbed me very much. I'm afraid to say it, but I must. Someone drew an ornament of a creature with an enormous phallus."

Reuben and I looked at Marcus, who seemed distracted by some piece of dust between his fingers.

"There is no place in the Gospel for an enormous sexual organ," Gormgal continued.

I admit I stifled a laugh and pretended to cough into my sleeve. Reuben said, "Well, Marcus?"

"I draw from life, from nature," he said.

"We draw griffins and lions with eagle heads and man-fishes. What do you mean we draw from life?" Gormgal asked.

Marcus shrugged. "I won't do it again, then."

Gormgal looked at me expectantly.

"Yes, don't do such things again," I said.

Gormgal looked deflated that there was no punishment. He pressed his fists into his thighs and bit his lip.

Despite the warmth of the overheated room, I pulled the hood up over the back of my neck. "We need another scribe," I said. "I have become too busy to continue doing my share."

"None of the boys are ready," said Gormgal. "It's a man's job."

I looked to Marcus, who cocked his head. "I think Brother Cellach has the talent," he said.

Reuben nodded. "Aye. He has learned a great deal."

Gormgal's neck reddened. "Cellach has procrastinated. He's made no commitment to us. He's more of a visiting guest than a monk."

I rubbed my hands together, eager to offer this blessed work to Cellach. "I think Cellach will commit. And I think contributing to our great work will influence him."

Gormgal raised his chin and scraped his teeth against his lower lip. "I think it's completely inappropriate."

"God brought Brother Cellach far, and he has had the opportunity to learn scribing in several schools. Let us not waste his education," Reuben said.

"I agree," said Marcus.

I said, "Let us pray for Cellach to join our mission. Let this holy work inspire him." I stood, signaling the end of the meeting.

"I will fast and pray," Gormgal said meekly as they left.

I awoke and my hand went to the lump in my armpit. Every night I resolved to stop feeling it in the morning, yet I did. For a while it grew rapidly but now seemed to be staying the same. I shifted and something was sore in my groin. There was another new lump there.

The day was frosty and in the church the breath of the monks made the chant visible. Then I went to the scriptorium. It might be the last page I would contribute. I filled the ink horn and propped it in the hole in the edge of the desk. I snapped off the end of the quill and slit the end. I want to try to express this.

The joy of effort, when all pain is forgotten. Blocked out, the rank sweat smell of the room. The sounds of phlegm clearing, the hoarse sound a grating rasp. The internal sound, the music stuck in one's head, rises and drowns out the rest, the constant chant heard all day and night like the sound of the sea. The blank space must be filled, as the sea fills the horizon, as the chant fills the air. Creeping in, at first, a draft chills the joints. Wind penetrates, bringing with it the scent of the fresh world outside, the memory of walking through the field of bedstraw, thyme, and tiny orchids with Oona, making a crown for Deirdre's hair. The breeze stirs the smoke from the fire and oil lamps, a thick smell, warming and heightening the other smells of the wildflowers and sweat, alternating layers of smell. But they will pass away, along with the cold and the pain. Away with the hunger, like a sharp stone in my stomach. My throat is dry, my parched lips chapped to the point of splitting, a tingling pain. It will pass. The hunched back aches, my wrist is almost numb, dully sore. Only when my fingers are numb and limp, unable to hold the pen, will I stop, because until the fingers can no longer pull the ink into fine curves and lines straight as taut strings, I will work.

The work is three hundred and sixty pages. It is the work of four men. The most ornate page takes a man a month of steady work to finish. The work is the Word of God. It is the Gospel. It is the Good News.

When the smells drift away and the draft recedes and the pain goes blank, it is the time of joy, a joy felt not even as happiness, because inside happiness is the contrast and memory of sadness, and this has no memory. It is the joy with no past—it is the joy *of* no past—it is the joy with no future—it is the joy of *no* future. It is the joy of emptiness, though the page is covered and filled with color and pattern more intense than any wild meadow, than any flower's center, than the iris of a hazel eye. The pattern soars to heaven, and the mind is blank as the beginning, the mind moves to a white unshadowed sky, into a steady gray ocean wave, into a black moonless night.

It is where all light comes together, where sounds rush until they drown themselves, where pain is an opiate of pleasure, where all joins together to form absolute emptiness.

It is layers of concentration. First the planning. The dividers walk down the side of the page to mark seventeen evenly spaced lines. If the page is text, then the decorations are only small bursts—initials and ornaments, each a bit of controlled wildness: A dragon's head spewing out serpentine spirals. A lion's tongue filling the circle of a P, an eagle's neck stretching around the letter S, an R ending in lion's paws. So many eagles, lions, and peacocks.

Other pages are a full design consisting only of a few words. The Q of "Quoniam"—"Foreasmuch"—the opening of Saint Luke's Gospel, is the entire page, the rest of the letters of "uoniam" nestled inside the rectangle of the Q. Steady rhythms of squares, everything filled with digging knotted spirals. Pages as brimming full as my stomach is empty. The patterning deeper and deeper, the pattern repeating and changing, turning on itself, like the spinning waves of the Corryvreckan whirlpool.

Quoniam is my page, tribute to my dear Luke. In the lower right corner, wrapped around the N and the M, the faces of my brothers, lined up to chant. Eight perfect small red circles inside the center of the Q on the left, the suggestion of a cross in half-circles around the edge, the hard straight lines in perfect balance with the smooth curves dancing and shimmering inside. The pattern going inward, inward, never stopping, pulling like a child pulling on my hand across a field, Oona long ago, saying,

"Come, look, see." It is eternity itself, it is a taste of the everlasting, born of the hard chair, the stiff muscles, the draft, the hunger, the ache, all fused into the blankness of the page whitened with chalk, once living skin holding blood and flesh, holding the course of a heartbeat, the blankness now becoming the dizziness of speed, of running across the blank white sky, unable to draw breath until the breath catches hold, the joy of the single Word, the one Word. The only Word. Love. The answer to the monk's question on Islay, and the reason God gave his only begotten Son, as John told.

## CHAPTER THREE: CELLACH CONTINUED

My Dear Sister Aedith,

How glad I was to say goodbye to you, however briefly, before you left for Kildare. Years ago it seemed expected that you and I would wed, but somehow I think we both knew our lives were meant for other, weightier things.

You once gave me a lock of your hair. It was stolen far away in a foreign land. I'd ask for you to send me another, but I know I should let go of all nostalgic things.

You might enjoy knowing about my new labor.

I have been assigned to help with the great Gospel of Columba, and my tasks for now are tedious but necessary. My chief labor is to cut quills. I cut them by the dozen. Like the hides, they come from all over Scotia. The best feathers are the flight feathers, from the right wing for a right-handed scribe and the left wing for a left-handed scribe, such as Marcus and I. There is the buzzing sound as I strip the barbs, the fluffy pith from inside pulling up as I tease it out with a tiny stick, then the curved cuts of the sides, the snap of the end, and the snap of the tiny center slit. The knife has to be quite sharp not to crush the end of the quill, and the cuts have to be perfectly straight. I ruined at least a dozen quills at first. But it came, and I cut quill after quill every day. I would like to chant or sing to keep the pace. It's hard to work in silence.

But I am in between worlds, because I have the decision yet to make. I have not taken final vows. I could take my place and rise to be a high chief. I could leave at any time. I needed an amchara to discuss it with, and Connachtach chose Marcus for me. There are times when I think I'll speak at length about it, but somehow he brings me into quietude, with the impression that great decisions are not made by lengthy discussion.

One day, we walked on the beach to find a shell or two to use as dishes for mixing the paints. Marcus picked up a shell and studied it. I asked if it was the creature that made purple dye.

He said, "No," and dropped it with a somber look.

I picked it up. Something tugged at my memory. "There was the boy on the Island of Women who died from the bee sting. Do you remember?"

Marcus looked up at the sky. "He was my stepson."

I stared. "How did I not know that?"

"You were busy with your own concerns, I suppose."

"Do the others know?"

"Perhaps. Though now that Brother Jeremiah has gone to be abbot on Tiree, no one seems to be so interested."

I looked over at the other island. "You never go there anymore."

"My wife took our child's death as a sign. She withdrew to a convent."

Thoughtlessly, I asked, "Do you think it was a punishment?"

He said quietly, "I don't believe God punishes people by taking the lives of little children. My penance is to live among people who do."

Ashamed, I didn't know what to say. I put my hand in his. He grasped it and looked at me with his dark eyes, which were always so intent and knowing. Before, the wisdom in his eyes had been mingled with a kind of pleased look, as if he took his lot at the monastery as an ironic joke at his own expense. But now he looked a little more tired, the humor drained away. I hoped whatever I had felt was in him was not entirely defeated. I said, "Perhaps working on the great book will ease your mind."

He took a deep breath and looked across the sound. The angle of the sun lightened his eyes and a look of acceptance turned his lips slightly up. "Yes, I do take that work with pleasure. And I understand that you can scribe."

I lowered my head. "I have done some lessons and letters."

"Perhaps I can teach you about the illuminations. You must ask Brother Gormgal to show you the Gospel of Lindisfarne. We still have it here for inspiration. You must ask tomorrow first thing after Tierce."

The next day after Tierce I approached Gormgal's desk between the locked bookcases and asked to see the Gospel of Lindisfarne. The librarian's head bobbed in the palsy of old age. He pointed his long bony finger at me.

"You have not taken final vows."

I wanted to see the book now very much, and I looked at his chalky white face, his watery blue eyes gleaming with some inner rage I always felt was there though I never knew what for.

"If I obtained the permission of the abbot, may I see it then?" I asked.

His thick tongue darted to the corner of his mouth. "I would not gainsay the abbot."

I went to Connachtach's office, kneeling before him as we all did in respect. He smiled at me, but there was something in his stiff smile and short breath that made me sense he was in pain or not feeling well. I was going to ask him if he was ill when he spoke first.

"Your scribing is quite mature and valuable to us. We would like you to contribute pages to the new Gospel. Brother Marcus will get you started."

I caught my breath. "I didn't expect this. I haven't yet taken the vow."

He replied, "I think you are afraid of any decision. You can't live your life in a half-world, half in one place, half in another. You are afraid of the cost of any decision, and so you won't decide."

"I feel I should take the life that best suits my temperament. Rising to chief and living a free life is probably what I'm fitted for, because for a long time I've been interested in power and all that it means."

"Then why don't you go?"

I pondered this for a few moments. "I feel that there is some question I haven't asked yet, and when that question is answered

I'll know what to do. I think it's here that I'll find that answer, for one way or the other."

I knew that my thoughts were strange ones, but he seemed to understand.

"You speak of freedom. I know you have met kings and emperors. Do you consider them free?"

I shook my head.

He continued, "Do you not know the greatest freedom of all is to give up the world?"

"I have heard that said. And in my mind, I understand that. But that idea has yet to penetrate my will and heart."

He reached out and clasped my hand. "I believe it will, Brother Cellach." He paused. "Some may resent such a long hesitation," he added quietly.

"Is that why Brother Gormgal hates me?" I blurted out.

"What do you mean?"

I told him how Gormgal had refused my request to see the Gospel. I hoped Connachtach would smile on me again and take my side to comfort me, but he did not.

"It is fitting that the Lindisfarne Gospel stay secure unless I grant permission. You shouldn't take it personally."

I blushed. "Brother Marcus told me to go to Brother Gormgal."

"At any rate, we will go. We can go now."

As Connachtach stood his knees gave way for a moment, and he leaned heavily against the desk. I quickly reached out and helped him up.

"Are you ill?" I asked.

He hesitated, and in the way he leaned on me, the answer was too clear for him to deny. "I must start to think about a successor."

A hard lump pained my throat. "It would be hard to stay on here without you." Mingled with my grief was the thought that Gormgal, as the oldest, might succeed him, and to my shame I felt I wouldn't want to live under his hard rule.

"I will show you, now, why you should stay on."

On our way to the scriptorium, he told me that the Gospel of Lindisfarne was made in honor of Saint Cuthbert, scribed by

Abbot Eadfrith a generation ago. When we got there, Gormgal knew what we wanted, and without a word raised his key to the lock and took out the book that meant so much to the monastery. The Gospel was in a wooden box decorated with silver in wondrous patterns, but the box was only a hint at what lay inside.

Connachtach opened it. Light dazzled from the first page. Gigantic letters flashed, outlined with thousands of tiny red dots. My eyes watered, and I had to rub them.

"They're called illuminations because they shine like light through stained glass," Connachtach said.

At first, I wasn't sure if I was looking at actual words. But as I stared I made it out. It was the letter Saint Jerome wrote to Pope Damasus to introduce his translation of the Gospel in the fourth century: "You ask me to make a new work out of the old, so that following copies of the scriptures scattered about the world, I might set myself up as judge where they vary, to decide which of them agrees best with the Greek truth."

"Do you think Saint Jerome had any idea that three hundred years later a copy such as this would be made?" I asked.

Even old Gormgal smiled and patted my shoulder.

I had to turn my head because at the very bottom, the last three letters didn't fit the line and were written sideways. "It's a shame the line didn't quite fit," I dared to say.

Connachtach gave a wry smile. "Titivillus was pleased."

He turned to a page at random, displaying a giant rectangular Q with words inside of it, the beginning of the Gospel of Luke. It was bordered with cormorants, twisting birds, and the corner terminated in a cat's head.

"A cat for Luke!" I said with a laugh. Our Luke had loved his Pangur Bán, who, old but still living, slept by the fire in the corner. He stretched and curled his nose under his paw.

Connachtach turned to another page, and it took my breath, the most magnificent of all.

"What is this?" I asked.

"The Chi Rho page. Chi and Rho are the Greek letters that begin the word Christ. This opens the Christmas story. Christ autem generatio sic erat cum esset disponsata mater eius Marie Joseph. Now the birth of Jesus Christ was in this wise: who as his mother was espoused to Joseph."

The Chi and Rho took up half the page, the top of the Chi ending in a trumpet shape, spirals, and eagles massed in twisting interlace. The letters of the text were filled in with regal purple, green, and yellow, richly outlined in deep black.

"Is this what we are doing?" I asked.

Connachtach smiled when I said "we." "Yes, and perhaps… perhaps…we will go beyond even this. I think for our Chi Rho page, the Chi and the Rho will take up the entire page, and the only other words will be 'autem generatio.' Now born."

One word suddenly leapt to my mind, to describe the wild and dazzling display before me: freedom. Under the Rule, with the strictness of obedient discipline in every daily task, this work was the place where their hearts knew unbound freedom. Connachtach had tried to tell me that to be a monk was to be free of the earthly ties that confine men's souls. A monk's life is like the tide that obeys in its God-given regularity. But here was the work of a soul as free as the boundless ocean.

Marcus drew a short straight line on the vellum. He took the dividers and measured the width of it, and then from each end of the line marked twice, above and below, making two x's, drawing a line between them to bisect the first line. Having established the center of the line, he drew a circle. The lead of the dividers marked the vellum faintly. He placed the point of the dividers at each of the four points where the circle met the two lines and created the corners of four equal squares. He had me practice this several times. Though I had been practicing lettering, I still felt clumsy with these fine tools. We laid out rectangles of various sizes, connected center points and angles, until the page was covered with circles, arcs, rectangles, and squares.

I thought I was only going to scribe, and by then I had produced several pages. Now I was taught the secret of laying out the decorative pages. Another day we began the secret of the knot work. We laid out a square, then divided it in half on all sides, and kept dividing the squares in half, marking all the intersections of these tiny squares with dots. These dots guided the weaving lines, measured only by the compass and straight edge, but precisely measured. I drew one line between the dots in a curling ribbon.

"Now, outline this line. Thicken it by adding a line on each side of it, equidistant. But pay attention to the intersection, as you will go over and under the original line. Alternate where it goes over and under."

I had to concentrate and got lost in it. Something quickly confused me. I started drawing the inner border, but as I brought it through, it turned into the outer border, and the outer border became the inner border. I couldn't explain it, but it was before my eyes, and I made no mistake. It was a fascinating puzzle that worked by its own rules.

I followed lines. I followed them around borders of a page and inside spiraling circles. I spent hours and hours following lines. When the patterns became more complicated, I lost the thread and made mistakes. This vexed me with frustration.

Marcus told me the mistakes were caused by a little demon named Titivillum, who gathered mistakes in his bag. He sought to fill his bag a thousand times a day to bring to the devil. I more than filled his goal.

Sometimes as I drew with my short, hesitant strokes, Marcus encouraged me to "Draw with the arm, not the fingers." I told him I was finding my way and didn't want to extend the line too far. Instead I drew with short little strokes. He said, "It's better at times to make a bold mistake than a hesitant decision." He wanted my lines to be sure, to be definite, so that the quality of the line was firm and clear, even if it went in the wrong direction.

"You can plan one on a waxed tablet, and if we approve, you may be asked to produce it for the great Book," Marcus said.

"And the Chi Rho page?"

"Abbot Connachtach himself will lay that out. I will color it. You will help by mixing paints. There is always something you can contribute."

I spent my free time designing a page of geometric design. I was partly inspired by the designs I'd seen in Baghdad, regular geometric forms with no figures. It was a page of crosses intersecting in circles, like patterns woven in an Arabian carpet. Whenever I showed my progress to Marcus, he told me how I could add more intricacy to the design until it seemed to explode on the page. After several weeks I was invited to show my design to the committee.

Reuben and Marcus were pleased by it and said so, remarking on the symmetry of the design and the colors I had planned. Gormgal sniffed and held it to the light.

"Symmetry is not the issue. Only, does it glorify God?"

Connachtach looked tired. "I will keep the design here, and we'll see if there's a place for it."

I had hoped for more commitment than that.

He seemed to divine my thoughts, for he added, "Commitment is more satisfying, as anyone knows."

It was a pointed remark. I heard Gormgal chuckle, and I blushed with shame.

That night on my cot, I turned it over in my mind. In the world I could be a chief and own horses. I could have the smith make silver cups for me, wear jewels. I could have power. But there was nothing in the earthly world that compared to the magical power of that holy book.

## CHAPTER FOUR: THE DESERT

"I'll tell you all, in time…"Nothing alive within sight. Not a wall or a man-made thing. I almost changed my mind, but could not retrace my steps. There was some relief in not having the choice. Surely I would find my way. God would not allow me never to see Deirdre again. Thoughts dried up in the simmering heat.

God would take care. *Take care of what?* Everything. How can it still be green at home, green and wet, Dermott slipping on the mossy bank, slipping now in the sinking sand, the sun so far from the gray misty fields? The sun is there, where it hides like the Lord's ways, here it shouts, sound swallowed by immense skies, there must be a sign, it can't be hidden, a sign in the sun, there must be a path, it's here, only buried, here the flesh never rots but only hardens on the bone, red and tough, cow hide, slaughter, Dermott tying the rope, Connachtach slitting the throat, flaying the hide, careful not to tear, slipping in blood, mud, dung, moist moss, wet walls, mossy stones, magic wells, lively water, juicy fruits, berries, cherries, stones, pits, wells, flooding streams, dams, signs of man, dark houses, shadows, shade, the moon rising over the wooden cross bright as my daughter's face, her face bright as a starry night, her voice like a summer breeze through leaves, will she remember my voice, in this silent sky swallowing sound, sandy steps shuffling sandals a soft scrape gone without an echo, no reply, no bird, no cry, no choice, no choice, fists by my sides, bleeding blisters, knives of sand.

Night. *When did the sun set?* Breathless cold, no dew, no ice, the stream cracking under my knuckles, still runs, the stream bubbling under ice along the frosted bank.

Sun. *When did the sun rise? When did I start walking? How did I rise?* No choice like the stream running like a thief like a horse ridden at midsummer games, the boys parade, riding like a thegn, dead in the sea, split throat, blood and salt, waves of froth, waves of dry froth slipping underfoot, pebbles in the well wishing for a new chance, for Deirdre, for Deirdre, wishing for grace, willing the blessed Virgin, willing an answer, willing to go on, willing every hard hand-wrought labor, willing without choice, her sight gone, swept away and lost like a gem fallen from a ring. Find me in Deirdre's golden garden.

Night. *When did the sun set? Am I asleep?* God almighty, let me wake in linen sheets, bandages on my feet, a voice singing, Deirdre's voice, birds trilling in the dawn, sun rise in the mist, glistening dew, a moist rag to my lips, words dry up. Day. *When did day break?* What will they find, dry leather-wrapped bones. Christ in the hot sun, vinegar for wine, blood for milk, I am the way and the resurrection, I am not ready, I am not ready, but.

Someone knelt beside me where I lay in the sand. He put his ear to my lips and a croak bubbled out that he would not understand. "My choice. Always. My choice."

I awoke in a cart that bounced hard over the rocky track. My legs were shackled. My head throbbed, and my tongue was swollen in my dry mouth. There was a bolt of linen under my head, my one comfort. Around me were casks, amphorae, bolts of cloth, and a cage with a bright blue singing bird. I looked at the bird and parted my lips. The bird's round eye glared at me, then with a little wing flap it turned away. With pain I sat up as far as I could, my face even with the cage. I tried to say, "Birdie, birdie," but could only manage, "Bir, buh."

The cart stopped under a sudden clump of trees at an oasis. Voices crackled. I couldn't sit up far enough to see the men. I lay back. A boy jumped on the cart and slid his arm under my head and put a cup of water to my lips. I choked, and he pulled it away.

I grunted to beg for it. He brought it back to my lips, and I sucked slightly at the water while he sat with me a while holding me until I could swallow the whole cup. A voice of rebuke rose, and the boy jumped off the cart again.

We spent the afternoon there, and at sunset I was given another cup of water.

In the morning we passed fields of wheat and vines, and the great round walls of Baghdad. I revived and sat up, looking in the street eagerly for my daughter's blue eyes.

We came to the palace, to the traders' gate. The boy jumped on the cart and unloaded the bundles and jars. They were careful with the bird, but as for me, they yanked me up and dumped me onto the ground, my knees buckling. My legs shook as I tried to stand, pain stabbing my raw feet. I sank back to the ground while the trading business buzzed around me, as wares were inspected and lists consulted. The camels and cart left the courtyard, and I sat in my shackles, breathing hard.

I closed my eyes. A breeze stirred, and I slumped over my knees.

A familiar voice woke me. "So you have shamed us."

I looked up at Rosa.

"You were given your freedom, and you return as a slave. So you shame Harun who freed you. So you choose to be a slave, and a slave you shall be under my charge. No one will know you here. Don't ask about your daughter. So beautiful and precious, so special, no? The special singing bird is away in her little palace. Some of us are not so lucky. You are lucky to be alive. You should be grateful every day for me to keep you alive, that's right. You won't deserve the bread you'll eat, but I am a good person, better than you. Come. I am a good person, I'll give you a day to heal yourself before you work. Come."

I stared, unable to move, and Rosa pulled me up by my hair.

## CHAPTER FIVE: SCRIBING, INTERRUPTED

Perhaps my dear Aedith, you are doing some scribing in the convent. I started to write down my feelings while absorbed in this wondrous work. I put this before you now, but I have terrible news, something I will only set down in fits and starts, as this dream of my work alternates with a nightmare. First, the work:

Lay out a large square. Bisect into four squares. Above and below that, the measure of half a square lengthens it into a rectangle. The upper curve of the Chi would go above the square, the tail of the Chi below. Everything based on a square or a circle. There is no ruler, only the compass for measure. Long invisible lines from corner to corner, from midpoint to midpoint, define the center of ornamental circles. Midpoint to corner defines the diamond center where the curve of the Chi goes into its stem. The correspondences all invisible, like the workings of God.

It must be perfection, this measurement, these perfect squares and circles. The price was blood, the sacrifice of everything we had in the world. The sacrifice of the monks who died at Lindisfarne. The lives we all gave up, for this. For what it represents. The sacrifice of over a hundred innocent calves, the pages curling, trying to become hides again, the skin around warm bodies, the memory of its life bending this page. The sacrifice of farms, of sisters and mothers, the loss of status and power, the martyrdom of separation. Gone. Gone, the green-gold fields of oat and rye. Gone, the feasts and the singing of ballads. Now it is penance and psalms. Solace in the church, the chant of God's word, the slow hush of voices sharing prayer. Wanting nothing.

Where are our sisters? Where are the women we might have loved? Abandoned.

Kings ask us to pray for them, for their souls, for justice, for prosperity. Kings may demand. But our sisters only said, *Go, if you will be happy, go.* She said, *Now you will be happy.* As if a lamb on the altar said it to the knife coming down. Sacrificed.

For the blood, this must be perfect. The tip of the pen crisp and clean. The vellum unblemished and white. The curves as round as the sun, colors blazing like saints that come to us in dreams. They speak with our sisters' voices. They sing soothing words. Ghosts or angels. The past beckons, and we sacrifice the past and the future for this age, the last age, to prepare for Christ's return. For all humanity we pray, for the sake of the soft, earthy world. Every day, every single day, every three hours, year in and year out. We offer this gift born of sacrifice, as any gift must be.

For the living and the dead, the ghosts of the past and the angels in our dreams, this must be perfect. All thought is gone, there are only squares and circles, perfect concentration. The world fallen away, for the sake of the world. A shaft of light falls across the page, the pathway to God.

I laid my straight edge across the page from the lower right, the midpoint of the square, to the upper left, and marked the diamond center, where the Chi crossed from curve to stem. I had been laboring all morning in silence, when a smell of drying and rotting fish crept into the room. I felt the hairs on my arms prick I put down the pen and looked up. Monks were studying their books, bent over in the dim light. Their hands gleamed, some tracing the words with their fingers. The stillness was palpable and the moment frozen in time.

I hurried outside and into the moment that the roar erupted, a storm of voices from the beach, and I ran down the Road of the Dead until I saw the source of the roar and stench. Six long boats, boats the like of which I had never seen, brightly painted, enormous, stinking of drying fish, were headed toward the beach. Was I the only one who saw? Was this a dream, a nightmare, was I not really inside still, staring at my page?

But monks sprang beside me, the church bell rang like a crow's warning cry. Some brothers ran toward the beach, others away. Cellach ran straight to me.

"The Book! We need the Book!" he shouted, and ran into the house.

## CHAPTER SIX: THE SLAVE

Rosa, who was sharp and learned the language quickest and whose confidence, height, and powerful will raised her up over the other slaves in the kitchen, ruled over us with a regal air. Though she did work alongside us, as hard as anyone or harder, her word was an order not to be disobeyed. Most of us, like Rosa, were from a pagan land, though we all converted to the heathen religion at Rosa's insistence. She told the others I was evil and that I worshipped the son of a prostitute. She made it clear no one was to talk to me.

Sometimes she said to me, "You are the luckiest of women, that I saved you and give you bread to eat. And your squeaking mouse of a daughter, she is the luckiest little princess. Yes, everyone loves her—because she is a witch, and she has cast a spell on everyone." And in the back of my mind I heard the cry, "Natalya, Natalya!" though Rosa never spoke of her dead daughter.

As I scrubbed the mosaic floor, I studied the complex pattern of twining leaves. If I were not a house slave, I thought I would like to be someone who made these tiles. In Dermott's Psalter there were a few pages with borders like this. Was Dermott reading the Psalter now and praying for me? I tried to remember his voice, reading aloud, but in my mind his voice was altered by the accents now around me.

I was in the hall outside one of the men's sitting rooms, their voices within like the scrape of metal on stone. But one voice was gentle, making even their rough, hard language sound like softly pelting rain. It sounded like Dermott. I hadn't realized that before. This was Musa. I strained to listen, kneeling on the wet tiles, squeezing the rag in my fist.

"What about Deirdre?" a man's voice said.

The rag slipped away. The breath froze in my chest. I was sure I had heard it. *What about her? What about her?* There was a jumble of voices rising excitedly, the words colliding. *Let him speak.* His gentle voice floated below the others, murmuring like a stream. Something about a feast. Something about a namesake. Something about a baby.

A sudden tap on my shoulder sent me forward onto my hands. Ali stepped around me.

"Go to the kitchen. You shouldn't be here this time of day."

I gazed up at him, unable to speak for a moment, thinking quickly. "Shall I take stock of the kitchen supplies for Musa's feast?"

"Yes, of course."

"When is the feast? When the baby is born?"

"Yes, next month." He began to walk away, then caught himself, realizing what he had given away. He had kept Rosa's secret to please his lover, but he looked as if he wished he could have nothing to do with it. He threw me an angry look. "I said go."

I stayed on my knees. He seemed to see all in my face, and his expression softened to a mixture of sympathy and exasperation. "The feast will not be here. We will be sending over food and slaves. Not you." He waved his hand impatiently. "She is happy. She is beloved. You can believe your treatment is a sign of how happy she is; one makes the other." His voice rose in frustration. "I don't know or care what happens between women!"

I clasped my hands in front of my chest, a cry stuck in my throat, but my eyes were dry. I waited intently, my eyes burning into his.

"He treats her like a foreign princess, and he has taken no other wives. That should tell you what you want to know. Now stop looking at me like a starving tiger and get to your work. Quickly." From within there was a sound as if the men were getting up, approaching the door.

I rose and picked up the rag and bucket. I turned and walked away, my head erect.

One day I started to enter a chamber but was stopped by the sight of a man sitting with his back to me. I recognized him by his black hair cut shorter than the others'. It was the man with the strange eyes, Jang, who was the son of a man captured in war between Arabia and a country even farther east. He was seated on the floor with his legs folded in front of him, his hands resting in front of his navel. The stillness filled me. He seemed engaged in some kind of prayer.

Peace washed over me for a few moments and then I turned to go, but I accidentally kicked the pail. He did turn, which I hoped he would, and he smiled, and then turned back to his prayer. I left, my heart beating fast.

Later as I was scrubbing a big pot in the kitchen, Rosa came up to me. "Ali wishes to speak with you." I dropped my rag into the pot and hurried, knowing Ali would not beckon me for any unimportant reason. He was waiting for me in the narrow back hall, his expression friendlier than usual, a thin, embarrassed smile below his mustache.

"You have a little break now, though it's foolishness. Jang wants to speak with you. Follow me."

I followed him through the dark passage and upstairs to quarters I had never visited. We went through cool rooms tiled in blue, to a men's sitting room with windows open to the courtyard. From outside came the sound of fountains and birds. Jang was sitting on a cushion at a low table, and another man sat to his right. Jang nodded with an encouraging smile. The other man, an official in an elaborately embroidered robe, spoke.

"Jang is interested in your foreign land. He wants you to tell him about your gods and your inferior beliefs. Tell us what you believe."

I looked from one to the other. Ali stood in the corner and folded his arms. There was a twinkle in his eye, as if he were expecting a fine joke.

I waited for words to come to me. After a long pause, my voice sounded strange in my ears, as if I were playing a flute rather than speaking.

"I could tell you what my people believe. It is that a loving God sent his only son to redeem mankind, sacrificing himself for the sins of world. I believe this story to be beautiful. But it is all strange to me now. You ask what *I* believe. I believe... that nothing happens for a reason. There is no order and no procession of events leading to any glorious ending. The world has become what it is, but it all just as easily could have been completely different. One truth is the same as any other, because such truths float above the world like stars; they do not really touch this world. I do not look up at them. The world could just as easily have been something completely different from what it is. But now it is what it is, and we are trapped in the box it has become."

I looked steadily at Jang. His eyes filled with tears, and he bowed his head. I didn't look at the other men in the room. In a moment Ali grabbed my arm and pushed me back out of the room and toward the stairs. I hurried back to the kitchen. My pot was where I had left it.

## CHAPTER SEVEN: THE REASON

I can hardly write this, but I must. The horror has come, and now the wind brings fear. We all glance to the water looking for the broad sails, for the shields burning in the sun. The deep peace of the running wave is shattered. We are shattered.

I was with the boys tending the vegetable garden when one of them shouted, pointing behind me, and we all turned. Six long boats knifed the water, pointing at our beach like daggers, bringing a stench of death. My first thought was to protect the boys.

"Run to the church and stay there." I grabbed their hands and pulled them away.

"What are they? What does this mean?" they asked.

"They are raiders." I wanted to say as little as possible.

"Let us fight," they said.

"We are men of God," I told them.

"Then we should not hide."

I rushed them into the church under the care of Nithard, ordering them to obey me.

The bell rang, loud and fast. The monks were assembling outside the church. I ran to Connachtach, who had just come outside.

"We need the Book," I shouted. I raced into the house, into the scriptorium.

Connachtach ran after me. "No, Cellach. Don't."

The Chi Rho page was laid out on the desk, the letters just outlined. I slipped it out from under the weights and held it over my head. Connachtach stared in astonishment. For a moment we paused, a heavy moment, as outside the bell clanged and a chant rose from the monks. Connachtach raised his hand toward the page, opening his mouth, his body tense with the urge to action. His face was baffled, then wincing in pain, then defeated. His poised body sagged, and he leaned against the desk, his breath draining away.

"No," he whispered.

"It is all we have," I said. We had no weapons, only the word of God.

I ran back outside, where the hundred monks had formed a chorus, lined up four abreast in the road, their voices deep and powerful, chanting the twenty-third psalm. *The Lord is my shepherd...* I took my place at their head to hold up the Chi Rho page in front. We marched chanting toward the beach to confront the white devils with prayer. The chant swelled, beautiful, calming us with the power of love.

And so we marched to the beach, where the heathen monsters were pulling their boats ashore. They looked at us wonderingly as we assembled before them and chanted, our voices growing louder, filling the air with everything we stood for, everything we had, with majesty, with mystery, echoing out courage that came from God.

The monsters stood back, holding the swords at their sides, listening with confusion. I held up the page as high as I could. Connachtach stood beside me, and I heard his voice tremble.

One of the devils took a step toward us. Another barked at him. He turned toward his chief and gestured in dismissal. He took another step and raised his sword.

They could have simply walked past us to steal what they wanted, our silver plate and crosses. They could have done as they pleased and left us unharmed. But that was not their nature.

The one devil looked confused and angry as he raised his sword above his head. We sang. The other monsters watched him. They seemed afraid, waiting for him to do something, as if they thought we might have some trick, some way to attack them, though they could see we didn't have the means. They did not believe their eyes, that a hundred defenseless monks would stand before them only praying. They believed other men were like them, cruel and violent, and they had no way to understand men of peace.

The devil took another step. We chanted. *Yea though in the valley of the shadow of death...*

Reuben stood at the end of the line. It seemed I could hear his voice above the rest. In a flashing moment, I remembered all my time with him, our journey on sea and land, his humor and his wisdom. In a moment I heard everything he had ever said to me. *Ah, quiet at last; the salmon must be for some waiting monk on shore; take care of the old man.*

The sword flashed like a memory. It burned in the sun as it came down faster than lightning. Reuben raised his chin to meet it, his neck stretched, his voice suddenly loud, and it was not my imagination, I could hear him. And then his neck was split and his voice stopped.

The sight of blood excited the rest of the stinking mob, like a school of sharks. They all jumped, roused to their violent urge at once, the spell of our chant broken. They rushed at us.

Who among us would run away? Who would turn first?

The first to move was Marcus, but he didn't run. Just as they sprang, he stepped forward and grabbed the one who killed Reuben—Reuben was Marcus's amchara. He grabbed the devil by the hair and punched him in the throat. The devil fell on him. But as the attackers ran at us, their chief tripped, and his sword went into Reuben's killer. The chief leapt back up, laughing. Marcus returned to his place, his arm bleeding.

We chanted still, our voices as loud as the devils' roar, answering their guttural heathen shouts with the peace of angels' music. They were as frenzied as we were calm.

And I? I wanted to run. But I could not be the first, and no one else ran. I waved the page, my voice growing hoarse with fear. Blood flew up like rain. I cannot describe the carnage. I long to forget. I will not describe the bloody defilement and cruelty launched at us, as our voices dimmed and one by one our brothers fell.

When more than half of us were down, the beasts had their fill. They seemed to suddenly remember what they were there

for and ran roaring up the path to the house and church. I
thought of the boys I'd tried to keep safe. Had I made a horrible
mistake? The church was what they wanted, for the silver. Smoke
rose in the air.

Still we chanted. Behind me, Gormgal put his arms around
my waist so that I could hold him up. Marcus sank to his knees,
inspiring us all to kneel among the dead, chanting.

The beasts returned carrying their burden of loot. I thought
of the burden of silver we carried across Francia. That is the fate
of wealth, to cause death and chaos. The beasts threw the silver
into the boats and pushed off. As they moved into the water, one
of them, who looked young and who seemed perhaps to have
some human feeling, stood up in the boat and raised his sword in
a salute to us as they rowed away. They were gone.

We stopped chanting.

Connachtach stood before us as we remained kneeling amid
the butchery. "First, look for survivors," he said.

We worked among the fallen to determine who was dead.
Marcus was injured, a gash on his arm, and a few others had
injuries they could survive if they did not become infected. Sixty-eight monks were dead. We laid them on the beach. It had
been known as the Bay of the Dead already because dead kings
landed there for burial. Now we would call it Martyr's Bay.

As we marched back up to the monastery to assess the damage,
a high chant rose above us. Old Nithard and the boys were at the
top of Dun I, singing. We learned they had thrown all the silver
out of the church and escaped up the hill. Inside, the altar was
broken and candles scattered across the floor, all the windows
broken. Otherwise the church was unharmed.

The house was smoldering, partially burnt, but the chest with
the Book pages was untouched. Gormgal sank to his knees in
front of the book case and pressed his forehead against it. I lay
the Chi Rho page back on the desk. Connachtach came up to me
and put his arms around me. We held each other in exhaustion.

We didn't have forty shovels, so we took turns, and those who
weren't digging brought more bodies, swept up the broken glass

in the church, and started to repair the house. Men brought wood from Mull, and monks came from Tiree to help.

The boys gathered moss to dress the wounds of the injured, and perhaps it was a small miracle that not one of the survivors' wounds was mortal. But I was in no mood to believe in miracles.

To dig sixty graves is hard work, and we worked until we were senseless, until the sight of the gore didn't sicken us but only seemed an unreal nightmare, in which we were the ghosts. We reassembled the bodies of those who were in pieces, gently as a mother cares for her child's broken doll. And then the child has died, and the doll is carefully wrapped and laid in the grave. The gore was too much. These were only dolls. They could not be men.

In the evening a warm rain fell through the still, windless air. The rustle of the drops was the only sound other than the shifting of the sandy earth. We had not eaten or drunk, and we rubbed the moisture over our lips with dirty hands. We were all filthy like hermits, muddy and matted and blood spattered, as if we had been punishing ourselves. And we wanted to punish ourselves.

I wondered if somehow I had brought this here. I had been near their region in Frisia. I had seen where they went. I had come from Lindisfarne, their first raid. Perhaps somehow they followed me. Perhaps they had always been watching me. Perhaps I had brought a curse from my travels. Perhaps I was evil.

Nithard stopped digging and leaned on his shovel. His face was white and sweating. He sank to his knees and looked peculiar. I hurried to his side. He raised his arms, and I held him, his head against my waist.

"Rest," I said.

"Yes, this is my rest now."

He slumped, and I eased him onto his back. He was sweating profusely and his face turned red, then white again. His breath was strangled in his throat. He died.

I did not bury him in the grave he had been digging. I would not do that. I dug his grave, and the shock wore off me. No longer senseless, I dug with rage and hatred in my hands, in my shoulders, in my legs. My empty stomach was tight with rage.

As it was midsummer, the sun didn't set until late. When it was dark, we held a mass and an all-night vigil. Though exhausted, we were wide awake. The chant of the remaining monks was quieter from the missing voices and thin with choking tears.

Finally, late in the morning, we were done with the burials. Connachtach had us eat some bread and cheese, which was like dust in our mouths.

The sky was gloomy and gray, but it was warm and the muggy heat oppressive. I walked across the island to St. Columba's Bay. How empty the island seemed. No monks in the gardens, none tending the cattle. I went down to the pebble beach where the monks often piled rocks into mounds, a rock to represent every sin. I began to make a pile. But soon I simply picked up the stones and threw them into the gray sea.

We could have had piles of rocks as weapons. We could have fought. The exercise only increased my fury. I picked up a red stone like a heart and threw it as far as I could. The humid clouds began to resolve into rain. As the drops fell, the colors of the pebbles came out, and the gray beach took on hues of green, yellow, red, orange, purple, and white. I thought of all the monks who wouldn't see this, who wouldn't see stained glass or paintings again, who wouldn't see the Book completed—the Book that didn't save them.

Marcus found me there and watched me throw the stones.

"Why didn't we fight?" I asked him. "Why didn't we try? Why did we respond the way we did? You started to. We don't have weapons, but we have pruning shears, we have plough shares. We could have done something rather than be slaughtered like calves."

Marcus took a deep breath and pulled his cowl over his head against the rain, shadowing his face. His eyes glowed, hard in anger like mine. He weighed his words. "We didn't fight because we are monks, and that is not what monks do."

"We are men. Did we give up everything? Our very manhood?"

"Perhaps."

I dropped the stone in my hand and brought my fists to my chest. "I could be a chief. I could lead an army against such monsters."

Marcus folded his arms and held himself. He spoke quietly. "That will not save the world."

"And how did we save the world yesterday?"

"By staying who we are, to the end."

Sobs came over me, sobs of both rage and confusion. Marcus put his arms around me, and I felt his body quiver with his own tears.

Days passed. We repaired the house and put skins over the church windows. Connachtach, who had been weakening before the raid, was able to respond with some renewed energy afterward. We conferred about what to do, and I urged the brothers to invite an army to live with us, but that was rejected. Instead, we decided to move. Our island, so remote, was too easy for the raiders to attack by ship. We would move to Hibernia, inland, and we would build a monastery of stone with a tower to withdraw to if attacked.

I went along with this, but my desire to respond more aggressively was frustrated. And there was more. I saw lines added to the Book, to the Chi Rho page, and as the book appeared like a vision through the dawn, I couldn't ignore my doubts any longer. My rage at the invaders was matched by another anger.

One day in the scriptorium, alone with Connachtach, I could no longer contain myself. "Of what use is this Book, this great Book? Was it not to protect us? I should have known better. I saw the Bible of Saint Boniface. I saw the scar that cleaved its cover and his head. Where is the power of the Holy Word? Where is the power of God in our work? What is the meaning of our labor? It is all for nothing. Why didn't we forge weapons, swords and shields, instead of grinding paint and straining ink? What is this for?"

Connachtach took in my questions. His face was gaunt and slightly yellow, the grizzle of his beard coming in white. His neck was thin and his jaw sharp, the skin close to the bone. His gaze was humble as he accepted my anger and despair. He clasped his hands and turned his gaze upward, eyes shining with the light of someone close to death. That moment, in his look so holy and shining, I saw how soon he would join our late brothers. I was gripped with remorse and sadness, but also a whisper of hope, that if anyone could tell me the purpose of our work, our days of prayer, of our very lives, it was he. He spoke just above a whisper, his voice like a wisp of smoke, his words penetrating the air like incense.

"You know how I had longed since I came here, since even before then, to create this great Book. But I was told over and over it was only my pride that inspired me. And that was true. It was only when I forsook my pride that I suddenly had the opportunity, like an unexpected gift. I knew I must treasure it, and let go of my frenzied emotions, my very self, to do this work. And I knew we must do it.

"When Daric came and told us of the attack on Lindisfarne, I knew one day the raiders would come to us. Some think the world is coming to an end. It is the final judgment. I don't know about that. Perhaps it is, perhaps it isn't. There have been three ages, the age of the Old Testament, the age of our Lord, and this final age as we await his return. I think, though, that perhaps the world is not ending, but that some change is happening, and will happen. There are places that don't know our Lord. There are people who live and don't know, and there are those who attack us like wild beasts. And as there are other places in the world, there are other times, past and future. I thought that there might be a future as foreign to us as the pharaohs of Egypt, as foreign to us even as these alien monsters who came and took the lives of our brethren only for a little silver and worldly gain so easily lost.

"And I thought this, only one thing: that whatever the world holds and whatever the future holds, people would know: We are here, and we love. That we live the word of Christ, that we made this Book to last forever, only because we love. We love each other, we love our fellow brothers and our fellow man, and we love God.

And this love is incarnate in our work. It is only out of love that any great work is done, and, if it is only a humble thing that we labor over hour after hour, that still it is something, something that tells the world of our existence, our sacrifice. We have left behind families and given up our birth-right. We will not have wives and children, but it is not because we don't know what love is; we know it keenly. And all the love we have sacrificed we gain back in our brothers and in our prayer. The Book is for all those we have loved, for our brethren who died and live in our hearts, and of our Christ who lives forever. This Book will last and tell this to the world. Our love allows us to do this work, and above all else, we love better because we do it. That is the final reason, that our labor makes us love better."

When Connachtach finished, I wiped the tears from my eyes. I rose and kissed his cheek, and I asked him to give me my final vows to stay on as a monk.

## CHAPTER EIGHT: A PROPOSAL

I fetched the water from the kitchen well. Then, in a small rebellious act, I took the long way around and stepped into the garden. White jasmine bloomed and scented the air among dark glossy leaves. I moved slowly between the manicured trees, noticing everything. A marble fountain sprayed in the center of a bed of tulips, scarlet streaked with white and purple. The flame-like petals were wild in the carefully ordered garden.

Jang sat alone on a bench on the other side of the fountain. I started to back away, but he beckoned for me to approach. I took small steps forward and set down my jug.

"I'm glad you're here," Jang said in his singsong accent, so at odds with the guttural language.

I knelt and folded my hands.

"I asked you a question the other day. But you didn't get to ask me anything," Jang said.

I gazed up. "Do all your people have eyes like yours?"

"We are a different sort. Your eyes are like the sky. Ours are like the earth."

"What is your land like?"

"Green. Vast. There are plains and beautiful, lonely mountains veiled in mist. Tranquil gardens. Farms where the grain grows in water. Cities where all is in order and harmony."

"There are no cities or towns where I'm from in Scotia. Only farms, monasteries, and some forts. Are there monasteries in your land?"

"Oh yes. Beautiful monasteries. We pray to Buddha."

"I've seen you pray. I liked watching you because you seemed so content."

"That is the goal of our prayer, only to be at peace and content."

"What do you say? You weren't speaking when I saw you."

"We chant sometimes and we say, 'However innumerable sentient beings are, I vow to save them. However inexhaustible the defilements are, I vow to extinguish them. However immeasurable the dharmas are, I vow to master them. However incomparable enlightenment is, I vow to attain it. But mostly, my prayer is my breath. We breathe, slowly, counting, and in that stillness is our prayer."

"I used to pray the Lord's Prayer: Our Father who art in heaven, hallowed by Thy name. Thy kingdom come, Thy will be done on earth as it is in heaven. Give us this day our daily bread, and forgive us our trespasses, as we forgive those who trespass against us, and lead us not in temptation, but deliver us from evil. Amen." I shrugged. "Now I pray to Allah. I pray what they tell me to pray."

"You no longer seek anything in prayer?"

"I've forgotten what to pray for. I don't know if I exist or if I am an echo."

He smiled. "That is wonderful."

I had been too long, and I rose. He bowed his head.

When I had poured the water into the cauldron in the kitchen, Rosa came up from behind me and boxed me on the ear.

"I saw you dawdling with that man. You are an evil devil! Wasting time and disturbing the men. You don't belong in the garden! You keep your place and don't put on airs—you are proud, that's what your sin is, evil worshipper of whores!" She pinched my wrist and shoved me away.

I was alone in the small hallway between the kitchen and the men's dining room, scrubbing the tile floor. My knees hurt where they grazed the tiles, but it was cool in the shaded passage. I heard footsteps approaching but didn't pay attention until a man cleared his throat. Ali was standing in the archway. Quickly I wiped my hands on my robe and stood up, bowing and keeping my gaze down.

"I have a message for you. Where can we talk alone?" he asked.

"We are alone right here."

He stepped closer, the bucket between us. Faint voices came from the kitchen; the thick walls muffled the sound.

"You have a change of fortune," he whispered. "I have come to ask for your hand in marriage. Jang is very impressed with you. He seeks to marry you."

I kept my gaze on the foamy water in the bucket. "I cannot choose my fate. I am owned."

"Yes, the court's permission is required. Jang is an honored guest, but still a prisoner. He has not the status of a citizen. It would be allowed. We could require it of you, but he wants you to choose. Think and accept it. He esteems you. You would have a little status, a different life in a new land. He is being sent back to his country. He wishes to take you with him."

I looked up and away, and saw this future. To be able to come and go. I could learn about the world, learn about yet another strange new place, as a free woman. What was the East like? We would go there. He said it was green and mountainous. No more of this dusty dry desert that turned everything its tan color. I looked at the ceiling and saw the blue sky of other lands. My heart began to pound. And I would be known, then, no longer would I be a blank space; I would be known and then perhaps they would let me visit my daughter and grandchild before I left.

"To be married is a better thing than to be alone," he said.

Startled, I looked up. The heavy brick ceiling was there. The floor that would never be clean of dust was beneath my feet, from wall to wall, the massive walls so close. I looked from ceiling to floor to wall, and there was nothing else to see. Behind me, pots clattered in the kitchen.

I looked into his bright face and showed him a face that showed nothing.

"I have a living husband. I cannot accept."

His face slowly dimmed. He backed away. "Of course," he said, and bowed low to me before exiting the hall. I fell to my knees and scrubbed.

## CHAPTER NINE: GLADIUM AND GAUDIUM

I worked at scribing the Book as Father Connachtach became weaker. He tried to perform his duties, but he was wasting away, and we all knew but didn't speak of it.

I was copying Matthew when I came to a verse that deeply troubled me. The line is, "I come not to send peace, but with a sword." Our Christ could have meant several things, perhaps the sword of division between unbelievers and the faithful; perhaps the sword of justice. But I was troubled. We had had enough of swords and enough bloodshed. I went to Abbot Connachtach after Prime to unburden myself.

He stood when I entered, and I begged him to lie back on the pallet beside his desk. He was in his office daily but sometimes had to lie down, and a pallet had been provided. The green light from the window fell on his hollow face. He looked old beyond his years, but his eyes were bright and sharp.

I told him my anxiety over what I had to write. He raised himself up slightly and put his hand under his head, his elbow bent out. This gave him an air of one casually relaxing in conversation rather than one struggling with death. The pain eased out of his face. "And perhaps, too, it was copied incorrectly in the past."

I gasped. "How could that be? The word of God."

"But copying still is the work of frail men. We often have to correct mistakes. And it does seem to me that 'gladium' is very similar to 'gaudium.'"

*Gladium*, sword. *Gaudium*, joy. "I come not to send peace, but with joy." I uttered this and thought about it. It seemed much more fitting, a marvelous and truthful thing to say. "Is that what I should write?"

"Do you feel it in your heart that God is telling you to?"

I looked at his gaunt face, which so often looked tense and pained, and which now glowed with the last of his vigor. Yes, I said, and that is what I wrote.

There came a day when our dear abbot did not rise from his pallet. He lay stiff because any movement brought him pain. He sent for me, and I took the vigil beside him. He raised his hand and said, "It will be done."

I said, "Yes, Dear Father. It will be done."

He said, "Not in my lifetime. But the Book will be done before the world ends."

Our dear abbot died, and to my surprise, before that he offered my name up to be voted on as his successor, perhaps because so many more worthy brothers had died in the attack. It is true I had been busy assisting him. There was much to negotiate and arrange during that year, with moving to the new habitation. Abbot Connachtach didn't live to move with us, and we buried him on Iona with lamentations.

And so the abbot's office became mine, and I have great responsibilities, but because I had gradually taken over so many duties, it is not a hard transition. After we buried Connachtach, I called a meeting of the Book committee. But Reuben was dead, and now it was only Gormgal, Marcus, and myself. We needed to train up another scribe.

The fight was sucked out of Gormgal. He agreed to everything with an absent look, reminding me a bit of Daric when he was so distant and ill. I expected him to oppose and fight me, but it was only my own vanity and self-importance which prompted my expectation.

We rose and Marcus left, but Gormgal asked to linger. When Marcus was gone, he sank to his knees, as one would out of respect to the abbot, to beg a favor or to receive chastisement. He closed his eyes and didn't speak for some moments. I stood over him and placed my hands on his shoulders. Tears squeezed from his eyes.

"Why am I alive?" he asked.

I stroked his hairless pate. "There must be more work for you to do. We will find comfort in the new place."

"I want to stay here. I want to die here."

He raised his hands, and I took them in mine. "There are some who are staying, but it will be a harder life with so few to do the work. I would consider it a blessing if you stayed to lead them."

He held my hands tightly, and I raised him up and pulled him into my arms. He was so slight, so frail.

"I think now you finally understand our purpose," he said. "I didn't have faith that you would. Forgive me."

"There's nothing to forgive. I was slow to understand. I believed much in vanities. I'm still learning, every day."

"So am I."

We kissed each other on the cheek, and he left, walking lightly as a fawn on his knobby legs.

Connachtach had almost finished the Chi Rho page before he died. There was still a blank area to fill in, on the lower left side. The page already contained all manner of interlace and imagery. The Rho ended in a man's head, to symbolize the humanity of Christ. Angels perched on the side of the Chi, and a grape vine bordered the edge on the right. The interlace was finely done with a crow's quill, and some of the painting done with a brush barely thicker than one hair.

It was up to Marcus to finish the one blank spot under the Chi. He is a mysterious man, and he always takes an unusual path in this lonely life, yet his painting surprised me. He drew two mice with the host between their teeth, watched by two cats with mice on their backs. Is it a bit of humor on this most sacred page? Does it stand for the life that continues beneath our vision while we pray? I never asked him.

When I had time, I continued work on the new Book. I had forgotten for a while about the lapis. Its use was no longer required; Mother Mary was already painted in royal purple instead of chaste blue while I was on my journey. But one day I ground and rinsed the lapis and made the paint.

There were places in the illuminations that were blank, just little spots here and there to fill in. I took the blue and filled in these small background areas, in between various designs and letters, and I thought how God might be like that, filling in all the small spaces in our hearts, all the small spaces in our lives. I thought of our late brothers whom I loved, old Daric, Reuben, and Connachtach. The woman Oona as fierce as the desert. Their memory fills the small spaces in my mind and brings peace to my heart. I felt very calm as I painted, and let the love of God fill me as Connachtach advised so that my love would be written into this Book as his was, and as was the love of all those who were any part of our lives in the humble monastery.

I have found my dear Father Connachtach's unfinished letter to you, ending with the moment I cried out for the Book to protect us. He grew too weak to write more. I will send all this together to you. I hope our brotherly love will inspire you on your journey of faith.

Tomorrow we make the journey to Kells, where we will finish our great Book, and hopefully find a peaceful home for our prayers and labors. I plan to resign as abbot after we are settled. This has been the story of my part of the great Book, my confession. Peace be to you, and may God fill your heart, as he has filled mine with the wonder of this remarkable world and love for all who have blessed my life on this strange journey of nightmares, dreams, and miracles.

With love in Christ, your dear Brother,

Cellach, Abbot of Iona

## CHAPTER TEN: COMING HOME

I scrubbed the floor of the hall outside the kitchen, my hands the color of the red tiles. When Rosa called, I answered without an accent, no longer tripping on the new language, my voice nasal as any native's.

"Go to the market and fetch some pomegranates," Rosa said. She handed me some coins in a little lambskin pouch.

In the beginning, Rosa hadn't let me go to the market. But now, after so long, I had earned her trust. Rosa's hatred had turned cold, hardened, her demeanor frozen. There was no more pinching and slapping, only a tired coldness. Rosa's skin took on a gray pallor like a sheet of lead. Her eyes were still fierce, their flashing blackness the only heat in her face.

I had kept up my obedience, our secret still kept like a cold stone in a well, like the root one can't dig out. It was unspoken as always, only there, never changing, a hard gray thing that quieted voices whenever I approached, that kept me apart though no one knew the cause. I was rumored to be some kind of witch or to have committed some unknown crime, but some thought there might be an injustice to their silence towards me. But silence was kept like a space around me, and they said to each other that I seemed to prefer it. And, after all, I seemed so proud with my erect walk and steady gaze.

In the crowd I was as anonymous as any native woman. I passed the spice stalls where the air was thick with the smell of cumin, cinnamon, and pepper. The men who measured out the spices were all familiar to me, but they did not greet me, because though I knew them, they did not know me. The market was a place I watched closely as I went about my business, but I never conversed. I haggled like anyone else, but always settled quickly on a price. If I were quick at it, I had time to walk and observe, and Rosa wouldn't think I had wasted time.

A stray cat rubbed itself against my leg. I reached down and stroked its red fur. It blinked light eyes at me. I could tell Rosa the fruit was dear today, so I turned to a stall of dried fish and bought a small one and fed it to the cat.

The fishmonger said, "If I had known, I wouldn't have sold it to you."

"Maybe you still don't know," I muttered.

"Women," he said, and came out from behind his table to firmly nudge the cat away with his foot. "Get off with you."

The cat carried its fish and ran away.

My eyes filled with tears, which surprised me; I had not been prone to weeping in years.

"I didn't hurt it, you crazy woman," he said, returning to tend his stall.

I wiped my eyes and turned. The nut seller looked up from the book he always read between customers and crooked his finger at me.

"Try this," he said. His face was tender as he handed me a few pistachios.

The earthy taste filled my mouth. I bowed my head and moved on, crunching the nuts one by one. A feeling rose in me, almost of happiness, a light sensation that something good would happen. Maybe I would find that cat again and take it back with me, keep it hidden in my room and feed it scraps. Yes, I must keep an eye out for it.

I continued to the fruit stalls, where the sweet smells of lemons and dates cheered me. At the end of the stalls where the road curved toward a fountain, a small crowd was gathering. I picked out three pomegranates, not stopping to haggle, then joined the current of the crowd, drifting toward the bend in the road. Something was happening just around it. A small drumbeat rose above the sound of splashing water, where the crowd was stopped. It was a steady tapping as if from a small drum, a child's toy.

A little voice rose above it, singing. I tried to get closer, as whatever the scene was, it was clearly enchanting to the people gathered. I squeezed ahead. There was something strange about the song, calling from the depths of the past, a song about a swallow flying to one's love. A song in my own language. Between the crowding shoulders I glimpsed a four-year-old boy with his drum. The crowd was commenting with amazement, praising his bright red hair and blue eyes, his strange, unearthly beauty. Musa stood proudly next to him.

I stepped back. I let shoulders and backs close off my view, but I could still hear the song, filling a space in my chest, emptied of breath, my heart pounding in empty space, airless. With the rushing sound of the fountain I felt pulled under, drowning, but all was dry, so dry, and the air was above me like an apple on a high branch; I couldn't reach the air.

O if my love
Were like the swallow
That flies, up in the sky—
Then with my love
I would now follow,
And kiss my love, or I will die.

I opened my mouth wide, and the air rushed in at last, too much now, and I felt dizzy. The sun beat down, so hot I floated, knees soft and collapsing, I started to sink. But I straightened up, raised my chin, and took another glimpse at the red hair shining like a midday star. There was only to breathe, my breath a prayer. I took three deep breaths as if about to dive in deep water. An idea rose in me almost without thought.

I nudged a nearby woman and pointed my finger. "For shame," I whispered. "This boy's grandmother is a slave in the house of Harun. For shame, that he lets the grandmother of his darling child work as a slave."

The old woman next to me bent and whispered to the girl beside her. A wave of murmuring arose. A wave that traveled like the river that had brought me here, like a current that flowed from Connacht across the sea and emptied into this ocean of a desert, the current of my life. The whisper grew, there was pointing, "t'sking," and the shaking of veiled heads. Someone whispered to Musa.

Musa's eyes widened as he gaped at the gathered women.

I disappeared into the murmuring crowd, the basket light on my arm; lightly I ran down the street.

While in the kitchen, I heard a man's shouts from outside, Rosa's shrill but ultimately feeble protest. The man entered and with bows, awkwardness, and haste, rushed me out into the waiting cart. We drove, winding around the white shell of the city, to a house and into a courtyard where a fountain sprayed amid vines of jasmine. The gate was open and I passed through.

You sat, looking downward at your son playing on the mosaic tiles.

"Deirdre," I said, afraid to come near.

You looked up. Your eyes shown in the dappled light. "Are you—are you a ghost?"

"I hardly know."

"Mama?"

"Yes, my love."

You jumped up and I ran to you, the sound of laughter and crying like a jangle of bells amid the rushing water and the tapping of a drum.

"How are you here?"

"I'll tell you all, in time."

At our feet, the little red-haired boy beat his drum.

### THE END

AFTERWORD:

On the Research, Chronology, and Acknowledgements

I read fifty books to research *Kells*. I titled the book *Kells* because the manuscript is now known as the Book of Kells, but it wasn't created at the Kells Monastery. I visited its home of Iona twice, the first time with the Rabbie's Trail Burners Tour, led by the wonderful Suu Ramsay, and the second time with Mull Magic. Suu Ramsay said that the stone now known as Scotland's Stone of Destiny is not the real one but was palmed off to the English, and that the real one was an Egyptian obelisk that found its way to Scotland. Mull Magic was especially enlightening thanks to Ruth Fleming and bird expert Stuart Gibson.

Vickie Rayhill of the Society for Creative Anachronisms showed me how to make the iron gall ink, and I also got help from calligrapher Peter Lynn. I took a Celtic art class from the Irish-American Heritage Center in Chicago. The Chicago Public Library has a full-sized facsimile of the Book of Kells in the Rare Books Room of Harold Washington Library, where it is possible to leaf through the Book. Trinity College, Dublin, has possession of the Book of Kells and used to sell a CD-ROM of the Book, which can still be found from online sources.

As a novelist, I took some liberties. For instance, the first raid on Lindisfarne was in the year 793, Charlemagne was crowned emperor in 800, and the raid on Iona that killed sixty-eight monks was 806. I compressed this timeframe. Additionally, the interment of the bones of St. James, inspiring pilgrimages to Spain, happened slightly later, in the ninth century.

In modern times, Scots and Irish people keep a distinction between their two peoples. In this era, the whole region might be referred to as Scotia, and someone from what we now call Ireland might be called a Scot.

In this time period, the area we now call Kells was known as Cenannas. I decided to keep it Kells in this book to make clear that this is The Book of Kells.

Many of the named characters were real people: Connachtach, Bresal, Cellach mac Congall, Liutgard, Alcuin, Arno, Isaac, the traveling monks Lantfrid and Sigimund, and Karl (Charlemagne). The missionary in Frisia was named Liudger; I changed it to Udger to be less similar to Liutgard. Connachtach's epitaph states he was a master scribe, but that's all we know. I made up everyone's background except Alcuin and Karl, about whom more is known.

The cat Pangur Bán was the subject of a ninth century Irish poem. I first came across this poem in Pierre Riché's *Daily Life in the World of Charlemagne* and the poem is also quoted in Thomas Cahill's *How the Irish Saved Civilization*. Bán means "white," so presumably the title refers to a white cat, but the white light of knowledge is a possible subtext. The version of the poem presented here is from Robin Flower's book *Poems and Translations*, from 1931.

The quoted prayers and hymns are from *Iona: The Earliest Poetry of a Celtic Monastery*, edited by Thomas Owen Clancy and Gilbert Markus. The little poem for the bees is from *The Year 1000*, by Robert Lacey and Danny Danziger, who got it from Eileen Power's book *Medieval People*, who in turn got it from *Althochdeutsches Lesebuch* in the Vatican Library. The Breastplate of Saint Patrick, or Deer's Cry, is from Cahill. The songs Oona and Deirdre sing are invented.

The monastery of Iona did not comprise lots of beehive cells as monasteries sometimes did. According to the archaeology, there was a round building sixty feet in diameter. That is the house I depict for the monks. This is noted in a footnote in Adomnan's biography of Saint Columba. I guessed the house was two stories to accommodate work and sleep. I don't depict the monks as vegetarians because the archeological evidence shows they ate plenty of meat.

I'd like to thank readers of the early drafts for their comments: Carolyn Sperry, Brian Mossa, Frank Klock, Sandra Amass, Joan Baranow, and special thanks to Elizabeth Wetmore for her copious notes. I thank Elizabeth Percer for helping me with the query letter. I'd like to thank Steven Yousha for his advice and Karl Lanocha for his long-distance support. My deepest gratitude goes to Susan Casanova for reading everything I write and for our long friendship. A heartfelt thanks to my tireless editors, Chelsey Shannon and GK Darby, and to Alex Dimeff for the book design and illustrations. Lastly, thanks to my husband Samuel Crider for being my best friend since 1981.

Photo by Stone Watters

Amy Crider is an award-winning novelist and playwright. Her first novel, *Disorder*, a murder mystery, was published by the University of New Orleans Press in 2021 after it won their Publishing Lab Prize. *Kells: a novel of the eighth century* is her second novel. Amy has been published in *Bayou Magazine, The Dramatist, Avalanche Journal*, and her editorial about *A Christmas Carol* for the *Chicago Tribune* was nationally syndicated. In 2021 her play *Fourteen* won the Tennessee Williams & New Orleans Literary Festival One Act Play Contest. She has been a semi-finalist for the Princess Grace Award. She produces a podcast called Continuous Dream Theatre. Her website is www.amycrider.com.